ISLAND
OF
REDEMPTION

DAN
I hope RETIREMENT IS ALL you hoped.
My next book, The final book in the
MANNA Chronicles Trilogy, will have
you as a character.
Good or bad ? TBD :)

A Novel by
Chris Reynolds

www.AuthorChrisReynolds.com

Retail distribution available through Ingramspark.com
© Island of Redemption Copyright 2022 by Chris Reynolds
ALL RIGHTS RESERVED
Published by Chris Reynolds Media Group; Boca Raton, Florida.
No part of this publication may be reproduced or transmitted in any form
or by any means without express written permission. Requests can be sent to
Contact@AuthorChrisReynolds.com.
This book is a work of fiction. Names, characters, places, and incidents either are
products of the author's imagination or are used fictionally. Any resemblance to actual
events or locales or persons, living or dead, is entirely coincidental.
Cover design by Chadwick Pelletier
Library of Congress Cataloging-in-Publication Data
Island of Redemption: by Chris Reynolds
ISBN Print - 979-8-88796-854-4
ISBN ePub - 979-8-88796-863-6

Contact Information:
11932 N Lake Drive
Boynton Beach, FL 33436
www.AuthorChrisReynolds.com

About the Author

Father, husband, writer, musician, adventurer, explorer, inventor, and faithful friend. I value God, country, family, friendship, loyalty, honesty, and integrity. Son of a sailor, raised in Maine, and schooled in Florida, at one time or another, I have called Bar Harbor, Presque Isle, St. Pete, Miami, New York City, Easton, Connecticut, Culver Indiana and Pacific Palisades, California, my home. My beautiful wife, Merryl, and I have been together since 1984, and we raised two extraordinary children who now live in New York and Miami.

An avid history buff who believes in research, and more research, I tend to look for hidden agendas that can be linked by common threads. So, it is only natural that my stories revolve around ancient mysteries, alternative histories, personal destiny, and shadowy figures that pull the strings of what goes on in the world.

Weaving together known truths, ancient myths, arcane facts, and legends, I try to craft tales of suspense and intrigue that can only be unraveled through the lens of unconventional insight. Remember, just because someone labels something a conspiracy theory, doesn't mean it's not true…

Other Books by Chris Reynolds:

<u>Young Adult Fiction Co-written with Jedd Birkner</u>
The World of Fizz Cola – Miramax
Through the Mind's Eye – Chris Reynolds Media Group LLC
<u>The Manna Chronicles</u>
Chris Reynolds Media Group LLC
Lost Secret of the Ancient Ones – Book One
Ghost Gold – Book Two
In The Time of Noah – Book Three
Due fall 2023

The Lions Gate – TriMark Press

In Memoriam

Keith Reynolds
David Nicholas
Wynn Lambert

These men have all had a great impact on my life and I miss them. Death being the silent river of societal consciousness, I am comforted that their faith in Jesus Christ has assured them the riches of Heaven. Knowing that one day, I will join them.

Acknowledgements

The creation of a book is a collaboration with many hands. Thank you to Chadwick Pelletier for another awesome cover. To Dawn Alexander for helping structure the story, James Gallagher for his insightful edits and Lisa Fenley, who fixed my abundance of grammatical errors. You guys have all contributed to making this book better.

To my friends I have used as characters in my book, I tried to stay true to your personality. For those friends not included, don't fret, the next book is full of dastardly characters. You will not be forgotten.

To my wife and family, thank you for the encouragement and putting up with me.

****LANGUAGE WARNING****

I want to apologize to my readers for the vulgar language. This ends after the seventh chapter. I tried to find comparable but less offensive linguistic options, and when possible I have inserted unfinished sentences. But I concluded that to completely sanitize the language did not align with the personality of the main character or allow me to show his transformation.

I also ask for forgiveness to those who may be offended by the casual regard in which the Lord's name is taken in vain. Nowadays, using *God* or *Jesus Christ* as a form of vitriol is not even given a second thought. Please note—I do not make this part of my personal vocabulary.

It is a sad state of our times, but crude language now permeates every level of our society. I, too, am guilty. It is one of my annual New Year's resolutions to swear less, but like most resolutions . . .

If I may, let me share a true story about how someone I knew and respected was able to address a language-challenged individual.

My deceased friend, Pastor David Nicholas, and I were playing golf one day with a retired trial lawyer. Both men were tall and robust. The golfer I had invited would use defamatory variants of the Lord's name to curse every bad shot. After one such exclamation, David finally walked over to him, put his arm firmly around the man's shoulder, and said, "Bob, I find if you talk to him before the shot, it always works out better."

Message sent, situation defused. Bob's golf, already far better than my own, went smoothly the rest of that day. Whenever the two crossed paths, Bob's language was that of a choirboy. The lesson for me was that humor without judgment always works better when correcting someone's behavior. So don't be afraid to help a person move beyond vulgarity by using a light touch. Gentle mercies instead of shame.

I hope you enjoy the story and understand why I chose to keep the original language in the first seven chapters. And that you will forgive me for doing so.

Chris Reynolds
October 2022

Only by the Cross of Calvary
Can One Find the Riches of Heaven.
—Hanri Fick, 1732

Chapter 1

"What the hell was I thinking?" Mark wailed. Fear overwhelmed him as mountains of water tossed his Bertram like it was a toy.

One moment he was being pulled up the side of a giant wave, the next he was crashing down into a trough a hundred feet below.

"Damn it," he cursed, desperate to hang on. White knuckled, he squeezed the wheel harder. The pounding in his chest raged as he glared through the salt-crusted windows. Spume blowing off the roiled waters was indistinguishable from the gale-driven downpour. Only the compass, spinning and bouncing, recalibrating, and fighting to establish a true north, offered him any sense of direction.

"If I don't get this damn boat turned around . . ."

A mammoth storm had appeared from out of nowhere. Huge rollers stacked one on top of another were driving piles of water into the vastness of the open Atlantic. Driving him farther and farther from home. Hope receding.

Mark Lambert was not a licensed captain, but he considered himself a decent boatsman. But now, as his vessel plowed down another gigantic crest, acidic bile soured his throat.

The waves had swollen beyond comprehension. Angry troughs boiled deep below the frothy towers. The forty-two-foot Bertram he and his friend had rented for the week was being ruthlessly slammed into the belly between the peaks, sending shudders through the hull. He wished Davey had not bailed at the last minute. Being alone only added to his fear.

"Son of a . . ." A searing pain tore through his body as he smashed hard against the wheel, the agony reminiscent of a once-cracked rib. He screamed a slurry of obscenities at the pain. This had turned into a death match.

Marshaling a false bravado, he unleashed all his anger at the storm.

"Is this all you got, you damn bastards!"

The fear in his voice was lost in the howling of the wind.

"Come on . . . ," he pleaded. "Come on . . ."

Ignoring the discomfort, he strained every muscle, trying to turn the boat around. As the craft neared the top of the towering surge, the wheel spun free, followed by the discordant scream of propellers breaching the surface. The boat plunged back into the churning bottom, heeling hard to one side, foamy waters pouring over the wheelhouse. Only the closed compartment offered any illusion of safety.

Leaning hard into the wheel, Mark gunned the throttle, willing the blades to bite into the sea. This was a zero-sum game. Win or die!

"You can do it, *Lil Darling*," he encouraged. The quivering needle bounced and gyrated, and slowly the compass began to respond. One hundred degrees, it read. One twenty. Then it lost some ground. A hundred and five.

"You mother . . ." The boat staggered like a heavyweight boxer, but the props bit. One thirty . . . one fifty, one eighty . . .

"Come on, darling, show me what you're made of . . ." She continued to turn. Drawing the boat broadside to the titanic surge, he felt her straining to stay upright.

"Don't roll, baby," he pleaded, knowing there would be nothing left but a stain of what once was. He willed her, cajoled her, and finally reverted to shouting a mixture of profanity-laced encouragements.

"Come on, you son of a bitch . . ."

Against the odds, the bow edged into the angry wall bearing down on them.

"Up, baby. Keep pushing. You can do it!"

Adrenaline juiced his fear as the seas challenged every thrust and every parry. But the compass kept staggering in the right direction. Two twenty, two fifty . . . and then—two hundred and seventy degrees. *Lil Darling* had turned into the maelstrom. West.

His heart pulsed in his ears.

"Thank god," he breathed out, easing his death grip on the wheel. It wasn't even close to being over, but his boat was now aimed back toward the islands. Back toward Bridgetown. And back toward Kay's, his favorite bar.

"I did it," he shouted with smug vindication. His exclamation summed up victory over everyone who had ever doubted him, haughty righteousness that exonerated every foolish risk he had ever taken.

From the top of the wave, he could see flashes of lightning in the distance. The air smelled of ozone, and he tasted the tang of salt upon his lips. Setting the autopilot, he needed to assess the damage. Opening the cabin door, he saw the deck was awash in gullies of seawater funneling through drain ports in the sideboards.

As the spike of adrenaline subsided, his arrogance got the better of him, and he raised his middle finger and flipped a bird at the angry sky.

"F—you," he yelled into the face of the storm. Without warning, his feet felt hot, there was a loud ringing in his ears, and everything went black.

Days earlier…

The long bar was three deep with tourists all clamoring for a drink. Spring break in Barbados offered lots of pretty girls and booming music, all reflected from the aged mirror behind the bottle-lined shelves. He was on his third margarita when a woman, not bad for her years, sidled up next to him.

"Hey, sailor." She smiled. "All alone?"

The rolled-sleeve bartender came over.

"I'll have what he's having," she said.

"Alone?" Mark repeated. The word hung with a question mark.

The bartender handed her the fresh pour and moved to the next customer. The clamor of voices, peals of laughter, scuffle of barstools, and clanking of beer bottles all blended into the cacophony of a Sunday in Bridgetown.

"Cheers," she offered with a raised glass. "To not being alone."

"Damn him," he muttered, rapping his finger on the bar, signaling for another drink. Stewing that his friend had canceled at the last minute, he was well into the throes of drowning his anger.

"Damn who?" she asked with an inviting grin.

"My friend. We were supposed to go out for a week of fishing. Boat's paid for and already provisioned. But he had a fight with his wife and . . . bitch," he muttered under his breath, seeking someone to blame for Davey abandoning him.

"Ahh, wives." She said this as if that was the universal answer he was looking for. "I'm not much of a fisherman, but I'm a hell of a mate." She reached down and squeezed between his legs.

He noticed the perfume she wore, the glint in her eyes, and the lust on her lips. Her signals were all green.

"Whoa," he said reflexively, holding up his hand to display his wedding ring.

"Oh, sweetie," she cooed with dismissal. "That just means disease-free."

Her hand lingered, and he hesitated. She squeezed a little more, and his male reflexology felt the stirrings of trouble.

"No," he croaked weakly. But he did not make any effort to stop her.

Giving her the once-over, he thought she had probably been a real beauty when she was younger. After all, even now, she looked pretty good. There was a battle waging inside him, weighed against his desire, the risk of getting caught, and the anonymity of the islands. The latter had an unfair hand on the scale.

He was roused by the cold ocean sloshing over him. He lay face down, and water squeezed in and around as it rushed into the main salon. His body straddled the threshold. He was soaked, his ribs hurt, and . . .

"No!" he shouted, suddenly awake enough to see what was coming.

Looming high above the mangled tower was a wall of water so menacing, so massive, and so . . . he nearly soiled himself. He braced against the jamb as the boat raced down the steep wave like a toboggan on ice.

He staggered back into the cabin and seized the wheel, gravity pulling him hard against the console. He pushed down on the throttle . . . nothing. He turned the ignition. Nothing. It was dead.

"Damn it." Slowly the fog of what happened opened wispy patches of recall. The boat had been struck by lightning.

Forcing down fear, he kept flipping switches. Cabin lights. Bilge pump. Radio . . . anything he could reach while keeping one hand on the wheel. But soon the illusion of hope evaporated. Everything was fried, including the power to the rudder. Holding the wheel was an exercise in futility.

And worse—all connection to the outside world was gone. He was alone, no one knew where he was, and the relentless surge of an angry sea was pushing him beyond the shipping lanes, farther from habitation.

"Please, I don't want to die . . . ," he wailed.

His fate was at the mercy of the sea gods.

With a trancelike grip, he fixed his eyes straight ahead. The titanic mountains of water seemed endless. One minute the boat plowed nose down like a dog, the next it hung precariously abeam the rising swells. The seas were enraged. Their rhythm unpredictable. The froth wailed violently. As the boat corked to the top of another wave, the unthinkable unfolded.

"Come on, come on," he willed over and over.

Mark raced with trembling hands to grip the captain's chair. His vessel was listing so far to one side that the port windows were kissing the waters. Then . . . the boat began to tumble. Once, twice, three times it rolled, until any sense of up or down was blurred. He held on for dear life while trying to cover his face. His nose was gushing blood, pummeled by loose objects flying through the cabin.

He began mumbling in prayer, piercing the walls he had built as a teen. God and all that mumbo jumbo had been relegated to superstition and dismissed long before ever exiting high school. But pray he did. It was all that was left. It was a prayer rife with humility, a prayer putting aside all his hubris, a prayer pleading that if fate would spare him, he would be better. He swore this as tears streamed down his face.

His heart raced. His face beaded with blood and sweat. Fear filled the cabin like a bad stink. When it appeared the boat could take no more punishment, the flexing of fiberglass cracking with yet another sharp report, his despair at its zenith . . . then and only then were his pleas heeded.

The craft found the bottom of the trough and miraculously turned upright in the spew of tumultuous waters. The cabin was in shambles, with everything stowed now scattered and ready to become lethal new projectiles in the next go-round. He spied the uninflated raft and plastic oars floating over the floorboards. Their futility mocked him.

He could only imagine what lay topside. There was nothing he could do. He was at the mercy of destiny. The pain of a broken nose simply offered the promise of more to come.

Admitting defeat, he moved across the littered galley and opened the door to the forward berth. Carefully stepping down the slick stairs, he tossed the loose stowage up the steps and locked himself in. Resigned to the probability of drowning and being lost forever, he wedged into the corner bunk, pulling pillows, towels, blankets, and anything else that was soft around his body. He hoped to ward off further pummeling until life escaped on the gurgle of a final breath.

He was painfully aware he would never see his wife or children again. His mind sought a bridge to hope. Anything. Anything at all. What he found were his uncaring memories for others who had suffered fates worse than his. Catastrophes the world had endured over the past year, from the massive earthquake that devastated Haiti to the volcano that had rained destruction on some far-off island, that he didn't really give a damn about.

It had always been someone else's problem. And, truthfully, he never dwelled on the problems of others. Especially those far away. But now?

"Will people even be concerned that I'm gone?"

Closing his eyes, he envisioned a funeral. His funeral. Any distraction from the current reality.

Where would it be? Who would attend? What would they say?

What unfolded was not a beatific tribute.

"Screw 'em . . . ," he said in anger. It was his answer for everything.

Exhaustion, defeat, resignation . . . his eyes grew weary, perhaps closing for the final curtain.

Chapter 2

"I'm alive!" he cried, untangling himself from the fabric cocoon. Golden shafts of sunlight streamed through the port window, the boat was no longer being tossed, and the screaming winds had become a whisper.

"What the . . ."

Relief turned to alarm at the cold, ankle-deep water sloshing from one side of the room to the other. Splashing his way up to the main salon, he saw a debris field strewn across the cabin. Every pot and every pan. Every can and every box. Beer, water, soda, everything. Scattered.

He felt his nose. It was sore and crusted in blood. he didn't care—the boat was afloat, and he had survived. He exhaled a long sigh, the pressure cooker of bottled-up fear finding an exit.

Still slightly disoriented, he eyed the windows. Like himself, they had somehow endured. Beyond the coated glass the sky was clear, and the waves had settled into a following sea.

The cabin smelled dank with seawater. He lifted an Evian from the scattered melee and stepped out onto the deck. As he inhaled large gulps of ocean air, the sun felt warm on his face.

Taking stock of his surroundings, he was not surprised that the tuna tower, wheel, throttle—actually, the entire top of the vessel—had been ripped free.

Now at the bottom of the ocean, he thought.

Watering parched lips, he took a long swallow, thinking how close he had come to joining the tower at the bottom of the Atlantic. It gave him pause to reflect on the one thing he had avoided thinking about for almost his entire life. Death, that thing he always imagined as being down a long road . . .

Pondering the what-ifs, he tensed at how close he had come. While absently gazing at his surroundings, he saw the fishing reel wedged into the outrigger. It had not only remained intact through the countless rolls, but the line was taut with prey.

The sight conjured up a long-ago memory of his middle school neighbor, Thomas.

It's been ages since I thought of him. His friend always saw everything as a glass half-empty, with life as unfair and him always in retreat.

Even when he and Thomas had gone fishing with his dad, when Thomas had hooked something huge and his dad had encouraged him to reel it in, Thomas's comments were consistent with his personality.

"Probably nothing but seaweed . . ."

Smiling at the memory, he offered up some optimistic sarcasm for his ancient pal. "Thomas, we've got ourselves one helluva fishing trip . . ."

After prying the rod from its hold, he moved to the angler's chair, a white polyurethane seat anchored to the stern floor. As the adrenaline-driven roar in his ears abated, he felt the quiet. There was no engine, the wind had dropped to a soft whisper, and the rollers moved with a silent rhythm. A rhythm that steadily pushed him east. Farther from home. Farther from rescue. Farther from hope.

"How long will they look for me?" He was a practical man, knowing that even if they did look, it would be for only a few days at most.

Working the line, careful not to let his catch slip the hook, he winced, as his ribs hurt, his hands were sore, and fatigue was gaining ground. Occasionally, his prey would break the surface and then dive deep again. It looked to be a large, bluefin tuna.

"Damn thing must weigh a hundred pounds."

Raise the rod, reel the line, dip . . . over and over. The battle waged for what seemed an eternity, but he could feel the struggle draining from his captive. As the end came near, the large, torpedo-shaped fish evacuated its bowels and vomited up chum. He had seen this occur a hundred times before, the final act of the defeated. It was honey to the predators who were always on patrol.

And as if on cue, a monster of a shark, at least eighteen feet long, rose from the murky depths and clamped onto his catch with massive jaws, tossing it back like a piece of sushi.

It glared at him before sinking into the deep.

"Holy mother of god!" He quaked as adrenaline coursed through his veins.

The creature vanished as quickly as it had appeared, taking with it Mark's optimistic demeanor. Facing the implacable reality of his situation, the beast was a wake-up call to stay vigilant if he was going to have any chance of surviving.

He stared out at the endless water, wondering if the predator was gone. Seeing nothing but whitecaps and unending fields of rolling seas, his inherent nature took over, and he set about to create order out of chaos. Opening the cabin to air it out, he began methodically stowing each item while taking inventory of what remained.

"Food, water, perishables, beer, alcohol, candles, tools, binoculars, fishing tackle—gonna need all this," he said, entering each item into a log.

Once righting the galley, he opened the engine compartment to see if there was a way to jump-start the engines.

"Now what?" He swore under pinched lips. Looking into the hold, there was nearly five feet of oily water flooding the engine room.

The motors were submerged, and the batteries were dry only because they lined a top shelf.

"No way these are coming back to life." The reality crushed any lingering hope. Running his hands through his hair, he stared down at the situation.

The air smelled of diesel, and greasy stains were floating over the water. His stomach bunched in knots at this unexpected turn, adding one more concern to the growing pile.

"Great. I survived the storm of the century so I can die in a fuel explosion."

Stripping to the waist, he climbed down into the engine room, found some goggles, and submerged into the slick water. After surfacing a half dozen times for air, he was mollified that there were no obvious holes or cracks in the hull, and he could not find any place where fuel was leaking into the compartment. As far as the water went, it must have drained in from the storm.

"Darling, you are one helluva boat," he said with admiration. After retreating topside, he lingered upon the uninterrupted vastness while considering what to do about the engine room.

"It's a ticking time bomb down there. One spark and . . ."

He had always been practical. One who could see several moves ahead. He had been a capable chess player as a kid, competing at the local YMCA. These skills had served him well sensing shifting winds, anticipating cause and effect. The skills had guided him through a long list of entrepreneurial endeavors where his successes far outweighed his failures. Right now, he was sorting his options and his priorities while weighing probabilities and outcome.

He hated it when people did stupid things. Acting, in his view, without thinking it through. His kids had grown to hate this particular rebuke: "What the hell did you think was gonna happen?

It was a constant source of argument with his wife. 'Think, then do,' he would constantly tell her. She never understood his ability to analyze and anticipate the probable outcome of his actions or appreciate how often he was right. She enjoyed the fruits of his success but always wanted him to shy away from risks.

How could he explain gut instinct? Risk and reward. He was always careful to notch up more victories than defeats. It was how they afforded their lifestyle and their big house back in South Florida.

They often argued about the investments he made. Just before leaving, she had opened their month-end stock portfolio, and she had jumped all over him.

"A river company?" he repeated, parroting her admonishment. "And now you're into fruit?'" As she rambled on, he recalled thinking, *Damn good thing you don't know about the other stuff.*

His departure had been acrimonious, her feelings got hurt, and he just wanted to get the hell away. *Distance to heal all wounds,* he had convinced himself. And now—well, here he was. Plenty of distance.

When will she find out I'm missing? After the charter fails to return? What about Davey? I'm sure it will sit like a big turd when she finds out he never came. Noooo . . . Davey had caved to his wife's demands. What about me? Thanks a lot, pal!

"Damn, damn, damn it," he unloaded in a wave of anger, releasing a latent part of him that was always there, always ready to give rise.

Slipping into a foul mood, he found the foot pump and hoses. After placing one end of the tube in the hold and the other over the side, he started working the pump with one leg, then another. Foot up, foot down. Up. Down. Up. Down. He focused all his fury into draining the engine room and bilge.

It kept him preoccupied for the next few hours. But time was now the one thing he had in abundance. Time to think, time to reflect, time to hope, and time to fear.

There was a lot of water, and it was slow going. He worked diligently into the afternoon, past the setting of the sun, and beyond the first twinkles of starlight. Meanwhile, the persistent rolling of the waves kept pushing him farther and farther and farther away from civilization.

"Son of a gun," he lamented as cramps fought for control of his hamstrings. But the water was gone. He had drained the boat's belly, the bilge emptied.

Climbing down into the engine room, the roof barely a foot over his head, the first thing to draw his attention was the strike where the lightning bolt must have hit. The fiberglass was charred and disfigured. After a careful inspection, he confirmed that the electronics would never come to life again, which forced him into accepting that the engines could not be resurrected.

After coming back on deck, a fresh wave of hopelessness washed over him, despair demanding to be treated as an equal partner. He waved it off, ignoring depression's incessant desires. Instead, he evaluated everything on his floating cocoon, coming to the conclusion that the only thing still working was the propane stove.

"The perishables are gonna go bad . . ." So he cooked the beef, the bacon, and the lamb, then settled in for a hot meal and a warm beer.

Once the galley had been cleaned and everything put away, he went up on the foredeck to sprawl out under the stars. Though not quite as level as the fishing transom, the extended prow was significantly larger and ringed by rails that had mostly survived.

He started picking out the constellations one by one. Cancer, his sign. Gemini . . . the bright stars of Castor, Pollux, and Alhena were always easy for him to spot.

"This is the way night skies are supposed to be," he said in awe. Relaxing into the rhythm of his surroundings, he had done all he could do for today.

The celestial highway blazed unfettered, the nebula of the Milky Way glowing like an opalescent rainbow. The grandeur of the night sky never ceased to give him pause at how insignificant humans were in the scheme of things.

Lying low on the horizon was Orion's Belt. Recalling one of the shows that had captured his imagination, he thought of how a theorist of alternative history had demonstrated that the three pyramids of Giza were aligned with the three bright stars of Orion.

Furthermore, though he was not a believer in any sentient being called God, he had found one thing that was almost impossible to explain in nature. Not only did the three stars of Orion align in exact angles, size, and placement to the belt of Orion, but the Nile fluxed and flowed in a precise spatial relationship with the contours of the Milky Way as if heaven had been mirrored on Earth.

"Coincidence?" This was the kind of question that kept drawing him in . . . the intrigue of ancient mysteries.

The endless sky resembled diamonds scattered upon black velvet. Unimaginable wealth if you could just reach up and grab hold of it. Often the great expanse of the heavens would send him off on one of his fantasies of having untold wealth. He would buy control of the effed-up media and own the politicians so that he could fix all that was wrong with America.

But not tonight. Tonight the reality of his situation pushed off any dalliance with fantasy.

"Will I ever see my family again? Am I going to die here, alone, where no one will ever know what has happened to me?"

As one unanswerable question followed another, fatigue pulled him into the world of dreams as the rolling sea rocked him to sleep. The stars above, the ocean below, and the nest of his meager vessel adrift on the wings of fate—these were now his only companions.

Chapter 3

Day in, day out, the seas continued pushing east. The swells remained manageable, and his boat showed no further signs of distress. Day—night—day, it all blurred into one. Each day, every day, in every direction, Mark saw nothing but ocean.

The sea was never the same two days in a row. Deep blue, powerful in its grandeur, rolling waves, choppy wind-spewed spray, gullies and plains, the swells changed their contours as often as the clouds scudding above.

Boredom was the enemy and survival the objective. His body was burned by the sun, and the salt-laden air kept him feeling clammy. Erecting a blue tarp to ward off the searing rays, he found that it also served to collect rainwater when squalls would blow through.

Mark had become a prudent caretaker, carefully managing his diminishing supplies. Augmenting his meager rations with fresh fish, he waged a constant battle against the sharks. They got about two of every three fish he hooked. The pattern soon became obvious. Anything hooked that was under forty pounds, he quickly pulled on board before they were even aware of the catch. But as the fish got bigger, the fight took longer, and the thrashing was more robust. Inevitably, this was when the beast zeroed in.

"You lazy prick," he screamed when the line snapped. "Go get your own dinner."

It was the same shark that shadowed him. With jaws the size of a car door, the creature would often bump the boat, doing exploratory reconnaissance. When Mark was busy washing down the deck or hauling in buckets of seawater, his nemesis would move silently, just below the surface, his massive dorsal fin like a periscope, always close.

Secure in the integrity of his craft, he had little worry as long as he did not do anything stupid.

One evening while drinking his last remaining beer, something magical happened. The ocean lit up like an airport runway. Long corridors of undulating light glowed for as far as the eye could see. It was spectacular. Bioluminescent plankton were acting in concert, streaking the ocean in rivers of light. This unusual spectacle of Mother Nature reminded him of another time nature had left him amazed.

"That trip seemed like a million years ago." He was getting used to speaking out loud. Surprisingly, the sound of his own voice helped ease the loneliness that was ever present.

Sitting on the prow, beneath the windows, he closed his eyes and let his mind drift back. Replaying memories was one of his ways of fighting boredom. Out here, all alone, there was nowhere to hide. Some memories revealed parts of himself he preferred to ignore. But this one he relished.

He and Davey had been sitting at the dock in Bimini, preparing to go out for the day when someone shouted, "Lobster march." Suddenly, there was a flurry of activity as every boat headed for the harbor's exit.

They followed them out of the well-protected inlet. With the shifting shoals of coral-bleached sand in the clear Bahamian waters, navigation was simply by line of sight. But that morning, the bright bottom had turned dark. A giant shadow moved as far as the eye could see. Locals started free diving into the water. Near ten feet deep at the channel's entrance, it dropped quickly as it sprawled out toward the edge of the Gulf Stream. Dozens of islanders were hauling out lobsters as fast as they could grab them.

It was another of nature's inexplicable reasons for doing what she does. Like the plankton that gave him the light show this particular night, no one knew why or when lobsters would gather and march. It was one of the most unusual experiences of his carefree life when he was a master of the universe.

Returning his thoughts to the current sight, he stared captivated at the long, luminescent highways. He followed a spoke out to the edge of his vision. There was a blip on the horizon, but it was too far away and too dark to see.

"I wonder what it is," he thought aloud and considered using the binoculars he had stowed away.

"A place for everything, and everything has a place," he repeated, triggering a memory of his dad. He had died not too long ago, undergoing a rapid but fatal bout with cancer.

His father had served most of his adult life in the navy. Enlisting to serve in World War II, he had eventually gone on to officers' candidate school. Rising to the rank of lieutenant commander, he was the commander of his own ship when Mom died.

"I was nine, Collette was twelve, and Misty was a mere child . . . ," he recalled. Thinking of his mother opened old wounds. He was too young when she died, and he had hardened his heart so that he buried any emotions of missing her. "What would it have been like to grow up with her being alive . . ."

The transition of life after his mom had died and his father had begrudgingly left the navy had been jarring.

"Dad enters the picture with no practical parenting skills and pissed off at the world for being forced to retire his career to care for his children. He treated us as if we were his sailors, using the same disciplinary protocols he had used in the military.

"And every time Collette screwed up . . . we were all punished until she confessed." Which, of course, she never did. He remembered all of them being made to keep their foreheads pressed against the wall for hours until the culprit who ate the entire can of Charles Chips confessed. His little sister dared not cry, but he had seen the bruise growing on her forehead.

His father's bizarre disciplinary devices had played a part in the loathing he had for his older sister. As adults, it simply worsened.

"What a selfish bitch," he seethed, once again overwhelmed with anger.

Anger at his sister, anger at his father, and, mostly, anger at this whole damn situation. He willingly settled into his flashback of resentment.

"That crap may have worked for grown men, expecting the crew to take care of their own, but not for kids and especially not for Misty. Cripes, she was just two years old . . . what a jerk." He spit, hocking a loogie over the side.

Anger slipped into the realization that another day of nothing to do lay before him.

"Is this the tenth or the eleventh day?"

It was a stupid question. He was still his father's son. He knew exactly how long he had been at sea. This returned him to thoughts of his dad. Though the recollection that appeared this time brought a smile as he recalled a bittersweet victory he had gotten over on dear ol' Dad.

He lay on the bow deck, the winds rustling over the waves as he relived his senior year in high school . . .

He had not gone the traditional route. With his father unwilling to help with college tuition, he had shunned the entire process. No forethought or planning, just screw 'em. But as it was a requirement at the time, he had taken his Saturday-morning SATs, albeit hungover and still smelling of beer from the night before.

He revisited his beliefs that the schools had dumbed down education. "I got high all the time but still managed to get Bs and a few Cs. It was like they were catering to the lowest common denominator. I just needed to show up.

"I applied the same work ethic to this test as I had to my classwork. It seemed pretty basic. Answer what I knew. Of the remaining questions, eliminate the obvious wrong choices and guess. I was done before anyone else. The teacher would not accept my paper, as it required I list five colleges where the results would be delivered. Like I gave a rat's ass . . ."

He smiled at the irony, thinking at the time the joke was on them. Harvard, UPenn, UCLA, University of Miami, and on a whim—Annapolis.

"After all—Dad's a navy man." He was enjoying the moment from so long ago.

"Well, fate had the last laugh. Apparently I guessed correctly on close to one hundred percent of the questions and scored in the top one percentile in the nation."

"'No effing way,' I recalled saying when acceptance letters began to arrive. I was pretty damn proud of myself—that is, until Dad came home all excited." My father had gotten a call from the local congressman. The secretary of the navy had informed him that a native son from his district was on his way to the academy. Dad was suddenly so proud of me.

"A-hole . . ."

What happened after that took on a life of its own. Autopilot with the inevitable ending. The military physical—passed. The navy requesting he have his wisdom teeth removed—done. Obviously, they didn't want to pay for it. Still, check the box. Another meeting and then . . .

"Holy crap. Now what do I do?" he recalled.

It was the moment of truth. While he waited outside in the buffed linoleum corridor, behind the closed door were three admirals who would decide his future.

"Mr. Lambert, have you thought about your career path in the navy?" He was a middle-aged man. Fit and in his dress whites.

"I want to be a fighter pilot. Top gun," I said, knowing my height exceeded the cowling maximums. My high school friend had told me that. The men looked at one another and shuffled papers, obviously aware of my particular vitals.

Another said, "Navigator?"

The top cowling sloped up as it sloped back—I knew this. At six foot two, my height as the rear-seat navigator would not be an issue. But fate was offering an opening, giving me the courage to speak plainly.

"No way am I spending one more day in the god-awful navy."

"Sirs," I said, my hands fumbling below the tabletop. My voice was hesitant, my mouth bone dry.

"I don't want to be in the navy. I have been doing this for eighteen years. That's more than enough. At least for me, anyway."

I was quick to add that last part, as I did not want to offend. Once in, they could make my life hell.

"Don't get me wrong. This is a great honor, and I appreciate your faith in me. I would fulfill every obligation and serve my time with dignity. But . . ."

I hesitated, trying to read their expressions, but they were implacable. "But when my commitments are fulfilled, I do not expect I would reenlist."

I rushed to add weight to my argument. Anything to fill the vacuum of their silence. "It seems like a lot of money to spend on a one-timer."

The look on their faces finally cracked. Humans after all. But they were clearly confused. I'm not sure they had ever heard such a thing before. Preempting their first question, I added something that surprised even me.

"Sirs. My father spent his best years in the navy. If he ever heard I was telling you this, he would be heartbroken. I don't want to hurt him, I just

don't want to mislead you. The navy has always been good to my family."
I was hamming it up a little, but the sentiment was genuine.

A week later he had received a letter from the Department of the
Navy—and what they wrote had shocked him. It was well thought out and
offered redemption. The specificity and personal nature of the communiqué
was definitely not boilerplate.

Dear Mr. Lambert,

As you know, these scholarships are offered to individuals who we feel
are uniquely qualified to become officers. But in closely reading through
your transcripts, one thing became clear. We applaud that you worked
full-time while in high school. It is what has made you the fine man you
are today. But we noted that, because of this, you have had little time for
extracurricular activities and experiences, to explore what life has to offer.

In light of this, we are withdrawing our offer—but only temporarily. If
you would like to resubmit your application next year, we will give serious
consideration to your situation. Take a year off—this is a big decision. We
can wait.

We wish you well and hope you will reconsider a life as an officer and
a gentleman—just next season.

Regards . . .

"Dad was pissed. I was elated. When the opportunity to graduate from
high school came six months early, in January instead of June, I shucked the
prom, senior yearbook, St. Pete, and everything else and split for Miami."

The memory faded as fast as it had appeared. He did not want to think
about what else he had forgone. Some of his antics alluded to an ugly part
of his character he always avoided examining.

Looking out at the sea, he wondered . . .

"What would my life have been like if I was viewing these seas from
the top of an aircraft carrier or destroyer?"

The sun was firming the shapes of morning. After retrieving the
binoculars, he returned to the deck. Flexing his hands at the residual
resentment, he raised the field glasses to his eye. He could make out a dark
mass reaching up from the sea.

"Land?" Quickly he calculated the rhythm of the waves, his trajectory,
distance, and . . . disappointment.

"We are too far away . . . ," he lamented. He was going to pass the land
and there was nothing he could do.

The life raft was wedged between the cabin and the starboard rail. He
had inflated it as something to do, thinking it might be an option if there
ever came a chance to get off this drifting mass. His focus shifted between
the island and the raft as wild ideas began looking for traction.

The thought of trying to make it in a small, floating piece of rubber
ticked at his heart rate, but practicality scoffed at the nonsensical notion.

"No way is this gonna protect me from Ironsides." It was the nickname he had given to the monstrous leviathan that lurked below, waiting to steal his catch.

Slowly the island was falling behind him.

He let his eyes sweep the rolling seas, and the receding speck of land melted into the horizon. He went back into the cabin and pulled out the navigation charts. Maybe there was an opportunity in the moment. He unfurled them onto the table, hoping to get a bearing on his location and find out what islands lay to the south.

"Of course not," he muttered half-heartedly. Not really surprised. With modern GPS and satellite, few boats would carry paper charts that covered an area this far out to sea. He set out to calculate his position for something to do.

"The seas continually roll at four to six knots—call it five. Twenty-four hours a day over eleven days . . . maybe thirteen hundred miles east of surviving . . . ," he said sarcastically.

Assessing his food and water, he knew it was simply a matter of a few weeks—assuming the gods continued to provide him with similar levels of sustenance and rain squalls before things turned really bad.

Chapter 4

"What was that?" Woken from a deep sleep, he jumped out of bed, his heart racing.

The boat had struck something, causing the hull to shudder. Taking the stairs two at a time, he raced onto the back deck. Shadows moved in the predawn light. His fears turned to wonder as the silhouettes firmed with the gathering glow.

Whales, lots of them. He found their presence oddly comforting. He counted the ones playing in and around the boat. There were others farther away, but in the dawn light they blended into the sea.

"Awesome," he beamed, exhilarated by the reprieve in his loneliness.

The ones closest were moving off in a southerly direction, following the rest of the pod. But a mammoth blue whale, more than twice the size of his boat, came close enough to shower him from his blowhole.

"Ohhh, that feels good." He smiled, the mist on his naked, sun-beaten skin was far more pleasant than the occasional bucket he used to rinse himself down.

The large mammal lingered, watching him. His eyes seemed intelligent and inquisitive but also sorrowful.

"Is this your family?" Mark asked. He had never really considered the lives of ocean creatures. Or that they might have family, feelings, sorrows, and pains. Now he wondered—*Do they have memories and hopes?*

It wasn't that he didn't love animals. Sometimes his wife accused him of loving the dog more than he loved her, but fish . . .

The sun crested the horizon and painted the sky with hues of red, yellow, and orange. In the distance, Mark spied a much smaller whale that the older ones were protecting. Mark sensed the big blue was the sentinel, taking stock while the others put distance between the boat and the pod.

"Come back any time—you're always welcome," he said, wishing for their company a little longer. It was a respite from the pervasive weight of solitude.

The one who had eyed him, the one he thought of as Big Daddy, blew one last stream of water, letting the wind wash it over him. Mark flushed in awe and thanks, waving back at the big blue.

He was glad for their company, even if it was fleeting. But eventually they faded into the rhythm of the waves. And again he was alone with the rolling ocean, endless sky, and the winds that tipped spray off the wave tops.

The pod brought thoughts of his own family. His wife and three kids. Alessandra was seventeen and preparing for college. Florida State. She had been so excited when she got her acceptance letter. Forest was two years behind, still in high school. And his baby girl—Victoria, she had come quite unexpectedly. But she was his joy, five, precocious, inquisitive, and not yet jaded like the other two.

"Rachael must be frantic by now," he murmured.

He was surprised that he had to wipe a tear. For years they had been growing apart, mostly held intact by their children. He knew she felt like he did.

"Perhaps my going missing will free her." It was maybe the only consolation to this entire ordeal.

Memories came and went, another way to pass the time. The swells rose and fell with a predictable cadence, the sun bore down with its tropical intensity, and he found shade under the tarp.

He willed himself to recall each child's life, recollecting every detail of every moment he could remember from the minute they were born to the day he left.

Each thought triggered another. Without distraction, an honest assessment began to weave a tapestry, some of which he was not so proud.

"Rachael was there for every scrape, wound, heartache, and problem. Where was I? When Forest was in the hospital with a kidney infection, Rachael would sleep there every night. I barely even visited. But someone had to watch the other two children, right?"

He knew he was kidding himself. "All my son ever wanted was my attention, and I meted it out like water in a desert."

It pained him to cut through the whitewash he had painted over his life. He had convinced himself in the past that his role as the economic provider was what made him an excellent parent. What he saw, instead, was that he had never been emotionally present for his children. And when he was around physically, his mind was always off somewhere else.

"How could I have ignored those who are most important to me? Do they know that I love them?"

The question was daunting because he truly did not know the answer.

"Do they even care that I am gone?"

As a true analysis of the man he had been came forth, the side of him he wanted to forget would not go away as another day slipped into another night.

"Maybe they will be better off if I just drift away . . ."

It was now past the second week since he had gone missing. He spied a pale-blue buoy wrapped in slimy rope floating up ahead. It was made of blown glass, about the size of a beach ball. These had been used for centuries by Greek fisherman to hold up their nets. From the thick algae, he knew this one was old.

"Probably been drifting out here for over fifty years."

He had read about such things. Back during World War II, the Germans had seeded shipping lanes with drifting mines and used these large glass containers as floats. They were temperamental and extremely dangerous.

Nautical guides warned boaters to stay well clear of them, and *Lil Darling* was on a path to overtake and ram it. With a fresh sense of urgency, the idea of being blown to smithereens obliterated his bout of self-loathing and firmed his resolve to live, to return to his family, and to repair his broken life.

"I need to push this thing to the side before something terrible happens."

After grabbing a gaff, he leaned out over the rail, his muscles tight with anxiety, his eyes peeled for his nemesis.

"Be careful," came the cautioning yin to his yang. He scanned the waters, looking for Ironsides. Since the arrival of the whales, the shark had not appeared.

"Almost got it . . ."

He stretched to the point that the end of the pole kept slapping the water just in front of the buoy.

A ginormous shadow raced up from below and seized the gaff.

"Son of a bitch!" Mark recoiled. He scrambled backward, and his breath surged with adrenaline—fear scorched him like a hot anvil. With stained teeth, Ironsides glared back before moving off into the waves.

"Damn it, you idiot!" He shivered at his carelessness, watching the giant dorsal fin race away.

The shark turned, and it began to charge back toward the craft, its mouth gaping with teeth longer than Mark's forearm. Mark expected the beast to duck under the bow, but instead it leaped from the water and crashed onto the deck, where it hung suspended, dead eyes glaring with hatred, until it slipped back into the sea.

"What the . . . " Mark screamed.

Biting his lip, he backed away from the edge, unsure what was coming next. His mouth twitched as he gasped for breath.

This time Ironsides went out farther, leaving the buoy in its wake. Mark watched as he lined up another run. Fear had buried itself so deep into his psyche that it left a void, one that terror had already filled.

"He's not big enough to sink the boat . . . is he?"

Thwack! Splintering shards of fiberglass sailed from the crumpled rail.

The killing machine thrashed desperately, trying to get to the human prey mere feet away.

"What the . . . how much more can this boat take?" Tremors of fear ran down his spine as he remembered that in *Jaws*, the shark sank the vessel.

Tasting the metallic bile in his mouth, he eyed the buoy, desperate.

"This bastard is gonna kill me if I don't do something."

After grabbing the other gaff, he pulled at the last threads of courage and shimmied out onto the crushed rail. With one eye on the beast, he extended his arms as far as he could reach. The pole grazed the algae-coated hemp.

"Damn it," he swore. Ironsides was making his turn. He slid out a little farther, presenting an easy target as his nemesis lined up for another run. Working the hook end of the pole, he could not get it under the rope webbing.

"Come on, come on, come on." He kept one eye locked onto his tormentor, the other on the slime-coated halter.

"Gotcha," he cried, snagging the buoy. Knowing the hunter had him in his sights, he crawled to the side, pulling the reluctant float closer and closer.

"Come on, you bastard," Mark chided, intentionally leaving himself vulnerable and exposed as he gauged the seconds.

Ironsides adjusted his attack angle and made the dive. Mark scrabbled away from the edge just as a giant whoosh erupted, lifting the bow out of the water. Shards of plexiglass and rail rained across the deck as the boat splashed hard back into the sea. Mark pulled himself up from his knees.

"Take that, you dumb bastard," he said, pumping triumphally at the spreading pool of blood.

The smell of death drew in hundreds of sharks of every make, model, and size, each vying for pieces of the fresh meat. One anxiety was replaced with another. More sharks, more threats, more . . .

As quickly as they had appeared, frenzied and frothing, they vanished, receding back into the sea. Though unseen, Mark knew they were still there, lurking and waiting.

That was a week ago. And the band kept marching on. Another day dissolved into another night followed by another morning when it would begin all over again. Day by day by day, never changing, simply varying. Though he was relieved that the sharks had gone, boredom was now the all-consuming obstacle.

This day began like many others, with wispy clouds high in the atmosphere painting the pale sky. The wind lifted salt off the waves, crusting his skin.

But this day would be different. Starting with a smudge on the horizon, dawn firmed the morning, and he saw an island to the south.

He felt a flicker of hope flutter in his belly. "Land!"

Fate smiled on him as subtle shifts in the current turned toward the landmass. Hour by hour, soft swells pulled his craft closer and closer. The land became more distinct. Time moved at a snail's pace.

There had been a squall two days ago that had filled his fish cooler. Even after topping off all the plastic bottles, he still had gallons of fresh water left. Rubbing fingers over the salt that laced his skin, he decided change was in the air.

"It's a good day to take a bath." And bathe he did. With the last of his soap, he scrubbed at his deeply tanned skin until, for the first time in weeks, he felt clean.

Let's see what we got here, he thought, coming closer still.

It was a long ways off, but using the binoculars, he could see cliffs on one end and a smaller range of mountains at the other. Sandwiched between were dark forests edged by a long black beach.

"No signs of habitation," he muttered, frustrated and angry. All his life he felt he was in control, his actions determining his destiny. But now...

"Will we get near enough? What if we don't?"

Wiping perspiration from his hands, he eyed the raft, memories of the shark-frenzied waters always near.

"We need to get close . . ."

Constantly calculating the wind, current, and trajectory, he was gaining confidence that the ocean was going to pull them towards the island—but how close?

The binoculars, now his second set of eyes, brought a long coral reef into focus. Upending the waves that rolled across the relentless sea, the reef created a neat little harbor where inside, gentle swells lapped black-sand beaches.

He watched, he analyzed, and he plotted. All the while, the flicker of hope had grown into a fire burning with optimism and fueled by desire. Calculating and recalculating his course, he determined the boat would approach from the south side of the island and drift outside the reef until passing the high cliffs marking the northern end of the cove. He eyed the raft.

"If I can get close enough, do I go for it?"

Chapter 5

Close enough to see with the naked eye, endless arrays of coral became evident, their arms of staghorn so close to the surface that it would slice his raft to pieces. The idea of getting too close to the coral and his boat being shredded conjured up visions of sinking into the swamp of predators he always assumed were nearby. In truth, the coral was just the first of potential problems he envisioned.

Looking at the lush island in the middle of nowhere, he had a funny thought about his old friend Thomas. Maybe not so funny, but more like a nervous deflection.

As kids, their homes were near a copse of woods. Though most of the kids in the surrounding area would enter to play hide-and-seek, Thomas would not. He would mutter on about all sorts of improbable creatures.

"What if there are headhunters? Or cannibals?" echoed his distant voice. He had read stories about unexplored islands in the South Pacific that still had tribes that engaged in these barbaric practices. But here, in the Atlantic…

"Stop with the bull," he admonished himself. "I'm gonna make this work, no matter what!"

It wasn't cannibals who drew his concern. It was his fixation with sharks. But he hashed it out, arguing the pros and the cons, the what-ifs, and the why-nots. His analytical self-versus his cynical nature. The banter had all the trappings of friends arguing politics.

The wind had kicked up, adding a little more speed toward his final decision. Practicality advanced a plan. Each rebuff was dissected and addressed until he reached a consensus with Thomas. Which, of course, was really just his conscience, but he enjoyed the idea of an old friend as a companion, even if he was imaginary.

"Okay, then. We tie a long line to the bow and place the anchor into the raft. We tie a separate line connecting us to the boat in case we get separated."

In his mind's eye, he saw himself rowing close to the reef and tossing the anchor onto the coral. The current would swing *Lil Darling* around and draw her even closer to the bank. If possible, he would then raise the anchor line, take it in toward the leeward side of the barrier, and set it into a more permanent position.

"It's a sound plan. If it works, we can ferry gear back and forth to shore."

His chin high, confident of the big picture, he liked his chances. But being the man who was always extolling risk mitigation, a hallmark trait when he built his companies, he dug deeper. Anticipating obstacles, he measured currents, waves, and unexpected bottom topography. Continually updating speed and path, he estimated he was just over an hour from launch point.

What should I take ashore? he thought with a bit of optimism.

Scanning the galley, he saw the boat was literally shipshape, demonstrating his need to exert control over so many variables he had fallen mercy to by stowing everything in its place.

Not knowing if the island was inhabited or if he would be able to return for a second run, he prioritized by assuming the worst.

"Food, water, tarp, bucket, skillet, blankets, shoes, clothes, fishing rod, and tackle," he ticked off, all weighing into his first choice. "And, of course, the Dundee knife, honing stone, and binoculars."

He had moved past possibility and into expectation.

"We will pull this off."

Gathering the items, he added a lantern and kerosene, then bundled everything up in blankets creating two rope bound parcels.

"Set the anchor, come back, and get the stuff. A good plan." Rarely did he second-guess his choices. But again, the Thomas of his cynical side still needed to get a word in edgewise.

"One more chance for the sharks."

"Shut up . . ."

Shaking his head at his bickering lunacy, he gave scant consideration to the question of sanity. After nearly a month and a half of solitude, he justified that the manufactured alter ego actually helped to keep him sane. But he did note with amusement at how different the two sides of his personality were unfolding.

"Well, me is me. And I am I." He laughed. Talking to himself had become a game, something to relieve the monotony and to have fun with. And hearing another's voice, even if it was his own, helped lift the weight of being alone.

He grabbed a bag with two hundred feet of rope. Attaching one end to the raft and the other to a side cleat, he placed the oars in the oarlocks and secured them. He had never used this type of raft before, so he practiced procedural dry runs on the deck.

Closer, closer, closer, until . . .

He hoisted the raft over the rail.

"Time to go!"

Mark lowered the anchor into the center of the raft. It wasn't that heavy but instead was designed to claw into the bottom and hold fast. He eased himself over the starboard rail. With the rafts rubberized folds, his weight creased the bottom but helped to stabilize the boat as it rolled with the swells. He scanned the waters, looking for any shadows lurking below the surface.

"I know you guys are there," he warned them with his less-than-confident voice. Settling between the oarlocks, he unleashed the line from the rail and let the current pull him toward the bow.

The water was clear, and his anxiety kept a steady vigilance. It was his first time leaving the boat in over forty days. He never swam. His baths were generally from buckets of seawater. And his phobia of prowling predators was ever present.

"Damn!" he swore through pinched lips. He saw an open gash at the bow, just above the waterline.

"Fricken Ironsides. Good riddance, you prick!"

The wound wasn't mortal, but it was nasty. If the ocean kicked up another storm, it was an opening that would take on excessive water. A good reason to expedite maneuvering his boat up onto the reef.

He looped the line through the grommet and tied it off. Once satisfied, he pushed off and set the oars in motion. He angled toward the reef, the current assisting as the rope spooled out a bit too quick.

"Shoot! I've gone too far." There was not enough slack in the line to set the anchor. As he fought against the current, the stiff breeze was making it difficult. Waves splashed over the side, sloshing water from end to end.

"Failure is not an option," he told himself. He pulled harder, paralleling the underwater barrier until he regained the slack he needed. The reef was made up of thousands of coral heads interspersed with sluices and gullies, just like in all the other reefs around the world where he'd dived. He was aware that the canals were big enough that predators could easily move in and about the reef.

He continued to work the oars, ignoring the cramping in his hands. He was winded and breathing hard, but the clear waters revealed a coral head that could work. He tossed the anchor, and the weight dropped straight to the bottom. With a little luck and a bit of skill, he maneuvered the line until it was secured behind a hard pillar.

Lil Darling drifted past the fixed spot until her bow turned into the oncoming current. The line tugged as she adjusted to the rhythm and flow of the water.

"It's working! Damn it, it's working . . ." Then the line came free, and *Lil Darling* was once again adrift, the stern leading floating forth on the endless river. *God dang it . . .*

"Grab the damn bottom," Mark yelled, willing the dragging anchor to do its job. But the boat kept drifting. He rowed furiously, being pulled north by the mother ship. The reef below dropped off, and he found himself in deep water. A pass that split the reef in half. He worked through the new information, looking past fear and seeking any possible leverage.

"It's a channel, which means there is a way to get to shore without shredding the raft. Should I try?"

Working the oars with a frantic pace, he grabbed the line and pulled the anchor that was bucking along the bottom. He aimed toward shore, the mother ship as compliant as a mule, bucking and kicking until . . . the current had gone slack.

Lil Darling was in limbo.

"I'm inside the bay," he shouted with exhilaration.

Calculating the amount of line left, he looked for a place to reset the anchor before the tides reversed his fortune. The slack water made it easier to move the larger vessel, and the current was pushing *Lil Darling* toward the northern wall of coral.

The water was so clear he could see everything below him. The channel was well defined, with spires of ancient coral bracketing the open flow of the tides.

The Bertram scraped the wall, then did so a second time. She was breaking coral fingers, and the drag was becoming immensely difficult.

"There," he decided. It was a large pillar that had no doubt lasted for ages. He could see fish swimming among the blue polyps as his sea mistress wedged onto the shallowing coral. Lowering the anchor, he worked it until he had a sufficient number of wraps to hold it secure, but he left enough excess for the tides.

"No way you're gonna snatch my *Lil Darling*!" he hollered at the ocean, triumph coursing through his veins.

With the work completed, he rowed alongside her. He was already pinning hope on her that she would be his beacon to the outside world, that a passing vessel would see his white goddess and think, *Someone is stranded here.*

He looked at the beach and he looked at his boat. He was zealous about going ashore, but being a prudent risk-taker, he needed to be sure she did not come unfree during the night. He had already gotten away with that mistake once and was fortunate the boat had crossed the channel and wedged on its north side.

And besides, the day was almost over, with the sun low on the horizon. The sky was a hundred shades of red.

"If there are people here, they'll still be there in the morning." His instincts, though, were not as optimistic as the words coming from his lips.

Not long after the stars had emerged from their hiding places, he drifted off into a world of dreams. His dreams were filled with hope that the island would solve all his problems, hope that he could get back to being Mark Lambert, as well as other dreams which were a bit more lurid . . .

He was interrupted by the first rays of sunrise. Stiff from sleeping on the deck, he lingered until he remembered where he was.

"The boat! She held fast on the reef."

There was a slight tilt but no rocking. A small tide had pushed her higher onto the inside barrier. He could see she was nesting in a cradle of broken coral.

"Mark Lambert, you are the man." He was rightfully pleased his plan had been executed to perfection.

Eating a breakfast of warmed-over beans and his last can of hash, the excitement became tempered by the what-ifs.

"What if the island is deserted? I've stranded my boat here permanently." This slipped into the what-if fears of dying all alone in the middle of this godforsaken ocean. *What if there is no food or water? What if the . . .*

"Snap out of it, mister," he told himself. After grabbing his backpack, he collected his wallet, cash, credit cards, cell phone, and, of course, his passport.

The blue cover embossed with the seal of the United States of America did not have a single mark on it. He had renewed it less than two months ago.

Opening to the photo, he reviewed his vitals. "Mark Austin Lambert. Male. Brown eyes. Brown hair. Six foot two." It had his birth date, issuance date, and expiration date. A lot of dates.

He flipped to the lone immigration stamp, and it felt like forever since he had been away. "Barbados, forty-six days ago." He closed it, put it in his backpack, and gathered up his toiletries, adding those to his ditty bag.

Readying to go ashore, he checked his anchor one last time.

"Mr. Lambert, two more points for you."

He thought it funny that all his thoughts were now verbalized.

"I guess I just love to hear myself talk." He laughed.

Success always gave him a warm feeling, an affirmation that fueled him, that gave him a semblance that he was in control of his world.

Staring at the line of seaweed pushed up on the beach, he knew that the closer one got to the equator, the less severe the tides. He had calculated the tidal spread in Barbados when he had allocated the length of slack yesterday.

"Pretty darn close," he said with smug satisfaction. With his hands on his hips, he surveyed the deck one final time.

"If I need these, I'll come get them." It was a large plastic bag full of the empty water bottles he had used and reused.

Being a creature of habit, he made one more reconnaissance of the vessel.

"Shipshape and ready to roll. Time to go see what this island has to offer."

He hefted the dinghy over the rail and carefully lowered each bundle, his toiletry bag, and the backpack into the raft. As he climbed off what had been his home for the last six weeks, the suppressed anxiety of the unknown was no longer suppressed. Biting his lip, he made promises to his beached friend.

"Don't worry, *Lil Darling*. I'll be back."

With minimal currents and smooth water, rowing to shore proved simple. He spotted a grassy knoll beyond the sand and headed that way. Within minutes he stepped from his raft and drew the dinghy up onto the black volcanic sand. It was hot under the tropical sun.

"Land!" he extolled, raising clasped hands in a form of mock prayer. His legs wobbled, and he stumbled to his knees.

"Sea legs," he laughed, while his eyes darted one way then the other, absorbing everything around him.

The beach ran about fifty feet from the water's edge to the line of palm trees, abundant with coconuts and leaning toward the sea. He knew from living in Florida they were full of nutritious water. Beyond the palms was a knoll covered with coarse grass, a large boulder, and, behind that, forest that ran off into the island.

"Hellooo. Helloooooo," he called out. "Anybody here?" His voice died on the breeze. Other than the scurrying of lizards and the songs of birds in the forest, there were no signs of habitation. But he did not let that discourage him. Not yet anyway.

"Maybe on the other side of this island. How big is it?"

He removed the gear and carried it up to the grass, where he could still see *Lil Darling*.

"I'm right here, baby. No need to worry."

She gave him comfort. Her body being so large and white and so anomalous to the setting, it was his beacon of hope that the outside world would notice and eventually rescue him.

The knoll dipped inland and muted the roar of the distant surf. Near the edge of the forests, he could hear the buzzing of insects, and along the beach came the soft lapping of surf that serenaded the black volcanic sands.

He closed his eyes, taking deep breaths to fully absorb the feeling of finally being back on solid ground. After a spell, he opened them and looked north. The question of how big suddenly seemed crucial, or perhaps curiosity was now king. Either way, the jutting cliff was about a mile down the beach.

"We could get a better view from up there . . . ," he said, eyeing the top of the mountain.

"And leave our stuff here? Is that smart?"

Thomas had quickly adapted to his every thought. In this case, he was weighing whether to set up camp or see if there might be others on the island. He gave scant consideration to the voice concerned with his stuff. What was important stayed with him in the backpack.

"If there are people who want to steal our things, then there are people who can connect us with the outside world."

Adding the binoculars and large knife, he headed north. The sand was firm, the waters to his left were clear, and to the right a thick jungle was filled with the sounds of squawking birds. Scents of exotic flowers drifted down from the slope.

Approaching the mountain, the promontory marking the north end of the bay extended out hundreds of feet into the ocean. The walls were variegated, craggy rocks splotched with guano from the seabirds. He angled toward a gap in the trees.

He logged every detail, knowing survival would demand total awareness, and his gut told him he was alone.

"Still no signs of human intrusion. No paths, no cut or broken plants, no animal tracks, burrow holes, or residual animal droppings. Seems we have the place all to ourselves. Let's climb the mountain to be sure."

He was not as disappointed as he should have been. His instincts had been priming him for this eventuality. Instincts he had learned to trust years before.

"The forest is pretty thick. I don't think we should go in," responded the naysaying Thomas of his childhood.

"You know we share the same brain, right?" He started laughing. The presence of Thomas allayed the boredom and masked the loneliness. It was too soon to start analyzing this side or that side of himself.

He wielded his knife like a machete, cutting a path along the outcropping. Vines hung from the walls, intermingled with roots and thorns on the forest floor. He made slow progress, eventually rounding a point that cut off his view of the bay. He stopped to wipe sweat from his brow.

"Man, it's hot."

The humidity clung to his clothes, to the vegetation, to the air itself. He assumed it was because he was used to the constant ocean breezes. He sucked in gulps of heavy air while fingering flowers on the hanging vines.

"What's this?"

There was an opening behind the stringy creepers dangling from above. Pushing them aside, he peered into a gap that penetrated the rockface.

"Looks pretty big. Hello," he called into the opening. Nothing.

Cutting away the bramble, he ran his hand over the stone, and flecks of mica glistened on his fingers.

"It's an old lava tube."

Cutting away enough vegetation that he could step inside, the first thing to hit him was the temperature change.

"Nice." He reveled in the unexpected luxury.

His skin tingled from the cool air, and he enjoyed his first respite from the tropical heat since the boat's air conditioner got fried along with the other electronics.

"Anybody home?" he called. "Hello, hello." The vegetation implied there was no habitation, but he wanted to give fair warning in case any large animals had made a nest in the darkness.

The echo of his voice was muted, an indication that a larger space lay beyond. But the depth of the darkness could not be penetrated by the feeble light seeping in from the opening. After a dozen more steps, he stopped and listened. Again nothing.

"I can't see squat!" he said, thinking perhaps sound could glean more about this place.

"Hello," he whispered. Then a bit louder: "Anybody home?" Finally shouting at the top of his lungs, "Bubba, you in there?" Nothing.

But the echo did reveal that the cave continued back a ways. What he could assess was mostly positive. The floors were dry and relatively flat, it was spacious enough to store his gear, and it was naturally cool.

"That's the big plus. But the downside," he said, balancing the scales. "From here we cannot see the beach." Meaning he could not keep an eye on *Lil Darling* in case a boat appeared.

Stepping out into the sunlight, he logged the data, parked the debate, and studied the face of the cliff. He was glad of the discovery—it might make a good shelter, but he needed to get back on task.

"Let's go see what we can see."

The vegetation was thick, but it was less foliated close to the rockface. Steadily he ascended. At one point he could see the entire length of the beach, including his white companion anchoring the south end of the reef.

Inland treetops sloped up the island's incline. He wasn't up far enough to see what lay beyond, but he was getting a feel for the surroundings.

"No towns, no people!" Disappointment was catching up with his gut instincts. The island was deserted.

Coming upon a small ledge, he stopped to catch his breath. Whipping out his manhood, he let loose a long yellow stream. As it rained onto rocks far below, he burst out laughing.

"In the distance category, the gold goes to America's Mark Lambert."

It was from an old movie about Japanese factory managers trying to train American auto workers. They had all gone out drinking together and decided to have a literal pissing match. The Americans argued they should score for distance—the Japanese argued for accuracy.

After zipping up, he took a swig of water and returned to his climb. Slowly and begrudgingly, the vegetation gave way until there was just old volcanic rock. With hands flecked in mica, he reached the top.

"Phew," he exhaled, letting out a winded breath. The dome-shaped top was roughly a football field wide. And the view . . . unobstructed three sixty.

In one direction he could see the length of the island, the outlines of the reef, the beach, and the cliffs at the other end. He noted the topographical coloration changed near the far point.

"Looks to be about two miles, give or take," he calculated aloud.

Inland was thick with jungle, and ahead the sea was as blue as blue could be. He followed the current beyond the coral barrier until it rounded the point below him and continued on its journey out into the vast Atlantic.

He took out his binoculars and peered at the high point along the eastern spine.

"Agriculture?" The contours looked artificial, kicking up a flutter of hope.

"I'm telling you its cannibals."

"Really?"

"Or chupacabras."

"Oh brother."

Mark flexed his hands while imprinting the topography to memory. The island ran north to south about two miles. The bulging mountains capping each end had the look of a dog's bone. The bay was protected by a reef that bowed out toward the deep blue. The south bay looked relatively shallow, though the water grew deeper as one approached this end.

From this vantage point, the jungle looked dense and the topography uneven. He would need to explore it later. His attention was drawn back to the unforested rim that ran along the spine of the island. Beyond the hillock he could see ocean. Of course, that would make sense—it was an island. This led to some probability and speculation.

"If this side of the island has a wide forest angling down from the ridge, does the other side have the same?" Could there be a town, maybe even a harbor?"

His gut instincts were telling him that nobody had been on this island for years. Still, hope flickered like a candle's delicate flame.

Chapter 6

Coming down the mountain, Mark had a few missteps, with loose gravel putting him on his butt a couple of times. But mostly the return trip was uneventful. All the while, he was exploring the idea of using the cave as a permanent shelter.

"I need to check out the rest of the island, but it looks promising."

With only the sound of birds cawing in the forest, he considered the real possibility he might be here for an extended period.

"Find out what food is available. Look for fresh water. Make a secure base camp and . . ."

Looking out at *Lil Darling*, he churned through all the stuff still onboard.

"You have nothing to say?" he chided. Thomas had been silent for a while.

"Umm, nope. You seem to be doing a surprisingly good job of figuring it all out."

Mark gave a smirk. "Yes, I have."

With the afternoon ahead, he went to explore the other end of the beach. Camp had been struck at the closest point to the reef, which so happened to be the beach's center. He guesstimated the area as being about two miles end to end. Thus, he had a mile walk.

The onshore breeze was cooling, and the air felt clean. Feeling clammy and crusted with sweat, he eyed the turquoise waters.

"Man, I could go for a swim . . ."

"And get us both eaten by sharks," came the instant retort of his skeptical self.

But in this case, he heeded the sage advice of Doubting Thomas.

He walked the water's edge, sidestepping the lapping rhythm of the sea. To his left the lush jungle began to thin. Boulders were replacing trees, the inland view growing deeper, and with each step a dank odor grew stronger.

"What the hell is that?"

The terrain had flattened into a marshy swamp that extended to the water's edge. An unpassable barrier separated him from the southern peaks.

"Maybe circle around?"

As he looked inland, something was rustling the marsh grass. He froze—nerves taut. From this distance, it was hard to distinguish if the grass was moving or simply swaying. He envisioned a large animal stalking through the bramble. Being alone in a strange place had taken the reins of his imagination. The place was giving him the creeps, and the pounding in his ears made him only more wary.

"It's a chupacabra, I'm telling you," Thomas piled on.

Adding to his unease, an undulating mass came from out of the bog.

"Ow, damn it!" With unexpected viciousness, an insatiable cloud of mosquitoes swarmed him.

"Get off," he screamed over and over. The scent of his fresh blood carried on the wind, and the swarm grew until every part of his body was covered. They just kept coming.

"Run," he yelled with all he had. And run he did. Racing along the water's edge, he sought distance between himself and those bloodsuckers.

Winded and out of shape, he kept running. He gulped air, and they kept coming. Little by little, he sensed the cloud was thinning, but he dared not stop to look. Eventually, once he was past the boulders and back in line with the thick forests, most had given up. He suspected the ocean breeze helped.

"Keep those bastards pinned down there," he spit, vowing to stay clear of that end of the beach.

Winded, he slowed to a walk, squashing greedy mosquitoes still hanging on, his tanned skin now covered with a thousand dots of red.

"Screw this place," he shouted down the beach. Only the roar of the waves offshore responded.

Under a heaving breath, he wandered back to camp. Lingering on fears of malaria, typhoid, and other mosquito-borne diseases, his thoughts found their way to stories about people being swarmed in the Maine woods by black flies so intense that they were drained of blood before they could ever get away.

"That ain't gonna be me," he swore.

The world suddenly felt shaky—the mosquitoes had unsettled him. He cast his eyes out to the reef. Seeing *Lil Darling* helped to calm his spirit, and he'd been unaware of how important her presence was to him.

As the shadows of afternoon grew long, the smart thing to do would be to build a fire, set up camp, and put up the tarp. But, truthfully, the sky was that kind of blue that turned into a night full of stars. His intellectual barometer told him no rain tonight.

"Let's go see what's topside."

He had always been driven by curiosity, and deep down he still harbored hope there might be people. After adding a couple of water bottles and food to his bag, he entered the forest.

Wary after the last experience, he was attuned to every sight and every sound.

"Are there people here? Will they be friendly? What language will they speak?"

The going was gradual, and the vegetation tore at his legs. Roots hidden underfoot and creepers dangling from trees thwarted each step. There were birds cawing in the branches but no signs of larger animals, no paths they may have established, and no source of water he could see.

"At least there are plenty of coconuts," he acknowledged, denting his disappointment.

The foliage was dense, and the deeper he plunged, the damper it grew. There were bugs aplenty, but not akin to the tornadoes near the swamp. His shirt was soaked and sweat beaded off the end of his nose. He was determined, however, until he came to an unscalable wall of rock.

"Well, if you can't go over it, and you can't go under it, then go around it," he reminded himself, returning to an old business axiom he harbored.

As an entrepreneur, he had learned every new business encountered problems. His answer was to find a solution, not an excuse. It was the mantra that separated those who succeeded from those who quit. In this case, his only option was to try to go around.

As he followed the wall of errant boulders and hard basalt, the ground gradually began to rise. Soon the rocks had become manageable and continued to diminish in size.

"Ahh."

Stepping onto the top of the ridge, he was covered in sweat and coated with cuts. The first thing to strike him was the flatness of the ground in front of him. Behind, the hillside was lined with tall hardwood trees, like sentinels guarding the forest. But to the east, grass grew among an orchard laden with spiny green balls.

"Bread fruit," he exclaimed joyously. Surprise lifted laugh lines that crinkled into a smile. "Food! Acres and acres of it."

The green melons were a great source of protein used throughout the tropical world. They would definitely help him to survive. And there was an almost unlimited supply.

"Great, we can die of scurvy instead." Thomas was back . . .

"Negatory, my doubting friend," he said, going on to explain to him why this was the mother lode of survival.

"Plenty of vitamin C as well. Breadfruit is a universal food. It was used to prevent scurvy, is hearty, and obviously doesn't need a lot of tending. For us, it is manna from heaven."

He had read a book in high school about settlers to the West Indies who had planted breadfruit as the ultimate food source for survival.

Their presence, though, did raise questions. Where did they come from? Who planted them? Are there people here? Maybe below the hills on the other side? Or maybe slave traders back in the day? It didn't matter. This was a huge find.

With the sun's rays angling lower, Mark was eager to keep exploring. Crossing to the windward side of the island, he looked over the edge.

"Crap! No boat's gonna get on the island from this side."

Crestfallen, he saw there was no town. There were no people. The ocean was hundreds of feet below with nothing but a continuous pounding of waves against the base of the cliff. Disappointment dashed away his hope of there being others on the island.

"I'm alone," he admitted.

Solitude was an omnipresent weight, and he was not built for having himself as his only companion. He had always been the life of the party, and it had been easy for him to engage others.

"We got each other," Thomas offered in a poor attempt at humor.

"I'll sleep here tonight," he said, resigned. His failing enthusiasm lingered on the reality of his situation. "Here, there, the cave, what does it matter? I'm going to be here for a really long time."

With the sun sinking fast, he located a soft patch of grass to lie down upon. With weeks and weeks of boredom, sleep was one of the ways he had passed the time. But this was the first time sleeping on solid ground since departing Barbados.

He was alone, scared he would die here, and that no one would ever know. The thought of irrelevance, of passing and no one caring, felt oppressive.

It was not long until the lingering twilight was gone. A deep darkness covered the island. One by one the stars appeared until, like a bowl of jewels, they were as bright as they had been out on the open sea.

Finally starting to relax, he heard a sound. A rustling. Something was lumbering through the branches below the rim. His hands grew clammy and his shoulders tight. His imagination ran down every fear he could muster.

"Headhunters! I knew it!"

Mark was in no mood to argue, especially with himself. His concern centered on a more probable possibility like wild dogs or pigs. Either way, both could be dangerous. One saving grace was that the adjacent escarpment was too sheer to climb.

Over the rapid pounding of his heart, he could still hear the noise prowling below, and he relaxed only when it moved off toward the southern end of the island. It was another reason to avoid that place.

The next few days were a busy blur of activity as he shored up his survival in the middle of this unforgiving world of wind, water, and the unrelenting heat of the tropics.

Accepting that it could be months before he might be rescued, he set out to provide the basics he would need to survive—food, water, shelter. Fortunately, the breadfruit would provide him with both the protein and the vitamins he needed.

There were thousands and thousands of coconuts—pipas, the local Cubans back in Miami called them. Light orange on the outside, they were full of a thin watery liquid that was supposedly good for the kidneys.

Regarding a more permanent shelter, between the good weather and explorations of the island, he had put off returning to the cave, at least until it began to rain. And rain it did. Tropical monsoon–type rains. The water spilled from his tarp so quickly it overflowed his cooler.

"Gotta get the bag of bottles . . ."

"And the other fish boxes to save more water," Thomas added, saying something constructive for a change.

"First things first." It had been forever since he had taken a decent shower. He stripped and let the rain pouring from the tarp wash over him.

"Ahh, simple pleasures . . ." Salt on the skin was a constant problem, as it caused rashes in areas prone to moisture. He reveled in feeling clean. But the water kept falling, and soon his gear was soaked.

"Thomas! We are not getting out of here anytime soon, so let's gather up our stuff and move to a more permanent home."

As he headed north, the mountain that jutted out into the sea cast a shadow onto the beach. Washed against the base of the cliff were scattered piles of driftwood. Some big, some small, most bleached by time, all would be perfect for a fire.

"Probably been washing up here for centuries."

With machete in hand, he hacked a trail. As before, rounding inland, the humidity index skyrocketed because of the lack of a breeze, but as soon as he entered the cave . . .

"Ahh." He flipped on the flashlight. The walls appeared solid, but he could feel a minute breath of air flow into the cave from the rear. He had read that some volcanic islands had rivers of ocean water coursing deep below, in this case providing a natural air-conditioning system that kept the place cool, dry, and free of must.

"Plenty of room to store the gear," he assessed aloud. "But light is going to be a problem. Batteries will only last so long."

Still, this was going to be the place. The trade-off of not seeing his boat which he began to refer to as his girl, lost out to maybe the only cool spot in this part of the tropics.

Over the next few days, he widened the path from the beach and produced a decent landing at the front entrance. Here he set his tarps, sheltered a fire, and stored wood for cooking.

After slogging all his gear, he confronted two facts that had to be addressed. He could not sleep on the floor. It was too hard. And he needed a more permanent answer for light.

"I told you I would return," he said as he climbed aboard his grounded vessel. Talking to *Lil Darling* was a way of personifying his sea mistress. He was comforted by the fact that his old friend remained wedged hard on the reef. Not only was she not about to abandon him, but it reduced any sense of urgency to strip the boat. Instead, he could take things in a slow, methodical process.

He recapped his priorities: remove the mattress and find a more permanent solution for light. The latter was a problem he was still exploring.

The sun, a constant in the tropics, was already hot on his face. He imagined relaxing in a hammock with a cold drink.

"Maybe an ice-cold Fresca," he said with smacking lips. He settled for a bottle of water and surveyed his domain. The beach, the mountains, the ridge beyond the tree line. Back on the boat for the first time, he now had a broader perspective of the island.

Turning his gaze out at the ocean, the endless horizon was filled with tame whitecaps. But he knew how angry she could be if she was riled.

The thought of those monstrous peaks reminded him how fortunate he was. He vowed that whenever he felt depressed, he'd remember it could have been worse.

"I should be dead," he admitted, truly thankful for his survival. "Your strength saved us. And standing here day and night, you will be the reason I will get rescued."

Wiping sweat from his palm, he did a quick survey. Finding a possible light source was the first priority he was going to address.

"Let's start below."

Climbing down into the engine room, he had not expected the water that covered the floor. It was dank and had the cloying smell of grease. Daylight spilled in from the gash in the bow. It was the hole where Ironsides had done his worst. Rainbow sheens of oil glimmered on the surface of the water.

After gathering some old rags from a box on the shelf, he stuffed them into the hole. Though reducing the sunlight to a haze, hopefully it would prevent any more water from sloshing in.

"That should do the trick."

The engine room had a number of storage compartments. There were tools, which he placed topside, diving gear, a small amount of emergency rations, and basic first aid stuff. Dozens of items that would be useful. And then . . .

"Well, what do we have here?" It was a solar charger used in case the batteries died.

"A solution to my lighting problem?" His pulse quickened on an idea: remove the batteries, set up the solar charger, and create a lighting system.

But what little he knew about electricity told him there was a problem. You cannot hook up AC lights directly to the batteries.

The sun peeking through edges of the cloth-stuffed bow offered inspiration.

"Remove the bow lights. Of course." As a seasoned boater, he knew they were connected by a direct current.

"I can take three batteries, keep two on the charger, and put one inside. Rotate them as necessary. This could work." He was suddenly full of optimism.

Had someone been watching, they would see the sparkle in his eyes. Maybe it was pride, maybe hope, or perhaps a little of both, but he had found a viable solution.

The next couple of hours were spent removing the batteries, the bow and running lights, the mattress, and the two coolers.

"Don't tip the raft over," he scolded himself. The bed dominated his Zodiac, making rowing difficult. But he managed. Load by load, he ferried items to shore. Soon he had perfected his conveyor belt, completing five trips before stopping for a bite to eat.

"Amazing how much stuff *Lil Darling* can hold," he gushed as he viewed the beach arrayed with a broad assortment of foodstuffs, diesel fuel, tools, flares, tackle, and more. The pile was eclectic and bountiful.

He was stiff from all the lugging but did not want to interrupt the roll he was on.

"Plenty of daylight left, and the weather is cooperating, so when in Rome . . ." He settled into a rhythm, climbing aboard again and again to retrieve another load.

He found additional fishing gear, two flashlights, and a few remaining D batteries. He gathered up plastic plates, cups, silverware, pots, pans, aluminum foil, and the remaining plastic sandwich bags - basically anything that was loose. He took the bathroom mirror off the wall and removed two of the deck chairs. He realized this was a bit optimistic but justified the addition as a backup in case one broke. He took the cushions for floats and even removed the table.

Doing a final run-through reminded him of all the times he and the family would check out of a hotel, making sure one last time that nothing was left behind.

"The last trip we took with the kids was . . . Disney World," he said, recalling it was a few months before he had left on this trip. "Man, that was ages ago."

He had scoured every cabinet, and the only things left were a few drawers in the bunk room. Opening the first drawer of a night table, he saw a couple of books—the King James Bible and a fiction thriller by Chris Reynolds called *Lost Secret of the Ancient Ones*.

The Bible brought back memories of all the hotels where the Gideons had placed free copies.

"Great. Something to pass the time." He took them and looked into the other drawer. There were unused notepads and a box of pencils. He assumed these were left over from a previous charter.

It had taken all day, but by the time he left his grounded friend, he had removed more stuff than he could have ever imagined.

"What a pile," he marveled, dragging the raft high up on the sand.

The colors of late afternoon shifted to a brilliant red as the sun sank into the horizon. The birds were darting in around the edge of the trees for a final dinner run. When night came, it came quick and was all encompassing. The night was going to be clear, and it appeared no foul weather was on the near horizon.

"Most of this stuff can wait," he said.

His hands on his hips, he stood, fatigued from a long, arduous day. But he worked diligently to get his bed and light set. He moved the mattress to the cave, careful not to damage it. Once set inside, he returned for the blankets, sheets, and pillows.

The lighting project was more challenging. The batteries were heavy and could only be carried one at a time. It took three trips, plus a fourth for the lights and charger. Dripping in sweat, he labored under the exertion, his breath growing ragged. But once he was done, the feeling of success was sweet.

"Now let's see if we can get some light."

He attached the wires of the lamp to the battery diodes, and the bulb produced an instant glow.

"Bingo!" he exclaimed with a fist pump, satisfied that once again he had been right.

After hooking the other two batteries to the solar charger outside, he assembled the three lights inside on a single switch. Spooling out the line, he placed one by the bed, one near the back, and one along the other wall.

"Let there be light."

For just a moment, concerns of being stranded on the island took a back seat to victory.

Day by day, weeks turned into months. Taking stock of all that he had accomplished, he considered the bamboo lattice gate he had made to place over the door at night. It was something that helped allay fears of roaming predators. Though in truth he had never seen any evidence, it was simply the recall of hearing something in the bushes.

With the hundreds of plastic bottles always full, it was constant proof that his tarp collection system worked just as he planned it.

Of course, there were also failures along the way . . . like the cooking pit. That had been a bit more of a problem. Cooking in the cave had proved futile. With a single egress, the smoke just lingered until he was choked out.

Eventually, he reasoned the fire would need to be kept outside but also safe from the rain showers. Using four poles dug into the ground, he constructed a gazebo with a stone firepit. He covered it with the tarp and incorporated his water system alongside the cooking center. Adding a couple of logs to create a counter and an outdoor seating area, he found it perfect.

"All the comforts of home," he said with satisfaction, sorting his cooking gear and organizing it on the log made into a stand.

He had set up the table with the two chairs inside to protect them from weather. The boat cushions became indoor shelves for the old travel bag that contained his passport, wallet, and phone, as well as other essentials he wanted kept safe, such as the binoculars, his two books, and writing materials.

And he adopted routines. Each evening he would mark the wall with a new day added to note his time on the island. And each morning he would check on his mistress, as he did today.

"Good morning, *Darling*." He waved, half expecting her to wave back.

His alter ego Thomas would sometimes have some fun, answering back with an imitated female voice. "Hey, Marky. I'm still here."

The rhythm of bantering, talking, and arguing with himself steadily increased. Thomas was his only companion, a solace that warded off despair.

He had plenty of time. Without all the distraction that made up the modern American life, windows of self-realization often opened.

Though he did not notice it at first, he was proving quite adroit at keeping a lot of his life safely tucked away, not wanting to confront certain personality traits or events from his past . . .

Chapter 7

About a year after landing on the island, he woke to an unfamiliar sound. Pulling on shorts, he was startled to see thousands upon thousands of black-snouted terns. They filled every branch of every tree as far as he could see. It was March.

He had heard of birds that left Africa and migrated all the way to Greenland.

"The breadfruit." He panicked, wide-eyed with the realization they could be eating it all. There were certainly enough birds.

Hurrying to investigate, he witnessed more birds than he had ever seen in his entire life. And the farther south he ventured, the thicker the clusters became.

"I hope you guys are eating the mosquitoes," he said with a grin. Over the past few months, he had cleared a path to the orchards. Entering from the beach, he reached the top of the ridge, expecting the worst.

"Thank God," he breathed out, seeing the birds had no interest in the breadfruit. Looking south, he saw more and more terns were congregating beyond the tree line.

"What the hell . . ."

"That place spells trouble," Thomas reminded, his voice notching up their anxiety.

Before today, that part of the island was off limits. But his curiosity was piqued at the tens of thousands of birds . . .

"Why there?"

Experience had taught the hard lesson to stay clear of the beach at the southern end. The jungle was too thick, the mosquitoes too voracious, and, truthfully, all he could see was swamp and marsh and more swamp. Once or twice he had ventured along the ridge, but thick curtains of bamboo made the forest impenetrable.

Today, curiosity trumped fear. Reaching the variegated impasse at the south end of the ridgeline, he started hacking away at the bramble. By the end of the day, he had made some progress until he reached a field of giant boulders that blocked any further passage.

Meanwhile, thousands of birds continued to land and depart as though it were an international airport.

"What are they doing?"

He started climbing, myopically focused, fingers cramping, sweat soaking his shirt. He heard a rush in the foliage—something below him was crashing through the underbrush. Fear stuck in his throat as goosebumps blossomed. Then . . .

"Noooo!" he screamed, falling, flailing to find something to grab on to. But there was nothing. He landed hard onto an uneven pile of rocks.

Pain shot through his body. His back was twisted and his head bleeding . . . darkness blotted out the pain. How long he was out, he would never know.

He was woken by a gentle rain, his shoulder was killing him, and he could not move his left arm.

"Screw this place," he bellowed in agony. "I'm never coming back here. Ever!"

He struggled back to the beach, and the throbbing was so severe, simple things like gathering the breadfruit or managing his drinking water . . . these were all going to be far more difficult, and he depended on them for survival.

While walking in agonizing pain, he recalled his wife had once had something called frozen shoulder. She had said she would rather go through childbirth again before suffering this ailment. Truthfully, he had not been very empathetic, thinking she should suck it up and stop whining.

"Rachael, I'm sorry I was such a dick. I promise if I ever get out of here . . ." He never finished the thought, the weight of despair icing any thoughts beyond the pain of here and now.

His thoughts segued to their friend, Barb. She had always suffered from chronic back pain. In a rare bout of honesty, he admitted to never really having had much empathy for others' anguish. Now that this shoulder hurt like a son of a bitch, he was having second thoughts.

Day after day the pain lessened, but his shoulder was useless. The birds began leaving, heading on a northern trek. Then one night while lying in bed, he heard a pop so loud it woke him up. His shoulder had come unfrozen. And suddenly, he had his full range of motion back.

"I can't believe it," he said with genuine thanks. Days and days of unfathomable pain fled in an instant. He was grateful beyond anything he had ever felt in his past. "If I ever get off this island, I will never dismiss another's pain. When we suffer, it is all-consuming."

Time marched on, and months turned into years. The white terns would arrive like clockwork every March, which became his seminal marker. The rains had a seasonal rhythm, and the storms would come and go. The candle of optimism often flickered, but it never died. With the rain-collection system working great, the abundance of fish, the breadfruit, and the coconuts, he had a stable diet. Boring but nutritious. Food, water, shelter—all the basics accounted for.

Never one to sit idle, he had traversed most of the island, but he'd stayed clear of the south end. He knew every plant, boulder, root, and seasonal flower. Always looking for possible foodstuffs, he often experimented with roots and berries to add flavor to the otherwise bland breadfruit.

One day while hiking deep in the canopied forest, where the humidity clung perpetually to the vines, he came across an unfamiliar tree. It was of medium size and had dark, glossy leaves with tiny yellow flowers that emitted a pungent aroma. There were clusters of nuts that clung to the thorny bark. He gathered both the nuts and the flowers, eager to experiment with something different.

He was always careful to try new things in small quantities. The last thing he needed was to poison himself. He had learned that experience was a harsh master, having gotten very sick on a local berry. He had cobbled together a small cache of herbs and pseudo spices for the breadfruit. No matter how many different recipes he used, it mostly lacked flavor.

"Something new," he said with anticipation. Back at the cave, he cracked the yellow nuts and removed the meat from the shell. It was kind of gooey. He dabbed a finger in the juice and touched his lips.

"Ach." He winced. It was strong and had a bite like a hot chili, but, surprisingly, it left a satisfyingly greasy aftertaste.

"Tonight, my newfound condiment, you will gloss the freshly cooked breadfruit."

Along with Thomas, *Lil Darling*, and the world at large, he was now talking to his food.

"Add fresh grouper, a little lemon grass, and voilà, Chez Mark, ze superb chef of Lambert Island will create yet another masterpiece."

Snacking on a piece of salted fish, he considered his latest innovation. He had always been a carnivore often indulging in big steaks and lots of bacon.

"You can never have too much bacon." He laughed. The memory of sizzling meat caused his mouth to water.

But with nothing but time and the fact that he caught more fish than he could eat, he began to experiment with salting to make it last longer. This, of course, required salt. But that was no problem—he had an ocean full.

Having retrieved baking pans as part of his haul from the boat, he filled them with seawater and let evaporation do all the work.

Easy-peasy.

Once he had enough salt, he went through processes of trial and error. Taking a portion of each batch of fish, he tried different ways of salting it and setting it in a cool place to see how long it would last until going bad. He eventually mastered the art of salting fish that would last for weeks and, in his opinion, tasted excellent.

"Feeling pretty, pretty good," he said as the warm tingle of evening washed over him. There was a sense of serenity he hadn't felt in years.

As he prepared dinner, he considered how far he had come since his arrival. He was regularly blessed with fresh-caught grouper and snapper. Cleaning it beachside, he threw the entrails back into the water to attract more fish. Learning to extract hearts of palm from certain species of trees, he used them as a mild substitute for greasing the frying pan. And, of course, he had an abundance of his staple: spiny melons of breadfruit.

"Not bad, buddy. Not bad," Thomas said, adding his own thoughts to the warm and fuzzy feelings.

He cut thick slices of the melon and swabbed it in what he called "yellow extract," which he used to cook the fish and carb loaded breadfruit to a perfect golden brown.

"One of the best meals I ever prepared," he exclaimed with a rub of his satisfied belly. After drinking a cup of tea made with lemongrass and putting everything back in its place, he moved into his chambers, securing the lattice door.

He relished the cool air wafting through the porous lava. Today the sensation was especially pleasurable. He did not know why, but it felt luxurious.

After undressing, he climbed naked into bed. Lying on his back, he pulled the covers up to his armpits and rested his arms at his sides.

"This is my bed, my home, and my island." It was his mantra that reaffirmed. A form of prayer, one might say.

Time had stripped away most of the anxieties that had kept him awake back in the real world. They had fallen off one at a time. No more worries about money, his job, or any of the other nonsense now so unimportant. He closed his eyes and started dreaming.

As night deepened, he had the odd sensation that he could feel his cat. She was kneading his arm, as if curled into the crux of his body. The claws worked gently, doing that thing that cats do. He missed Maya. Truthfully, he had completely forgotten about her. When he thought of his pets, he had been entirely focused on his chocolate lab. But he enjoyed the connection Maya made in the middle of most nights, a cat's way of giving something in return for room and board.

The next morning he sat up, hopeful, sure his cat was going to be there, waiting for her magic bowl to miraculously refill itself.

"A dream? It felt so real . . ."

Maya had opened the box of loneliness he tried so hard to keep closed. He checked his right armpit, just to be sure.

"No claw marks . . ."

He thought of Thomas, quiet this morning. As wild as it seemed, Thomas beat the hell out of being alone. He did not care that he might be going a wee bit nuts, because solitary confinement was used as a punishment for a reason.

Five years had passed. He knew because the wall was marked with a modified version of the tally system. But instead of five-day intervals, he marked thirty-day increments, twelve across. He stood looking at the engravings as if they were a form of art. Five years, two months, and five days since he had left the United States.

His kids would now be twenty-two, twenty, and the youngest, Victoria, would be ten.

"Do they even remember me?"

He smiled as he recalled Ally, his oldest, taking his phone and changing her name to "My favorite child." This had irked her brother to no end. Surprisingly, he had never changed it. *If I ever get my phone charged again, it would still be there. After all, she was our first.*

He looked at the old traveling bank bag. It held his wallet, cash, passport, phone, and charger. The battery was long dead. For him, the photos stored inside were priceless, yet unobtainable. It was time to find a solution.

"Somewhere on that boat there has to be a converter . . ."

"Dude—lightning—fried—duh!"

He ignored Thomas and returned to thoughts of his kids. He wondered about Ally's college experience. This segued into memories about his own days at college, about his time at the University of Miami.

"What a joke," he reminisced. "In high school I had been on the school newspaper and written an article on the rise in popularity of Rollerblading, concluding it was mostly due to the advent of polyurethane wheels and ball bearing systems. When I graduated and fled to Miami, unknowingly to me, my teacher had submitted the article to a national writing organization. It won me a scholarship to UM. The U." He chuckled, holding his thumbs together and fingers up in the iconic symbol.

"I enrolled mostly in business classes with a major in girls and a minor in drugs. Lots and lots of drugs . . ."

As his thoughts drifted down memory lane, they became less about his children and instead focused on the different chapters in his own life. He considered his new fear of the water. Or more specifically, his aversion to the predators waiting for him to dip his toe into their domain.

As sure as he was that they were out there waiting, there was one fact that did not support his narrative. Inside the reef, nothing ever stole his catch. And often he would sit and watch dolphins playing in the bay.

"Dolphins mean no sharks." Which led to all the times he had been diving. The pleasures and the work.

"In college I augmented my income collecting tropical fish in the Keys. I formed a company called Sea Capture."

It had become apparent that fish were abundant in the summer, when Northerners were least interested in their hobby, and least abundant in the winter, when hobbyists were most ardent. It was a classic supply-and-demand issue.

Always a problem solver and able to see opportunity where others saw obstacles, he had established collection stations throughout the endless summers of the Caribbean. It allowed for abundant travel, daily diving, and adventures that could fill a book. That was, until the day two Colombians walked into his warehouse with a suitcase full of cash—and just like that, he was out of the biz. Next stop NYC, to build a recording studio.

"I bet the reefs are loaded with tropicals . . ." He paused, envisioning his daydream.

He recalled how free he felt when diving. How beautiful the reefs were and how exceedingly large things were at depths of over a hundred feet. Still, though dead, the image of Ironsides glaring at him crowded his thoughts.

As the days drifted one into another, Thomas was his only friend. Yet like an old married couple with nothing new to say, the tone had begun to sour. There were accusations of stupidity and acrimony, and the lines between humorous banter and schizophrenia began to blur. And to top it all off, he could not rid himself of his alter ego. There was no privacy.

"Something bad is gonna happen," he said, sitting up. The night had been filled with uncomfortable dreams. Fueled with a sense of foreboding, he could not recall any specifics.

He kindled the fire under the thatch and went down to the beach. The sky was ominous, and the clouds were thick. The wind blowing over the island was picking up. Hour by hour it gained in strength until it was fevered. The fronds bent and vegetation snapped. Leaning into the gust, he hiked to the top of the ridge. To the east, the sky was dark, mean, and tinted green. He could feel the pressure dropping.

"Of course, it's July!" he stated in realization, his South Florida roots drawing the connection.

"Happy fricken birthday," retorted his acrimonious colleague. The voice of sarcasm, doubt, and fear always had something to say.

"It's the middle of hurricane season, you idiot. They form off the coast of Africa and work their way across the Atlantic."

"So?"

"Man, you are daft. There's a hurricane out there, and it's coming right at us!"

Mark rushed to the beach and began collecting all the gear. Anything that was important. He deflated his raft and trundled it to the cave. He took down his tarp and moved the empty bottles, extra batteries, and solar charger to the rear of the cavern. He was relieved that almost everything he owned was safely stored at the back of the lava tube.

The rain began to fall harder and harder until sheets became so thick it was impossible to navigate. Securing the few remaining items, he raced against the howling wind pummeling everything.

As the ferocity of the storm rampaged unimpeded over the island, his lava tube proved a worthy sanctuary. With only one opening, the ambient pressure prevented the storm from entering. But beyond, the wind wailed, rain poured, and a small tornado swept away his thatched covering. Chaos reigned and landslides obliterated parts of the island.

Rubbing nervous hands over a scraggly beard, he sat staring out at the endless torrents of rain. A wave of depression washed over him. Like so many times before, he asked the same question, "Will I ever be rescued?"

The next question was so out of character.

"Is this my fate?"

He mulled the idea of fate and destiny until his thoughts were broken by an unidentifiable sound. He had never heard anything like it. Able to penetrate the maelstrom, it started out as a low growl, almost a whisper. But it grew louder and louder, becoming a cry so mournful and haunting that shivers ran down his spine.

"What is that?" He froze, pulling the spear he had made from a sturdy branch close to his side. His heart raced, and a sour taste filled his mouth, a taste his water bottles could not wash away.

With a mixture of intrigue, worry, and dread, he sat watching Mother Nature unleash all her fury. Beyond the entrance, the air was thick with debris creating a death trap for any creature that could not find refuge. And the noise . . . like a thousand screaming banshees. His skin prickled.

"Thomas, what untold destruction will we find when this is all over?"

His worry centered on the orchards. Would they survive? And *Lil Darling* . . . his lifeline to the other world.

"Stay strong . . . ," he murmured. A growing anxiety that something terrible was happening bounced from possibility to possibility.

Day and night merged into the storm, but eventually the winds began to subside. The rains moved offshore, and the cyclone's rage was now out to sea, where the warm waters of the Atlantic would fuel its furor for the next victim.

This made him think of home. The impact glass he had installed, the generator and all the food and supplies.

"Rachael always kidded me about being a prepper . . ."

But as the son of a military man and a Boy Scout from his cub years, it was in his nature to prepare for the worst, just as he had done here on Lambert Island.

And he knew Rachael was happy to always have power and for the family to always feel safe. This was one of the things that had drawn her to him. He was a good provider. But even after their love had drifted into something more akin to roommates, she would always be the mother of his children, and he would always do what he could to make sure they were always safe.

"Let's go see what the storm has wrought," he said, trying to remain upbeat. But he was gravely concerned with his primary food source.

Debris was piled everywhere. He had to untangle the pathway to work his way down to the water's edge. Turning the bend, he was struck at how changed the topography had become. The beach was awash in rivers of runoff, leaving deep furrows in the sand for as far south as he could see.

After he rounded the escarpment that afforded a full view of the bay, confusion, disbelief, and then realization struck at his heart.

"*Lil Darling!*" he cried. She was gone along with his hope of ever getting off this island.

"Was she swept out to sea?" Anguished tears poured unchecked.

He did not know how long he stood there. A minute, an hour, half the day. His mind was paralyzed. Standing on unfamiliar ground, the bout of depression he had been feeling opened into a deep, dark well. He kept waiting for Thomas to say something, anything. But he remained uncharacteristically quiet.

"Huhhh." He let out a long sigh.

"Goodbye, my friend. You were faithful for all these years. May you rest in peace."

He stared blankly at the milky waters spewing from the runoff. He noted how currents were pulling the cloudy lagoon north until it poured a silted river out into the deep-blue sea.

"That would explain why so much wood has washed onto this end of the beach. The current comes from that end and exits here."

The process of analyzing helped bring him back to the moment. Wiping away his tears, he set out to see what other damage had been wrought. His worry centered on his main food supply - specifically, the orchards. He ascended the trail he had worn over the years. Mud made walking difficult. Everything was loose, and it would be easy to slip and fall.

A crashing branch off to his left was a reminder that any accident out here, any broken bone or infection, could be lethal. So he slowed his steps, methodically placing one foot before the next.

"Damn, damn, damn it," he wailed in anger. Cresting the ridge, his worst fears were realized. The trees were stripped bare. The fruit was scattered everywhere, most of it broken and smashed.

He knew that this island had likely suffered this fate many times over the centuries, and the fruit would grow back. But in the interim, he would need to collect as much as he could and try to store it.

Continuing to survey the damage, he noticed that to the south the bamboo forest had taken the brunt of the storm. What was before unseeable was now open sky. For the first time since falling years ago, he approached the forbidden end.

"What the hell?" Straining his ears, he homed in on an unfamiliar noise.

"Falling water? Runoff? Doesn't sound like it."

Getting closer, he heard it grow louder. He was drawn to the edge, and he saw the once-impenetrable forest had collapsed into a ravine. A chasm that, truthfully, he did not know had even existed. And with the view now unobstructed, what he saw shocked him. On the other side of the gorge was a waterfall. It was the source of the noise.

"Fresh water!" he said, surprised but thrilled.

It poured into a lake, maybe a hundred feet below. And in the middle of the lake something was moving. His eyes grew wide. He blinked once, twice, wanting to believe what he was seeing.

"Holy crap! There's somebody swimming."

The outline looked feminine, but she was too far away to be sure. His heart sprinted at the sight of another.

"Am I hallucinating?"

Chapter 8

Descending to what he prayed was not a mirage, he trod over loose ground. Mud caked his sneakers, and the vegetation obscured his view.

An opening in the trees offered a view of the lake. And what he saw caused him to slip and fall hard on his rump. It was all the catalyst he needed. Scrambling to his feet, he threw caution to the wind.

"Hello there! Hellooo . . . ," he called to the woman swimming in the lake.

She made no signs of acknowledgment.

"Please be real . . ."

He stepped over fallen trees, errant logs, and other debris washed down by the storm. His heart pulsed with anxiety. His mind told him this was just his imagination. It had been so long since he had seen another, it caused all kinds of conflicting emotions. His entire system was a dichotomy of hope and hesitation. Near the bottom, he saw she was still there. She seemed to be naked, alone, and . . .

"Oh my god, she is fricken gorgeous."

He pinched himself to make sure this wasn't some sort of dream.

"Hello . . . ," he called again. He did his best to sound friendly.

She stopped swimming. Treading water, she turned and flashed him a brilliant smile. With no signs of distress, she swam to the far side and stepped out.

"She's completely naked." His jaw dropped, stunned at the sight.

He had not seen a woman's bare body or, for that matter, any woman in over five years. Unabashed and unashamed, she neither displayed modesty nor provocation, and he sensed she felt no discomfort. She looked to be about twenty-five. He could not have imagined a more beautiful woman. She was glorious in her nakedness, and part of him expected this was more fantasy than reality. She was just too perfect.

With his heart pumping wildly, he exited the trees and approached along the shore's edge. She was still there. He let out a deep breath.

"Calm down," he told himself.

The lake was housed within a hollow. It was fed by a waterfall cascading over rocks that were aged and weathered. She was sitting on a clump of grass, running her fingers through her thick blonde hair.

There was a slope behind her that ran up to a ridge rimmed with ancient hardwoods that felt ancestral. He heard birds cawing somewhere in the treetops, but the sound competed with the rush inside his ears.

He approached cautiously, not wanting to spook her. He put on a wide smile, though his insides were in complete turmoil.

The inviting sparkle in her eyes added a bounce to his step. When he came close enough that his shadow touched her, she looked up but made no effort to stand. Everything about her showed a lack of concern.

It simmered his turmoil, but her nakedness had a different effect. He fought to keep his gaze on her face. Her cobalt eyes were powerfully deep, like an ocean. All of this consumed his attention and held the question of his rescue at bay . . . but only for a moment.

"Hi," he said with an unsure voice. "My name is Mark Lambert."

She said nothing, appearing as if his words did not register.

"I've been trapped on this island for over five years, and, well, you are the first person I have seen since being here. Do you live here? Do you have a boat or a way to communicate to the outside world?" The words fumbled out of his mouth.

She simply looked up at him, saying nothing.

Maybe she does not speak English.

"I'm sorry," he apologized, speaking a little louder and trying to elicit a response and also to convince himself this was real. "Seeing you, here . . . it was so unexpected. As I said, my name is Mark Lambert. And who might you be?"

She laughed, apparently unconcerned that her womanly parts were not covered. He became more flummoxed.

"Who might I be? Well, I might be Saraf. But then again, I might not . . . be."

Her voice was teasing and full of confidence. And why not? She was exquisite and no doubt knew it. Again, her eyes . . . he could not recall ever seeing such depth in another person. They were inquisitive yet mysterious, simultaneously revealing nothing but inviting trust.

"Saraif?" he repeated, bungling her pronunciation.

"Sara with an *F* at the end." She chuckled, as if it was a joke.

She was playing with him. It was so weird. Her being alone, in the jungle, with a man twice her size.

"Sa-hair-riff . . . ," he said, trying again. The way she pronounced it was not to simply add a letter to the name *Sara*. Her cadence intoned three syllables.

"Sar-re-ef? Sair-ra-if." He tried a few more times and began to feel foolish.

With a friendly smile she offered a lifeline.

"You can call me Angel."

"Angel . . . I like that."

"Perhaps you should sit down. You seem a bit . . . ." She hesitated and placed a thumb under her chin, resting a long, slender finger upon her mouth. It was as if she was searching for the right word.

He looked at her moist, succulent lips. It had been so long since he had touched another or engaged in something so simple as a kiss. He realized he was staring and fumbled for an answer as camouflage.

"Discombobulated?"

"Yes. The perfect word." He felt like a child in her classroom.

"I am not sure if you saw my boat that was out on the reef until the storm. It is how I ended up here. I'm a castaway," he explained, the words feeling awkward and unsure.

He sat across from her, trying to avoid staring at her naked body but failing. *Don't be that creepy old guy,* he told himself. *I'm at least twenty years older than her.*

"How long have you been here?" he asked, bending away from his spiraling thoughts. He hoped to glean if she was stranded or if he was going to be able to get him rescued.

"An hour."

No boat could have survived that storm, so either she misunderstood what he was asking or was unwilling to give up anything to a stranger.

"No, I mean how long have you been on this island?"

"Probably not as long as you."

Her answers were never revealing. Searching for something to help him burst the bubble in case this was merely an illusion, he continued. "Are you real?" He was so desperate for this to be true, it was all he could think to say.

She pulled her long hair over one shoulder, her arm crossing her breast. To avoid staring, he looked away and focused on the waterfall. It fell from the top of a large, moss-covered spire.

"There's no source? No river or anything else."

"Are you?" she challenged, causing him to turn his attention back to her. The lines around her eyes crinkled with humor.

He wasn't sure if she was kidding or just being evasive. But he answered anyway.

"Of course, I'm real. What do you think, I'm a ghost or something?"

He tried to act like her, his tone teasing, but it came out hollow.

"Maybe you had an accident or something and you're in a coma. Maybe none of this is real."

Her grin had an impish quality. He could not tell if she was mocking him or questioning him. Or . . . what if? She was very sure of herself. The idea of one so young keeping him so off balance was not something he was used to. Of course, it had been so long since he had talked to anyone but Thomas.

Considering her question, he felt his nose, the unset knob from where it had been broken. He thought back to the lightning strike on the boat. And then he looked back at the falls.

How long had I been out? Was I rescued and now I'm lying in a hospital—in a coma? A burden to all those who love me?

Rumbling around inside his head was a line from an old song: "Did you leave your role in this world for a lead part in a cage?"

"No way . . ."

"How did you get here?" The practical part of him was looking for tangible answers. He returned to the hope she could help him get off this island.

"The same way as you."

"On a boat?" His excitement rose at the prospect she had a vessel.

"By fate."

Again vague, again annoying. It was all she had to say on the matter. She had a distinctive expression that made it clear when she was done. She pressed her lips together, which created little dimples on her cheeks, but it was her eyes that said, "Move on."

He caught himself staring, but why not? She didn't seem to care, and her body . . . oh my god—what a body. His mind wandered, and he felt the bulge that was starting to grow. Being lecherous and scaring her away was the last thing he wanted.

Walk softly, he vowed. It was a reminder to be charming, debonair, and likable. His specialty. Still . . .

As hard as he tried to avoid leering, he was doing a lousy job of it. But she never seemed bothered or worried or threatened in any way.

Getting up, she took a white garment hanging from a limb, a sundress like he had seen the girls in Charleston wear. She slipped it over her head, and it fell perfectly around her body.

"Want to hear a joke?" she asked, sitting back down on the grass. Her voice pulled his wandering eyes back up to hers.

"A joke? Uh, sure . . ." He decided acquiescence was the best path forward if he hoped to receive some solid answers.

"One day this man was stranded on an island . . ." Her voice had a lilt with hints of Irish, dreamily exotic and disarming.

Keeping his eyes on hers, he fought the urge to let them slip and explore the contours of her dress.

She continued. "Months passed and he was a mess. Unkept, undernourished, and without hope. Then, to his wonder, he spotted a beautiful woman who was half-naked, walking along the beach toward a boat made of reeds."

"Sounds familiar," he said as she sat a little taller. He could not help but notice the fabric of her dress stretch tighter, and he knew she had nothing on underneath.

"'You look terrible,' the woman said to the castaway. 'Come with me. I have built a home on an island not far from here.'"

"'This boat is yours?' the man asked."

"'Yes, I made it.' She oared expertly, and soon they approached a small island, where he spied a beautiful house. It, too, was made of local materials, with a thatched roof and a wide covered porch."

"'It took me almost a year to build that,' she told him, giving him a tour. As she continued with her story Mark was mesmerized by her, the house, everything."

"'Why don't you get cleaned up in the bathroom? There is a shower and some honed shells you can use as a razor. I will pick vegetables from my garden and make us dinner.'"

"He was in heaven. A house, a boat, a garden. A beautiful woman, this was amazing."

"She laid out some fresh clothes she had made. After he was bathed, she asked, 'Would you like a cocktail? I fermented some coconut juice with lemon grass. It's quite refreshing.'"

"Everything was perfect."

Mark tried to recall where this was going. It felt familiar, as if he had heard this before. Maybe long ago.

"After a dinner of wild boar, vegetables, and some sort of potato-like tuber, they retired back to her exquisite living room. A few more drinks later and soon the atmosphere grew lusty. She stood before him, moistening her lips with the tip of her tongue. Her body exuded a woman who knew what she wanted. Her voice grew husky, and she dared state the obvious. 'It has probably been a while since you've played around. Am I right?'"

"The atmosphere was perfect, the drink ample, and the beautiful woman was wanton. His eyes grew wide, his breath shallow.'"

"'You're suggesting . . .'"

"'Yep,' she said with a lascivious wink, her signals clear and inviting."

"'I mean, for real?'"

"She smiled invitingly."

"'My god—you're telling me you built a golf course!'"

Thoroughly amused, Angel fell back onto the grass, laughing. "Played a round. Get it?"

Her simple quip had defused his embarrassment without shaming him.

Though he was finding it difficult to take his eyes off her, his hope pressed him to find out who she was or where she came from.

Perhaps I should take a different approach.

"Are you a golfer?" he deflected, side-dooring an approach to learning anything he could about her.

"Are you?" Her gaze was less penetrating and more as though she offered him her undivided attention.

He considered that most times when he had talked to people, his mind would be somewhere else. Or he was thinking of his response. This was a new experience. It was a bit unsettling, but it was growing on him.

"I love it," he admitted. "I miss playing with my buddies." It was a strange conversation to be having. He had not thought about golf for years.

"Are you any good?"

She had shifted onto her right side, stretching out her long legs, her elbow on the grass and a hand holding up her head. Blonde hair cascaded over her arm, catching rays of sunshine.

"Probably better than average, but I'm no single-digit handicapper." It was an honest assessment. But he wondered, *Does she even know what that means?*

"Do you cheat?"

It was a straightforward question. Unexpected, for sure, but he saw no malice—it was just odd.

Who asks these kind of things?

"Cheat?" he repeated.

"Like moving your ball in the rough if no one is looking. Stuff like that. The little things."

"It's not like we were playing for big money or anything," he said a bit defensively.

She kept hitting soft spots, and he fought to hide his irritation. She did not judge, but he got the feeling she could see what he was thinking. He needed to take the spotlight off himself.

"Do you play golf?" he asked.

She sat up and crossed her legs in the classic lotus position.

"Integrity is a funny thing, isn't it? What is the old saying? It is the moral code you adhere to when no one is watching."

Her smile had returned to that impish twist, where one side of the mouth raised like a single eyebrow. Inquisitive and inviting. But not in a sexual way.

"I guess if you thought someone was always watching, you would reconsider some of the things you do in private."

His mouth hung open, but nothing came out.

"Are your parents still alive?" It seemed an abrupt change of subject, but it wasn't.

"Are yours?" He adopted her technique, trying to get more than he gave, but she was smart beyond her years. He shifted in his seat. His back ached a little, and he was growing uncomfortable . . . in more ways than one.

"I asked you first," she said. "But I think not."

"Why would you think that?" She was right, of course, both his parents had passed.

"You flinched when I asked. Subtle, but there nonetheless."

She doesn't miss a thing.

"Why do you ask?" He tried a different tack.

"What if the dead are watching us? Like when we cheat on the golf course. Or indulge in self-gratification and sexual fantasy. Or every other thing we try to keep hidden from the world at large."

"Jesus," he said, thinking of some of the kinky porn he had engaged in over the years.

"Him too. Especially him."

Oh brother . . . this conversation was making him really uneasy. And he still had no answers to his most pressing concern.

She stood to straighten her dress. He could not tell if the material was some kind of tightly woven cotton or an unfamiliar synthetic cloth. It shimmered but did not wrinkle. It hugged her curves but did not pronounce the feminine aspects beneath. Like her, it was perfect.

She looked down at him.

"I must go now," she said without explanation. "Can we meet again tomorrow?"

"Of course," he blurted out. "But, please, tell me. Do you have a house here? Or a boat?"

"Tomorrow then," she replied, ignoring the question. Seeing the distinctive waggle of her finger, he inherently understood her message: *Do not follow me!*

Then she was gone. He knew to his very core that if he ignored her wishes, he would be alone again. All that remained was the sound of the waterfall and the birds that flitted in, drank, and flitted out as rainbows dissolved in the mist.

"Is she real or am I going crazy?"

He recalled the first night he had slept on the island. Something was moving through the forest. "Was it her? How long has she been on this island? Why am I just meeting her now?"

He looked south, the only part of the island he had not explored. It had always been so foreboding.

"That must be where she lives . . ."

He wrestled with taking a look but instinctively knew it would be a colossal mistake. If he chased after her, there would be no tomorrow.

"I'll ask her when I see her again," he told himself.

So instead he settled on the idea of a good bath. Scanning the shoreline, he checked to see if she was watching, his modesty a little more discerning than hers.

"Angel?" he called softly. There was no one.

After removing his shorts, he waded into the water. It was cool and clear, sweet to the lips, and the bottom was firm and sandy. It sloped down toward the middle. The pond was about half the size of a football field and rimmed with old-growth trees.

He plunged headfirst, and the soft silky water fused him with vigor. He breaststroked to the falls and found he could stand. Letting the cascade rain down on him, he closed his eyes and gave in to the sensation of being scrubbed.

He ran fingers through his hair, over his body, pits, and pelvic area. He grabbed handfuls of sand from the bottom, like a luffa, and he scrubbed every part of his physique. It was the first real cleansing in over five years.

"Oh my god, this feels sooo . . . good."

Fully refreshed, he returned to the grass and lay fantasizing about Angel.

"Those full breasts. The pert nipples. And that perfect . . ."

Aroused, he'd grown accustomed to taking care of this, but the thought of someone always watching had stuck in his craw, and now it irritated him.

"Really . . ." He felt uncomfortably angry and embarrassed. With the thought that his mother might be looking down on him, he pulled on his shorts and followed the trail back to the beach.

As he trekked along the water's edge, thoughts of Angel crowded out everything else. Tomorrow couldn't come fast enough. Again, the question surfaced.

"Is she real? Who cares?"

Out in the lagoon he saw the dolphins. The runoff had turned the waters to milk, but it appeared they didn't care. Looking past their frolicking, he stared longingly to where *Lil Darling* had rested.

"I miss her." He could not help but wonder about the coincidence of one friend leaving and another one appearing.

"So, Thomas, what do you think of Angel?"

The only thing he heard was the wind sighing over the waves.

Chapter 9

The next day, and the day after that, and the day after that, Angel was always there, waiting. No matter what time he showed up, early or late, she was sometimes swimming, sometimes lounging. But always she wore a radiant smile. She never seemed bothered, always sought the bright side. And it was becoming contagious.

His probes of where she came from, where she went at the end of each day, or whether she could help him to get off the island never found a firm answer. It was as if she intentionally did not want to answer these basic questions. Without uttering a single word, she made it known to him to accept that she was here now and that should be enough. *Be here now.*

It was frustrating, never getting any solid information. But the trade-off was her companionship. It filled a deep hole, and he found himself more and more wanting to impress her.

One morning he got up early and watched dawn sifting light through the trees beyond the clearing. Taking a mirror off the cushion, he gave it a long look. Perhaps he wanted to see what she saw. No illusions—just an honest assessment.

It was clear he had let himself go soft. His belly had no definition, and his arms and shoulders had no meat.

Gazing at the reflection, he could not believe how unkempt the guy looking at him had become. His hair was long and straggly. It sat atop a face matted by a scruffy beard that was uneven and sparse. And the wild whiskers coming from his nostrils and ears made him look like Ian Ballantine, an old friend who looked like a hermit from a fairy tale.

"Time to make some changes." An announcement, proclamation, and declaration, all rolled into one.

He retrieved the scissors and shaver from his toiletry kit. The leather was brittle from years of salt air. The zipper was rusty but still worked. There were twelve blades when he started. He had vowed that under no condition would he use the last one. That was reserved for the day he was rescued.

It was symbolic. A beacon of promise. Like a bottle of champagne one saves for celebration, it was a sacrament that was important to his well-being. He had employed them sparingly over the years.

"Still three blades left."

Taking a seat at the table, he propped the mirror against a tackle box pulled from the back. He got a bottle of water and poured it into a bowl. He did not have soap, but he had made a weak substitute out of mashed breadfruit and coconut water. He shaved his face until it was smooth, exposing white cheeks surrounded by his deeply tanned body.

Next, he attempted to cut his hair. This was a bit more taxing. He had shaved his face enough to ingrain it as habit. But cutting one's hair—that was altogether different. He gave it a go, cutting the long tail first. Next he tackled the sides, clipping up and around the ears, and finally imitating the comb-through cut technique his barber Alex had always done.

"Not bad, eh, Thomas?" He admired himself, peering at his reflection. His doppelgänger had been missing since Angel arrived, but he was still reluctant to let him go. It was like tossing away an old friend.

He gathered up all his clothes, sheets, and towels and took them outside. The clear blue sky offered the promise of a beautiful day. He sorted the three sets of shorts in various states of repair, some jeans, a number of tees, and a half dozen pair of underwear. Everything was a little looser—time on the island had taken its toll. And nothing had ever been properly washed, but the lake changed everything.

He considered the chinos and loose linen shirt held in reserve, his island casual for the bars in Barbados, but decided they did not need cleaning.

"I'll save that for the day I am rescued," he said.

He filled the chest with water, adding some of the pseudo cleanser. It did not get soapy per se, but it did leave a hint of coconut and was great at removing sweat. Scrubbing everything, he added extra emphasis to the sheets and pillowcases.

"I need to make a clothesline." He was surprised it had taken him five years to see the obvious. Grabbing some cord, he set a line to dry his things. As he worked the stains, he thought back over the things Angel had discussed with him, one of which was her assertion that he had wasted his time being on the island.

"Time is a luxury," she had told him. "You are blessed. You just don't see it."

His life before the island had always felt overwhelming due to work, family, and social obligations. Not to mention the never-ending distractions of news, politics, and the rest of the crap that made his blood boil.

The hindsight-triggering realization that so much of the discordant banter he had with his friends and colleagues about politics and religion was stupid. Now opting to adapt Angel's view of a glass half-full, he was gaining respect for her wisdom and admiring her pragmatism. In most things they were of two like minds. And he knew she was always right.

"I'm gonna get in shape. That's what I'm gonna do!"

Telling himself it was about time management and self-improvement, in his heart he knew he wanted to impress Angel. Though old enough to be her father, he did not want her to see him as a middle-aged guy going to pot.

"Sit-ups and push-ups . . . ," he began. Then standing with sweat shimmering on his skin, he spied a perfect limb for pull-ups. Standing on his toes, he reached and grabbed the sturdy branch.

"One, two, three . . . dang." He dropped to the sand on *four*. But unlike in his past life, instead of feeling defeated, he doubled down on his vow.

"Buck up, Mark. You got nothing but time, so don't be a pussy."

Motivated to impress Angel, he committed to six days a week until he could do two hundred sit-ups, fifty push-ups, and twenty pull-ups. At the age of forty-seven, he had worked out enough to know that his body responded quickly to exercise. He would not give up—not this time.

Through the years, he had procrastinated at maintaining a regimen. His life was littered with on-and-off bouts of exercise, diets, and binges. And to compound things, his social life, TV life, and home-alone time with his dog had all been bookended with more alcohol than was responsible. One of his favorite drink-alone excuses made him crack a grin.

"What's the old saying, 'It ain't drinking alone if the dog's home'?"

This triggered a different memory, reminding him how much he missed Carson. His female chocolate lab had just turned one when he went on his trip. Though he had had dogs all his life, he had never bonded with another as he had with her. Other than Pica, who had passed of old age, this was the one who stole his heart.

Missing his dog caused him sadness. It was a different feeling from that reserved for his children or the feelings he had for his wife.

"Rachael, hope you are holding up, babe." He looked skyward—perhaps someone was listening.

Barefoot, wearing only shorts and a T-shirt, he went down to the beach. "Time to start running."

He made his target the footpath a little more than a mile away. But reality was a swift reminder. Not even a hundred yards out and he was laboring for air. He stopped to catch his breath.

"Damn, boy. What's happened to you?"

Sucking wind, he was drawn to the ocean. Always there, always changing, it was familiar and yet . . . it did not seem as lonely as it had when *Lil Darling* had first vanished. She was gone, and apparently so was Thomas. But Angel was here.

"Perhaps life has given me a quid pro quo." He wondered at the odd timing of it all.

Up the trail and down into the bowl, when he reached the clearing, Angel was in the water. Naked, as always. And once again he was letting lust get the better of him.

Wringing his hands his tongue moistening his lips, he knew he had to be careful not to scare away the one thing he now cherished more than anything else.

She watched as he circled to their spot, giggling at him as he tried to hide his bulging discomfort.

He took her dress from a twisted branch. As she stepped from the water, he could not take his eyes off her. He noted that her skin was flawless and tanned as he followed the curves of her hips, the fullness of her breasts. As his eyes drifted to her more private female parts, he quickly looked away, but the sight burned within. Blue eyes sparkled and danced with humor. Her skin smelled like a June night. All of this was framed by her long, flowing hair. Desire became so overpowering, it suppressed reason. Longing upending caution.

We are not young and old, but man and woman, he foolishly told himself.

Stepping closer, dropping the dress, he reached to pull her in.

"Mark," she said with a sharp retort. Her voice was firm but without rancor.

His arm stopped midair. Her rebuke woke him from the slumber of desire.

"You are married. And I don't do married men . . . ev-ver!" Her inflection left no room for negotiation.

He deflated, literally and figuratively. The desire that coursed through his veins was replaced with defeat and rejection. Until . . . grasping at the specificity of her words, he straightened, seizing on the idea that it was not him but his marital status that was the obstacle to his desire.

"How do you know I'm married?"

She lifted the dress and pulled it over her head. Shaking out her hair, she stepped into what should have been his personal space and took hold of his hand. Her touch was soft, the first contact he had had with anyone in over five years. It sent a warmth through him that he had forgotten. Being touched by another offered reassurance that he was not alone in this world, that someone cared, that . . . well, it meant a lot of things. He fought against tears leaking down his cheeks.

She stroked the ring. Gold, worn, feeling like an ancient relic, it had been there for so long he no longer thought of it.

"This speaks volumes," she told him and released his hand. Moving toward the grass, she crooked her finger for him to follow. "Let's talk."

Uh-oh. It was what his wife used to say when he was about to be read the riot act. Sweat glistened in his palms. *Did I go too far?*

"Damn, damn, damn," he mumbled.

"We should talk about this." Her demeanor did not exhibit any signs of anger.

"I'm sorry." The regret was genuine. "It's just that I have been here so long, I guess I let urges get the better of me."

"Is it normal for you to start with contrition and close with an excuse?" she asked, her face like marble.

"Uh, I, umm . . ."

"I mean, it's not like you haven't pleasured yourself plenty while being on this island. So your"—she used her two fingers in a hashtag notation—"'urges' have had plenty of attending to. Right?"

Mark was tongue tied. *Is she spying on me? Is this why she said things about someone watching? How? From where?*

She waited for an answer. With none forthcoming, she continued to prod.

"You know nothing about me, and yet you are willing to break your marital vows. Have you done this often?"

"Done this?" Words kept sticking in his throat.

"Slept around. Cheated on your wife. Tried to have sex with a stranger. I find that men who objectify women are more prone to cheat. Do you cheat?"

It was the second time she had asked this, he thought a little defensively. *Is this what she really thinks of me? That I'm a cheater?*

"What about the woman at the bar in Bridgetown?" she asked before he could form a proper denial.

"Nothing happened. I swear!" *How can she know about that?*

"Come on, Mark . . . we both know that the reason you did not follow through with having a one-night stand with that woman was because she wasn't young enough or pretty enough for you. When I look inside you, I see nothing but a zoo full of lusts."

Pfffffttt . . . . deflating again.

"Do you love your wife?"

The tone of her question was not seriously weighted, seeming merely inquisitive. Shifting into a cross-legged position, she waited for him to reply.

His eyes were transfixed upon the hair caressing her neck, and the silkiness of her skin. His tongue felt thick. His mind raced for a safe response.

"How about Marcia?"

He narrowed his eyes, wondering where this was going.

"You know, your high school sweetheart."

"Of course . . . ," Mark said, shifting to a fond memory. His shoulders relaxed, not realizing he was holding himself so tightly. "You never forget your first."

"First?" Her expression bordered on amusement and doubt.

"Love," he added defensively. "My first love."

"Riiiiiight. Love." She was mocking him. He tried to anticipate what was coming next.

"You knew you were moving to Miami for over two months but did not tell her until the night before you left. I mean, this girl was your first lover. Your sweetheart. It lasted for almost two years. And yet you waited until the day you were leaving to spring it on her."

"That's not fair. I went back and forth every weekend," he defended, embracing an aggressive posture.

She put up her hands in mock surrender. "Hey, I'm just the messenger. But, really, let's see this through. Every week, every two, then it was three weeks. Then a month, etcetera. She ended up marrying your best friend, didn't she?"

Mark could not fathom how she could know these things. As she pressed on his speculation ran the gamut.

"It has been said that love is to give, but lust is to take. Did you ever care? Was there ever any emotion? Or was she just the first in a long line of desirable objects?"

Like a prosecutor presenting a case for the jury, she laid bare his soul. Or, more specifically, the callousness of his self-centered nature.

As the morning turned into afternoon, with the sun warming the glade and the dragonflies buzzing the top of the water, she drew out of him every woman he had ever slept with.

Some were taken from fuzzy memory, others resurrected from the sands of time. One-night stands he had taken home from the clubs in Coconut Grove. Waitresses he had worked with. The Saturday-morning call from Julie's roommate that she was going to have an abortion. Him not even knowing she was pregnant and never offering to be by her side. The cheap affairs, the friend's wife. The television star. The list was exhaustive—and damning.

"Can you tell me anything about them? Their hopes or dreams, fears, and concerns?"

His memories could recall their looks, the sex, their quirks and kinks. But he fell short when seeking much about their wants or desires. Her case was so compelling and methodical that there was no denying he had been insensitive toward women.

He liked these girls. Or most of them, but he never really cared about them, not really. Only as far as his own needs were concerned. And sometimes simply to impress those who measured him by the girl on his arm . . .

"What a dick," he muttered under his breath. It stung. Never before had he ever thought of himself in this way. He always held himself up as a righteous guy, a good person.

"What was, was. And what is, is," she told him, neither agreeing nor disagreeing. The comment was simple but powerful.

The rays filtering through the trees announced the waning of the afternoon. She stood, and he knew it was time for her to leave. *Where does she go?* She would not say. *Follow her?* He dare not. Truthfully, he was afraid of what he might find out.

"Mark. You are a nice guy. I am sure there are dozens of friends and colleagues back home who feel the same way. But not God. He sees us for who we really are. And so should you. Not objects, not colors, or races, just people all trying to find their path and reason for being."

"There are never coincidences with the people who enter our life. Even for just a moment, at a traffic light, or passing on a sidewalk, like you, they are where they are because they are supposed to be there."

"Ask yourself this question, Was your marriage an accident or a seminal moment in your time here on Earth? There are no coincidences. I suggest you consider this . . ."

Chapter 10

The next morning, he was up before the sun. Thinking about his marriage had him thinking about something else, something he had left behind years ago, but something he now wondered about.

"Is that my edge?" After stirring the coals in the firepit, he prepared the lemongrass for his morning tea.

When he and Rachael were meeting the pastor the day before their wedding, he was asked if they were Christians and had accepted Jesus into their lives. His wife was quick to affirm her belief, but when he had remained silent . . .

She filled the void that he was once a Rosicrucian. The look on the man's face was not judging but curious. He asked a few questions, making sure I wasn't in some sort of cult or something like that.

"And now?" he had asked. After a few more questions, that was the end of it.

"But was it?"

The topic was something he was looking forward to discussing with Angel. She was morphing into his shrink. Probably because she had made it clear that as long as he was married, nothing else was going to happen. And as long as he was here, well . . . lack of information left a deep pool of stagnant history.

"Am I still married? Has Rachael moved on with her life? Don't know. Might never know."

He would return to the nugget he had recovered from his past, but first things first. He finished his morning brew, not quite the coffee he loved, but it was acceptable. He changed into the blue shorts he called his gym clothes and commenced the morning ritual.

"Sit-ups, push-ups, pull-ups—nine this time." He was gradually improving. "And then run . . ."

"The work is beginning to show," he noted with open satisfaction. "The flabby handles are gone. My belly shows some abs. Will she notice?" Deep down he wanted her approval, even if she would not allow their relationship to be physical.

He changed up his diet—more fish and less breadfruit. He could run farther and soon added sprints to augment his routine. Unlike at any point before, he actually looked forward to his workouts. He had reduced them to five times a week, so his body had time to rest. Sometimes he experienced the mythical endorphins athletes would talk about. It was a high that was almost as good as sex.

"Ahh, sex . . ." It was never far from his mind. Gulping lungful's of air, he redirected his mind away from his lusts and pointed it toward questions for Angel.

His routines adapted to the presence of the lake. Once done with his exercises, he would load his backpack with empty bottles and fill them at the falls.

Today was no different. Walking the beach, the sun sparkled on the rippling waters. Dolphins frolicked in the bay. Their unbound joy always made him smile. They were his friends. Maybe a dozen or more came by every few days, jumping and diving, probably corralling a school of fish.

"Hey, guys," he shouted, smiling—knowing that dolphins mean no sharks. It was a reminder he told himself each time he saw them.

He was torn between rushing to talk with Angel and watching his aquatic friends. As always, Angel won out.

"Not today, fellas." He waved, and they responded as dolphins do, leaping out of the water with turns and spins.

"Now you're just showing off. Maybe later?"

When he arrived at the lake, she was not there. His mouth felt dry, and his palms grew sweaty. It was the first time she had not been there waiting.

Did I offend her, coming on the way I did? What was I thinking? "Please God," he asked, his heart pounding with worry.

As if someone was listening, a soft breeze floated down from the ridge, carrying a hint of frangipani, her scent.

"Everything will be okay," soothed a voice inside his head. His heart began to find a normal rhythm as he took in slow, deep breaths.

He filled his bottles and put them aside. Entering the waters, he set out to do his laps. Overhand crawl to one side, breaststroke back. Crawl, breaststroke. It was his focus, perfecting his technique, going for quality over quantity. He loved the feel of pulling forward as his hands stroked down on the resistance, the muscles of his back filling with blood at the exertion. His shoulders and chest had grown in size and strength. He knew he was looking the best he had in years.

When he reached the day's goal, he swam to the falls and let the cascading waters cleanse his body and clear his mind.

From the top of the grassy knoll, Angel stepped from the forest, her stride elegant, meaningful, emanating complete control. Once reaching the shore, she removed her dress.

But she was no longer naked. Instead, she was wearing a pearlescent-white, two-piece bathing suit that hugged high on her hips. Though not quite as provocative, she was still incredibly sexy. Diving into the water, she moved with smooth, languid motions, joining him under the falls.

"Nice suit," Mark complimented.

"You too." Her thousand-watt smile was always on display.

"Macy's?" His tone kept it playful.

"Neiman Marcus."

Mark smiled. His wife was also a Neiman's girl. As always, the sound of Angels voice and cadence of her accent were hard to place. He wasn't a linguist or any such thing, but she sounded a lot like people Rachael had grown up with in Utah. But also like a woman he had met when visiting Ireland. *An Irish Mormon?*

"Come on. I want to show you something."

She submerged and Mark followed. The water was glass-clear, silky, and smooth. Through churning bubbles, he could see her legs parallel the cascade falling overhead. She turned and he followed.

The water grew shallower, the ground firm underfoot. Standing waist deep, they were inside a hollowed-out cavern behind the falls.

"Cool," echoed his voice. "It's like something from a James Bond movie."

Ascending the gentle slope, he found the floor was made of fine sand. The granules clung to his wet feet, leaving two sets of imprints.

Mirages don't leave footprints. Do angels? It was the type of question that he would ask himself over and over, again and again. Often his mind would go down one avenue and then the other, never quite finding clarity.

The area was the size of a large bedroom. Sunlight diffusing through the aquatic window flickered translucent patterns upon the walls and ceiling.

"Look."

Following her gaze, he saw a cross etched into the wall. It looked to be about ten inches from top to bottom. By the depth of the carving, it was apparent that whoever made this had gone to great lengths to see that it survived.

When he first discovered the orchards, his instincts were that slave traders had planted them. This was only the second piece of evidence that humans had ever been here before him.

"What do you think?" he asked.

"Many of the slave merchants were Muslims," she told him, echoing his thoughts. "They would not allow Christian worship. Perhaps this was where those who could came to pay homage to their Father."

"You mean God?" Mark clarified.

"I do. Speaking of which, how's that Bible of yours?"

Her questions were never benign. He knew they were all designed to lead somewhere.

"Skimming," he admitted. He could not explain it, but intuitively he understood she was somehow privy to even his deepest secrets. Accepting that her observations were both helpful and insightful, he saw no reason to lie to her, something that for most of his life had been second nature when he wanted to keep secrets from the world.

Angel sat down on the soft sand, her back against the wall. She patted the ground, and he joined her. They sat quietly, listening to the muffled sounds of the water splashing beyond the aquatic curtain.

"Do you believe in God?" she asked.

71

"Not really. At least not in the aspect of a benevolent being watching over us. Someone who is in control of everything." He studied her face, looking for a reaction, but she simply continued unhurried without any signs of judgment.

"So you think life is simply random." Her tone was laced with doubt.

"I believe we shape the events that affect our lives. Every day we make decisions based on input. The better we are at process, the greater our success. Matter of fact, I want to talk to you about something related to that."

His thoughts that morning led him to want share an idea with her.

"Hmm," she started, "so process gives one better control over events, and thus we are the arbiters of our destiny."

"Something like that," he said. The walls created a soft reverb, like singing in the shower.

"Of course there are obvious things we cannot control."

"Like the weather," Mark conceded, enjoying the discussion, and seeing no need to rock the boat.

"Personal things that define us. For instance, we have no say in what century we are born. Right?" She sat casually, twirling her hair with two fingers.

He could see his weather comment had strayed far from her mark. And he acknowledged this with a nod as she continued.

"We don't control which continent we are born on. Our color or ethnicity, our choice of parents or our siblings. We have no say whether we are born rich or poor., have good parents or bad, or grow up in an orphanage or nurtured by a loving family."

He acknowledged these were valid points, but this was not moving him any closer to conceding the idea of the existence of a benevolent god.

"We have zero input into the diseases we are prone to, the color of our eyes, our gender and height, our body type, natural abilities, or which hand is dominant. The list goes on and on. It seems to me like ninety-nine percent of what shapes our lives was never in our control."

Her presentation made it hard for him to argue her conclusions.

"Okay, you are right. I never really gave it that much thought. But what's it got to do with God?"

"Everything. If we are born for a reason, which some call destiny, then God has given us the necessary skills and attributes to fulfill his plan. Sometimes the winds of fate may blow us off course, but he always finds a way to return us to his path."

"Like this island. Blown off course. Is he going to autocorrect that?" It came out with an unintended edge.

"Mark," she said, her voice soft. "I do not know what God's plan is for you. But as long as we are here on Earth, God is not done with us. Have you ever considered the philosophical question? Which came first, the chicken or the egg?"

It was not at all what he expected. And it seemed like a childish riddle. Without thinking, he responded with crude sarcasm. "I always thought it was the rooster who came first."

She did not laugh. From her passive expression he now wished he could put the words back in his mouth.

"If you look beyond merely cracking the Bible, you will see that God finds foul language and crude jokes sinful. And I find them distasteful . . ." Her face registered disappointment in him. "Those who can only express themselves with vulgarity have a weak mind. I never thought that of you. Am I wrong?"

"Sorry," he lamented, the point scoring a hit.

"May I continue?"

"Of course. I'm sorry," he repeated. *Idiot.*

"This question gets to the heart of everything," she explained. "Where we came from, where we are going, and what we should do about it. Creationism versus evolution, it exemplifies the adage 'What you believe to be true will dictate your life.'"

"Okay?" He had never given weight to a childish riddle, but right now he focused on good behavior.

"A chicken would come first if God created all the animals, the creation theory of a benevolent God. Whereas the egg would come first as the casing of any new evolving species in accordance with the tenets of evolution. Random events, cause and effect, elements, and adaptation, you can see the life-altering ramifications by which of these two concepts you adhere to."

She never gave him a chance to answer. But, of course, they already knew where he stood.

"The illusion of control is contrary to the precepts of destiny."

He was left to wonder, *What am I supposed to do with this?*

She altered her course ever so slightly. "A new truth can only rise within the destruction of an old truth. Which would seem for you is in need, so we can deal with the fundamental point of life. If you are still here, He is not done with you yet. Have you ever heard the quote, 'The arc of the moral universe is long, but it bends toward justice'?"

"Sure. Martin Luther King," he said, satisfied he knew the answer.

"Close." She smiled. "He borrowed it from Theodore Parker."

"Meaning what?" he asked, surprised.

"Do you believe in right or wrong?" Her question sought a simple yes or no answer.

"Of course."

"But within the constructs of evolution, there is no such thing as a moral decision. Right or wrong does not exist. As Darwin stated, 'survival of the fittest.'"

Mark had never considered this, tucking away the idea for further inspection.

"Our conscience comes from God. Morality is what distinguishes us from the animal kingdom. You do see that?"

Before he could answer, she went down another avenue, following the same direction.

"Now tell me, Why did you pray when all seemed lost? When the boat was rolling and the end inevitable?" Her eyes grew soft yet expressive.

The question unlocked the vows he had made. With a sharp breath, he recalled every harrowing minute.

"Right," she said with that distinct curl of her mouth. "If you survived, you promised you would change. Have you? You still swear and use crude language. You still lust. And you still avoid acknowledging God. So—are you working at becoming a better man?"

He was silent. Her words were like a firehose, something you tried to withstand without drowning.

"I guess."

"Your prayer was a hope. Without God there is no hope. You see where randomness takes you." She let the idea dangle and gave him room for introspection.

Shifting in her seat, she brushed hair off her face. "You know the Bible is full of great stories, ancient history, allegories, and poetry. You would be surprised how many times angels and other cosmic emissaries are described across the pages of time. If you want to find out God's plan, start there." Her final two words did not invite any comeback.

Angels? Angel. If you are still here, then He is not done with you . . . There were so many innuendos at play.

"So what's that thing you wanted to talk about?" she asked, leaning back onto the wall.

He was growing used to her mode of operation. Plant an idea, then move on. So he moved on.

"When I was a teen, I was a seeker. Always looking for a greater truth. Believing there was more to our reality than the mere physical we could see and touch."

She smiled. "Like God . . ."

"Perhaps," he conceded in a gloss over. "Eventually, I was drawn to the Order of the Rosy Cross. Better known as the Rosicrucians."

Her silence encouraged him to continue.

"After signing a pledge to never share the materials they would send me, I began what they called the process of enlightenment. It was a series of daily practices used to develop my pituitary gland, which is known in ancient circles as the third eye. And to train my thalamus, the gland attributed with filtering out ninety percent of everything we see and hear. In effect, the gland that creates our reality. This process is designed to bring the initiate closer and closer to the Akasha, where they will obtain the nirvana of metaphysical insight."

She smiled, showing genuine interest. This emboldened him to dive deeper.

"One of the techniques was to light a candle and meditate on the flame, clearing the mind of all thoughts."

"I bet that was hard," she stated, as if knowing what he was thinking.

"For sure. Humans have a knack for distractions. But over time, I did get better. Anyway, they claim that one of the benefits of this practice is that initiates would begin to have a greater clarity and new understandings of what lies beyond the mental horizon."

"You mean like clairvoyance?"

"I'm not sure that is the right word. More like insight into possibility, discerning cause and effect—seeing around the corner."

"I see." Flashing her thousand-watt smile, she grinned. "No pun intended. You believe this was the gift that enabled you to be so successful in business. To see what others could not."

"I don't know—but maybe. Right?" The thought had been percolating since this morning. It was what he wanted to believe, hoping she would affirm this.

"And how were you drawn to this, and why did you quit?"

"It was an ad I saw in *Archaeology Today*. I responded to an 800 number."

"A random ad that somehow moved you to action. Hmm. Like God whispered an idea into your head and you responded."

He was not going to spoil the mood by arguing.

"Eventually other distractions caused me to let go and forget. But now—I wonder . . ."

"*Archaeology Today*? That was some pretty heady stuff for a teenager." The way she said it felt like a compliment.

"I have always had a fascination with ancient humans. Even as an adult I watched shows about alternative histories, vanished cultures, and their ancient astronaut theories."

She shifted on the silky sand, tucking her legs underneath her.

"You realize that every single theory of ancient astronauts arriving on Earth could also be attributed to angels and other emissaries of God. In Ezekiel there are passages some attribute to historical recordings of flying saucers, but . . ."

He saw a sparkle in her eyes, as if an idea suddenly burst upon her.

"The Book of Daniel . . . you should definitely read that. There is a passage where the angel Gabriel says he was sent by heaven to answer Daniel's prayer but ran into trouble. 'The prince of darkness that reigned over the kingdom of Persia withstood me for twenty-one days.'"

"I'm not following," Mark admitted.

"This prayer was not answered by aliens, but by angelic beings."

Mark digested her comments, letting the sound of falling water and his beating heart play out their duet. After a few moments of soul searching, he felt a pressing need to ask why she was here. It covered a deep-seated fear that one day she would leave him.

"Angel."

"Mark," she echoed his tone.

"Can I ask you something?"

She answered before he asked. "We are both children of the same father . . ."

Again he was left to dissect a reply that could have two entirely different meanings.

Chapter 11

Angel was the highlight of each day. Over the last eighteen months, Mark had grown accustomed to her dissecting and disassembling every facet of his life. She always found a way to enlighten him without judging him. Gentle mercies instead of shame. And strangely, he felt the process was transforming him. He once told her, "This may be the first time I have ever really liked myself."

He enjoyed the clever ways she incorporated every conversation with elements which showed that life was more than a series of random events—to the point he no longer dismissed the possibility of a controlling force that organized the universe.

And she would end every conversation with the same reminder. "If you are still here, then He is not done with you yet."

Of course, this usually led him to a question that was never far from mind. "Will I ever get off this island?"

Though Angel occupied most of his thoughts, he still had many other things that required his attentions - things like survival. Pragmatism had ingrained daily routines that only varied with the weather and the seasons. Nature's patterns had become a form of an annual clock.

"Summers are too damn hot, too much rain, too much humidity," he expressed, marking the season as his least favorite time of year. "But then in the fall, the whales always return." He could hear them when they cruised offshore. Their presence always cast him back to the few fond memories he had when he was adrift.

"I love the blue of the winter sky, like an ancient grotto. But it's the spring I love most. The annual return of the black-snouted terns, the way they come, drink, rest, and depart."

As an afterthought, he always considered the evidence of their presence. "They leave a lot of poop. The annual fertilization of Lambert Island." He chuckled, but it was a truth.

Because of Angel's insistence that "you only live once," or the constant reminders "to embrace every moment." That "Life is not about playing it safe, it is to be experienced." More and more he gave in to the exploration of curiosities, willing himself to make use of his time instead of putting life on hold, waiting…

"I'm gonna dust off my old meditation practices."

He recalled the look on his marriage pastor's face when he described expanding his third eye, so it gave him pause. In the book *Lost Secret of the Ancient Ones*, he had read about government programs involved with remote viewing, the process of letting one's consciousness leave the physical body to see things far away and then return with the retained data.

"Obviously, if it's funded by the government, there must be some science behind it, right?"

He had nothing to lose and time on his hands, so he decided to give it a try. As a teen, he had meditated on a candle. But here there were none, so instead he focused on the flickering fire, maintaining his sole attention on the yellow glow as it wavered in the heat.

Setting his mind upon thoughts of home, his children, and his wife, a month passed. So far, he could not see any success, but with nothing else to do, he kept practicing.

"One day at a time," he told himself. "One day at a time."

As the calendar moved forward, the way he viewed Angel changed. Originally, lust had framed her as nothing more than an object of desire. But as days together turned into weeks, then months, their relationship shifted more to the comfort of a companion. And now he wanted to believe this had matured to what he hoped was a lasting friendship.

He often toyed with the idea of exploring the path she would leave upon, but she had let it be known he should not. And for him, the value of the companionship far outweighed the need to know if she was real or imagined.

Arriving at the lake, the cool turquoise waters glimmered in spiraling rings radiating from her leisurely strokes through the water. She was no longer wearing that sexy white bikini. Instead, she had on a black one-piece, more functional and less enhancing, like those worn by Olympian swimmers.

He considered the evolving nature of her wardrobe and juxtaposed this against the changing nature of their relationship. Angel's arrival coincided with Thomas's demise. He assumed this was no coincidence. *One imaginary friend for another?*

"Come on in. Water's great," she hollered.

Well, she's real enough for me.

Suppressing the thoughts, he joined her, and they began to move in unison. This gave strength to an idea that had been percolating for a while—to enjoy the freedom of diving once again.

Five years and no sharks. It's time to get over my fear.

He smiled, plugging in the mantra she had ingrained into him. *If I'm still here, then He's not done with me . . .* Right?

Exiting the water, stretching out on the grass, she lay on her side with one hand propping up her head. The sun was warm but not hot. The wind was a faint whisper through the trees, and a wide palette of birds came into the glen, had a drink, and flew away. The day was turning out perfect.

"Mark," she began. A long grass straw hung from the corner of her mouth like one of those cigarette holders used during the Roaring Twenties. Her casualness was one of the attributes he had grown so fond of.

"There are no creatures on this island. Other than us, there is nothing larger than a rabbit. No predators, no chupacabra, no monsters or wild dogs."

He sat up. *How is it she always knows what I am thinking?* She had just unpacked the core of his morning's thoughts: fear.

"What about the sounds in the bushes? Did I imagine those?" He trusted her, but he knew what he had heard.

"Do you know the expression 'energy follows thought'?"

He nodded.

Running his hand through wet black hair, his mind drifted.

I'm gonna be fifty soon. A little gray, but all in all, my hair is full, my body fit. And I'm in the best shape of my life. He licked his lips in smug satisfaction, forgetting she never missed a thing.

Locking eyes on him, she continued. "It's a scientific explanation for why the power of prayer works," she said. "It is a highly focused form of thought energy."

"Okay . . ." he agreed, settling in for the day's lesson.

"Throughout history, going back for thousands of years and across every culture, there have been mythical creatures manifested by man's darkest fears. If enough people conjured up a beast, then these energies would become manifest."

"So you're saying what I heard was simply the power of suggestion?"

"I am saying there are no beasts or creatures or even natural predators on this island."

There was no equivocation. Her tone was definitive—it was a fact he should accept.

"What about the howling I heard on the night of the hurricane? That was real, and it creeped me out. Even now I keep by my bed a spear that I carved from a long stick."

She fell back in the grass and started laughing. It was infectious, and soon he could not help but join in.

"I would submit that there are lava tubes just over the ridge. If the wind blows across them correctly, as with an empty bottle, it will create a mournful sound. Find that and you will find your monster."

He felt she was hinting at a challenge.

"Why are you telling me this now?" He knew she always had a reason, and she was always strategic. Sometimes he saw the bends and fluctuations of the road she was unfolding, but other times . . .

"Fear is the Enemy's greatest tool. It causes anger, it blinds us with distraction, and it acts as a shield for the agents of darkness to keep us from

79

basking in the love of God. Did you know that there are three-hundred-and-sixty-five references in the Bible instructing man not to fear? I do not think that is a coincidence. Fear is a tool used by evil to rob us of joy. And joy is the serious business of heaven," she reminded him.

It never ceased to amaze him how she was able to direct every conversation back to God. By now he had read the Bible cover to cover. He could identify the Old Testament passages about the coming of the Jewish messiah. And truth was, he loved the tales of angels among men, the hints of the ongoing cosmic warfare, and even those biblical patriarchs like Enoch who had learned the secret of transmuting off the planet only to return.

But for him, they were just words. He could not grasp the New Testament's message of Jesus Christ, the Holy Spirit, and the Trinity of God. Three in one? It defied logic. And evil? The personification of beings battling for humanity's soul? It felt like an excuse for lacking accountability—

The Devil made me do it. But he wanted her to be happy, so he continued to read, question, and let his curiosity wander while suspending his disbelief.

"For though I walk through the valley of the shadow of death, I fear no evil," Mark quoted to impress her and affirm he was paying attention.

"Exactly." She stood. "Tomorrow? Same time, same place?"

"Every day," he replied, producing an easy smile that mirrored hers.

She ascended the grassy knoll. Shafts of sunlight cast an ethereal halo around her golden tresses. At the top of the glen she turned and spoke softly. Though no longer near, her words were as clear as if she were standing right next to him.

"For those who don't know where to begin wading into scripture, there are thirty-one proverbs and usually thirty-one days in a month. Today is the eighth . . ."

What she imparted was odd because he had already admitted to regularly reading the Bible.

She smiled, the crook of her mouth signaling mischief. "It might answer some questions for you."

As Mark exited the forest, he was met by the breeze wafting in from the ocean, cool fingers picked up from the deep waters. He could see his friends frolicking in the bay, which reinforced the desire repressed for far too long.

"I used to love diving, scuba, snorkeling, whatever. I miss the beauty and quiet below the waves . . . dolphins mean no sharks!" he emphatically reminded himself. "They hate each other!"

As the creatures played, their antics were joyous and carefree. They were simply having fun. Two in particular reminded him of his two oldest when they were young. Sometimes after work he would take his kids to the park, which would be full of children and moms, strollers, and nannies, and he would watch how uninhibited his kids played.

"They lived for the moment. Free of concern. Uncaring of what other people thought, simply being where their feet were. What do they look like now? What are their interests and hobbies? Does Ally have a boyfriend? Does Rachael approve?"

He felt a sudden need to connect with his family. His phone was dead, but the pictures were still in there. Knowing he may never see them again, the photos were all he had. And yet they remained elusive and out of reach.

During the dark of night, he had played out scenarios of what had happened to *Lil Darling*. And all the logic, and perhaps a little intuition, said she had slid off the reef into the adjoining pass.

Often, when he would stand on the beach looking out over the waters, he wondered, *Is she still there?*

"If I retrieved the power converter, maybe I could charge my phone."

From somewhere deep within, an idea germinated and would not be ignored.

"Angel's right!" His voice projected out over the waters rippling in the bay. "I won't let fear rob me of my life!"

The walk home gave him plenty of time to talk himself out of it. But he had become resolute. Find *Lil Darling* and get the converter. Donning his gear, he pushed the raft into the calm waters.

This drew the attention of his buddies, and it was not long before they were jumping and chattering all around him.

"You guys crack me up." He laughed. Over time, he had assigned names to each. And, of course, his favorite was Flipper.

Rowing through the promontory's ever-present shadow, he looked down and peered into waters that were deep and clear. He realized that an ocean-worthy vessel could easily find safe harbor here. But the thought was fleeting. Flipper's jumping and spinning vied for his attention.

"Come on, guys, let's go diving."

Hearing them cack, cack, cacking in that unique voice of theirs, he imagined they were encouraging him to return to the water and rekindle his love of being under the sea.

Rowing with a sense of purpose, he found *Lil Darling* sitting upright on the bottom of the cut a mere ten feet below the ocean surface.

"So that's where you went," he whispered, relieved that his friend hadn't been taken out to sea and broken apart. Seeing her for the first time since the hurricane hit him with an onslaught of emotions. Joy, sorrow, relief, hope, loss, but mostly comfort.

"She never abandoned me."

Letting his eyes wander, Mark watched the dolphins swimming below the waters. Circling the boat like they were playing musical chairs, they would randomly pop their heads up as if they were encouraging him to come in.

"No sharks today," he whispered, and cast a thankful glance upward. He realized the action attested to the fact Angel's teachings were making him more open minded.

"A mind so open your brains fall out." He laughed. It was a random memory that in the past he had used to mock those whose politics he found loony, but now . . .

He was thinking how closed he had become, letting fear dictate his life.

"There is nothing to fear but fear itself," he quoted while slipping on his fins and mask.

Entering the water, he found it cool with a mild current. As he submerged, the bubbles cleared, and just like that he was back in a world of undersea wonders.

Below him *Lil Darling* sat nestled on a sandy bottom. Adjacent was a wall of living coral. The railings crumpled from Ironsides were still affixed to the bow.

Swimming with the raft line, he tied it to the dilapidated rail. Memories of the hundreds of times he had gone diving stripped away the anxieties. He relished the return to his aquatic cocoon.

I have returned to the sea. Let's go take a look.

Not quite sure where to start, he did an assessment of his old friend. Other than sitting submerged, she seemed relatively intact.

Surfacing for a gulp of air, he dove down to the engine room. The water was clear, his movements raising silt that had seeped in along the floor.

Seeing the three batteries left behind, he reasoned there would be lines in from the generator and lines out to a converter. All of this would pass through the battery housing. After coming up for a second and for a third breath, confident his sentries were on guard, he returned to the compartment and determined which was which. The lines to the converter passed up through the hull into the cabin.

Surfacing for air yet again, he spied tentacles of green algae trailing in the current, the boat was not an impediment to the channel's flow. It unlocked what should not have taken him years to understand.

"The sea enters from this end, flows inside the reef, and exits at the end closest to my cave. Nature's way of flushing the bay and replenishing the cove with fish. This is why the dolphins love it here so much."

Taking three large gulps, he plunged below, this time entering the main salon.

There you are. It was the DC to AC converter. A blue metal box a bit larger than a shoe box, albeit much heavier. It was held in place by four screws.

Examining what tools he would need, he noted a standard outlet built into the box. He had to surface three more times for air, but eventually he retrieved the box and placed it in the raft.

"Work done—time for play." Flipper did a backflip, calling out his joy.

He had been diving the world over, but this reef was the most pristine he had ever seen. Being so far from the destructive wastes of humanity, everything thrived.

Pancaked layers of color stacked in shades of yellows, blues, and a hundred other hues. Corals with grooves reminiscent of a human brain sat like large boulders. Anemones swayed in the currents, their tentacles filtering the never-ending flotsam. Fish darted in and around the fire coral, through the extended arms of staghorn, and under the ledges that made up the cornucopia of an alien world.

Five-dollar queen angel, he thought. Grammas—two bucks a piece. Foolishly, he reverted to old habits. When he collected tropical fish in college, he had reduced each fish to a price tag. Money had turned joy into work and beauty into greed.

This reef was the perfect way to rekindle his lost passion. It was abundant with every tropical fish found in the Atlantic. Tangs, rays, angels, eels, even giant sea turtles roamed over the coral heads. He was getting reacquainted with the magical world below the waves, recapturing the lost joy that had started long before his fear of sharks.

Each time he submerged, he got deeper into his comfort zone. Yellow tangs schooling with blues. Neon-spotted damsels flirting with the anemones. With Flipper as company, he dared move farther from his raft. Farther from Lil Darling, he explored the underside of the coral heads. More fish, more diversity, more . . .

What do we have here? Two antennae protruded from beneath a ledge. He was an old hand at tickling these wily crustaceans out of their hole.

Lobster tonight. Do I need a permit?

Ach . . . note to self. No laughing underwater.

Surfacing with dinner, he played out an old memory sparked by the permit joke. In hindsight, he knew Angel would be ashamed at how reckless he had been with other people's lives. At the time, though, he justified it as bold, youthful audacity.

He had borrowed his dad's thirty-two-foot Sea Ray. Along with two friends, he had taken them and their girlfriends down to Soldier Key for the overnight Columbus Day Regatta, an annual event that enjoined over seven thousand boats for a weekend of unbridled partying.

We gotta drink, we gotta get drunk, because—regatta . . .

Across the bay was Turkey Point Nuclear Power Plant. And leading into the plant was an artificial canal cut into the shallow waters for barges to come and go. All of this was inside Biscayne National Park, where lobstering, as well as any other form of ocean harvest, was a federal crime.

I didn't care. I had a plan . . .

When we were anchored inside the canal, the three girls sunbathed topless while we plotted to get a bag full of lobster tails from right under the Feds' noses.

"Rules are for the other guys. The difference between courage and stupidity is success." Hoisting a dive flag, we slipped into the water in full gear. The walls had thousands and thousands of lobsters in holes they had made in the soft sides. Literally condos of crustaceans.

The bottom was littered with carcasses where the sharks had come in and feasted. Today we were the sharks.

Removing lobsters by the dozens, we popped off their tails and threw them into a bag, adding to the detritus on the bottom. And, as expected, it was not long before the shadow of a boat had pulled alongside our own.

Marine Patrol!

We tied the bag to the anchor as planned, and I surfaced to meet our fine friends in law enforcement.

"Can I help you?" I had asked.

"Is this your boat?"

"My father's," I informed.

"Tell your friends to surface."

I had noticed they must have instructed the girls to put their tops back on. What a sight that must have been for them. Especially Ariana . . . oh boy. Her breasts would mesmerize any man.

We all entered the boat, removed our gear, and sat down as directed.

"What are you doing here?" one asked.

Truth was always the best defense.

"Looking for lobsters," I replied, unconcerned.

"I see. Did you see any?" The larger man was trying to suppress a grin—the gotcha look.

"It's like a zoo down there," I told him. "Thousands."

"And did you catch any?"

"Not yet, we just got here when I saw the boat overhead."

"Hmm . . . may I search the boat?" I could tell he was not sure if I was lying or telling the truth.

We looked at one another, concerned, as there was some pot on board. But it was well hidden. I hoped. I'm a fairly good actor, straight faced. It was the others I worried about, so I made sure the attention stayed on me as they searched the boat. Fortunately, they were not overzealous.

Then the shakedown started. All I could think was, Thank god Dad is a navy man.

"Life preservers." Enough for six. Check.

"Floats?" Check.

On and on. The list was extensive. Who knew there were so many rules and regulations for operating a boat legally? Finally they got to the last item.

"Do you have a backup whistle as required in case your horn breaks?" I smiled. Actually, we did. Good old Dad. So I showed them.

They conferred with one another, and then their body language shifted. "You don't know how lucky you are we got here when we did. Had you harvested a single lobster, we would have confiscated the boat, arrested all on board, and your father would be fined ten thousand dollars."

I knew all that, but I was arrogant enough to be sure I was smarter than them. And in the end, I guess I was.

Or God had other plans for me. If you are still here, then He is not done with you yet.

Once the Feds left, we pulled the anchor with the bag attached and raced across the bay to get lost in the thousands of boats of the regatta. That night was a lobster feast for us and everyone anchored around us. What happened after that . . .

Ditching a replay of his debauchery, he untied the rope and headed back toward shore.

The dolphins showed their pleasure by splashing and playing all the while with that perpetual smile on their faces. He knew what they were saying, "Job well done . . ."

"Delicious," he said, smacking his lips on the last morsel of lobster. "I'm gonna add this to the menu."

Glad he had gotten past his phobia, it gave him an excuse to keep diving. He finished cleaning up and, once done, tossed another piece of wood onto the fire. Sparks rose on the heat, the glowing embers setting the dry wood aflame.

With his back against the log, his thoughts returned to Angel. They always found their way back to Angel. Today she had planted a seed that evil was personified. Evil was not just a concept—there were spiritual beings in a war for the souls of humanity.

"Evil uses fear as a tool," she had told him. "To distract us from the joy God wants for us." That simple lesson was the catalyst that had unlocked the day. It encouraged him to dive with the dolphins, and it allowed him to feel free again.

The fire crackled, and shadows danced against the rocks, against the fish rack, and against the bamboo gate leaning near the entry.

Fear, he thought, never once considering how much power it had over him. He turned it over and over, his mind metaphorically tasting it, touching it, holding it, and smelling it, appreciating how it had robbed so many aspects of his life.

"She's right! I let it put me into a cage. Well, no more!"

Gathering a blanket and pillow, he set out for the beach. With his chin high and his shoulders back, he walked with a sense of purpose. As if the heavens were welcoming him back, the sky was clear and the Milky Way bright. Its nebula glowed as it always did.

"I forgot how beautiful you are," he whispered in awe. His old friend Orion was also there, his belt heavy with stars.

He arrived at the spot where he had first landed. He thought back to that day.

"Geez, that was a long time ago. Over seven years."

He spread his blanket and settled onto his back to gaze up in wonder. For years he had spent his days exploring the island. But the nights . . . almost from the day he had arrived, fear of the unknown had kept him sequestered inside his cave, but not tonight.

"I trust her. If Angel says it is safe—then it is safe."

The air was comfortable, with a slight breeze sighing through the palm trees. The water lapping on the beach mingled with the distant muffle of ocean crashing out on the reef, an island chorus that filled the night. No animals, no beasts, no predators, just Mark Lambert.

He thought of Angel. He thought of home.

"Will I ever be rescued?"

Just before the world of dreams took over, he found his comfort.

If I'm still here, then He's not done with me yet . . .

Chapter 12

Mark woke to a dawn streaked in crimson. "Red sky at night, sailors delight," he murmured the old sailors' axiom about pending weather. The other stanza, "Red sky in morning, sailors warning," hastened him to gather his bedding and get home before the rains let loose.

Once there, he fueled the fire, heated some water, and added lemon grass to brew a weak tea. "God, what I would give for a cup of coffee."

More and more he missed the little things. Like strong coffee in the morning, a cold can of Fresca in the afternoon, or maybe even a bag of Fritos.

"When I get back . . ."

The idea that he would be rescued fueled an optimism that his days here were numbered. But, of course, being pragmatic, the possibility came with questions attached. *Is this simply hope, or has intuition given me a glimpse of the future?*

He finished his breakfast, and the sky tipped its hand to the storm that was coming. Lightning within the tall cumulus clouds put on a show worthy of the Creator.

"Time to get the gear inside."

After so many years on the island, he was familiar with the types of weather that nature was bringing. Through observation he had learned what to expect and how to prepare. In this case, he took down his tarp and moved all loose items into the cave.

With nothing else to do, he headed for the lake. Walking the beach, Mark peered out to the horizon. The idea of rescue would not go away. Once again, he wondered if this feeling was just wishful thinking or something more.

When he arrived at the grotto, the rains let loose. Angel was nowhere in sight, perhaps because of the rain.

"Will she come?"

Their thoughts like one, she stepped from the trees. Her smiling face was dripping with water, as was his own. She waved to him.

"Hey, Mark."

She was the yin to his yang. Though there was no ignoring her beauty, he was becoming more drawn by her intellect and reason. He mostly savored the companionship. Lust had run its course, something that surprised him.

Perhaps I have changed.

"How about we sit in the cave today?" she suggested and plunged headlong into the waters.

He followed after her, and together they surfaced behind the falls. He noticed his footprints from before. But only his. It triggered the same internal debate. And again he told himself the same thing: *Who cares?*

While he used his hands to sluice water from his chest and legs, she twisted her dripping hair, letting the wet run down her body and onto the floor.

The air felt cool, the sand felt soft, and the lighting was muted by the rain. He studied her silhouette. He had long ago given up on where she went. Somewhere along the way, he had accepted it was better not to know more than he already did.

Most people really don't want the truth. He chuckled as he thought of an old cartoon. *They just want reassurance that what they believe is the truth.*

When it came to Angel, this was his gospel.

"A penny for your thoughts," she prodded, leaning back on her hands.

"You'll need at least a dollar."

Saying nothing, she tilted her head to one side, encouraging him to continue.

"The invisible world . . ."

Truth was, he was wondering about her, his recent feelings of precognition, and about reality itself. He was hoping she might offer him some insight. Perhaps even a clue about herself. Though on the latter, he knew in his heart that this was never going to happen.

"The invisible world . . . ," she mused. She placed a finger to her lips, thumb under her chin, and he knew this was one of her tells, that she was giving the idea serious thought. And generally what followed was another one of her lessons. He sat back and listened as she began a new topic for the day.

"Did you know that back in the fifties the Soviet Union did a number of experiments to explore the unseen realm? For instance, they took newborn rabbits away from their mothers and placed them in buildings that ranged from next door to miles away."

"They would hook the mother rabbits up to an EKG, and at the other locations, they went about violently killing their babies. Over and over they did this, and over and over the results were the same. At the exact time of the death of their individual children, the mother's EKG would register a significant spike."

He smiled inwardly. He loved that when she was serious, her intensity almost had a glowing affect. Like now.

"How could they have known their child had died unless there was some form of link we cannot see or hear? Navajo call this the Golden Rope. The stronger the relationship, the more binding the cord."

"Shamans once held the reins of society's connection to the invisible world. Unfortunately, today it is relegated to science fiction or conspiracy."

The conversation reminded him of a book, *Recollections of Death*, written by an emergency room surgeon who had interviewed hundreds of people who died while on the operating table and then came back to life, and he focused on their experiences and the spiritual connections they revealed.

It was a long time ago, but Mark remembered thinking the evidence had been compelling.

"Do you know who Ingo Swann was?" she asked, bringing his attention back to her.

"I do. He was an early pioneer in the practice of remote viewing."

"And you know his successes were the basis for the government funding numerous psyops programs. The creation of psychic warriors," she pressed.

Mark recalled reading about the Red Brigade, an Italian terrorist group that had kidnapped Brigadier General Dozier, an American attached to NATO. Using remote viewing to track his aura, Swann mentally formed a picture of a town and street block where Dozier was being held. Using this information, analysts located the exact building, and the general was rescued, giving birth to the American psyops program.

"Yes."

As she readjusted her position, he scooped up some of the fine sand, letting the granules pour through his fingers. The lull in the conversation seemed to amplify the pattering of the water falling beyond. He knew her well enough to see that the dimple she formed when deep in thought meant more was coming.

"The Russians did different experiments on humans," she said in a low voice, introducing her next point. "They had invented Kirlian photography, the ability to record images of one's aura. By taking prisoners who were close to death . . ."

She paused. He discerned from her expression that those used in the experiments were victims who were murdered by the state.

" . . . they would place them on an atomic scale and film them with their Kirlian cameras as they passed from life to death. At the time of death, the aura began moving slowly from both hands and feet up into the body cavity until all that was left was a light centered in the brain. There the glow would remain until roughly the third day, and then it extinguished. When the light was gone, the atomic scales would recognize a very slight decrease in weight, as if the soul had traces of mass."

Mark thought of all the cultures and religious ceremonies that required waiting three days before cremation or burial. Even Jesus waited three days to rise again. Could this be related? How about those people who died and came back to life? Many claimed their lives flashed before them.

He wasn't really thinking about souls when he asked the question of the invisible realm, but since they were on the subject . . . "So what about reincarnation? If man has a soul, do we get to come back again?" His curiosity was genuine. *Might I have another chance?*

"Sorry, Mark, no mulligans in life. One and done. Make the most of it while you can."

Feeling slightly rebuked, he considered the rigidity of her worldview. We have only one life. It has a reason. And if we are still here, God has not finished with us yet.

"But that's not the question, is it?"

Once again, she cut to the chase.

"No," he answered candidly. "I have been doing my Rosicrucian meditation exercises, and over the last couple of sessions feel like I have started having some visions. Fleeting, for sure, but could this be related to that type of mental travel?"

"Mark," she began. Her tone and expression suggested she was about to impart something important. "Trust in your intuition. God gave each of us unique talents for a reason."

The last thing she had said before they exited the cave was about the weather, how it was going to rain for days, and they should wait until it ends to meet again.

He had become so comfortable in their relationship that he took her suggestion for what it was—a practical solution to avoid the inclement weather. He never doubted if she would be there when he made his way back to the glen.

That was two days ago, and she was right. It had not stopped pouring. To pass the time, he pulled out the converter and tried to make it work. Truth was, he didn't know jack about circuit boards, so he had no idea where to start.

Confined by the unrelenting downpour, he often stared out from the protection of his fortress at the unrelenting rains. It was August, and heavy downpours were common. He knew the heat of the equatorial tropics daily pulled so much moisture from the ocean, it was a hit-or-miss lottery of where it got dumped. This week it dumped and dumped and dumped on Lambert Island.

As luck had it, the batch of salted fish he recently cured was ready. That was good, for cooking was on hiatus. With lots of time and little to do, he made an extremely small fire just inside the doorway and gave additional time to his meditative practice.

Deep in thought, his mind clear, an insight appeared. Concentrate on the question—nothing more, nothing less.

How do I fix the converter?

He had oft had some fuzzy images come and go, visions that shimmered and dissolved like a heat mirage. He was sure he was on the right path, each time adding a minuscule grain of confidence to keep going. But tonight he experienced an entirely new level of success.

"What are these weird images? I'm on a small craft floating upon a river, the current specific, moving, and impeded by obstacles, then flowing again.

"What is this place?"

The question filled his head. *How do I fix the converter? This is the answer.* Containing his excitement was becoming difficult.

"Nothing straightforward like an owner's manual. Instead, allegories of streams feeding into rivers, sources of flow, and obstacles diverting the current."

As he framed the allegory with the context of an electrical current and impedance, a vision slowly unfolded.

"That's it!" he exclaimed, retreating back into his body.

Mark took out the converter. The screws were already loose, so he removed the blue housing and ran his fingers along the integrated circuit board. Tracing solder lines, he intuitively felt where the currents flowed, the impedance modulated, and where circuits merged and converted.

"Here," he said as if an invisible force was guiding his hand. The connection was loose. He wiggled it, and a piece of solder came free.

Holding the small bit of metal between two fingers, he retrieved a tiny piece of aluminum foil. Since being on the island, he never threw anything away. Casting an eye over his random collection of odds and ends, things he would use again and again, it reminded him how wasteful his world had been.

"Use once, toss, buy another. We are a very disposable culture," he lamented, wrapping the small piece of foil around the diode.

Returning to the table, he gently worked the item back into its slot. The slight increase in size formed a perfect wedge.

Still, optimism was muted—this really wasn't his jam.

"Let's see what happens."

He connected the DC lines from the converter to one of the unused batteries. A red light came on.

"Whoa!" He gave a fist pump filled with profusive thanks.

Errant thoughts that this information had come to him from the ether did not go unnoticed. But right now he had bigger fish to fry.

The bank bag with his phone and charger, unused for over seven years, sat on a cushion. He held the black piece of glass-covered plastic in his hand. Inanimate and cool to the touch, it was static. Lifeless.

"Man, my life used to be glued to this thing . . ." Daring to raise expectations of unlocking the past, he plugged in the phone but nothing happened. The gravity of disappointment left him staring. The blank nothingness reflected his drawn expression in the glass.

"Of course. A battery dead this long . . ."

Wishing on the empty screen, a blur filled his reflection as a white logo rose, as if drawn from the bottom of the deep.

"It's working. My god, it's working." He repeated this over and over, convincing himself it was real. Squeezing the device between trembling fingers, the manufacturer's logo materialized, followed by an icon showing the phone was now in charging mode.

Impatient and unmindful, he tapped the photo icon. "Nothing. Dang it. Just needs more juice."

It had been a long time since having to navigate the various kinks, quirks, and protocols of his electronic umbilical cord. Waiting reminded him how addicted he had become, pulling in a memory of an old cartoon.

Hey, Johnny, a bunch of us are getting together tonight to sit around and look at our phones. Want to come over and ignore each other?

He had been as guilty as the rest, always checking, looking for updates, a need for gratification as if being rewarded. But now, impatience stretched time like taffy. The minimum charge elusively infinitesimal. Every few minutes he would try, and every few minutes he would have to wait some more. Try, wait. Try . . .

"Finally!"

The photos opened, unleashing a tidal wave of joy upon a torrent of tears. He swiped past the stupid screenshots he thought important at the time, until . . .

He locked eyes onto his children for the first time in, like, forever. Smiling, laughing . . . engulfed in waves of emotion, his heart longed to tell them how much he loved them and missed them.

"God, I miss you guys so much." Tears flowed as silent testimony to the desires of his heart.

"Rachael, you are so beautiful. I should have told you that more often."

Taking his time, ignoring the storm drowning the world outside his door, he scrolled through the photos one by one by one. His children, his wife, the family at Christmas, Disney World, Yellowstone, the kids' first time riding horses in Wyoming. Each image unlocked additional memories such as a specific day or a different trip they had taken. Some unspooled like a movie in his mind while others led to more memories.

He landed on the day they had gotten Carson, Ally cradling the new arrival. With her pretty red collar she was about the size of one of his shoes.

"Is she still alive? She would be, what, eight, give or take? How long do labs live?"

He had a sudden ache in his heart. For her, his children, his wife, he missed them all. The gloomy weather highlighted the dark feelings as all that he was missing came flooding back. He fell to his knees and cried.

He let his practical side indulge in wishful thinking. Stepping just outside the door, he searched for a signal. His service was probably cut years ago, and here in the middle of the Atlantic, he wished with all his heart. Nothing!

"God—help me get off this island? I will do anything," he lamented. The anguish raged like an uncontrollable river. As the emotion ran its course, the answer came on wings of an idea.

Start planting biomorphic suggestions out into the universe!

That night was one of the longest since being on the island. He could not sleep. His mind raced, his heart played a rapid duet with his pulse, and he could not calm himself down enough to find solace in meditation.

He tried sleep, tossing and turning. He got up again and again. He willed his mind to send out messages to loved ones, throwing out thoughts like prayers.

When morning came, he tried something else. Determination had been born, and he was a stubborn man.

"Failure is for those who give up. Maybe a message in a bottle."

Ready to try anything, he composed a note.

Hello,

My name is Mark Lambert, today is . . .

He calculated the exact number of days since he had left Miami—seven years, three months, and five days, and inserted the date.

He went on to describe the island's size and the mountains that marked both ends. He finished with a plea to please reach out to his wife and let his family know he was still alive. He wrote down their number, inserted the note into the bottle, and closed the cap with a twist.

Later that day the rain came to an end, and the sky cleared. Gathering the three bottles with notes inside, he exited his cave to a world dripping in moisture.

The ground was soft, the air felt scrubbed, and the heat of the summer wasted no time in bringing the humidity to a boil.

He was not the only creature glad the rains had ended. Birds filtered over his path as he headed for the beach. Every living creature on the island welcomed nature's respite.

"Dummy," he chuckled, seeing his raft brimming with water. His vocabulary was finding new ways to express himself without using vulgarity. It was another of those little things that changed him toward being a better man.

"That Angel of mine. Always in my head."

Before dumping the water, he chided himself that for the first five years before discovering the lake, he never thought of using the raft to collect rainwater.

"Imagine the number of baths I could have taken. Maybe you're not so smart after all."

Putting the boat in the water, he rowed until the current caught him. It was pretty strong with all the rainfall looking to escape the bay.

"Don't go too far, Bubba," he cautioned.

Calculating the speed and distance, he figured this was far enough. Last thing he needed was to get dragged out to sea. With a kiss and a prayer, all three bottles were launched into the sea. He watched until the current carried them beyond the point and out of sight. All that remained was hope.

He returned to the cave, grabbed his phone, and set off to see Angel.

"Can't wait to tell her the universe provided me insight to fix the converter."

He laughed, hearing her in his head. "Not the universe. It was God."

He shook his head. "Whatever!" Success fueled excitement about where his quests might go next, and he wondered what they might yield. But for now he focused on reuniting with Angel. He missed her and longed for her company.

From the top of the hill, he watched her slicing gracefully through the water. Raindrops clung to the trees, and the path was slick with mud. Picking his way carefully, he parted a few branches, aimed his camera, and took some quick pics.

"My Angel." Grinning with satisfaction, he arrived at the lake. "Uh-oh." Something was wrong, and he suspected what it was. He opened his phone to the photos of her swimming. They were blurred—a raindrop must have obscured the lens. He deleted them.

She exited the water, wringing moisture from her hair. Her face was stone cold. His approach was hesitant.

"Consider me like an exile in the witness protection program," she said coldly. "I do not like to have my picture taken."

His shoulders sagged, and he felt like a scolded puppy.

"Hand me the camera." She reached out her hand in demand.

"Please," Mark pleaded. "It's all I have of my family."

Her hand remained. He knew the choice was her or them. Reluctantly, he gave it to her.

"No more photos then?" Her face softened.

"I promise."

"Okay. Go stand over there."

Confused, he did as he was told.

"Closer to the falls," she directed.

Holding her fingers and thumbs the way a director would frame a shot, what came next totally surprised him.

"I know you think you're quite the stud muffin." She grinned, raising the camera. "Don't think I haven't noticed."

Stud muffin? Really?

He smiled and puffed up his chest. She took the photo, and his world fell back into its natural order.

"I see you figured out the problem of the converter," she concluded, handing him back his phone.

"Yes. Yes I did. I focused on the question, and the solution came to me."

Had this been why she suggested I stay home during the storm? She always had a reason, a road that twisted and turned but was going somewhere.

"So you have finally tapped into the Akasha. Good for you."

He knew she meant the Akashic record, that cosmic vault in the dimension of the spirits that held every thought, emotion, and deed ever created. Like everything else associated with such things, he had mostly just paid it lip service. But now . . .

"Perhaps." He lingered. "I sent out some psychic suggestions to those I love as well as a message in a bottle."

She eyed him up and down, pausing as she stroked her chin with her forefinger, causing him to wonder if his revelation might annoy her.

"Well, then, we better get busy. 'Cause I darn well know there's a pony in there somewhere."

The line was so out of character it caused him to laugh. It was more like something he might have said. It was a quote of Ronald Reagan's that he had read in a biography, and it had lasted through the years.

If you dig through a pile of manure long enough, you are bound to find something of value.

"Remember," she reminded.

"I know, if I am still here, then He is not done with me yet."

Chapter 13

One night in July, near his birthday on the twelfth, he was out walking on the beach when he spied a number of sea turtles coming ashore.

"Nesting season has arrived," he observed, watching the loggerheads come and go. It was another of nature's markers in his annual calendar.

Without an abundance of aerial predators, most of the hatchlings made it to the sea. In other nesting places like Florida and Costa Rica, tens of thousands of seagulls would swoop down to eat them. Only a small percent made it to the sea, where they had to survive the creatures of the deep blue.

"Life and death," he mused, aware at how far his own views on the matter had shifted.

"I wonder if God has other places around the world as safe incubators for his creatures?" It was simply another aspect of the incredible uniqueness of his island.

The moon was full and sparkled on the bay. Beyond the surf, he could hear whales calling out. Shadows and silhouettes moved against the night. It brought back that morning when the family had bumped his boat.

"They had a calf," he recalled. "He would be at least seven now." He knew that whales could live for up to two hundred years.

"Then what happens? Do they die and go to whale heaven? How about the turtles?"

Angel had touched on the soul a few times, most recently when discussing those experiments the Russians had done on humans. As with all things Angel, she was laying down a path that at one point or another every human explores.

What happens when you die?

He recalled what scripture said about the soul and what happens after death. "One and done," just as Angel had told him. He recalled the many passages in the New Testament about Jesus having conquered sin and the grave, but Mark still didn't get that part. Just that there seemed to be an afterlife, and one's choices on Earth determined where one spent eternity.

Were my choices so bad? Something else to discuss with Angel.

"She loves this God stuff. Maybe she really is an angel."

Mark woke before sunrise. The room was dark, and only the faint light outside differentiated the opening from the walls.

The yearning to rejoin society was growing. Willing to try anything, he decided to climb the mountain and cast thoughts out onto the waves. He had succeeded in fixing the converter through a mental connection with the universe. Why not see if he can connect with another human being the same way?

He considered the number of different businesses he had started over the years and all the naysayers who had been quick to point out, *You don't know anything about this, or you shouldn't do that. Stick to what you know.* It was one of the things that drove him to succeed, to prove them all wrong.

He never stopped venturing into new fields and remained unafraid to try, to learn, and to adapt when necessary.

"You'll never swim if you don't get your feet wet," he reminded himself.

He put a few things in his pack and set forth. After so many years, he knew the route by heart and could do it in the dark.

He was atop the mountain as magic unveiled the world around him. Fuzzy shadows came into focus. Soft silhouettes firmed and the ocean separated from the horizon.

Watching the rising sun defeat the night, he reflected on his conversations with Angel. More and more they centered on what she referred to as the invisible war, the eternal struggle between light and darkness. She had said man was merely a pawn in the cosmic battle between good and evil and that most people were not even aware it was going on all around them.

As the morning rays crested the eastern ridge, he surveyed his realm. It became a ritual each time he ascended the mountain. The orchards were an orderly contrast to clusters of mahogany and laurels that forested down to a beach. To the south, the peaks curled out to the end of the reef.

He considered the source of the water that fed the falls, speculating on the mechanics of how it was replenished. He concluded the falls originated from an artesian well, upwelling from below the ground. Why? He had no idea. Another of God's mysteries. From here the waterfall and glade were hidden from view, as were the lands to the south. Ostensibly, this was the location where Angel would retire at the end of each day.

Once the soft glow of morning gave way to the firm light of day, Mark sat in a cross-legged position facing the sea. Starting with morning prayers, he finished with a deep meditative focus.

I am alive. I am ready to be rescued. Hear my plea and feel my presence. Find your way to this island . . .

"Good morning, gorgeous," Mark said when Angel stepped into the glade, the wattage of her smile amplifying everything around him. He never grew tired of the light she brought to the dell and to him. If there really was such a thing as an angel, she was the embodiment of everything he imagined one would be.

"So what's on your mind today, Mr. Lambert?" Wearing a white pullover, she had her hair tied in a loose ponytail.

She always knew when he had questions. He often wondered if her thoughts and his were the same, or if everything she had discussed with him had simply been things he had read and forgotten. He had always been a prolific reader, even as a kid. It was probably the reason he had snagged the Bible and *Lost Secret* from the boat.

He got comfortable on the grass near where she was sitting.

"No swimming today?" she inquired with a knowing smile.

"I hiked to the top of the mountain, which is enough exercise for one morning."

"Upon the mountain of wisdom I will seek understanding." With pursed lips she was being playful, but he knew there was a nugget of truth in everything she said.

"Perhaps," he mumbled. Becoming serious, he straightened his spine and looked her in the eye. "I do not want to die on this island."

Her expression turned somber.

"Is there a reason you would consider that a possibility? Are you feeling all right?"

"I feel fine. So I don't know."

"Perhaps your thoughts are not at all about dying. Instead, the hope of rescue has fostered a new desire to live. After all . . ."

"If I'm still alive, then He's not done with me yet . . ."

They said this in unison, and he burst out laughing.

"If you are an angel, then tell me what happens when you die."

Mark had never addressed her in this way, even though early on she had suggested he read up on angels in the Bible. He noted she did not flinch or attempt to contest the notion.

"Death is what defines a culture," she said in her familiar tone. "It is what drives everything. It is the silent river of societal consciousness. Death is a fact of life, but awareness of mortality is a social, not a biological, reality. According to the Bible, death is not the end of life but the separation of the soul from the body. Scripture clearly speaks of both eternal life with God in heaven and eternal separation from God . . ."

"In hell?" Mark suggested with a trace of scorn.

"Perhaps," she said, ignoring his skepticism.

He was warming to the idea of an all-powerful God, loving and compassionate, but the concept of an eternal hell—it was a barrier he found difficult to accept.

"So you are saying that if one dies and has not accepted the proper faiths or rituals or beliefs, he will be punished forever?" His tone was dismissive to the point of argumentative.

"The short answer to this question is that the Bible says we literally die after death. We don't go to heaven or hell or maintain any conscious state. Dead people 'sleep' in unconsciousness—they don't think or feel anything. But the good news is that the sleep of death is not permanent."

"If we wake up after death and are consciously aware of our surroundings, is this God's ever after? And if we never wake up and never again know the presence of God, is this a form of hell or simply the end?"

There was a lull in the conversation. Angel's eyebrows showed mischief, something he had come to appreciate—the foolishness she would sometimes employ to alleviate the sting of her words.

"Mark, you know that when you are dead, though you are not aware, those around you still are?" She paused, that impish grin of hers lining up a punch line. "Well, it's the same with being stupid."

She fell back into the grass, giggling at the absurdity of her comment.

"Nice. Really, really nice." Mark appreciated that she always found a way to use humor and nonsense as a tool to keep his mind straight. He knew she was not referring to him as stupid, just playing. They shared so many of the same traits.

"Honestly, over the years I have read many accounts that have common themes described by those who died and then came back."

"Clinically died," she corrected. "Enough for today, I'm going for a swim."

"What a dufus . . ."

He woke up starving and had forgotten to replenish the breadfruit. And to add insult to injury, he was also out of dried fish. The only thing he had was the pile of yellow nuts he had shelled the day before. The fluid he put in a bowl, and the kernels he usually dried and beat into a type of baking flour. But today they were breakfast.

"Ach . . . better than nothing."

The kernels were slimy but filling. After eating the lot, he put on his sneakers and headed out for the orchards.

"Did it rain last night?"

The foliage glistened wet, but the dirt was dry. He ignored it and followed the path to the ridge. Everything about the morning seemed brighter—the plants, the trees, even the fleeing geckos were all greener. He felt good. Content was the best way he could describe it. It was the antithesis of the melancholy he experienced yesterday when they discussed death.

Ascending the steps that he had fashioned at the top of the path, he crested the ridge and was amazed. Thousands and thousands of yellow-spotted butterflies inundated the plain for as far as he could see. Undulating on invisible currents, the fields were a carousel of never-ending movement.

"Beautiful." He gawked. "Simply wonderful."

He had once read that certain species made long migrations, but how could they have crossed thirteen hundred miles of ocean?

"You guys must be whupped," he said with admiration, thinking of the winds these delicate creatures would have had to combat over the open ocean.

As he walked through the gentle maelstrom, they parted like dust motes streaming through sunbeams.

"Angel has to see this! She'll love it."

Racing to the south end of the plateau, he picked his way through the boulders, traversing the shortcut to the lake. When he entered the glade, the sun was shimmering on the water, creating an ethereal effect.

"Mr. Lambert," Angel announced with a genteel greeting. "If I might say, you look a wee bit flustered."

Her words always put him at ease. In this case, they tempered his excitement.

"I have never asked you this before," he began, nervous but hopeful. "Would you come with me to the top of the ridge? There is something I want you to see. Something glorious."

It was a major deviation from the totality of their times together, but he really wanted to share this with her.

"I'm assuming that if it is so…glorious, it must have come from the hand of God."

"One of his masterpieces," Mark affirmed with a happy nod.

"Well then, do lead the way."

Bursting with excitement, his heart pumping wildly, he led the way, and she followed close on his heels. He found himself laboring with heavy breath, whereas she had nary broken a sweat. But when she saw the soft-winged invasion, her face lit with delight.

"Mark! They truly are glorious. Thank you for thinking of me."

He tingled on the warmth of her joy.

She began swirling and twirling, creating soft eddies of dancing butterflies. It was contagious, and soon he was doing the same. She had set free the little boy who could leave behind the worry of what someone else might think.

When dizziness caused him to wobble, he lay down on the sweet-smelling grass. The scent triggered memories of a wild weekend on a Montana horse ranch when he and Rachael were early in their dating cycle. They had been two young lovers wanton in a barn filled with fresh-cut hay. As suddenly as it appeared, the memory crusted with sorrow.

"Regrets are the past crippling the present," Angel said, falling in alongside him.

He had long given up agonizing over how she knew his every thought. He simply accepted it as part of the package. He instinctively understood this helped strip away his tendencies toward even the most casual of lies. With her, it was best to simply tell the truth or say nothing at all.

"I am glad this has brought you such joy," he told her as he lay on his back, looking into the sky. There wasn't a cloud in sight, and the blue was as blue as he had ever seen.

"Joy," she said, "is the serious business of heaven."

He recalled she had said this once before. Propping himself on an elbow, he turned toward her. "You've been there, haven't you?"

The tone was both question and statement. He did not expect she would give him an answer. But she did.

"Of course." She smiled.

He sat up, wide-eyed. "Really?"

"We all have. It is where we were conceived and from whence we came."

"Of course." He didn't bother to frown or feign rejection—he had come to know this was her way. Sinking back into the pasture, he saw her smile. They lay there for hours. Two friends enjoying one another's company.

Today has been so different from before, which caused him to wonder . . . "Would you join me for dinner tonight?"

She caressed his face, her eyes growing soft.

He inhaled the contact. Touch from another was so sparing on this island, and a reminder of much he missed.

"Not tonight." She stood, and the sun cast a halo from behind. "But you could walk me back to the lake." Her voice was demure. His reply not necessary.

Everything seemed enhanced and each moment uniquely elevated. The butterflies followed them into the forest until they were replaced by flitting birds with iridescent coats. As they darted in and out of the branches, he watched the dissipating trails of their flight. It reminded him of times he had moved his hands through photovoltaic plankton at sea, the movement leaving behind a translucent wake in its aftermath.

Exiting onto the black sands, he beheld the sunshine rippling on the bay. No sooner had he settled into the tranquility of sky and sea than the cacking arrival of Flipper and friends replaced the silence with a cacophony of frolic and glee.

"Oh, Mark!" Angel exclaimed, pulling him close with delight.

Mark could tell from their frenzied behavior that his relationship with these creatures might be special, but they adored Angel.

She waded out, and a trio of dolphins came up and out of the water by her side. Upon tails they danced until they fell backward into deeper water. He had seen something similar at the Seaquarium when his kids were young, but never in the wild.

Breaking into a grin, he found himself clapping.

The sound lingered with an inexplicable reverb as the blur of his moving hands loitered like an echo. Everything felt heightened. The warm rush of happiness that filled him was akin to ecstasy. The day was magical, the creatures of the island were magical, and his companion, she was the most magical of all.

Eventually she bid goodbye to her aquatic friends, and they ambled down the beach to the trailhead.

"Thank you for thinking of me today," she said, giving his hand a soft squeeze. Her body language signaled she would take it from there.

"Will I see you tomorrow?" he asked.

"Of course, we have a lot to talk about ."

"We do?"

"For heaven's sake, Mark," she said.

"For heaven's sake?"

"Exactly."

"Exactly what?"

"For heaven's sake."

"Oh." He laughed. She was a clever wordsmith.

"I get it."

Chapter 14

Still groggy from the night before, he finished his morning exercise and set out to replenish the food he had meant to get yesterday. Disappointment greeted him at the orchard.

"And just like that," he lamented with great regret, "the butterflies are gone."

He'd been thinking their allure might entice Angel to break their routine for a second time. It seemed they had left as quickly as they had come.

Finding scant evidence of the soft-winged creatures, he retrieved a couple of spiny melons and set off to gather more nuts. They grew in a certain spot near the plateau, easily located by the abundance of bromeliads that flourished nearby.

Different flowers grew on different parts of the island. He knew them all—the orchids, birds of paradise, hibiscus, plumeria, and a host of others whose names he didn't know and so made up.

Arriving at the bromeliad patch, the humidity cloyed as he shimmied to the top of the tree. The yellow nuts grew high in the canopy.

"Gotcha," he said, triumphant hands pulling a large spiny cluster free of the bark.

Back on solid footing, he wiped his palms and headed for the beach. Winding through patches of wildflowers, he considered the magic of his island paradise.

The arrival of the butterflies. How playful and unafraid the dolphins are. The seasonal return of the terns and the moonless nights when the green and leatherback turtles would come to lay their eggs. And, of course, Angel. She was an enigma who was always in his thoughts.

Dropping the foodstuff off at the cave, he moved to the next item on the agenda. Early in life he had developed the habit of getting the day's most important things done before the unexpected whirlwind of life consumed his day. This trait had never left him.

He moved his two fishing poles out toward the end of the point and reset the lines in deeper water. It was clear that the previous spot had been played out. Last on his list was to gather up enough wood for the day's fire.

"Maybe six more months," he calculated as he stood before the greatly diminished pile.

Taking stock, his mind already considering other options, he wound his way back to the cave bearing the load of wood. Once finished with his chores, he got cleaned up.

The breakthrough with Angel yesterday caused him to be a little giddy.

"Time to go see my lady."

Every day on his way to the beach he would round the corner and hear the roar of the ocean. Today the crashing waves rolled in from the reef like cannon shots fired from a distance. One of the features of his home was how quiet it was. There was no sound of the ocean and barely the presence of a breeze. With the mountain sitting between the cave and the shore, only the insects in the jungle and the birds waking with the dawn ever invaded the silence.

"What's got you so roiled today?" he called out at the angry sea.

The sand between his toes and the primeval forest behind him, the island gave Mark a sense of security. His home was a fortress, and he had plenty of food and water. And most important, he had Angel.

He had thought it was all he needed, but now . . .

Angel's touch yesterday had unlocked a suppressed desire to hold a woman in his arms. To love and to be loved. It was the underpinning of his hopes to take yesterday to another level.

But the pragmatist in him exhaled a deep sigh. Discharging his longings, he made his way to their morning place and watched as she effortlessly swam through the water.

"Are you coming in?" she asked.

He hesitated, clinging to a hope that yesterday was the beginning of something new.

"The butterflies are gone," he expressed with sorrow.

He expected some sort of reaction, but her face was noncommittal.

"So . . . are you coming in?"

She basically dismissed the butterflies, and his hope for taking their companionship to a new level cooled. He removed his shirt, and soon they were matching stride for stride. All the while, his mind drifted from the butterflies to her departing comments from last night.

"For heaven's sake, Mark," she had quipped.

The comment had felt like a culminating precursor to the path she had been laying down. Each morning their conversations would touch on the idea of an afterlife, often mentioning heaven as if it was a real place. She was pulling together a worldview about how one's beliefs should impact how one lived their life.

Anticipating the morning, he had spent hours scanning the Bible, looking for answers. What is Heaven? Does it really exist? Are there animals, trees, and flowers in heaven? Are there majestic mountains and wild rivers, or is it tame and sedate? Does one eat or have hunger on any level? He had never given much thought to the existence of an afterlife before, certainly not heaven. But now . . .

Finishing first, she stepped from the water, twirling her tresses.

"Almost done?" she called, squeezing out the remaining drops.

"For heaven's sake," he yelled back with a grin. He expected a smile, but instead she knit her brows in bewilderment.

It's like she wants to pretend yesterday never happened, dashing any lingering hope for more.

Fueled by feelings of frustration, he raced through his final laps. Back and forth. Back and forth, eight more times. Once finished, he exited, winded from the exertion. As he sucked down gulps of air, she patted the ground for him to sit.

"For heaven's sake?" she asked in a professorial tone.

He couldn't tell if she was asking a question or making a statement. But from that particular voice, he knew the teacher was about to launch into one of her lessons.

And she did . . .

"God will hold us all accountable at the final judgment," she began. "You, me, all of us. No one will be spared."

He repressed an urge to smile, recalling how early in their relationship, when she had first used this voice, it always triggered a sexy-teacher fantasy. He'd imagined her sitting at the edge of her desk, wearing a short skirt and horn-rimmed glasses, the buttons of her tightly stretched blouse ready to pop open as her tongue seductively ran over moist lips . . .

Stop! he reminded himself, regressing into old habits. He changed his flow of thoughts by immersing himself in an old Bible passage. *God loves a sinner . . .*

Wading through the transition to clear his lust, Angel reprimanded him, once again gleaning what was going on inside his head.

"That's not what it says," she corrected. "God loves a sinner but hates the sin. And even that has limitations."

With a kindness he knew he did not deserve, she cast no judgment upon his longings.

"You are a smart guy, Mark," she said, drawing him in. "But time is running out."

His heart ticked at the comment. "What do you mean 'running out'?"

"It means we need to get your life on a firm foundation if you hope to withstand the storms that are coming." Her stare was unrelenting, demanding that he pay attention. "You do not want to end up stuck between two worlds."

"Two worlds?" He knew parroting was a defense mechanism, but this change in their relationship was not what he had had in mind when he woke up this morning.

"The physical world and the spiritual world," she said in a no-nonsense manner. "The life of humankind is wrapped in both whether they know it or not."

Her comment caused him to consider his meditative practices. The more he explored his art, the more real the spiritual world seemed to be. Apparently, she caught wind of his reflections.

"How are your dream journeys going?"

He knew what she meant. Remote viewing, out-of-body consciousness, there were a few other names, but he liked the visual of "dream journey." She often questioned his progress and encouraged him, positively alluding that this skill was something given to him by God.

But like the vacillating conundrum of 'Is she real or a figment of my imagination?' he often wondered the same thing about his viewings.

Am I having an out-of-body experience, or is my mind just playing tricks on me? As he considered how best to answer, she framed a question with a comment.

"Scientists would have us believe man is nothing more than a collection of chemical reactions. But that is too limiting. It simply addresses physicality. When you free your consciousness and begin to roam, is that your mind, your spirit, or simply a chemical reaction?"

The last part sounded a bit snarky.

"I'm not really sure," he admitted. "Maybe a sixth sense?"

She laughed at this, and he felt a little embarrassed.

"That is much closer to the truth than you realize," she said, softening, seeing his reaction.

"Meaning?"

"As I said, there are two distinct worlds, the physical and the spiritual. Generally, the sixth sense is attributed to the spiritual world. I would suggest as an initiate you are starting to straddle both."

He looked at her.

"Look, I know you grapple with the concept of the Holy Trinity, three entities separate but also one. But until you figure this out, we may never get you to heaven."

He wasn't sure if she meant the topic or the place, once again leaving him looking at two different possibilities.

Stretching out his legs, he leaned back into his palms. The grass was dry and felt soft on his skin. A slight breeze carried hints of frangipani.

"Your dream journeys throw cold water on scientific assertions of our chemical limitations. It does not address the complexities of the mind where our senses intersect to form our reality. And it completely ignores the existence of our spirit."

"That's true," he accepted. It made sense.

"So perhaps humans are better defined as the sum of mind, body, and spirit?"

"Humans are definitely more than chemical reactions," he agreed.

"Good. So now can I weave this into a bigger picture?"

"Sure."

While she was talking, he looked out at the water, at the misty rainbows that formed and faded. It was part of the hypnotic rhythm of the glen. *How many centuries has this recurred over and over and . . .*

"As an avid reader of the Bible, you know it says man was made in God's image."

"I do."

"Well, let's game this out. The trinity of God and the trinity of man. God is all knowing, omniscient, omnipresent, and omnificent. He is the mind. Jesus is the one who came down to Earth as a man to die for our sins—he is the body. And the Holy Spirit is the 'who' that enjoins us with the spirit that God has breathed into each of us. Our spirit, this breath of God, is what separates man from the animal kingdom. It is where morality and conscience come from. It is the antithesis of survival of the fittest."

"And the spirit is immortal?" he asked. Weighing her case of eternity against his own beliefs, he began to see he had never formed a solid theology one way or another.

"To a point your body is immortal as well," she teased. It was that smile and mischievous dimple, but mostly the playful pump of her eyebrows that clued Mark to her joke.

"If you are still here, then He is not done with you yet," he said, the phrase now ingrained into him.

"That is correct. He is not done with you yet." Her mouth curled at the corners, almost as if it was a sign of satisfaction.

She was a good teacher, planting ideas, following up with questions. A pattern of layering, guiding him in a direction he could follow and letting him get there on his own terms.

But the day had grown long, and the sun had grown hot. Mark stood and arched his back to stretch the cords of his muscles.

"Let's go for a swim."

"Into the cavern," she suggested with a hint of mystery. She dove in and he followed.

As they surfaced behind the falls, the air felt cool on his skin, and the sound of the water provided the rhythm for the light that shimmered on the walls. They sat beneath the cross.

"You know, this cavern could be seen as an analogy of God's entire plan for humankind," she told him.

"Really?" Wiping sand off his legs, he got comfortable, expectant of the lesson that would follow. He loved the way she spoke and never tired of looking at her. The translucent lighting made her only more beautiful.

Angel, he thought. *How appropriate.*

"In the beginning God created the heavens and the earth. And the earth was without form. And darkness was upon the face of the deep. And the Spirit of God moved upon the face of the waters . . ."

He recognized the verse. It was the opening of Genesis.

"And God said, Let there be a firmament in the midst of the waters, and let it divide the waters below from the waters above. And God called the firmament heaven."

"Waters above heaven and waters below?" He could see the cave-firmament allegory, but the passage itself seemed confusing.

"The waters above and the waters below are not references to the physical domain," she explained. "Eventually, yes, once the earth had been formed, but in this case, the waters above show God's omnificence. Knowing the end from the beginning."

To him it sounded like a bunch of gobbledygook, but he held his tongue.

"Okay, I can see I need to explain this differently."

She paused, probably looking for a different angle, bouncing her index finger against her lips until she found it.

"Instead of building a case point by point, I'm gonna give you the whole enchilada. The big kahuna, the history of creation, and the meaning of life. All of it in less than five minutes. I can see that is more your style," she told him with a wry smile. "Ready?"

"Sure." His reply carried her enthusiasm.

"God's realm is full of heavenly creatures. There are hierarchies of angels and seraphim and hosts of heaven. It has been this way long before time was ever created. There are worlds within worlds abundant with his creations. Layers and layers all created by the hand of God."

"At one point, one of God's favorites rebelled and wanted more . . ."

"You mean Satan?" Participation, he hoped, conveyed that he was genuinely interested.

"He has many names, but you are correct. Satan gathered a third of the angels to side with him, and they rebelled at God's authority. Revelation tells us those are the ones cast down from heaven. Now back to those waters God revealed in his opening chapters. Being omnificent, omnifarious, and omnipresent, he knew what would unfold, so at the very beginning, before time itself, he created a vault above the station of heaven reserved for his newest children. He then started the process of creation He completed with the making of humankind. When Satan fell and learned these creatures were being granted a station higher than his own, he became livid, and as time passed it festered into pure hatred. The true history of humankind is driven by this hatred, by Satan's desire to thwart as many of God's children as he can from ever making it to the vaulted waters above."

Mark envisioned the saga as a prototypical good versus evil movie.

"The Shining One had already fallen when he appeared in the Garden of Eden. After he corrupted Adam and Eve, he then corrupted the angels who were tasked to look after them when they were pushed out of the spiritual domain of Eden into the harshness of the physical world."

"The Watchers," he murmured, recalling having read about them in *Lost Secret of the Ancient Ones.*

Maybe there is more truth to that book than I gave credit, he thought.

"With their unbridled lust, these fallen angels corrupted God's creation and soiled the gene pools of both man and animal. It is why God had Noah create the ark. Only those humans and animals with untainted DNA would be saved from the great flood to start again."

She paused only long enough to catch a breath and tuck a strand of errant hair. Then she continued as though she were on the clock.

"The offspring of women and angels were called the Nephilim, giants who were the vile corruption of God's plan. It was another angle of attack orchestrated by the Enemy. The flood destroyed their physical bodies, but their angelic DNA survived."

"And being stuck in the spiritual world, they are still conspiring for ways to get back their physical bodies to reengage their carnal lusts and appetites. These creatures are known to most as demons."

"Possessed." Mark considered this with new insight. She had simplified the world into a tapestry that was both easy to follow and had an organized thread running through it.

"What was it you used to say when arguing politics with your colleagues? Something about hidden powers."

She had a way of continually engaging him, so he racked his brain until it came to him.

"The simple will argue which political ideology is better. Those with a broader view will see the fingerprints of globalism controlling both parties. But the truly observant will see the subtle control exerted by those who stay in the shadows."

He had been thinking Rothschild and conspiratorial names like that when he would say this. But he suspected she was going further up the food chain.

"Imagine who those might be who stay in the shadows. If you assume most things that happen in the world are neither random nor coincidence, you will understand why the spiritual world has a direct bearing on how you interpret events and, more importantly, how you conduct your life."

He felt like he was seeing the world from a long lens as he began to rise above the noise and distraction. He inherently could feel the threads of change recasting the way in which he viewed the world. Slow, subtle course corrections that seen in real time would be imperceptible. But taken as a whole . . .

"Your worldview must acknowledge that evil is not an abstract concept, but an army led by the Enemy. Each person, no matter who they might be, is in the same battle as everyone else. As comrades in this struggle, you must become a light in the darkness."

"And how do I do that?" he asked.

"We save Mark Lambert."

Chapter 15

Days turned into weeks. But no matter what time he showed up, Angel was there waiting with encouragement and a smile that felt brighter than the sun.

"You've come such a long way," she had told him as they prepared to leave for the day. "You are almost ready."

But ready for what? This was never discussed.

As the days melded one into another, less and less he employed tactics to get a reaction about the butterflies. Either she didn't want to discuss it, or he had dreamed it. Or worse, he was lying in a coma somewhere, and this entire island odyssey was merely a fantasy.

"Imagine if all this is a dream." The fire in front of him responded with a log collapsing into the embers, sending a flurry of sparks into the night.

Full from dinner, enjoying his herbal tea, he had an odd thought about his wife's book club. The first Wednesday of every month, Rachael would get together with her friends to discuss the latest assignment. He eventually realized it was more about wine and gossip than reading, but these women chose great stories. Rachael would suggest books she felt he would enjoy. And most times she was right.

Thinking of the island as a mere fantasy reminded him of a book called *Life of Pi*.

"It kind of parallels my own story," he thought aloud.

The main character had been stranded on a raft for months and months. The tale of his survival was fantastical, yet his survival was akin to a miracle. In the end, there were two plausible explanations, one grounded in a dark reality and one filled with whimsy. The reader was left to decide.

"Is Angel simply my imagination or is she an emissary from God? Is this even real, or am I locked inside my mind dreaming?"

On more than one occasion, he had woken out of a sound sleep to shake the feeling that none of this was real. It still harbored a little secret room inside of him, but he never let it get any real traction, not then and not now. The consequences of him being someone else's burden would be too great,.

Listening to the resonance of his voice and the crackling of the fire, he gave himself a good pinch.

"Ouch." He grinned with satisfaction.

He never really considered this was all a fantasy, but he was relieved, nonetheless. As far as the part about his companion being simply his imagination or an angel here to rehabilitate him, each day the scales would tilt one way and then the other. He had no solid answer.

But today when he was with her, she was real.

"One day at a time."

He threw another piece of wood on the fire, sending more sparks to the stars. There was a change taking place, within him and with Angel. He was still trying to put his finger on it. But for him, he no longer had any doubt about God and his grace. Today she had told him a simple truth referred to as the bad news and the good news. It was what she termed the Gospel, the core message of salvation. And in it, he felt stirrings.

"The bad news, Mark, is that we are all sinners," she said, personalizing her message for his benefit. "It is in every errant thought and deed. God cannot allow sin to enter Heaven. But the good news is that he loved the world so much, he sent his only son to Earth to die for the transgressions of man. And by a simple act of faith, accepting that Jesus died on the cross to save you, the Holy Spirit will come and indwell inside you, and you will be sealed with the protection of God for all eternity."

He had heard the words before. Read them a million times. It always seemed too simple. He had asked a ton of questions like, If I am saved, will I still be judged? How will I know when I am saved? On and on. He wanted to believe.

He had formed this lasting visual.

Jesus hung between heaven and the earth.

They had debated why God allowed such awful things to happen. Her response always returned to free will.

"If God had not given us free will, our love for him would not be genuine. But in return we suffer from our choices. God often intervenes—it's just that most times we are not aware."

She patiently answered each question until they had all been exhausted. He spent hours going over the conversation, rehashing each question and each answer. Only when the fire was down to coals did he finally call it a night.

Entering the cavern, shadows created by his lighting system danced over the walls, a marvel of ingenuity that still gave him joy. Psychologically, the light represented one of the two things that he felt separated him from being just another castaway. That and Angel.

The shadows flickered across his daily carvings. Rows and rows of days and months showing he was well into his eighth year. Taking his awl from the cushion, he carved another day. There were now two thousand, seven hundred, and fifty-five marks.

"You have been here a long time, my friend," he said to his silent witness.

He turned off the light and savored the smothering darkness. With the room made of black basalt and the angle of the door aimed up the slope, it was so dark that he couldn't see a hand in front of his face. The only sound was his breath. He had come to appreciate the silence. Back home, even though they were miles from I-95, at night there was always a background hum of interstate traffic.

He crawled under his blanket. The cool air seeping in from the porous rock usually put him right to sleep. But tonight he lay there, his brain scrolling through his time on the island. He knew he had changed. And he knew, even before Angel, the absence of distractions had fostered more and more introspection. In the end it had resulted in an honest assessment of the entirety of his life.

Some of the things he saw in himself were not things he was proud of. At first he had suppressed unsettling memories, always putting them back into their box. But Angel helped him to embrace self-reflection. With a need to impress her, it became a personal challenge to figure out ways to become a better person. "Tending to my issues," he called it.

Alone, with only darkness his companion, a voice inside his head interrupted his reverie. "Judge not, lest ye be judged."

The voice generally came when he was lying awake in bed. He knew he was guilty as charged. It was one more arrogance that needed tending. In the past he often groused about the lack of accountability that had permeated all aspects of society. He had blamed the politicians, government largess, the leanings of the universities, and a host of other things for the world's inability to step up and be accountable, at least not by his standards. Now he wondered.

"She told me I would start viewing things differently. Has the world become less accountable because people no longer view God as real? Is this the aim of Satan's distractions?"

He could feel the shift that was taking place. His point of view was definitely changing.

"If there is a God, and an afterlife, and a place called heaven, why are we here? Why am I here?" He fell asleep to the imaginary strains of Angel's voice.

"If you are still here, then He is not done with you yet . . ."

Chapter 16

It had rained uninterrupted for five days. Their relationship allowed for the whims of Mother Nature to create periodic separations. With time to reflect and time to consider, Mark no longer worried if she would be there when he returned to the lake.

Perhaps it was the hypnotic rhythm of the rain outside his door or perhaps the time alone, or maybe it was the accumulation of wisdom that had finally penetrated his armor, he did not know. But suddenly everything she had been leading up to became clear. The fog of doubt, the clouds of denial, and the din of distraction, all of this had been lifted.

Settling in for his evening meditations, he focused on the flame he made just inside his door. After luxuriating in the sensation of freeing from his body, he began to see things, shadows with outlines.

It feels so different . . .

He calmed his rising excitement. He knew from experience distraction was the quickest way back to the physical body.

This time the contours were of an unknown place. They would sharpen, then blur, then come back stronger, then drift out, like a distant radio station that floated in on a breeze.

This is real—I know it!

Suddenly he was back, staring at the fire. He failed to heed his own advice. "Dang it. Stop thinking. Just observe."

But he could not help but feel he had passed another milestone. Again, the linchpin of one of Angel's questions sought an answer. *Is it mind or spirit that traverses outside the body?*

As a pragmatist who struggled with accepting the unseeable and untestable, he was seeking a tangible way to explain what he was feeling, or seeing, or thought he was seeing.

He needed a way to validate his experience. And it was Angel's voice that drew him closer to accepting the spiritual world, and with it, she was drawing him closer to God.

This insight is a gift God has given to you. Trust in it. He gave this to you for a reason. All of one's gifts have a purpose.

The following morning the sun returned, the humidity lifted, and the world had a fresh-scrubbed feel about it. He started his day like every day, with exercise. In his old life this had been a chore, but now . . .

Sit-ups, two hundred. Push-ups, fifty, and then the hard part: pull-ups. "Thirty-eight"—*grunt*—"thirty-nine . . . come on, man, one more. Forty!"

Releasing the branch, he rubbed the calluses on his palms. "A new record."

Usually he would run to the lake, then swim, and then they would spend most of the day together. But he needed to gather firewood and rebuild his cooking fire.

Prior to the rains, Angel had come earlier and stayed later. There was a sense of urgency about her business that on one hand was exhilarating, learning what she called a firm foundation for living, but at the same time, a cloud of concern lingered that their time together may be coming to an end.

Like the pile of wood, he thought. The stack stood less than waist high.

Walking toward the glade, he took his time, appreciating every little thing. Birds swooped in and out of the trees along the sand's edge. The sun mottled the small waves in the bay. Far offshore the ocean seemed placid, the waters blue and deep and reminding him of her eyes.

Ca-ca-ca-cack, cack, cack-cack-cack. His friend was treading water with his perpetual smile. Farther out, the rest of the pod was fishing for breakfast.

"Letting me know you're here today," he said with a hello smile. "Maybe later I'll come join you. I could go for lobster tonight."

Flipper gave his approval with a leap high above the water and a smirk as he splashed back in.

"God, you have created an awesome place," he said in admiration, for perhaps the first time really grasping how magical and wonderful this island truly was.

When he arrived, he noticed she wore a different set of clothes, something he had never seen before. It was a white, short skirt cinched at the waist. Her hair was braided into a single tail, and her lips appeared a darker red than usual. But it was her eyes, as radiant as ever, the ones reflecting the depths of the ocean, that always held his attention.

"Good morning, Mr. Lambert," she said with that special lilt in her voice. "Did you use your time wisely and reflect on the foundations we are building under your feet?"

He had, and he was eager to tell her so.

"It is because of your unwavering patience that my eyes are now open," he said with sincerity. "God's love, his offer that merely requires a childlike faith. The trappings and distractions of the world, all an illusion to misguide and misdirect us, it is all falling into place and building the foundation upon which I will stand." Saying this aloud, he felt both elated as well as a little foolish. He had never been so humble to say such a thing to another in the past.

"You must feel different," she inquired.

"I do. I can't explain it, but, well . . . I feel more at peace. It's like the exits have been clearly marked, even though we knew they were there all the time."

"That's a very interesting visual, Mr. Lambert. I like it."

She turned and walked past their normal spot. A little higher on the slope, the grass was long and soft underneath. "Shall we?"

They both sat, and she settled in for the day's lesson.

"Love and death. These are the final things we must unpack. Then you will be ready."

She paused and then launched into .the Lord's Prayer.

"'Our Father who art in heaven, hallowed be thy name . . .' The line is the recognition, praise, and glory we should always give to God. 'Thy kingdom come thy will be done on earth as it is in heaven.' An acknowledgment that there will be a day of reckoning and we need to practice obedience here on Earth as they joyfully do in heaven. 'Give us this day our daily bread . . .' This is the supplication that fulfills our asks. To give us what we need, not what we want. Never think of God as your cosmic genie.

Weeks ago she had explained to him that this was the only prayer anyone ever needed. It covered everything. He was slowly coming to appreciate the power of this simple prayer.

"And for today's lesson," she announced with a roll of her hands, drawing his undivided attention. "'Forgive us our trespasses as we forgive those who trespass against us . . .'"

"Yes. Perfect," he interrupted, eager to share. "I want to tell you something. During our hiatus I recognized that judgment was one of my issues. Something I intend to address."

He gave her a self-satisfied smile, but from her frown, he saw she was having none of it.

"Why do you hate your father?" she asked, broadsiding him. "Have you ever considered how much pain he must have been in when your mother died? That he blamed himself? Yet you judged him. Instead of choosing love, you hardened your heart. The world is made up of two types of people—those who take it out on others and those who take it out on themselves. Which are you?"

The serenity of the glade gave rise to a tornado of emotions. All the times they had been treated unfairly, his father's obscene disciplinary techniques. The way his father would simply shut them out and not say a word for days on end, as if to make some point.

What—we are not worthy? It was all crap and more crap.

"You never even considered your father's loss, did you?" Her words were poignant and damning.

Her words felt like he was being hit with a club. She was right, of course. He never considered the loss his father must have felt. He simply cast blame and then seized on every little thing he could to use as a weapon against him.

"Forgive our trespasses as we forgive those who trespass against us," she said. "Let's repeat this together," she suggested, her voice soft, her eyes sympathetic.

"Forgive our trespasses as we forgive those who trespass against us," they said in unison.

"Again . . ."

Tears ran down his cheeks as he choked on sobs, embarrassed to cry in front of her but unable to stop.

"Love is the gauge in how God will judge us," she said with soft compassion. "Things like lust and sin, pride, and arrogance, all humans struggle with these. But love, how we dispense it, how freely we offer it, that is the coin of the realm that God will weigh when we stand before him."

Mark felt small and meek. He had let pride of how far he had come get in the way of seeing things that still needed seeing. He was appreciative of the compassion she emitted when she looked at him . . .

"Your father is in heaven along with your mother."

Embracing her tone, it was like she was merely relaying an observation, and it moved the scale of his conundrum toward that of a heavenly being.

"They are not looking down in judgment but with love. They are proud that you have opened your eyes to see and your ears to hear. Now we must open your heart to love, and you will be ready to rejoin the real world."

"What does that mean, 'we will be done and ready to rejoin the real world'? Please, can you just give me a straight-up answer? Are you leaving me?"

He needed to know. *Is my world about to come unglued?*

That creeper nonsense that maybe he was in a coma and none of this was real found a gap and poked its head in for a quick hello.

She smiled and placed a hand on his heart. "I will never leave you. Not now, not ever."

He exhaled with relief but again was left wondering.

"You know the Western world is broken into three main religions. But all three adhere to the same book Christians call the Old Testament. And note the word about the vault above heaven was written thousands of years before Jesus came as the Messiah to free the world from sin. Yet the prime directive of God then and the word of the Lord now is the same. 'Love thy neighbor.'

"I can't teach you how to love—that comes with your walk with God. But I have been showing you the path to get there. Now that you understand that fear is the tool of the Enemy, and that fear causes anger, which leads to hate, you can see it is the antithesis of love. And with your broader understanding of the spiritual world, your view of reality should open your eyes to the fact that this world is merely a drama being played out on a very small stage within a very narrow window of existence. Shift your thoughts to the long view, and the notion of 'love thy brother' will begin to flow naturally.

"Consider that hate cannot cast out hate, and darkness cannot cast out darkness, and that the only outcome of an action is the consequence. Choose the actions bound in love, and the consequence will be a path to God and a path to a mind at peace with whatever the world throws at you."

His tears were abating. He felt her aura of love. He couldn't explain it. He just knew.

Has she manifested this for me to see, or am I awakening to things before unseen?

As he pondered the message, she continued. "We talked about death months ago."

He recognized the transitions she so often implored and the "keep up" tone she slipped into.

"You told me that culture is driven by death. It underpins everything and is buried by almost everyone," he reiterated like a dutiful student.

"Yes," she affirmed. "Today and throughout the history of man, there is no person who believes they will not die. Even the young and naive know this. Still, people go to great lengths to distract from the inevitable. Until one is looking directly into the abyss, they will continually surround themselves in the diversions of their era. And because you have been enlightened about the who and why of those who hide in the shadows, you can imagine the extent of distraction they are fostering."

"The Enemy," he murmured. Shaping his views of cause and effect were inclusions of the invisible war. The war for man's soul. His soul.

"People have an innate desire to extend their mortality. The more wealth and power one accumulates, the greater the need to be remembered, but we all owe the debt of one death. And it will be paid. No matter how many monuments one erects, or buildings are named after you, or statues, foundations, or anything else, time will erode them all. There is no rich or poor when you stand before God. He is all that matters. How you love and forgive is all that matters. Worrying about storing your treasure up in heaven is all that matters. If you have but a single takeaway from our conversations, never forget that love stands alone and is the sole coin of the realm in God's eyes."

The lesson was finished, and she stood. The sun's rays filtered from below the tree line. He watched as she crested the ridge. He was alone. Simply the creatures of the glen and the forward march of falling water were there to witness his remorse.

"Dad, I have been so unfair. Please forgive me. I was angry. I blamed you but never thought of your own pain. I love you. Please tell God I am sorry that I was so blind."

Approaching his end of the beach, he saw the flag waving at the end of his fishing pole. The rocks were wet with spray, jagged and jutting out into the sea. The sky was layered with brilliant hues of reds and yellows as the sinking orb hovered on the horizon. It would be dark in an hour.

Carefully traversing the uneven crags, he knew he had something large on the hook. He kept the line taught and slowly managed his prey until it came to the surface. Thoughts of Ironsides never entered the picture.

"Mahi!" he exclaimed. It was a rare excitement. He pulled the large iridescent fish out of the water. The bullnosed, yellow-and-green fish felt to be about twenty pounds.

Resetting the hook, he returned to the beach and retrieved the filleting knife he kept on a flat rock. He cleaned the fish, tossed the entrails into the bay, then hastened up the trail to prepare a feast.

He had eaten so much snapper and grouper, tonight he would simply dress the filets with a small amount of salt. The balance he would fry in palm oil and preserve for later.

As he satiated one hunger, another grew like a fire inside.

"God, I want to want more of you."

Chapter 17

Walking along the beach, the wind felt different. It seemed to caress him, wash over him, and swirl in and around him. He imagined it was dancing and he was the rhythm. It caused him to stop. The sun was warm on his face. The tranquility of having spent the day with Angel still had its afterglow, and a deep sense of peace felt all pervasive.

"Hello, son," whispered a feminine voice.

He turned, the sound filling him, but he could not see anyone.

"Please know that I did not kill myself," the voice continued. "Those people in our town were wrong. I would never leave you or your sisters that way. I love you too much."

Caged memories escaped their long captivity.

"Mom?" he questioned, circling, looking, seeking. Nothing.

The air stirred, its breath the strains of an ancient voice carried on a childhood memory.

"I had been sad for a long time. Your father was away at sea more than he was ever home. Back in those days, the barbiturates I took to sleep were cumulative. One night I went to sleep, and when I awoke, I was on the other side. Please know I have always loved you."

"Mom," he wailed, dropping to the sand, longing for that relationship that had been absent for almost forty years.

The wind was picking up, coming in off the ocean. He felt it but noticed that the leaves did not stir.

"I love you. Yesterday, today, and tomorrow . . ." The sound of her voice raced into the forest, the Doppler effect like that of a passing train until it was gone.

Was she here?

He noted that all around him the wind continued to grow, still swirling through him. A change was taking place—peace had fused to his every molecule and every atom. His body was being recast. The wind that came was not from the ocean or from the heating-and-cooling effect that typically stirred the air.

"It's the breath of God," he intoned with an intuitive sense of awe and humility. "The Holy Spirit has found me and blessed me with its presence."

Today with Angel, he had finally stopped questioning the maybes and what-ifs and truly believed. The moment remained as a flood of feelings cleansed much of what had been lingering. Soot of the past. The term *reborn* now so obvious. Walking home, he let familiarity guide him as he explored this new sensation.

All through meal prep and the act of eating, he embraced the new clothing of salvation, wondering why he had ever been so resistant. An odd thought appeared, the melding of the spirit world and the indwelling of the Holy Spirit.

"Will remote viewing feel different?"

After cleaning up from dinner, he added a piece of driftwood to the fire. It was important to have a sustainable flame if he hoped to succeed in freeing his mind to roam.

His progress had steadily improved, and he was now at the point where his vision casts encompassed a wide range of experiences. Still, he had difficulty discerning if he saw things in real time or simply glimpses of some past or future moment. And then the question, why this vision? They were often so random, and all of it was propped up in doubt.

"Is this real or is my mind just keeping me entertained?"

He considered the last eight months. His discussions with Angel had kicked around concepts of the invisible realm, his visions, and even aspects of the human spirit. This led to the conversations about what it meant to be a human. Her argument was that to understand the world that God created one must understand the true nature of humanity.

"We are the sum of mind, body, and spirit," he rehashed.

She asked, "When Mark Lambert goes on a mental journey, which aspect goes walkabout?"

It would not be the last time this question would be asked, or his experiences would be held up for examination and contrasted with the spiritual realm.

Recalling how she had used logic to let him come to his own conclusions, it had taken her years of infinite patience for him to finally understand that mind, body, and spirit were analogous to the Holy Trinity. At some point along the journey, long after Angel's conversations on belief and fate, and death and heaven, he had come to accept that salvation lay in simple faith.

Faith that God came to Earth as a man, freeing humanity from the yoke of sin and the grave. For him, this was now an unassailable truth.

Looking back over the years of his transformation, he liked what he saw. "You've come a long way, Mark Lambert."

Settling against the log, he began his session as he always did, with prayer. He recalled one of Angel's jokes. "God answers all prayers. Just most of the time the answer is no."

The thought of her calmed his spirit and made him smile. He settled into focusing on a single flame, letting his mind go blank, allowing only a single sensation, the air entering and leaving his nostrils as it caressed the space between his nose and upper lip. It provided clarity and allowed his mind to replace the clutter of distractions with what he called a runway for departure.

Once he achieved the nirvana of stillness, he felt the sensation deep within him, almost like his consciousness was being unstuck as it sought to pull free of the physical bonds.

He loved the rush, that sensation of no longer being caged by the husk of a body. No aches, no pains, no heat, no cold, just pure energy.

Tonight he found himself in a chapel. There was a wedding, and the bride's back was to him. The train of her dress swept long. People were gathered. The groom was taking the ring as the pastor asked the ceremonial questions. The woman turned, revealing her profile to him. He now saw both of their profiles. They glowed with a radiance he had learned to discern as love. It had its own aura, a shimmer like that of quicksilver. Theirs was genuine, and he felt happy for them.

She seemed familiar. There was something about the aquiline nose. He had seen it before. The image was fuzzy, the features soft and gauzy. Then it hit him. And with it, the emotional cascade jolted him back into his body.

"Rachael has remarried!"

His heart began to race, and he struggled to breathe. He had never had a panic attack before, but as he began gasping for air, short gulps, any gulp, he considered this was what it must be like. He kept trying to breathe deep until the panic abated, and he could inhale normally again.

"What did you think, she would pine for you forever?"

He almost imagined Thomas popping in for some quick commentary.

Her wedding played against so many emotions. Slowly the realization that she was happy stabilized the jolt of her remarrying. It hurt but for reasons he did not expect.

He wasn't upset she had found happiness. It was the punctuation mark that he was gone and never expected to return. Was he now just a fading memory to his children? His friends? The reality was that the world moves on.

We are just actors who spend a brief moment on stage playing our role and then departing.

Angel was at the lake when he arrived. When he stepped from the trees, he could see she knew.

She always knows.

Hastening to greet him, she wrapped him in an embrace.

Surprised by her advances, old Mark would have felt sexual stirrings, but he knew her touch was to offer comfort.

"I am so sorry, Mark." There was nothing more to say.

Taking his hand in hers, she used the other to gently remove his wedding ring.

"You no longer need this," she told him.

He understood. He also knew that old Mark's first thoughts would be to wonder, *So now that I am not married, can we have something sexual and physical?*

But that Mark was gone, someone from his past. For many reasons, this question never entered their arena.

They walked quietly to their spot and lay on the grass. His mind was a cacophony of thoughts yet void of substance. The emotions were thick as water, his mind a liquid blur. Clouds dampened the sun, their shadows drifting uncommitted as they passed on their journey.

Angel said nothing, giving him room to roam.

"What next?" he asked. It was rhetorical, not truly seeking an answer.

His thoughts harkened back to the day he had arrived on the island. The man who was full of piss and vinegar had just been humbled by the sea. His mind then had been a cauldron of lusts, inflated concepts of self, and a master of self-delusion. For five years he had lived alone, simply waiting to get back to a place that, he now understood, was no longer there.

He thought of the allegorical river. Like life, it was never the same place twice. The water was always moving. A current seeking its destination. You can dip your toe in or take the plunge. But each day the waters are new and different, the before, no more.

He had wasted those years on the island. Now accepting that man is deeded only one life, he understood we can grasp it with all we have, or we can wait, hide, or shrink before change.

His life began the day of that hurricane, the day he let go of Thomas and *Lil Darling*.

"My life changed for the good the day God put you into my life."

She remained still while he thought back over the last few years. It didn't matter if she was an angel or simply his imagination. She was an emissary, and he no longer doubted that God had put her here.

"Angel. I want you to know how much you mean to me. You have been patient, kind, helpful, firm when necessary, and you always showed me what beauty wisdom has to offer."

"You know wisdom is the goddess God created at the beginning." She emphasized this with a quote from scripture: "'The Lord possessed me at the beginning. I have been established from everlasting, from the beginning, before there was ever an earth. I was brought forth. When He prepared the heavens, I was there . . .'"

He knew the verse by heart. He had taken her suggestion to read Proverbs 8 way back when she coyly mentioned how these verses were a way to wade into scripture.

"Had it not been for you, not only would I not understand what you are talking about, but I would never have considered the idea of Wisdom as a being. One more thing I am thankful for."

Angel lay on her side, propping her head on her hand. He had seen this so many times. Her golden tresses cascaded in the sun, the wattage of her smile outshined everything, and the brightness of his day was filled by the joy of her presence.

Slowly the turmoil of jumbled thoughts fell together, and like the river, he let them run their course. Sometimes you just needed to do that. Now was one of those times. He would occasionally pluck a thought from the waters, hold it, examine it, and then toss it back in. His breathing seemed to find a rhythm that matched the pulse of the glen.

The sky above was still blue. Birds flew in and birds flew out. Insects buzzed around the glade. Dragonflies skimmed the waters. And soft breezes rustled the treetops.

"You know, Mark, in life, sometimes one door must close before another can open."

Chapter 18

Yesterday, Angel had told him that today they would celebrate. "A new chapter," she had said. Then she did a whole spiel on numerology.

"Eight has many energies attached to it. For instance, eight marks completion. According to the Chinese, it signifies prosperity. And in the metaphysical world, a strong presence of the number eight envisions that a guardian angel is going to reveal that abundance is coming your way."

He knew she was referring to his time on the island. Last night he had marked the final line of the eighth row, at the end of his eighth year.

"The world has moved on without you, Mark Lambert," he admitted to the silent sentinel. "But God will always be at my side."

It was all the comfort he needed. That night he slept a thousand sleeps. Resigned to his fate, accepting life one day at a time, he woke refreshed and did as she suggested.

"Dress your best," she had said. "This is going to be a special day."

For the first time since being on the island, he put on his chinos and white guayabera. While a little snug in the shoulders from all the exercise, the shirt suited him pretty darn good.

He arrived at the lake to see Angel was already there. She had on a white dress with matching sandals and garlands in her hair. She was the portrait of a princess.

"My, now don't you look sharp," Angel said with admiration.

"You look pretty good yourself. New shoes?"

She blushed as she wiggled her toes.

"These ol' things . . ." It was something his wife would have said.

The banter carried comfortable strains of two friends simply enjoying one another's company. She took him by the hand. "Come, I want to show you something."

Over the years, physical contact had been minimal at best. His senses felt heightened. Her touch suffused warmth throughout. The sun shone a little brighter. The birds were a little more vocal, the frogs croaking by the falls were a little louder, and the dragonflies trailed wakes that were a little longer.

She led him to her path, the one she had departed upon each day for the last three years. Over a thousand times she had faded into the forest. And over a thousand times he was left to wonder *Where does she go, where does she live? Will I ever find out?*

This change was making him nervous. His hands felt clammy, and his breath was heavy. Whoever or whatever Angel was, she was his friend, his sanity, and the anchor of his reality. Was their time together coming to an end?

"Hurry," she told him, implying there was something she did not want him to miss. Her voice radiated calm, a tranquility pinned with a hint of excitement.

"She's not leaving me," he mouthed for reassurance.

The path was firm, the rocks weathered from the ages.

"Where are we going?"

"You'll see."

There were no coy looks or hints of subterfuge, simply an answer. They exited the trees at the top of the rise.

"You know I never dared follow you up here . . ."

"I know." She laughed, wrapped up in the gaiety of the moment.

Below lay a lush glade smaller than the glen behind them. Sunlight dappled the ground, and the smell of grass was sweet on the air. Beyond, the ground rose to meet open skies.

In the eight years he had been on this two-mile fingernail in the middle of the Atlantic Ocean, he had never come to this part of the island.

First, he had his run-in with the mosquitoes—then there was that nasty fall. All of it was encapsulated by a fear of something rummaging in the brush. And, of course, Angel was clear that he should not follow her. It was never verbalized, but it was a message sent and a message received. He would not risk losing her. Now his heart began to palpitate.

Why is she showing me this place? Why now?

He exhaled against a racing heart, pushing away one awful scenario after another.

"Come."

As she pulled him to the top of the incline, he could not believe what lay beyond.

"It's been here all this time . . . ," he marveled.

It was a surfer's paradise. Waves breaking offshore curled into white-sand beaches. Turquoise waters rimmed with bending palms. Birds skimmed the waters. In the distance, a point reached out into the ocean. And at its end was a building. It looked old and weathered, like something from another era.

"Is that where you live?" Mark mumbled in astonishment.

Angel gazed at him, her eyes deeper than the ocean, full of the tenderness in which he had drowned so many times before. "You know I don't live in a house."

The answer did not surprise him. Deep down he knew. He had always known.

A resurgent panic appeared. *Is she leaving me? Have I done something wrong?*

"Come, let's walk." Her tone was reassuring, a solace that everything was going to be fine.

Exhale . . .

"Okay."

Hand in hand they strolled down the beach. Beyond the headland, Mark gazed out at the ocean, seeing beyond the point.

"Angel, look!" The words tumbled out of his mouth in a rush of excitement. "It's a boat!"

She simply smiled.

Offshore sat a large white yacht. There was a motorized tender heading for the beach.

The pounding of his heart felt deafening—rescue was on its way. Then the realization that his reality was about to collide with his imaginary world rocked him.

"Angel . . ."

"Shush," she cooed. "It is time for you to choose."

As the boat drew closer, he saw a dog at the bow, its tongue lolling in the wash of breeze. Unexpected tears watered his eyes.

Angel gently wiped them away.

He knew he was a better man now than when he had arrived. The things he had thought important, she had helped him to shed. Things he had considered inconsequential were now the rock upon which his convictions were planted.

Angel had shown patience and wisdom in the way she was able to reveal to him what was important and what was superfluous, what was worthy and what was stupid. Explaining to him the meaning of life.

"Our one and only life, don't waste it, but instead live it to the fullest. Do not be afraid of death."

"God has plans for each of us, and we are all part of a bigger tapestry. Rich, poor, Black, white, gay, straight, male, female, liberal, conservative—these are all labels used to foster division. Tools of the Enemy, tentacles to expand the web of Lucifers energy."

He took her hand, and without saying a word, they watched the boat draw closer. There was a young couple aboard. He sensed a familiarity. She must have seen his recognition.

"It is time for me to go," she said with gentle mercy, accepting what they both knew was his only choice.

Mark shuddered, and she took both of his hands and looked deep into his soul.

"Please trust in what I am going to tell you. You have a wonderful life ahead of you. You are going to be incredibly surprised at how the seeds of your past have blossomed in the most marvelous of ways. I know you will harvest them with care and understanding. Remember . . ."

"I know, Angel. And I understand. If I am still here, then God is not done with me yet."

The phrase that started as a beacon of hope for that which was yet to come had morphed into a comfort, an acknowledgment of his relationship with God. The idea that there was a plan for him and for everyone.

She smiled. It radiated the supernatural life force that had sustained him for these last few years.

"Thank you. For everything. You rescued me."

"Put your trust in Him and don't let fear come between you and that trust. You are ready." Her smile beamed satisfaction of a job well done. Of . . . completion.

She placed a finger to her lips and then pressed it upon his own. Leaning in, she whispered one last secret. He nodded in understanding.

Without another word, she turned toward the forest. With a heavy heart he watched as she walked away.

From the corner of his eye he saw the dog leap from the moving boat, and he had an overwhelming concern for the canine.

"You're too far out," he hollered, upset his master would be so reckless.

The dog was swimming furiously for shore. With a rising anxiety, he followed her progress. As soon as her legs could touch bottom, she started running toward him. Mark gulped, wary. The dog was at least a hundred pounds and coming at him with a fury.

Without hesitation it jumped up and knocked him to the sand. With her paws on his chest, the dog revealed herself, and Mark's moment of panic evaporated. She lapped at his face, wagging her tail in ecstasy. Mark was astonished. God was having a great laugh with him.

"I have missed you so much," he told the lab. She showed no signs of letting up.

"Good girl, Carson," he repeated. "Good girl."

After the boat touched sand, an ashen-faced young woman leaped into the surf, running to intervene.

Mark was stunned. He knew by the assault from his old puppy who the girl was. But here? Now? How? Why?

A thousand questions were swept into the current of joy and the flood of mingled emotions.

"Carson, get off him. Now!"

The dog ignored her.

"I'm so sorry. Please, I don't know what's got into her. She has nev—"

The words froze midsentence, and the woman's face fell with incredulity. But her body was drawn like a moth to flame.

"Dad?" she asked, still gravitating forward. Her voice cracked with waves of disbelief. Mark eased out from under the dog, got up, and wrapped his arms around his oldest daughter.

"My favorite child," he told her, recalling how Ally had long ago programmed this into his phone.. "How much I have missed you."

Mark was riddled with so many competing emotions he felt as though he were being washed from the inside out.

"Dad?" she kept repeating beneath uncontrolled sobbing.

He pulled her closer and ran his fingers through her hair, whispering words to soothe her. "It's okay. It's okay. It's me. I'm here." Gazing up to cover his own tears, he murmured, "Thank you, God."

The man from the boat pulled the craft onto the sand and approached. "You okay, Ally?" he asked. He looked more confused than worried.

Mark noted his tone—caring with a hint of curiosity.

Ally let go. "Dan, this is my father. Dad . . . um . . . this is my husband."

He was not sure which of them was more surprised. After a pause, Dan reached out his hand, and Mark took it, impressed by the confidence projected by the man's firm shake.

"Mr. Lambert, I must confess this is a total shocker. But . . . ."

"This is real, right, Dan?" She reached out to caress her father's face, and he took her hands and kissed them.

Her words echoed his own thoughts. But in his heart, he knew God had delivered once again.

"I am real, sweetie. I have longed for this day. I look forward to calling home and telling everyone you found me. And that I am still alive."

A cloud passed over her husband's eyes, but he said nothing.

"Is everyone back home okay?" he asked, trying to cut through Dan's reaction.

"Everyone is fine. I can't wait to call them. But how did you get here?" Ally asked, her shock and disbelief short-circuited by the joy of the moment.

He could tell his daughter had a million questions. As did he, but his could wait. One thing the island had taught him was patience. As the roaring surge of emotions began to subside, she stepped back to appraise her long-lost father, apparently accepting he was not an illusion.

"Dad, you look great. I mean, it's been a long time, but . . . you seem younger." Looking around, she asked, "Are there others here? On the island?"

"We just assumed it was deserted," Dan added, as if it was an important admission.

Considering the questions to come, Mark wasn't sure what he was ready to share. He decided, for now, less was more.

"Darling. You are the first real person I have seen in over eight years." Pulling her close once more, the warmth of another human being suffused every part of his mind, body, and spirit.

In the harmony of the moment, the sounds of the bay were different from his side of the island. Still a concerto, just different instruments playing different melodies.

Fostering a feeling he could not describe, he lost all track of time. Minutes, seconds, hours, days, weeks, months, years, decades, these were all abstract measurements, inconsequential as the full weight of the day soared on wings of thanks.

Once again he cast his gaze to the heavens. Taking in the blue skies puffed full of smiling clouds, he relished the soft breezes gifted from a friendly sun. There were a million questions that stood in queue. At the front of the line was the question of why.

Why are they here and why now?

There was no urgency for answers, but when Dan finally broached the subject of returning to the boat, Mark considered the things he would need to recover. Entering back into the world would require his wallet, a passport, his phone, and a change of clothes.

Wiping sand from the shirt's wet paw prints, he asked what seemed most pertinent. "How long do you guys plan on staying here?"

He saw a silent message passing between husband and wife.

"That depends," Dan replied. "We have circled the island but cannot find a safe place to anchor. So, I suspect our time will depend on the weather and our hunt."

Mark had the solution to their anchorage problem.

"Did you see the large bay on the other side of the island?"

"Yes." Ally nodded. "We considered it, but the reef is too dangerous."

"There is a channel on the north end. It's hard to see because of shadows from the cliff, but inside is a safe harbor. I am sure it is more than deep enough for your yacht."

Dan considered this, biting his lip in thought. He looked to the boat, a twenty-four-footer with twin outboards.

"We should run it by the captain."

"Right." Mark scanned the beach for Carson. Always a nosy rosy, he saw her exploring the tree line at the top of the sand at the spot where Angel had stepped into the trees and out of his life. He did not expect he would ever see her again, her once telling him, "For all things there is a season." This was his new reality.

Mark let out a loud whistle, and Carson came running. She had not forgotten the familiar tune. Ally climbed into the boat. He lifted Carson over the gunnel and suggested Dan get in, and then he would shove them off the sand.

Hoisting himself into the craft, he looked toward the house out on the point. He imagined Angel waving goodbye.

"Is that where you stayed?" Dan asked, slowly reversing the tender.

Mark chose the simplest answer. "No—I am at the other end of the island."

Chapter 19

Approaching the yacht, Mark studied its contours. He had always been a boat lover. It was white, with three decks, a flybridge, davits for two boats, and an open area at the rear for dining and pleasure. Mark figured it to be about ninety feet. Though she had quite a few years under her belt, she was well cared for and, to him, simply gorgeous.

Serafina read the name painted on the side.

"Of course." He laughed and the universe laughed along with him.

As they pulled alongside, a barrel-chested man with a Hemingway beard, his age, he'd estimate, at about sixty, locked steely eyes onto him. Ally saw the man's wary expression.

"Captain Christakis," she called with a wave. "This is my father, Mark Lambert."

The man furrowed his brow. "You're that guy that went missing like, what, ten years ago?"

"Eight, to be exact, but yes, sir," Mark affirmed.

"Well, I'll be damned." His eyes softened to a good-natured crinkle. He smoothed his beard, and his demeanor became embracing. "Welcome aboard."

The yacht rose and settled under the swells. The wind coming from out of the west had freshened. Mark knew significant weather was not far off. He remained standing in the tender.

"Captain, there is a harbor on the western shore. If you like, I can show you the way in. I assure you it is large and well protected." He was going to add something about the coming weather but could see in the man's eyes he was already considering all the variables.

"Okay, why don't you and Dan take the launch, and we will follow."

With his boating knowledge getting a dusting off, Mark noted the captain had kept the yacht pointed into the oncoming rollers, knowing it added stability.

"Miss Ally, might I suggest you and Carson come aboard. The seas are starting to get a little rough."

"Right . . ." She laughed. "Good luck separating this dog from her master."

It was clear Carson had no intention to leave Mark.

"After all this time - well, I'll be doggone." The captain chuckled as he prepared to hoist the gangway. Once Ally was topside, Dan maneuvered the launch away from the ship while Mark sat in the back, letting Carson monopolize his every moment.

Mark weighed peppering Dan with questions, wanting to know who this man was, what his intentions were, how they met, and a full complement of other facts and choices that would impact his daughter's life. But a voice inside his head reminded him, *If he loves her, that should be enough . . .*

It was his old friend helping him to be the better man.

I will always be with you . . .

Carson nestled into his shoulder, her tongue slobbering drool onto his shirt. He pulled her thick brown coat in tight and nuzzled his face into her nape. His words ferried off on the breeze.

"You have no idea how much I missed you."

They rounded the southern point. He was surprised at the small tears that formed at the corners of his eyes. He knew it was joy but sloughed it off as effects from the breeze. The mountain dropped sharply to the water's edge, ending in craggy rocks pounded by endless waves. It appeared to be a collapsed volcano, created when plumes of magma spewed up from the bottom of the Atlantic eons ago.

Once beyond the point, the reef came into view. The arrays of staghorn reaching to the surface presented, to the untrained eye, an impenetrable barrier. Slowing to wait for the mother ship, Mark took a moment to remember the day he had landed, the boat coming free from its tether, the discovery of the pass, and slipping through the barrier.

"God brought me here," he whispered to his faithful friend. With a quick scratch behind her ears, he joined Dan at the helm. The yacht was coming around the point.

"Would you mind if I take 'em in?" He was more familiar with the channel and the contours of the reef.

His son-in-law shifted to one side, offering Mark the wheel.

"Dan, can I ask why you frowned when I mentioned calling back home? Is there something wrong that Ally does not want to tell me?" Mark asked.

"No, sir," Dan was quick to correct. "As far as I know, everyone is fine. It's just that . . ."

Mark studied him as he paused to find the right words.

"Well, three days before we got here, and up until today, we cannot seem to get a signal. Which is odd, since we have a global satellite receiver. It should work anywhere in the world. But not here. Something about the atmospheric elements, the captain has suggested. Truth is, right now we are dark."

Mark was relieved and intrigued. *Is God hiding this place?* He suppressed a smile and focused his attention on the channel.

The swells were particularly strong today, crashing and foaming outside the coral. Mark increased speed until they came to the northern inlet. Throttling back, he eased into the cut. Mark felt the outward current was pretty straightforward, with nary a drift toward the rocks. The waters were clear and the depth more than ample for the *Serafina*. He looked to Dan, who gave him the nod.

"Radio the captain and tell him we will guide him in. Last thing we need to do is increase the island's permanent population."

Dan finally cracked a smile.

The boat maneuvered safely into the harbor, and the anchor was secured. Once the bow had turned into the bay's gentle current, the stairs were lowered, and they tied off the runabout. Mark noted the Zodiac on the other set of the davits, thinking it would be more suitable. They were only two hundred feet from shore.

Boarding the craft for the first time, he was greeted by a woman of ageless beauty. Her smile was warm and engaging.

"Welcome aboard, Mr. Lambert. I am John's wife, Maria."

"My first mate," the captain added, joining her side.

"Your only mate," she corrected with a playful punch. There was no missing the love-light in their eyes.

A moment of melancholy washed over him. His wife was remarried, and his best friend was gone. But he embraced the here and now, letting it sink away.

"Come. I have lunch on the table."

Mark followed them to the stern, where a table was set.

"Please sit."

Ally came out of the main salon, changed and radiant. Dan moved to pull her chair out. *Old school.* Mark liked that.

There was so much Mark wanted to know about his family, the world, everything. But patience was a virtue, take each thing as it came and relish the moment.

Maria had set out plates of spanakopita and dolmades, along with hummus and pita bread.

"I hope Greek is all right," she said.

"No breadfruit?" He laughed, but they didn't get it.

"Fish, breadfruit, coconuts, and the occasional lobster, after eight years, Greek sounds heavenly."

The chair he sat in was very much like the ones he had taken from *Lil Darling,* teak, slat backed, and with a decent cushion. The deck was much more spacious than he had expected. Underneath the protruding overhang were two sets of sliding doors. A glance through the glass revealed that they opened into two different rooms.

Salons, he reminded himself, having always prided himself on his boating skills and nautical knowledge.

Maria opened a bottle of retsina. Greek wine. He considered his drinking days and how it had gone from an imbibement to a crutch.

"No, thank you," he politely declined.

"Fresca, Dan?" she asked.

"You know me so well."

"I would love one if you have enough," Mark asked, a bit more eagerly than expected.

"Coming right up."

"Before I met Ally, I had never even heard of Fresca," Dan confessed, placing a hand on top of his wife's. "And now she's got me hooked."

"I got that from my dad." She smiled, looking to make sure he was really here.

Maria never stopped moving. Serve the drinks, clear the dishes, serve the next course: moussaka, a Greek pasta. Clear. Then dessert: baklava, she never stopped but was always unobtrusive.

"Maria, you are an amazing chef. I can honestly say I have not eaten like this in years."

There was a hesitation. He wondered if she was deciding if it was a joke or a commentary.

"It doesn't look like you have fared too poorly," she said by appraisal. Her tone hinted at a hundred questions she wanted to ask but was too polite.

Captain John helped clear the dishes and then they discreetly departed. Mark could see they were a class act. He also had a hundred questions, but he did not want to leave Dan out of the conversation. There would be ample time to unpack all the lost moments.

"So, how long have you been married?"

"Actually, we are on our honeymoon," he began in a comfortable cadence. "We wanted to wait . . ."

Ally shot him a warning look, stopping him in midsentence. Suddenly, there was an awkward pause, an elephant in the room. Mark sensed what it was and saw no reason to beat around the bush.

"Sweetie, I know about your mother remarrying."

He thought back to the morning he came to know this and how Angel had reminded him that sometimes an old door must shut before another is opened. Wishing her good fortune and happiness was all he could do now.

At first it had stung, but as he prayed on her happiness, he felt better. Angel was right. Sometimes the past needed closure if you wanted to move forward.

He saw that Ally looked stunned at the revelation, her mouth agape, her words stuck on her tongue.

"Is she happy?" he asked.

"Um . . . she is. But how do you know?"

Mark sank back into his chair. Resting his hands on his belly, he felt full in more ways than mere food could provide.

"If I told you, you would not believe me. And I am trying to make sure that you don't go to bed tonight thinking maybe your dear old dad has lost it, being on this island for so long. For now, let's just say an Angel told me."

He patted her hand. And though she accepted his answer, a curiosity floated over her eyes. Perhaps seeing him in a new light.

"So, your honeymoon. Seems like an awfully long way to come. I cannot imagine you're here looking for me."

The subtle shift in their body language implied a decision was being made.

"No, Dad. We came here looking for buried treasure." Before Mark could respond, she added, "But in truth—I have already found far more than I could ever have hoped for."

"Amen," Dan added.

His comment was genuine, and for Mark it garnered him additional respect. Dan was all in for his daughter.

The old Mark would have seized on the idea of adventure, fantasized about treasure, and inflated it to untold wealth. But now it was a mystery that could wait. He wanted to know about his family.

"How are your brother and sister?"

"Forest is fine. He's got a girlfriend and works for a company called Barstool Sports."

"He works at a bar?" Mark realized his tone was judgey, already succumbing to old habits. "I mean, not that it's a bad thing . . ."

"Don't worry, Dad," she said, slipping into the "you're such a nerd" tone he remembered from her teenage years. "It's an internet sports company. Stats, fantasy games, merchandise, things like that."

"And Victoria?"

"Tori," she corrected, putting a faux gag finger in her mouth. "She's a Boca princess."

Mark raised an eyebrow.

"Don't worry, we still love her."

"I see," he said, amused there was still sibling rivalry. "I assume she lives with your mother . . ."

The questions about family had opened a door that streamed in and around past and present, weaving through milestone moments like college and holidays.

Mark intentionally drew Dan into their conversation, asking about his siblings and parents, education, where he grew up. He gleaned Dan was an only child, well-educated and quite smart.

When questions were directed at him, Mark would deflect from the things he did not want to discuss. Specifically, he steered away from Angel.

Ally was pretty good at this as well, often answering questions with a question. It amazed him how adept she was at saying a whole lot while really telling him nothing. *Angel would have been proud.*

"Carson looks like she needs to go," Ally suggested. She knew her well, and her concern showed him the kind of woman she was becoming. "Can we go see your house?"

House? He had never thought of it that way. The word triggered a memory of the first time he had met Angel and her story about the man stranded on an island and a beautiful woman who had rescued him, taking him to the home she had built from local materials. She had allowed him to save face in a moment of great embarrassment. She always had.

"Sure. That would be great."

Chapter 20

Earlier Mark had suggested that the Zodiac was more practical to use being this close to shore. It was different from the one he had. It was a bit larger, black, and had a small outboard attached.

The captain had accepted the suggestion. The launch had been moved to the stern and the inflatable fastened to the lower platform.

As they headed for the stairs, Carson wasted no time running down the gangway to secure her place on the bow. When they were all aboard, Dan fired the small engine, and in less than a minute, Mark was pulling the Zodiac up next to his own boat.

Faded but still legible, *Lil Darling* was stenciled on the sides. Ally paused, thinking.

"Dad," she began. "Everyone wrote you off. Lost at sea, and yet . . ."

She shifted her eyes between him and the raft. "You look better than ever. It's amazing."

"Thanks." He smiled.

She kissed him on the cheek. "Now show us your island retreat."

Mark led them along the cliff path. When the blue tarp of the gazebo came into view, he could see Ally inhaling every facet of his castaway life here on the island.

Dan brought up the rear. He, too, wore a bit of curiosity.

Mark was enjoying playing the accommodating host. In a caricatured French accent, he ushered them inside. "Apre's vous mon ami . . ."

Fortunately, but unexpectanly, the lights were still on. In his rush to meet up with Angel, he had forgotten to turn them off. But, of course, Ally seeing his working lights did add more sparkle to his sheen. The truth was that he had left in a hurry because Angel had promised this day would hold a surprise.

Boy, how right she was about that, but how did she know? It was the first time he had taken a minute to ponder it. But there would be no answer forthcoming.

Still . . . He shook his head. It defied both of his paradigms. Angel or imaginary friend? The scales were evenly balanced, but time would weigh heavier on one side than the other.

Watching them take in his home, he saw that Dan was fixated on the record of his time spent on this island—the eight horizontal rows with twelve clusters of diagonally slashed lines.

It was a powerful image that dominated the room, something Mark had long ago taken for granted. He was now glad he had kept up the daily routine.

"Eight years, Mr. Lambert . . . I have to hand it to you. You have more than made the best of a bad situation."

Ally wrapped an arm around her husband's waist. "Never forget, Lamberts don't survive, we conquer." With a huge grin, she gave him a playful punch.

Dan rolled his eyes, probably wondering, *What have I got myself into with this family?*

"Dad, this place is not what one would expect from an island castaway. It's like you've had an eight-year vacation. Can I . . ."

She sat on the edge of the bed. Carson sniffed his sheets, crawled up next to Ally, and started rolling on her back, mixing her essence with his.

"Happy dog," Ally said, further widening her big, beautiful smile.

"Yes, she is." Mark rubbed her belly, getting that sweet spot that started the leg thumping.

"Did you ever get lonely?" Ally asked, her expression shifting.

He spied the phone charging and used it as a diversion.

"Between old pictures of you guys and an imaginary friend or two, I simply lived life. I wasn't about to waste it wallowing in my circumstances."

He grinned at how close to the truth he was being. This was probably not the guy she remembered, but it was who he was now. "You guys up for a walk?"

Carson perked up—*walk* was an operative word. Her tail wagged in anticipation as she went to wait by the door.

"Well, apparently she is," Mark observed. It amazed him that after all this time it had taken less than a day for him and Carson to be inseparable again. She had never operated on a "Can I come?" mentality. It was always, "Where are we going?"

"Nothing's changed." He grinned, getting a curious look from Dan. He was still thinking out loud. "It's over a mile, but there is a place I want to show you."

Dan looked to his wife. "I'm game."

Exiting the cave, they got a different view of his encampment. The tarped firepit, the rack of salted fish, a pile of discarded nut shells, the black walls of the entrance, and forest that came to the edge of his clearing.

Dan walked to the fish rack for a cursory examination. He rolled a couple of nut shells in his palm while giving further inspection to Mark's salting process. "May I?"

"Please. I'm curious what you think." Mark was taking a shine to his new son-in-law, sharp and inquisitive.

Dan took one of the hanging pieces of fish and bit into it.

"Oh my god, this is delicious," he praised, wasting no time devouring the entire filet. "Did you know how to do this before coming to the island?"

"Trial and error," Mark explained, appreciating the compliment. "Shall we go?"

"Where are you taking us?"

Ally seemed eager for the next stop on the Lambert Island Castaway Tour. *Well, let's not disappoint,* he swelled with a sense of pride.

"For five years my fresh water came from a rain-collection system I had devised using a tarp, cooler, and empty plastic bottles." He played the host, narrating the tour.

"Then a powerful hurricane hit the island and destroyed a portion of what had been an impenetrable bamboo forest."

"That must have been scary."

He could see her imagination running through the ordeal. She had always been like that.

"Scary for sure. But my sanctuary proved impervious to the elements. Once the storm had passed, I went to check on the orchards that run along the top of the ridge. Remember, the breadfruit is my main source of food. The damage was extensive, but the orchard survived. But the biggest surprise was that the south end of the plateau was gone. Obliterated. And even more surprising, the opening revealed a waterfall. An endless supply of clean, fresh water. That day changed everything."

His eyes got a little misty as words stuck in his throat, but he said nothing about Angel.

"Limitless fresh water meant bathing and washing of clothes did not need to be with seawater. And offered a stable supply of drinking water." As he added texture to his ordeal, he saw their contemplative expressions.

Up ahead, Carson was splashing in the surf, chasing after seabirds. Her wagging tail and lolling tongue said it all. *Today, all is right in the world.*

He led them up from the beach and down into the ravine. The glen was washed in sunlit mist that created a canopy of rainbows. It was a magical place, and his family was enchanted. But his own emotions were different.

The light Angel brought to the glade was always brighter than that of Mother Nature. She had been life itself. Despite the vow, he was not sure that he would keep this secret forever. But he knew for sure she was gone. And his heart felt heavy. That is, until Ally tossed a small coconut into the lake, and Carson swam out and retrieved it, acting so proud when she dropped it at her feet.

Mark sidled up next to his daughter, and he knew she could see the mist in his eyes. He took her hand in his.

"It's beautiful," she said quietly.

"Here is where my life began. Five years had stripped away all the distractions of the world. Television, media, alcohol, arguments, toxic people, everything we absorb to feel alive. When I found this place, I was finally cleansed enough that the important questions of life could percolate. With no outside influences to cloud my mind, I was able to create a worldview I am now comfortable with."

Mark felt his daughter's hand tense. He realized he was getting a little heavy.

"Anyway, this spot will always be dear to me. Maybe tomorrow we can come back and go swimming. The water is especially luxurious, so soft on the skin."

"I would like that. Can we dive the reef too?" She turned to her husband.

"Dan, I never told you, but when my father was younger, he was a professional diver. He got me certified when I was ten."

"Tropical fish collector," Mark clarified. He did not want Dan feeling he had to compete with some larger-than-life superhero. "Yes, we can go diving. But let's wait for my friends."

"Friends?" Her tone raised a question.

"Yeah. My buddy Flipper and his pod. They come here every week. We have become dive buddies. You know what they say 'dolphins mean no sharks.'"

"Dolphins as friends?" she repeated. "Geez, what a life you've had."

When they returned to the beach, Mark suggested they head back to the *Serafina*. He would row out on *LD*, his nickname for Lil Darling's dingy, and meet them on board.

No one questioned his reasoning, but the truth was, he was already feeling a little claustrophobic about the changes that were coming.

Just take it slow. He is not done with you yet.

It was to become the mantra that helped keep him in the moment and remain focused on what was truly important.

"Sure, Dad. Dinner is usually served at seven."

Mark turned his wrist. "Hmm . . ."

Ally smiled. "Let's say in about an hour."

Dan fired up the outboard, the sound so anomalous to his time spent here. He watched as they slid over the top of the placid waters, quickly reaching the large, white, mother ship.

Mark sat admiring the linen, the fine China, and everything else. The Christakis's continually proved they were a head above the rest. Dinner that night was freshly caught fish with rice and salad. But it was the tomatoes dripping in vinaigrette he savored most.

"These are delicious," Mark said with satisfaction. "I grew tomatoes in a hydroponic system back home. I haven't tasted one in ages."

"Well, thank you, Mr. Lambert," Maria said with a gleam of appreciation. "May I ask, will you be sleeping on board this evening? We have a lovely room with your name on it."

Mark hesitated. It was one of the questions he had been tossing back and forth. There was a soft pleading in his daughter's eyes.

"Not tonight, Maria. Maybe in a day or possibly two. But for sure by the time you are ready to shove off, I will be here." He felt better seeing the relief on his daughter's face.

"Thank you, Mr. Lambert. I understand." She smiled and departed.

The interplay dampened the day's excitement. Dinner became a little more subdued. Sure that his decision to sleep ashore was worrying his daughter, he decided it was time to shift topics and rekindle the enthusiasm she had engaged in earlier. He placed his napkin on the table and pushed back his chair.

"Treasure," he said, lighting the fuse that animated Ally's expression. "Tell me your tale."

Dan opened his hands with the universal sign for "Have at it."

"Okay, then. I'll start at the beginning." She cleared her throat, pushed her dish toward the center of the table, and began. "One weekend Dan and I were lounging around, eating bagels, and reading the *Times*. We were looking for something to do. I saw an ad that Renard Rare Collectibles was auctioning off a set of first-edition books from an old professor of mine.

"I can't explain it, but I had this overwhelming need to attend. Like the page was calling out to me and wouldn't take no for an answer."

Mark wondered about this. *Could this have been when I put it out into the universe for someone who loved me to come looking?* It was a curious thing, and at this point, it was getting harder and harder to ignore coincidence. But he did not want to interrupt her flow, so he tucked the thought away to explore another day.

"I had to drag Dan kicking and screaming," she continued, messing with her husband.

"In my defense," Dan justified. "Saturdays are for college football. But when she makes up her mind . . ."

Mark hadn't thought of football in forever. But he understood Dan's point. In the fall, his Saturdays often followed the same routine.

"Is Alabama still a powerhouse?" Mark asked, finding a way to bond with her husband. Dan's grimace told him all he needed to know.

Meanwhile, Ally ignored them and continued. "When we arrived, the crowd was not very large. It seems that they did not find the items that appealing. But it was my first auction ever, so I found it all very exciting."

"After receiving our bid number and a list of items for auction, my heart almost leaped out of my throat. They were going to auction off the original diary of Hanri Fick." Her voice had become animated, and Mark was enjoying her reverie.

"I see," Mark said. Actually, he didn't. "So who was Hanri Fick?"

"She was a pirate. A female pirate. When I was an undergrad, her story was the basis for a history class I had taken. Back in the seventeen hundreds she and her partner, Nicolette Rey, were feared by the Portuguese slave traders, as they were wreaking havoc along the southern slave routes."

"Female pirates?" Mark had never heard of such a thing. The idea of something so unusual intrigued him, especially in light of the fact it was one more anomaly attached to his island.

"That's right. Hanri was South African; Nicolette's nationality was never verified. Anyway, their infamy was less about pirating and more about who they targeted and why. They had an all-male crew of rescued slaves, Black Africans they had freed over the years. You see, Captain Fick would patrol the slave routes from the coast of Africa to the eastern edge of the Caribbean, interdicting ships she believed contained captured human cargo.

"Her diary affirms what I had learned in my history class. When a target was determined, they would swarm the ships and seize the slave traders. Mostly Arabs or Portuguese. But she was not a murderer. As a matter of fact, she professed to be a Christian, and her goals were twofold. Free the slaves and return them to their homeland. And to rehabilitate the men she believed had lost their compassionate connection to humanity."

"And of course a little piracy, right?" Mark assessed. He liked the Fick character, gravitating to her willingness to chuck all conventions and do what was right. "Otherwise we would not be on a treasure hunt."

"Of course," Ally said dismissively and continued. "Somewhere between Barbados and the Horn of Africa was an island she describes in her diary as the 'Island of Redemption.'"

Mark thought about the name and how apropos it was to his own life. "So you believe this is the place?"

Ally nodded.

"And she named it Redemption?"

"She was a woman before her time. A crusader. A champion of the downtrodden. One to seek restoration instead of revenge. It was this quirk that captured the imagination of historians."

He was getting swept up in his daughter's enthusiasm. He was proud she gravitated to the values of this Fick person, though he knew this was more a testament to Rachael's upbringing than his own. Still, he beamed. "Okay, I'm intrigued."

"Once a ship had been commandeered, her crew would come aboard and free the captives. Then the freed slaves would be taught to sail, and the ship was pointed back to Africa, but not the traders and crew. They would be bound and taken to her island. Once dropped off, they were told, 'When God informs me that you have been rehabilitated, I will come back and make passage for you back to a civilized port.'"

"When God told her?"

Ally tilted her head, a quirk he recalled of his inquisitive child, accepting of things she wanted to believe.

"That's what she wrote."

"And did she return them to civilization?"

"Of course, but not all at once. She had an uncanny knack for knowing who was ready and who was not. She had given them breadfruit plants and showed them how to plant and harvest. She gave them gear for fishing and other survival materials. And, most importantly, she left them copies of the Bible written in their native languages."

Mark thought about this. It confirmed what he deduced about the orchard. And truthfully, three hundred years later, their lives here had not been that much different from his own.

"How long did it take for someone to be redeemed?"

"Her diary mentions a few specific individuals, who we assume are probably symbolic of types and nationalities. Generally, the consensus was five to ten years."

He considered that. Apparently, Angel thought he needed eight.

"She mentions the waterfall. I will recite the line that I memorized. 'The tears of God cascade over the cold world, offering life to those who want to be saved.'"

Mark knew it was a metaphor of duality. Life-giving waters to survive in this world and eternal life offered by the hope of Jesus Christ. Her reciting the waterfall passage made him wonder. *Does Ally believe in God?* He hoped she did, knowing he had been a poor role model when they were growing up.

"Well, the orchards are here," Mark affirmed, stacking the clues in order. "Without them, I do not think I would have made it. And your metaphor for the waterfall, you saw that yesterday. Are there any other characteristics she reveals in her diary?"

"Yes. A black-sand beach and a white-sand beach. She describes it as the grains of yin and yang. And then there are the mountains that make up the dog's bone."

"Funny, I used the same analogy when I first surveyed the island." He shared memories of the first day on the beach as he ran through a reel of thoughts.

"And, of course," Ally said, adding more weight to their decision to come here. "The location is perfect. Off the beaten path but near enough to her interdiction routes to be feasible."

"According to satellite images," Dan explained, "there are not a lot of islands in the greater vicinity and none that we could tell that have more than one of these characteristics."

"The Island of Redemption," Mark mused. He never doubted his daughter. If he learned anything from Angel, it was that God weaves many strands to create his tapestry. Apparently, Mark was simply the latest redemptive thread in the story of this island. *Who will be next?*

The thought gave him an idea. *Before leaving, I will stow everything in a safe place for the next person.* He was sure he would not be the last. *Perhaps a note.*

"What happened to all the people? There are very few signs that they were ever here," Mark asked. The story of God's unfolding hand was of far more interest to him than the lure of treasure, but his daughter was here on a quest. So he told himself, *Be where your feet are.*

She absentmindedly twirled ringlets of hair around her fingers. "In the end, it all came down to the treasure. She had to get rid of the people so she could hide what she alludes to as a king's fortune somewhere on the island."

Mark sank into his chair, inhaling the sweet smell of wildflowers carried in on the evening breeze. The stars above where shimmering in abundance, and the lapping of waves chorused with the crashing surf beyond the outer banks. The night was perfect, but he knew change was not far off.

Weather is coming.

He was an expert at the signs. Repetition had been a good teacher. He was glad they were not out on the open sea. Here in this protected oasis, the ship, crew, and his daughter were safe.

From the corner of his eye he studied the happy couple. His daughter was no longer a child but a grown woman and her husband, Dan, a fully grown man. At a little over six feet, he was fit and slight framed, with thick curly hair, brown eyes and a quick wit. His demeanor was casual but confident, intelligent but unassuming.

Ally looked a lot like her mother. Fair haired and fair skinned, faint freckles, medium build with an athletic frame. She was smart but also sharp with the tongue. He could tell she had little patience for stupidity.

She got that from me.

He recalled the line that had so infuriated his children when they were growing up when they did not look beyond the here and now. Of cause and effect.

What did you think was gonna happen . . .

No doubt there was an element of this about her. It was a lingering trait from an early indoctrination.

He was curious about Dan. The yacht implied he obviously had money. Did he inherit it or earn it? If the latter, how? This would reveal much about his son-in-law. As he let his thoughts flow, Angel appeared inside his head, reminding him not to judge.

Which opened up an old memory from his early teens. He was aware of a number of people in his neighborhood who had their own less-than-legal escapades in Miami. He used to justify this by saying, "In Hollywood, you gravitated to the movie business. In Miami, well, it had a reputation for something altogether different."

Don't judge, lest ye be judged.

148

This biblical passage elicited an inward smile as Ally launched into her tale of treasure.

"There was a Portuguese vessel that was returning from the Caribbean. Normally, ships heading east were of no interest to Captain Fick. They were unlikely to fulfill her primary calling of fighting slavery. But this particular ship was in trouble.

"According to her journal, the seas were gathering under a tempest, and the Portuguese vessel *Leanora* was listing heavy to one side. It was clear she was carrying too much cargo. Hanri ordered her crew to approach to see if they could offer assistance. Nicolette took her position on the top deck to survey the situation."

"All seemed fine until they were within hailing distance. Suddenly, a door opened on the broadside of the *Leanora*, and a cannon ball was fired, striking the upper deck and killing Nicolette instantly. This enraged Hanri and the crew. Being experts at ocean warfare, they responded with overwhelming force. Within the hour, the ship had been commandeered and the crew bound and gagged."

"Hanri personally inspected the hold, uncomprehending that their nonaggressive offer of help had ended in the death of her best friend. What she found were a dozen large chests full of gold and silver. But what intrigued her most were the hundreds of priceless religious artifacts that had been made of jewels and precious metals. They had been fashioned in the New World as gifts for the Holy See. The Catholic Church of Rome."

"She understood why they fired but not how they came to gather such a fortune. These were not religious men. So, she began interrogating the crew one at a time."

The story Ally unfolded was brutal even by pirate standards. "They had attacked a small Spanish fleet made up mostly of brown-robed monks returning home after years of missionary work. Under further interrogation, she learned that all of the monks had been tortured for the mere sport of it and then sent to a watery grave."

"Barbaric," Mark muttered, bringing a balled fist to his mouth.

How little life was valued on the high seas back in those days.

"This changed everything," Ally continued, her voice subdued. "Her heart was broken, and her anger enflamed. Apparently, her relationship with Nicolette was more than that of just friends. And these men were nothing but butchers, a blight on humanity with no redemptive value. She moved the treasure to her ship, and then each man was made to walk the plank. There would be no Redemption Island for these barbarians."

Ally paused, which Mark assumed was to allow him a moment to appreciate the scope of her ordeal.

"Her anger was reflected in the graphic description she had penned. But for now, I will spare you the details except to say, in keeping with her character, she gave each man a final opportunity to accept the Lord as their savior before they were sent to the bottom of the ocean."

"Then what happened?"

"First they stabilized the *Leonora*. It took them ten days to get to the island. As we sit here, I assume it was this very bay where the vessel was repaired and loaded with fresh stores of food and water."

"It was time to empty the island. She went through the motions of interviewing the island's prisoners, something akin to a pardoning hearing. Truthfully, it was all theater. She accepted their lies of salvation, and every person on the island was packed aboard the Portuguese ship and sent home."

Her face lit as if with a dawn of revelation. "You might be the first person to have landed here in over three hundred years."

"Perhaps." Mark juxtaposed his own experiences against those she tried to redeem. "It must have been very painful for her to have lost her true love," Mark said sorrowfully. His thoughts harkened back to his time with Angel.

His comments about Hanri and Nicolette elicited a look of surprise on his daughter's face.

Does she think my accepting of two woman as lovers is something I would have rejected? Love is love. He didn't judge. That was the role of God, not man.

"That was her last foray on the high seas," Ally continued. "She took the religious reliquaries as her and Nicolette's share of the booty. According to her diary, she buried them here on the island."

"It was blood money. She wanted no part of it. And she had no use for a religion that had fostered the Spanish Inquisition using God as an excuse to terrorize those they deemed unfaithful. This treasure belonged to no one. Never would the spoils of thievery from the native people of the New World be theirs. The balance of the gold, silver, jewels, and doubloons were divided among her crew."

"What happened to her?" Mark felt her loss, which touched him at the core as he projected his feelings for Angel onto the story.

"Some say she returned to her native home of South Africa. Others suggest she migrated to the New World. We will probably never know."

"Did she say anything about where the treasure is buried?"

"Sure. But not how you would expect. It's as if she was having fun when writing the diary, teasing anyone who got a copy. The treasure's location is an enigma wrapped in a conundrum sealed with speculation and intrigue."

"What do you mean?" Mark furrowed his eyes.

"She never gives clues about where the treasure may be buried. Instead, she offers riddle after riddle of where it is not buried. The only affirmative fact is that it is on this island somewhere!"

Holding a thumb and forefinger to his jaw, he stared out at the reef. He could feel Ally and Dan waiting for him to respond.

"That is a broad swath of possibility. How much time do you have to look?" he responded, then realized it was an unintentional foray into his son-in-law's background, something that would come up when the time was right. Here, now, it did not seem pressing, but . . .

Does he have a job? Does Ally?

Dan straightened up. "We have leased the *Serafina* and crew for three months. It took us two weeks to get here, and we should assume at least ten days to return to Bridgetown."

Mark did the calculations and determined that two months remained. Plenty of time to conclude his time here on the island. He longed to speak with his family, but after eight years, a couple more months was not really going to matter. After all, he had his favorite child here. And, for now, that was a gift he would keep enjoying.

It was getting late, and Ally yawned. Mark took this as a cue to wrap up the evening.

"Why don't we call it a night? I'm gonna head back." Carson's ears perked up, and she immediately stood. She always knew when he was going somewhere.

"Can she come?" he asked.

"Dad, she's your dog. Apparently I was simply a temp."

They both smiled. It was true.

"Dan, I am sure the captain knows this, but there is strong weather coming tonight. He might want to throw out a second anchor."

Dan looked at the sky. The stars were out, and the pale moon that had risen earlier was now sinking into the west. There were no outward appearances to bolster Mark's claim.

"I'll let him know," he said. But Mark noted the hint of doubt in his voice.

"Even if it rains, come for breakfast," Ally said, her smile a plea.

"Do you have coffee?"

"Duh?"

"Then I will be here. Come on, girl."

Chapter 21

Returning with Carson, he noted the breeze was growing as fresh clouds scudded across the night. When he arrived back at the cave, he did something he hadn't done in a long while. He retrieved the bamboo gate from the back. He told himself it was to keep Carson from wandering, but in his heart he knew he wanted protection from the coming unknown.

Do not let fear rule you . . . Angel was always there to remind him.

Carson crawled into the bed, taking over half the mattress.

"Geez, what a bed hog." After undressing, he turned off the lights, slipped under the sheets, and considered the day.

In less than twelve hours my prayers have been answered. Yet my best friend has left me. He continued by looking at a future of uncertainty. No job. No money. No credit. Acclimating to the new world was going to be far more complicated than he had ever considered.

Is this what I really want?

He recalled Ally's comment. *You have everything you need right here.*

Anxiety tossed and anxiety turned. Sleep was an orphan. For the first time in years his thoughts would not leave him in peace. There were so many what-ifs . . .

If you're still here, He is not done with you yet.

With Angel's calming spirit he recalled her comments on the beach. *The seeds of your past will bear surprising fruit. Do not let worry separate you from the peace of God.*

His heartbeat found normal, but he was too wound up to sleep. He got up and removed the gate. Carson came to his side.

"You always know." Mark smiled. "Let's go for a walk."

He wound up back on the beach staring out toward the sea. The captain had taken his advice and set a second anchor to keep the boat from swinging if the wind became unmanageable.

A crescent moon rested on the western horizon. Clouds to the east were gathering. He had seen it all before. There was nothing to worry about, but he was glad they had taken his advice.

He closed his eyes and tuned out the chorus of swaying treetops, crashing waves, and lapping waters. Quietly, he recited the Lord's Prayer. "Our Father, who art in heaven . . ."

Completing the biblical stanzas, he felt the need for additional prayer. Today was mostly centered on thanks. As he explored the path of gratitude, he recalled how much he had been given, where he had come from and where he was now.

He felt better. Anxiety had been stilled.

"Come on, girl. Let's get some sleep."

Sometime during the night, the rains had let loose. When he got up, the tarp was dangling from the frame, and the rack of fish lay tipped over. He had slept through it all. He looked forward to reclaiming a lost indulgence.

"Come on, girl, I've waited eight years for a good cup of joe. Let's go get some breakfast."

After he brought *LD* alongside the gangway, Ally looked over the rail. "Just in time."

Carson leaped onto the deck and bound up the stairs acting as if she was still a youngster.

"I guess she still knows who feeds her," Mark said as he finished tying off the raft.

When he stepped onto the deck, the sun was peeking over the top of the island. Dan was already seated at the table. Mark noticed two nutshells from his refuse pile. He also sensed something was wrong.

Ally took a silver server and poured him a cup of coffee.

Gawd, how I missed the joys of a simple cup of coffee, the aroma, the unique taste. One of life's true pleasures, he mused.

As he savored his first sip in ages, Dan was looking at him over the top of his own cup.

"Seems there's an elephant in the room. Care to tell me what it is?" Mark asked, cutting to the chase.

Ally sat nervously, her hands restless.

After a long pause, it was Dan who took the lead. "Mr. Lambert . . ." He, too, paused, his lips exposing the tongue pressed against his teeth in hesitation.

From the gravitas weighted on the word *mister*, Mark expected something serious was afoot. He took another sip from his cup but never broke eye contact. He let Dan unfold his concern at whatever pace was comfortable for him.

Dan took the two shells from the table and played with them in his palm. He seemed nervous. "I have a degree in botany," he began, clearing his throat once and then a second time. "One of the sub-studies I focused upon was that of hallucinogenic plants native to the Americas. For instance, these shells . . ." He steadied the flat of his palm. Mark noted a sheen of Dan's sweat glistening on the casing. There came another pause.

"Botany," Mark said to fill the void. His tone must have hinted at suspicion, projecting all the pot-growing "botanists" he knew back in the day.

Dan clarified. "Native people have been creating medicines for thousands of years. Today's pharmaceutical industry is finally waking up to this. I hope through my research to contribute to alternative cures for humanity."

Mark felt rebuked. *You deserved that . . .*

"So as I was saying, these come from the Virola tree." He set them on the table and tented his fingertips.

"They are members of the nutmeg family, Myristicaceae. There are some three hundred different species, but this particular variety is the most often used by the native people of South America for hallucinogenic rituals. The nut yields a very potent resin."

Mark was stunned. Threads of the story of his usage unfolded like an old-time movie reel. Finding it prior to the hurricane. Using the resin as a cooking oil for the fish and chopping up the nut as flavoring for the breadfruit. It had become a staple of every meal.

Was it all a hallucination?

The warmth of the rising sun upon his shoulders contrasted with the cold shudder running down his spine. *She appeared only after I started ingesting this?*

Which reminded him of the lake yesterday. His first impression was that, without Angel, the glimmer on the lake seemed to have much less shimmer. Then there was the day he had ingested the entire pile. The day of the butterflies. Without warning, a wave of vertigo washed over him. He almost toppled over.

"Dad, are you okay? Your face, it's turned white."

Mark stood on wobbly legs. He went to the rail and took slow, deep breaths as he stared out at the water.

Was she simply a drug-induced hallucination? Never real?

There was a buzzing growing in his ears. He was standing at a crossroads and had to grip the rail tight. Somewhere off in the distance, he heard Dan and Ally asking him questions, but they were too far away. And right now, he did not care.

His thoughts were thick with the cotton of competing concerns, and he heard Angel speak to him, her voice clear like a church bell on a Sunday morning. It was familiar, settling. He became oblivious to anything else.

"Yes," he mumbled through soft lips. On a hushed breath he repeated the line that saved him. "If I am still here, then He is not done with me yet."

Unmindful of his companions, he repeated this over and over. "If I am still here, then He is not done with me yet." Each utterance steadied him. Eventually he let out a long breath and returned to the table.

Sitting down, he patted his daughter's hand. She looked awful. He could only imagine the thoughts going through her head.

"Well, then. Enough of that, eh?" There really wasn't much more he could say. Did he need to? He could see his son-in-law wasn't satisfied. Perhaps humor was the only course of action.

"Best damn fish you ever had, right, Dan?"

The man's mouth opened, but nothing came out.

"You got me. Now you know my secret ingredient."

He put a big grin on his face, in part for their benefit, but also because no matter what the truth really was, once again she was there to save him from himself. Whatever pent-up fear or worry or imagination of some other unexplained worst-case scenario, the fish quip seemed to puncture the balloon, and the levity brokered a nervous kind of laughter, but laughter, nonetheless. He knew that now was the time to put this to rest once and for all.

"When I discovered that the resin made a fairly good cooking oil, it became a basic ingredient of my diet. Along with some palm oil, it's how I fried the fish. No wonder I had such a good time." He slapped his chest with a big "Who knew?" grin. It sealed the deal.

"My dad, the stoner." Ally giggled.

"Yeah, who knew?" Dan repeated, not quite as enthusiastically.

Any remaining concern dissipated with the familiar cacking of his friends. Carson started barking and ran down the gangplank. Next to his raft, Flipper was treading water, vying for Mark's attention.

"Looks like they want us to join them," Mark said, peering over the side rail. "You guys up for some diving?"

"Dr. Dolittle," Dan said, brooking a bit of lightness.

This caused Mark a small smile. *The elephant had left the room.*

"The stoner who talks to dolphins," Ally finished for him. "We'll get our things."

Mark descended the stairs, giving a shout to his friend. "Where is everyone?"

Four dolphins burst up from below, then fell back, soaking Mark and Carson.

"You did that on purpose." Mark laughed.

Two heads popped up, cacking away at their prank.

Labs love water. Carson's tail was wagging faster than her bark could bark. The cacophony of dog and dolphins was a chorus of joy. Mark felt drenched in good fortune.

Ally stood on the rail, watching. Happiness, thanks, wonder, and awe were encapsulated in her expression.

Dan appeared in a Speedo, dragging more gear than a sporting goods store could support. Mark had to stifle a laugh. They loaded it all into *LD*. And, of course, you-know-who had no intention of being left behind.

Mark rowed them to where *Lil Darling* was submerged. All the while, Flipper became infatuated with Carson, Ally dragged her hands in the cool water, and Dan greased himself in sunscreen. It was all so perfect.

Mark donned his gear and dove in to secure the line. The water was calm and the current mild. Carson could not contain herself and followed.

Soon the other dolphins gathered round, treating her as if she were royalty, the star of the show. One by one they came up beneath her. She eventually figured out that if she widened her legs, her belly could rest on the creatures' backs, and off she went—riding them.

Mark was amazed at how quickly they melded. It was the funniest thing he had ever seen. All of them sported earsplitting grins.

"Dad, this place is so magical," Ally gushed. Any hangover from his hallucinogenic past had evaporated.

"Yes. Yes, it is." He let his words trail off. Angel gave a wink within his mind's eye.

He wondered about the dolphins. *Perhaps, being so far from a fallen world, all things worked as God intended.*

Mark encouraged them to explore. He was going to stay topside, keeping an eye on the kids. It was the only thing he could think of to describe his dog and the dolphins interacting.

Carson would bark with glee, and when she fell off, another would come up under her and take its place. She was never in danger of drowning or even submerging.

It was not long before Dan surfaced with a couple of lobsters.

"Not bad," Mark encouraged.

Dan tossed them in the raft and went looking for more.

It reminded him of his early days of fish collecting, the thrill of the hunt and gratification of the capture. Eventually, it became about money, and the thrill felt more like work.

"Come on, girl, let's give your friends a rest."

As if understanding his every word, the dolphin carrying Carson came up next to the boat, and Mark helped his furry friend into the raft.

"You stay here. I'm gonna go join Ally."

Carson affirmed this by shaking off the water, covering everything in spray. More antics, more smiles, more perfect.

For a good part of the morning, they explored, hunted, and enjoyed the sea's underwater beauty. Together they had collected five, good-sized lobsters.

"Tonight I will cook and ask John and Maria to join us," Mark insisted.

When it was time to return, Carson and Flipper were engaged in a back-and-forth cack and bark—as though they were deep in conversation.

"What do you think they are saying to each other?" Ally asked.

"Another of nature's mysteries," Mark replied with a contented smile.

Chapter 22

The afternoon was blue skies and sunshine. Ally and Dan lathered up and moved out onto the yacht's deck to catch some rays. Mark remembered that when he lived back in Florida, Northerners were always trying to work on their tans. These two didn't need it, as they had been in the Caribbean for a while, but the sun chaser in them was not going to be denied.

Once they settled into their chaises, he turned his focus back to finding the lost treasure of Captain Fick. They had been at it for ten days. As Ally had rightfully assessed, the diary held more clues about where not to look than where to look. Success would rely on a process of elimination, a little luck, and maybe some intuition.

With his familiarity of the island, some of the clues were obvious, while others were more opaque. There were a number of references that, if you had not spent time here, you would never have figured out, such as, "'When the wounded beast cries upon the north wind, it is time to retreat.' I know where that is," he said under his breath. Another clue that would need to be marked.

Years ago when he and Angel were discussing fear, she had suggested the wailing sound he had heard the night of the hurricane could be explained if he explored the ridgeline. She was right. There was a small lava tube that acted like a bottle when you blew across its top. In this case, the sound was an eerie moaning that mimicked a wounded beast.

Had I figured that out by myself? Was she simply an internal voice repeating what deep down I already knew? Even now the scales were unsure which way to tip.

With wandering thoughts and roving eyes, he stared at the easel under the fly-deck. Dan had pinned a large map of the island onto foam board. Each unraveled clue was marked with a red pin. Thirty pins showed where the treasure was not buried.

We have barely scratched the surface, he worried.

He eyed the diary on the table. It was old and the pages fragile. Carefully lifting the book, he could feel the weight of its antiquity. The cover was made of faded brown cowhide. The pages were bound by punched holes looped with knots of frayed string, all of it quite brittle.

Written in a large, flowing script on the inside cover were the last words of Hanri Fick.

In the year of our Lord, 1732, the end of my adventures are near. I hope I have pleased the Lord, for I long to be with him and reconnect with the lost love of my life.

The right-hand page contained a single phrase that summed up her devotion, poetically defining the core message of the Gospel.

Only by the Cross of Calvary
Can one find the riches of heaven.

He was in no hurry. He had already read it through and through to the point where the words had been exhausted. With a jaundiced eye he immersed himself, looking for clues beyond the written word. He lingered on things like an odd passage or its placement and wondered at the things she had left out.

He sensed there were hints and traces just waiting to be unraveled. Twice she had marked a very deliberate backward *Z*, perhaps to unlock an anagram or a code of some sort. They seemed out of place.

Some of the inscribed expressions were stilted, yet her command of the English language appeared impeccable. There were random dots throughout the book, but they could just be errant droplets from the quill she had used.

But are they? He made notes of the page numbers and locations of each droplet on a separate pad.

It was an enigma, undiscerning of any meaningful patterns. All the while, the look on his daughter's face was one of anticipation, as if to hold her breath and wait for him to have an 'aha' moment.

He knew his survival had given her a misplaced belief that he was some sort of a superhero. And though he did not want to disappoint her, he was stymied by Fick's diary.

"A remarkable woman," he uttered, closing the cover and deflating the balloon of his daughter's anticipation.

"Hanri Fick has no doubt left clues for those who persevere. So we will persevere."

He got up, crossed the teak deck, and placed an additional pin into the map. It was the swamp where all the mosquitoes were. He recalled the first time he had encountered the marauding squad of bloodsuckers.

"The reference to the cloud of anger, I believe, refers to the swamp at the southern end. It is a haven of vicious mosquitoes. Trust me. I know."

Mark had spent each night since their arrival sleeping in his cave. Slowly, he was overcoming the anxiety of an unknown future, but he told himself this place was familiar, and he wasn't ready to let it go, at least not yet. He never expected the idea of returning to civilization would cause him so much unease.

"Sometimes baby steps are the best way to proceed," he whispered, thankful they still had some time before leaving. Thinking out loud was a habit his kids were getting accustomed to. He had explained that being alone, he needed to hear the sounds of human voices, so he had improvised. Ally laughed, and Dan simply shook his head and said nothing.

Each day he would move a portion of his belongings to the room appointed for him aboard the *Serafina*—things like his wallet, passport, phone, and the few clothes that were still intact. This helped to allay his daughter's unvoiced concerns, and it helped him to accept the inevitable.

It was time to make the leap from castaway to citizen. Time for him to stop avoiding what was inevitable.

"Tonight will be the last that I sleep on the island," he told her. He saw the muscles in her neck soften.

"Would you keep Carson for me?"

After eight years, it was time to leave his home, his fortress. With ample food, water, and the grace of good health, the time alone had allowed the distillation of distractions to boil down to what was most important in life. His old worries about work, money, and the quest for success had all drifted away as the years passed.

In hindsight, he could see how much anger, angst, and accusations he had accumulated. Back home he had never recognized how concerned he was at how he was viewed by others. It was one of the factors that drove him. Now he could see it was vanity and ego.

The moment of reflection reminded him of a parable Angel had told him about all the useless political arguments he had gotten into with friends.

Reminiscing, he recalled the beautiful lilt of her voice as she retold the tale of the donkey and the tiger, a tale he vowed to remember when he reentered the world.

"The donkey told the tiger, 'The grass is blue.'"

"The tiger replied, 'No, the grass is green.'"

"The discussion became heated, and the two decided to submit the issue to arbitration, so they approached the lion."

"As they approached the lion on his throne, the donkey started screaming: 'Your Highness, isn't it true that the grass is blue?'"

"The lion replied, 'If you believe it is true, the grass is blue.'"

"The donkey rushed forward and continued, 'The tiger disagrees with me, contradicts me, and annoys me. Please punish him.'"

"The king then declared, "The tiger will be punished with three days of silence.' The donkey jumped with joy and went on his way, content and repeating, 'The grass is blue, the grass is blue . . .'"

"The tiger asked the lion, 'Your Majesty, why have you punished me, after all, the grass is green?'"

"The lion replied, 'You've known and have seen the grass is green.'"

"The tiger asked, 'So why do you punish me?'"

"The lion replied, 'That has nothing to do with the question of whether the grass is blue or green. The punishment is because it is degrading for a brave, intelligent creature like you to waste time arguing with an ass, and on top of that, you came and bothered me with that question just to validate something you already knew was true!'"

"'The biggest waste of time is arguing with the fool and fanatic who doesn't care about truth or reality, but only the victory of his beliefs and illusions.'"

"'Never waste time on discussions that make no sense. There are people who, for all the evidence presented to them, do not have the ability to understand. Others who are blinded by ego, hatred, politics, and resentment, and the only thing that they want is to be right even if they aren't. When ignorance screams, intelligence moves on.'"

At the time, he had laughed at his own folly. She always found a way to cut through his armor using humor.

"Angel or imagination?" he asked himself. "I doubt I will ever know."

He lay in bed, his mind churning through things he had not worried about in years. The arrival of his daughter was supposed to be the answer to his prayers. But with the arrival came the outside world of worries that go with modern society.

Whereas before he could crawl into his bed, bring the covers up under his arms, and drop into a deep, peaceful sleep; now he lay in bed and worried.

What will I do when I return? I have no job. No money. I'm sure Rachael isn't expecting to go through some formal divorce procedure or revisit a division of assets. Had she declared me dead so she could remarry? What will my kids think if I made demands on her? Have all my friends moved on? Will I ever fit back in?

He was working himself into knots when Angel's soothing voice once again came to his rescue. *If you are still here, He is not done with you yet.*

Staring at the wall, it stared back. He had not marked it since Ally's arrival.

"Days on the island or days stranded?" There was a twelve-day gap between the two.

"On the island," he finally decided. Today would be the last in which he would actually live here, so he marked his record one final time.

While doing this, he considered the story of the Island of Redemption and those countless souls from the past along with himself. The island was magical—he knew this firsthand. It did not take much to figure out how to survive. It offered all the sustenance one would need.

"Has Angel always been here? Did those men who traded in human misery find change in their life?"

He suspected many did. And in that vein, he wanted to impart hope to the next person in God's redemption plan. He opened the plastic baggie with the few sheets of paper left on the pad he had liberated from *Lil Darling*. Another thing coming to its end. Taking a well-worn pencil, he crafted a letter.

My name is Mark Lambert.

I was stranded on this island for eight years until my rescue. It has taken this long to strip away that which is not important. Hopefully, I'm leaving in place a man who sees what is right and true and no longer worries about the things of this world, but in turn hopes to store up his treasure in heaven.

I've had to lose everything to gain much. This place is known as the Island of Redemption. If you have become stranded here, you are chosen to be blessed. Might I impart what an old friend reminded me of. "If you are still here, then God is not finished with you yet."

These are the words of Angel, the one who guided me. My friend. To this day, I do not know if she is real or imagined, but it does not matter.

Do not despair. All your survival needs are here in abundance. There is a lake on the south end with ample fresh water. There is an orchard of breadfruit on the eastern ridge, and I have left you fishing lines and tackle. The fish are abundant and waiting to be caught.

You only have one life. Do not waste it waiting or worrying. Be here now. Take advantage of the wealth of time that is free from the curse of distraction. Exercise, meditate, and explore the corridors of your mind. Consider the things of worth. Life, death, love . . .

I wish you well and encourage you to open the Bible that I sealed in a plastic bag. Shed your worry, pray for redemption, and it will come.

Good luck—Mark

He put the note in a plastic bottle, sealed the cap, and placed it on the bed. He packed the towels, sheets, shoes, and clothes he planned to leave behind inside the coolers and stored them at the back of the cave, along with the pots, pans, fish rack, tarp, and assorted other gear.

Once everything was stacked, he did a final review.

"Well, it looks like I have done everything that I can do to help the next person who comes to the island." He felt satisfied. Strapping the latticed door to the entrance, he headed to the beach.

The trail was well worn from thousands and thousands of trips to and from. He felt a sense of loss, a sadness that he was leaving the place he had called home for so many years. It had served him well. But change was coming, and he would adapt.

With his senses heightened, he relished the touch of sand between his toes and the soft breeze floating in from the sea. The waves in the distance played their familiar song as moonlight dappled silver on the placid waters. He had no idea what lay ahead, but it did not matter. Life was for living, and he vowed to savor every moment.

Wandering under the starlit sky, thoughts weaved through moments spent with Angel. He recalled the days when she was unabashedly naked, to that final day, when she was so elegant in the simplicity of her dress. He remembered the lessons she taught him, the lilt of her voice, even the scent of her hair.

Before he knew it, he found himself at the edge of the lake. Light filtering through the trees glistened on the waters. He took off his clothes and walked into the cool liquid. It felt fresh upon his body and soothing to his soul. He considered the cave behind the falls, but it would be pitch black.

"Tomorrow I will show the kids the sanctuary behind the falls."

He knew in his heart that he was still seeking proof of her existence, hoping her footprints would be imprinted in the sand. He had been so sure when he was with her, but now, no matter what piece of evidence he seized, he could always find an avenue to explain it away.

But that was not the only thing. There was something else. A hint, or clue, something unrelated percolated just below the surface. The harder he tried to tease it out, the more elusive it became.

Returning to the beach, he noted a single light glowing in the darkness.

"Old school." Mark smiled, appreciative of the captain's attention to detail. On a deserted island in the middle of the Atlantic in a safe harbor, John knew the law says keep a bow light on at all times so traveling crafts are aware of your location. He liked John and Maria and felt fortunate to have met them.

He rowed out to the *Serafina*, tied off, and was greeted at the top of the gangway by Carson.

"Hey, girl, why don't you show me to my room?"

Chapter 23

Watching dawn's magical transformation, the sky was clear, the colors gorgeous, and the world full of promise.

Mark had slept better than expected. The gentle strains of the ship's light rocking and the patient familiarization of getting acquainted with the room pushed any lingering claustrophobia overboard. The unfamiliar mattress had a fresh scent of clean, the pillows were full and soft, and the curtains blocked out most of the external light.

What was going to take a little getting used to were the sounds. The steady drone of air-conditioning. The bilge coming on for a brief spat in the wee hours. The chimes on the hour for the night watchman. Mysterious pings, clicks, and whirls attributed to the never-sleeping mode of modern electronics. For most, this was relegated to background noise, filtered into nonexistence. But for someone who experienced nothing but pitch black and absolute silence for eight years . . .

All in all he felt rested and content with a sense of closure.

What will the new day bring?

"Good morning, Mr. Lambert. Can I get you some coffee?"

"Thank you, Maria. That would be wonderful."

He thought he was the first one up, but the perfect hostess was well ahead of him. She returned with the freshly brewed pot and poured him the first cup of the morning.

Savoring it, he recalled a question once posed by Angel. *How would you describe what coffee tastes like to someone who has never tried it?*

It was during a conversation about how sometimes you must experience something, for mere words cannot capture its essence. Pondering an answer, he stared across the transom at the map sitting on the easel. His thoughts sifted the pattern created by the pins. They did not feel random, but more strategic, as if they were part of the message.

"But what?" He had counted them at least a dozen times, but he counted them again. ". . . thirty-one, thirty-two, thirty-three."

"Dad?"

Dressed in black leggings and a gray pullover, Ally came through the sliders, delighted to see him.

"I heard you come aboard last night," she said, leaning in with a kiss.

"And here I thought I was so quiet."

Her presence made him happy, a contentment welded by a father's love for his daughter.

"Actually, it was Carson. She was waiting for you. The minute you boarded she left our room."

Thump, thump, thump. Hearing her name, Carson started whapping her tail on the deck.

Sipping his coffee, Mark saw a silver cross hanging around his daughter's neck, secured on a filigree chain. He had never seen it before. There was something about it that caused his eye to linger. *Is she religious?* But that was not it.

"Thirty-three pins!" he exclaimed, sending a jolt into the morning. Returning to the board, he counted the pins one more time. The tally remained unchanged.

"Jesus Christ was thirty-three when he died on the cross. The Cross of Calvary . . ."

In his excitement, his face tinged red, and his breathing became relegated to an afterthought.

"Are you all right?" Ally asked.

"All right? Yes, yes, I'm fine. Really, I'm fine. Only by the Cross of Calvary can one find the riches of heaven," he repeated.

He could see the pattern, imagining each pin as a bead of light creating a celestial crown. The face centered on the lake. "It has been staring at us the whole time."

His enthusiasm was contagious, and Ally was getting swept into it.

"What's been staring at us?" Dan asked, coming in on the tail end of the comment.

"Yeah, Dad. What is it that is staring at us?"

"I know where the treasure is." He swelled with a sense of pride, thinking he had achieved victory at solving their enigmatic puzzle, but also chastising himself that the truth was so blatantly in front of him. *Why had it taken so long?*

It was the bombshell encapsulating everything they wanted to hear. What they had come for and what had so far eluded them and their faces grew wide eyed and expressive. Ally embraced his words as gospel and acted as if ready to go and get it that very minute.

"Let's eat some breakfast first. Then we can grab some shovels and our bathing suits."

"Shovels and bathing suits?" Ally repeated, fidgeting.

Dan was not quite as quick to dive in. He looked at Mark with more than a hint of uncertainty. Taking a sip of coffee, he tried to mask his doubt.

"It's at the lake," Mark told them, an intuitive truth coursing through him like wildfire.

"I'm game." She shuffled, ignoring her husband's skepticism.

"It's been there for almost Three hundred years, so I don't think a few more hours will matter."

But this was akin to asking a child for patience on Christmas morning. With the holy grail within reach, Ally had become animated, bursting with excitement, and raring to go.

Mark was sure they were on the right track. And with that came a slew of questions that did not seem important a mere hour ago, concerns that until now he had ignored.

If we actually find the treasure, who has legitimate claims of ownership? What are the legalities?

He imagined Angel whispering a different point of view. 'If you find it, what is the right thing to do?' But the thrill of the hunt nudged aside the moral implications.

"Dan, do you know what country lays claim to this island?"

"It's nebulous at best," he said, implying he had done his homework. "It holds no strategic value. It sits too far from anywhere. As far as we can determine, no one has bothered to lay any claim."

"Interesting," Mark mused, rubbing his chin with a thumb and forefinger. He could not imagine any other place on Earth that someone hadn't laid claim to.

Ally returned to the prospect of finding the treasure, unconcerned about who might own the island. "Why the lake? I mean, other than the fact that there are no pins there."

Considering what to say, he found himself once again wondering at Ally's necklace.

Dan cleared his throat with impatience.

"On the very first page of Captain Fick's diary, she tells us where to look. 'Only by the Cross of Calvary can one find the riches of heaven.'"

Dan still seemed perplexed.

"There is a cave behind the waterfall," Mark explained, filling in the blanks for them. "A small room with rock walls and ceiling, but with a floor made of sand. Inside the room there is a cross that has been carefully carved into the stone."

A glean of intrigue could be seen flickering in their eyes.

"Dan, are you familiar with the story behind the crucifixion of Christ?"

"I'm Jewish," he deflected.

"So was Jesus," Mark teased with a good-natured smile. He hoped his son-in-law understood that as long as he loved his daughter, that was all that mattered to Mark.

"Calvary refers to the place where Jesus was crucified. *'Only by the Cross of Calvary . . .'* And recall that in the diary, most of what Hanri said she buried were exquisitely crafted religious artifacts. *'Can one find the riches of heaven.'*

"As soon as one opens the diary, she gives you the location of the treasure. One simply needs to know the island to see it." The flicker became a flame.

"Damn," Dan said, rubbing his hands together.

They paused while Maria set out plates of croissants, cheese, and meats. Mark had come to learn Ally didn't eat meat, but she had no issue feeding it to Carson.

"And . . . there's something you want to ask me?" Mark knew his daughter. As a child, she had formed a habit of biting her lower lip when she wanted to know something but was hesitant.

"I don't remember you ever being religious. I mean, Mom was, but . . . you?" she asked.

Kids never miss a thing, he realized, not expecting that question.

"No, I wasn't. At least not until I came here."

She fingered her cross, her lips pressed tight, the "you're not making sense" query.

"Someone had placed a Bible on the boat, and I took it. I guess if you study something long enough, the content will penetrate even the thickest of skulls." He chuckled. He saw the conversation was making Dan a little uncomfortable.

"I had a lot of time," he reminded her with a tone of finality.

"So what do you think, Dan?"

Suddenly all hell broke loose. Carson leaped to her feet, barking loudly. There was a large commotion, and the dog raced to the aft.

Mark saw immediately what was causing the uproar and let out a broad grin.

Captain Christakis stepped through the sliders. He must have heard all the ruckus. He smoothed his beard, and smile lines crinkled around his eyes.

"You know, it's a good omen when dolphins appear."

Flipper was cacking away as the others began putting on a show for them.

"Yes it is," Mark agreed.

Carson ran close to the water's edge with dolphins mirroring their trek along the beach, additional magic further fueling the aura of anticipation.

When it was time to turn into the jungle, Mark waved with a shout. "We will be back . . . wish us luck."

Ca-ca-ca-ca-ca-cack, sang the aquatic chorus.

In their own way, these marine friends had been part of what had kept loneliness at bay. He was going to miss them.

When he reached the glade, rainbows kissed the misty falls. Dragonflies buzzed the lake's surface, and the steady drone of falling water rounded out nature's symphony. With the sun warm on their faces, they shed their clothes.

Ally set her things on top of a basket of food she had brought. Carson's olfactory sense were already investigating what might be inside.

"Don't even think about it," Ally admonished, shaking her finger. Carson just wagged her tail.

The ship had been equipped for the mission with picks, shovels, wheeled dollies, and a range of other related gear. Today they had simply brought two shovels.

Entering the water, it occurred to him how easy it was to let distraction defer exercising. Normally, he would have started with laps until Angel stepped from the trees, disrobed, and joined him. He gazed up the slope with a longing. There was no Angel.

"Grab the shovel and follow me." The anticipation was palpable, and even Carson felt the current, running and barking as they entered the lake.

"You guys ready?" As they stood under the falls, their expressions said it all.

"As I explained, we submerge below the falls and come up on the other side. No worries, totally safe."

As he wiped the water from his eyes, two faces broke the surface next to him.

"This is so cool," Ally said. The translucent shimmer of filtered light added an illusion of movement to the lingering echoes of their voices.

As Dan and Ally eyed the cross, Mark examined the sand, looking for traces of Angel's footprints.

None.

Was there any evidence she ever existed?

"Here we are," he told them, letting it go. Every nerve in his body said this was the right place. What he had not resolved, though, was when they found the treasure, what should they do with it?

Please trust me with what I am going to tell you. You have a wonderful life ahead of you. You are going to be surprised at how the seeds of your past have blossomed in the most marvelous ways. I know you will harvest them with care and understanding.

"Is this the seeds from my past?" he asked, letting his thoughts keep her real.

"What?" Ally asked.

"If we are right, this should be the spot," he said, unmindful he had been thinking out loud again.

Driving the shovel below the cross, he moved the conversation in the direction of their objective. Dan joined, and together they began to dig. Ally stayed on top and helped push the detritus away from the edge.

The sand was compacted but manageable. With sweat on their brow, they dug and the hole got deeper to the point that the tossed soil began seeping back into the pit.

"Keep digging. I'm gonna help Ally and move the pile farther away from the edge," Mark explained.

After a while the atmosphere had grown solemn. Ally's hands had little cuts, and Dan's grimace showed he was reaching his wit's end.

"You guys want a break?" Mark asked, but neither of them were takers. By their body language, he was worried that the toil was crumbling away belief and adding to thoughts that maybe this was a wild-goose chase.

"Ally, could you go check on Carson for me?" He knew she would not go on her own volition.

When she had left, Dan stopped digging. He was covered in sand and glistened with sweat.

"I'm not so sure about this," he complained, confirming what Mark had discerned. The drudgery had all but extinguished his enthusiasm, and his son-in-law was reaching the end of his rope. Mark needed to bolster his confidence.

"Hanri's not going to make this easy," he encouraged. "But it's here. I can feel it."

Dan said nothing and they continued. Dig, toss, move, dig, toss, move, the sound blending into one as it resounded off the walls. Only the slow-moving ripples of light gave any measure of time.

When Ally returned, Dan stopped digging. Frustrated, he wiped his brow with a dirty arm and glared at his father-in-law. To punctuate the point that he had had enough, he jabbed the shovel into the ground.

Thunk!

"What the . . ." He thrust it again, this time a little harder. Thunk.

"Holy crap," Dan exclaimed with a renewed surge of optimism.

Mark jumped in with the second shovel. Ally stood looking from above.

"Wood!" Mark exclaimed.

Ally could not contain herself and climbed down into the hole. In tandem they worked, brushing, clearing, soon exposing thick brass strappings. The more they cleared, the more they revealed.

"It's huge," Ally said, her excitement bouncing off the walls.

Working different sides, they pushed away dirt until they found four edges of what they hoped was the buried treasure. It was not one massive box, but four individual chests wedged together. Each oversized, each massive, and each waiting to be opened.

"Let's separate this one from the rest," Mark said, tapping the near left.

They worked it a few inches at a time until Dan stopped, arching into his back ache. "Damn thing weighs a ton."

"You okay?" Ally asked, concerned by her husband's grimace. "You guys should take a break."

The two men burst out laughing.

Dan grabbed a shovel. "Watch out."

He smashed the blade down on the three-hundred-year-old lock. The wood splintered, breaking apart the rotted lid.

"Holy moly." Mark whistled under his breath. The glitter of so much gold dwarfed his wildest imagination. There were piles and piles of Spanish doubloons, gold bars, and cut ingots. The density made it impossible to dig down. The gold was too heavy, too abundant, and too tightly packed.

"That's a lot of gold," Dan marveled, leaning on the shovel.

"Let's open the next one and see what's inside," Ally implored impatiently.

He was as caught up in the euphoria as they were, like kids on Christmas morning, ready to tear the wrapping off the next package.

"Dan, whack the lock off." Ally gestured with breathy impatience. Again, a hard clang later and the rotting wood splintered. With a sweeping gesture, Dan affectionately bowed to his bride.

"The honor is all yours, my love."

Opening the decayed top, they saw there were no coins, but instead layers and layers of aged cloth. Ally unfolded a corner to reveal a series of crosses made of finely polished gold and encrusted with large green emeralds and red rubies. There was an exquisitely detailed Byzantine cross the size of her forearm that rested among meticulously crafted chalices portraying biblical moments in the life of Christ.

Ally methodically removed the wadding, revealing more indescribable artifacts.

Mark's mouth felt dry on the adrenaline rush of such a discovery. "This could be the greatest find of the twenty-first century," he exclaimed in a raised voice.

"The craftsmanship is incredible," Dan agreed, holding a chalice in the diffused sunlight.

"It's like some lost art," Ally added, awed by a jewel-studded cross she had lifted.

The fabricated pieces of gold and silver had intricate ornamentation and fine engravings that re-created three-dimensional scenes from stories in the Bible. The shifting light simply added to their elegance and beauty.

"These are priceless," Mark said in reverence. In total, there were 133 items, a collection every museum in the world would covet.

"Which one next?" Dan asked, shovel at the ready.

"The one on the left," Ally declared for them.

They took up positions to move it, but the combination of it being well wedged, heavily crusted from years of dirt, and their overall fatigue from the dissipation of an adrenaline high took its toll.

"Let's take a break and get something to eat," Mark suggested to a willing audience.

Carson was a polite beggar. Her expressions of longing and the pleading in her eyes were impossible to resist.

"Here—finish it," Mark said, letting her devour the remains of his sandwich. Mission accomplished, she moved on to Dan.

"Have you given any consideration to what you will do with all this treasure? It could be worth hundreds of millions of dollars, maybe more," Mark said, stretching out the muscles of his back. The morning's toil reminded him of his age.

"Yes," Ally said, wiping an errant crumb from her mouth. "We're giving half of it to you."

"What?" It was an incredibly generous offer, and normally he would jump all over it, but in actuality it presented him with an opening he directed at Dan. "Can I ask you a personal question?"

"Sure," he shrugged.

"About money?" He had avoided the topic of his son-in-law's apparent wealth since meeting him, mostly because it was easy to arrive at preconceived judgments about a person based on wealth, prestige, and even how they made their living. He wanted to have a view of his son-in-law free of prejudice and based on observation. So far, he approved and was proud that Dan was now part of his family.

"What do you want to know?" Dan asked with a hint of caution.

"You said you studied botany, but the yacht . . . that must be costing you a pretty penny." He wondered how direct he should be. "If I may ask, what do you do for a living?"

Dan rubbed the lobe of his ear and smiled.

"Whatever I want." The comment was a tease, of course, but it said a lot.

"Dan has made tens of millions of dollars trading crypto," Ally interjected. "He got in way ahead of the crowd."

"Crypto?" Mark was unfamiliar with the term.

"Bitcoin," Dan clarified. "I got in around two hundred."

"Two hundred?" Mark wasn't sure he had heard him right.

"Do you know what Bitcoin is?"

Mark could see by his look Dan was calculating how long he had been on the island and trying to calendar the data.

"Yes." Mark smiled. "It's just that you said you got in at two hundred dollars. So if you made a killing, I was wondering, what's it worth today?"

"About sixty-five thousand dollars, give or take." Dan's answer had a hint of pride.

Mark considered the vast sums while continuing his questions. "So if money is not an issue, what do you guys think should be done with the treasure?"

"One thing for sure, we tell no one until we figure it all out," Dan responded emphatically. Ally's nod concurred with her husband.

"And the Christakis's?"

"We offered them a hefty bonus if we are successful."

"And had them sign a nondisclosure agreement," Ally reminded him.

"I see."

It was all he could think to say as his mind ran through the gamut of potential issues. How best to maintain secrecy, where to store the treasure, who to trust, which governments would want a piece. A thousand other thoughts came, got mulled over, and then made room for the next wave.

As they finished eating, while pondering what to do with the treasure, he stood and looked at the waterfall. For the millionth time his thoughts shifted to wondering where the water originated. The grotto was ancient and the flow abundant.

There has to be a massive underground reservoir. This he could understand. *But what forces are pushing it out with such consistency and volume?*

"One more piece of the island's magic," he quietly marveled as he considered all the unique attributes this enchanted place had offered.

Ally came alongside him. He pulled her close.

"We have hundreds of bins," Ally informed, transitioning the mood. "We can remove the items from the cave and carefully pack everything up. No need to decide anything else at this point."

She was right, of course. It was a logical decision. The last few weeks had given Mark plenty of time to see a broad array of his daughter's personality. Like her mother, her Gemini nature was contradicted by many sides of the same person.

The no-nonsense, methodical approach to reasoning she had gotten from him and the whimsical, emotional exuberance she often displayed in her carefree mode, like her mother. Though seemingly a dichotomy, it was the tapestry of who she was.

His body was tired, and as she said, they did not need to do it all today. Considering what they had already found and anticipating what lay unopened, Mark made a suggestion. Even a hint at a challenge. "Let's leave the two remaining chests until tomorrow and let our imagination percolate overnight at what the balance will unfold. The one who comes closest to describing what is inside the two other chests gets to choose any item they want as their own."

Ally immediately agreed, always one for a challenge.

Dan simply shrugged. "Sure."

It was the catalyst he used to call it quits. Tomorrow was just fine.

Chapter 24

Returning to the boat, Dan and Ally retired to their room. Mark, on the other hand, retrieved his phone and went to see if he could get it connected to Wi-Fi. He found Captain Christakis reading a book in the small private salon. The reclining leather chair he was in was worn and cracked and covered with brown duct tape. Mark assumed it held a special place for the man. Perhaps the piece was an old friend that was hard to let go, which was sort of how he felt about his cave.

"Afternoon, John."

"Hello, Mark." The captain rested the book on his lap. "It looks like you guys had some success today."

Mark raised a questioning brow.

"It was the pep in their step," he said with a grin. "I know victory when I see it."

"You are a very observant man, Captain. Tomorrow we will begin retrieving one of the greatest treasures ever found."

"Wow," he said with genuine surprise. "An appraisal like that coming from you . . . it must be something!" Shifting back to his role as the accommodating host, he advised, "Let us know how we can help."

"Actually, I was hoping for a password so I can access the internet."

He looked at the phone in Mark's hand, and his eyes furrowed with doubt.

"I'm sure it has long been disconnected," Mark explained. "But I think the apps just need access to the internet."

"Hmm, you might be right. But as far as email and texts, those won't work without an active account. But the password is Gstakis@1." He spelled it out for him.

"Thank you."

"No problem." The captain returned to his book, and Mark went out to the back deck. The sun's dying rays evidenced the onset of evening. While looking at the western sky, Maria appeared with a cold drink and a smile.

"John is a lucky man."

"Yes he is," she chuckled.

Accessing the internet, he connected with the outside world for the first time in over eight years.

"Another step on the road back to reality." He sighed.

With his stock tracker the most prominent app, it triggered his last conversation with Rachael. She had chided him about his investing strategies, complaining he was putting their money into risky investments such as fruit companies and river conglomerates.

"She owns it all, but I wonder . . . how'd I do?" Opening the app gave him quite a shock. "Dang! Bet she's not complaining now."

He felt a warm gush of accomplishment. His investments in Apple and Amazon had risen so much that she would be a millionaire many times over if she had held on to the stocks.

Winning always felt good. But that was not the reason he had gotten the password. It was something the day's conversations had wrought. Something that was far more important, but something that could spell opportunity or peril.

Most of his life he had used the same username and password. After he plugged in the right information, the digital domain responded, and the app opened as if he had used it just yesterday.

"Holy fu— . . . smokes," he corrected. Waves of disbelief, winds of hope, and every possible emotion in the book washed over him. With wobbly fingers he performed a simple transaction.

And in that moment he recalled Angel's parting comment.

You are going to be very surprised at how the seeds of your past have blossomed in the most marvelous ways.

"Is this for real?" Staring at the screen, he wondered aloud at the impossibility looking back at him.

"Is what real?" Dan asked. With a glass of wine in each hand, he was dressed in shorts, a faded blue tee, and sandals.

Mark closed the panel. "Amazon and Apple . . . I bought stock in these companies years ago and now . . ."

"They are trillion-dollar companies," Dan said, completing what he assumed was Mark's unended sentence. His expression bore a hint of approval at his father-in-law's investing prowess.

Mark pushed that train of conversation. "Even though it belongs to Rachael now, it feels good to have picked a couple of winners."

Mark eased back into his chair, relaxing the muscles in his neck as he put the phone in his pocket.

"From what I know, it seems she held on to it," Dan said in a passing tone.

Ally came through the sliding door carrying an opaque bin with a split-hinged top. Carson was right behind her. She set the empty container on the deck and pulled up a chair. Dan handed her the chardonnay.

"Gracias, mi amor." They clinked their glasses.

Dan saw Mark eyeing the bin.

"We have a dolly and two four-wheeled pull carts. The bins are fitted to hold in place."

"Good thinking." It was all he could do to stay present. The app on his phone called him like a siren's song. *Steady on,* he told himself to no effect. Instead, he repeated his mantra quietly in his head until calm once again reigned.

Letting out a long, slow breath, he shifted the discussion to some of the problems they would face tomorrow. "We're going to have to swim the treasure out of the cave, and there is a lot of it," he began. "Especially the doubloons? The water won't hurt anything. But the gold coins will need to be broken up into transportable units."

Ally set her glass on the table and tucked loose strands of hair behind one ear. "I have a box of oversized freezer bags I use for dirty clothes when I travel. We could use these for the coins," she offered.

"That should work," Mark said with a wink. "Did you guys come up with any ideas of what might be in the other chests?"

Dan seemed indifferent or didn't really care. Ally, on the other hand, was being cagey. He knew she was taking the contest seriously. It was the competitive streak he had witnessed early on when his daughter played soccer. She always had a "the point is to win" philosophy.

But Mark was feeling confident based on his series of deductions. He assembled the known data, which in this case were the few lines written in the diary and Hanri Fick's comments about blood money. But it was the reversed Zs noted on the pages where she had described the treasure that led to the foundation of his answer.

Outside left. Outside right. Inside left. Inside right . . . instinctively he knew he was correct. She had laid the chests least to best.

"Remember," he reminded, trying to give them a fair chance. "She gave most of the coinage to her crew and only took a portion for herself, so I personally don't think there will be more doubloons."

He held back that the cavern she chose had the spiritual presence of God anchored by the Cross of Calvary. So she would have chosen the absolute best pieces and placed them there in her sanctuary.

"I believe the best is yet to come," he concluded. "Logically we removed the chest on the left, which I believe is of the least value. Then we naturally progressed to the right chest. Its contents are beautiful, but not the premier pieces in the collection."

"Tomorrow we will open the chest on the back left first, and if I am right, expect to be stunned. But . . ."

He had captured their imaginations. They were attentive, expectant, and eager for what magicians call the great reveal. Of course, all of this was merely conjecture, but he was glad they were humoring him.

He had always loved to tell stories, spin tales, and let his imagination run wild. He often said to his wife, "I don't exaggerate, I think big." She would often correct his telling's with "Never let facts get in the way of a good story." So he put the final tassel on their imagination.

"The chest on the right will be the pièce de résistance. Her favorite items. The most priceless and precious. Her offerings to God. Here is where I expect I will select my prize."

He finished with a showman's flourish, full of confidence, having painted an expectation upon their imagination that was larger than life.

"You seem pretty sure of yourself, Dad," Ally said, giddy at the prospects.

"Yep." He smiled.

Mark was up early, his head swimming through things that before yesterday had been nonexistent. The lesser concern being the right thing to do with the treasure. *Who is the rightful owner?*

Two factors weighed on his thoughts. One was that the kids were already well off, so cashing in was not critical, and the second, he could not dismiss Hanri's wishes. The treasure should never be returned to those who had enslaved indigenous people for the sake of gold.

What the church doesn't know the church doesn't know.

"Morning, Dad," Ally greeted, interrupting his reverie. "How'd you sleep?"

She was wearing a robe, but underneath she had on her suit and was ready to roll. He deflected the sleep question by glancing at Carson and rolling his eyes, casting false blame to mitigate questions about the dark circles under his eyes.

"She's a bed hog." Ally nodded. "But she's your bed hog." There was a note of transfer in that statement, a final clarification.

"Are you sure?" He had not meant his eye roll to create the current topic. But he was happy it had. Ally almost spit out her coffee, stifling a laugh.

"Really? No way she's letting me come between the two of you."

Carson sensed she was the object of discussion and came over to lie at Mark's feet, sealing the covenant.

"Morning, guys." Dan took a seat as Maria arrived and served a continental breakfast, adding a bowl of Greek yogurt for Ally.

Over the top of his mug, Mark watched Captain Christakis bring the motorized tender alongside the gangway. He had already set a substantial portion of equipment on the lower dock.

They finished their breakfast and loaded the gear into the boat. Dan and the captain drove the tender to the spot where the path entered the forest. Ally, Mark, and Carson followed in the Zodiac. Today was going to be a workday.

Once the gear was on the sand, the captain reminded them, "Bring the full containers back to this spot. Once they are all gathered, we can load them onto the *Serafina*." He continued in a conspiratorial voice, "I made ample storage in the engine room away from prying eyes and curious customs inspectors."

Smart, Mark thought. Whatever they decided to do should not be dictated by greedy bureaucrats.

"Bonne chance," he told them. Dan and Mark pushed the boat off the beach and watched as he turned back toward the yacht.

"Let's place the empties in the wagons and see how they fare on the trail," Mark suggested. Ally had the plastic zip bags and tossed them into one of the bins.

There were two wagons. Ally followed, and Carson, being the most impatient, took lead. She knew exactly where they were going and wasted no time getting there.

Fortune smiled on them. The softly inflated wheels traversed the ground without problem. Mark knew they would need to watch the weight, but time was on their side, so they could allow for fewer boxes and more trips. They parked the gear next to the lake.

"Shall we?" Mark said, removing his shirt. Curiosity was king. But before anyone entered the water, Mark marshaled their desire by using discovery as the carrot to get some of the stuff moved out of the way.

"Guys, before we open the other two trunks, let's move the coins and chalices to the beach. This will give us more room to work, and we need to do it anyway."

Their faces sagged. Intellectually, he could see they knew he was right, but he also knew anticipation had been building all night.

He grinned. "How about a compromise? We leave the chest of coins, but we move the big pieces out and set them here by the water's edge."

Détente was achieved. He let them settle on the outcome that he had basically wanted.

Negotiation 101—aim higher than desire.

Piece by piece, the works were taken from the cave, brought under the falls, and arrayed by the lake. The sunlight refracted rainbows of color from the large rubies, emeralds, sapphires, and opals.

"The men who created these masterpieces must have gathered the best stones that the continent had to offer." The awe in Mark's voice was amplified by the dancing facets of light playing off the stones.

"Yes, but let's not forget," Ally reminded him. "Most of those men were cruel and treated the local people as if they were animals."

She was right, of course, but he could not fault the beauty and artistry they had achieved.

It took hours, but aside from the chest of gold, every piece had been moved to the beach. He could tell the kids were ready, their patience now boiling.

"Okay, let's memorialize this with a picture."

Mark held his phone and took photos of Dan, Ally, and Carson standing behind their trophies. For him, this moment marked the end of his time on the island. For them, it was the conclusion to the greatest adventure they would ever undertake.

"Before we reveal the balance, let's recap our opinions." Mark enjoyed drawing out the suspense a bit longer. "Ally says the boxes will contain more chalices . . ."

"And crosses," she added.

"Right. And Dan said more doubloons." His nod was perfunctory.

"And I said the box on the left would be more amazing then either of the two we have opened so far. And the box on the right will surpass everything else. Does anyone want to add or change their thoughts? Last chance."

They were not being ambivalent. It was just that there were so many priceless artifacts to choose from that being first, second, or third to pick seemed inconsequential. They swam under the falls and climbed down into the pit.

"Okay, Dan, let's move this one away from the other."

Anticipation collided with reality when the chest did not cooperate. It would not budge, and as if by design, the clasps were facing each other and inaccessible.

"Push," Mark called out. Ally scraped away the dirt in front of the chest. "Again . . ."

This went on and on until the forward end was free enough that they could reach the latch.

"Phew . . ." Mark exhaled, coated in sweat. He handed Dan the shovel.

Thwack. Splintered wood revealed another pile of deteriorating cloth. Ally removed the fabric.

"Figurines," she said. "Large statues, maybe platinum."

Mark reached in to remove one. It was so heavy he needed both hands.

It was an angel. A male whose wings reached from above his head down to his feet. The details were so finely etched that the statue radiated supernatural power.

"This is the Archangel Michael," he said, getting a little help from the name *Miguel* engraved on the bottom.

The next piece was scaled the same, two feet tall, solid, maybe thirty to thirty-five pounds. It was another angel, but his appearance was entirely different.

"Gabriel," he read.

One by one they removed one sculpted angel after another. Though each name was carved into the base, Mark had seen many of these before, when Rachael would drag him to various museums.

Gabriel, Michael, Raphael, Uriel, Azrael, Phanuel, Camael . . . they resembled depictions from the sixteenth century masters whose paintings resided in the world's greatest museums.

All told there were seventy-two statues to match the seventy-two angels listed in scripture. All were made of platinum. All were of the finest artistry he had ever seen. And all were different. The sizes varied, and Mark assumed they dovetailed into a biblical hierarchy, something he kind of knew from his reading of scripture.

"Okay, Dad—you win," Ally said, glistening with perspiration. They were all coated by the exertion, but it was a labor of love.

"Let's take a quick dip, see if we can carry these to the beach. I want to check on Carson." He didn't wait for an answer. Instead, he grabbed Michael and plunged under the water. Swimming with thirty-plus pounds was difficult. Fortunately for most of the way he was able to touch bottom. The two youngsters followed, and in minutes three of the statues sat upon the sand. Ally started back to the falls.

"Coming, Dad?"

"Gotta go, girl. Sorry." Carson sat, looking at him with her brown pools of longing for him to just play. Back inside the cave, Dan was standing with a shovel in hand, waiting and eager.

"Go for it," Mark told them.

Clang. Nothing. Clang—clang—clang.

This chest proved defiant. He tried again and then again, and once more. Snap. Instead of the wood, it was the lock, iron brittle with age that broke

Dan removed the broken U-bolt, then turned to Mark and with a roll of his hands offered . . . "I believe the honor is yours."

Mark took in a deep breath and let it all out. His heart raced with the adrenaline of expectation. Ally's eyes sparkled in anticipation.

The lid was much heavier than the others. This chest was made of metal, not wood. With hundreds of years of dirt caking the top, no one had noticed until now.

"Hanri Fick closed it back in 1732." Mark paused. We are the first ones to look at whatever she found as her masterpiece. Here goes." Lifting the lid took both arms, and the initial impressions were less than desired. Unlike the other three, this chest felt almost empty. Actually, that wasn't the right description. It simply contained two items.

But as the expectation of bedazzlement adjusted to the light of what lay before them, the theory he had construed became validated a hundredfold.

The bottom of the rusted chest housed a massive Bible made of gold. Its cover was so phenomenally detailed, mere words could not capture its essence. Unabashed in his staring, he relaxed his shoulders as he took in a series of deep breaths. Shaking off the awe, Mark tried to remove it from the chest.

"Dan, help me get this out."

They struggled but ultimately were able to remove it and place it on one of the other chests.

"Magnificent." Mark traced his fingers over the top. Marveling at the detail, each page was a sheet of exquisitely fabricated gold so thin as to be flexible, but strong as metal. And enduring forever. It was ornated with pictures so exquisite that it seemed to be a work of angels. Rare stones were used to form mosaics, and the results were beyond lifelike. It was truly a lost wonder of the ancient world.

"It's like the Book of Kells," he admired.

"Like what?" Ally's gaze darted from him to the artifact.

"The Book of Kells. It is the most important icon in all of Ireland," he explained. This was without a doubt the most magnificent item of the entire lot.

"The Book of Kells was created in either Ireland or Scotland around AD 800," Dan cited. Proving a bit of a history buff, he added some texture for Ally's benefit. "It is a masterwork of calligraphy and illumination. The manuscript takes its name from the Abbey of Kells north of Dublin, now housed at Trinity College."

Mark once saw it before heading to the Temple Bar for drinks with colleagues. But it did not compare to this.

Though the pages were written in Spanish, Mark was still able to recognize books that were not part of today's Bible. Two in particular had caught his attention: the Lost Books of Eden and the Book of Enoch.

While he was examining the work, Ally looked into the chest to see what else it contained.

"Dan, can I get a hand?" Ally asked.

Mark watched as they removed a large female figurine. But this one did not have a set of wings like those of the angels.

"Look, Dad," she said, resting it on the edge of the chest. Dan tilted the statuette to read the engraving on the bottom.

"My Spanish is a little rusty, but I believe the translation goes like this. *'I am Wisdom. The Lord brought me forth as the first of his works, before his deeds of old . . .'*"

Mark's mouth fell open, but nothing came out. Tongue tied, he tried to unscramble the thoughts that rushed at him.

"May I?"

Dan turned the statuette. Mark used his fingers to trace the face, her hair, and even the dress she wore. He could not take his eyes from the figurine. It reminded him of Angel.

Choked up, he became transfixed.

"Dad," Ally said softly.

"I'm sorry. It's just that she seems so familiar. Like someone I knew long ago."

He realized he wasn't being fair to them, so he added some kernels of truth without breaking his own vow.

"When I first started eating the hallucinogenic nut, I had an encounter with a beautiful woman who called herself Angel. Even through the drug-induced haze, I knew this was not real—but when you are as lonely as I was, you don't look a gift horse in the mouth."

"What I cannot fathom is why she would look like this statue. It has to be at least Three hundred years old . . ."

As his brain worked for an explanation, he mumbled possibilities. "Perhaps the Goddess Wisdom is an archetype described in the Bible or some other ancient manuscript. I really have no explanation."

"Of course Wisdom would be a woman," Ally said with a touch of levity.

Dan rolled his eyes, and Mark put a bear hug around his oldest child. Unknown to them, he was shielding the tears in his eyes and letting them mingle with her wet hair.

"Well—let's put her here so she can watch us work," Dan said, closing the lid and setting Wisdom on the chest.

She watched as piece by piece they moved the items to the beach. Carson came by, gave the items a cursory sniff, then went back to the edge of the bushes to do what he remembered she loved so much—hunting for lizards.

It took them three days to extract everything from the cave and move it to the beach. Each bin had been carefully packed and placed on the trolley and taken two at a time up the trail and down the trail. Over and over and over this was repeated until all two hundred and ten boxes had been safely tucked aboard the *Serafina*.

The Bible, its pages made of thin sheets of gold, its pictures created by an inlay of precious stones, and whose weight was considerable, had been the most difficult to retrieve. The water was not an issue as far as the relic was concerned. It was just that it was so large and heavy it took all three working together to get it back to the boat.

A full inventory had been logged and photographed. The repetition of oohs and ahhhs from each of them, including the Christakis's, had the hallmarks of a heavenly choir. There was still no decision on what they would do with the treasure, but Dan made it a point to assure John and Maria that they would never need to work again unless they wanted to.

The one thing they had all agreed upon was that the Bible was too special to hide from the world. It would not become part of someone's private collection, but instead a home would be procured in a proper museum, where it would reside on loan.

Mark knew his time on the island was coming to its end. The only thing left to do was to remove the Goddess of Wisdom from her perch inside the cave.

"Have you decided?" Captain Christakis asked him. He had come to learn of their wager and understood at least some of the drama around the statuette still in the cave.

Both he and Maria had accepted the invitation to enter the hidden sanctuary. Of course, Mark had enlisted them into the recovery efforts and had no doubts that they relished every minute of their part in the greatest discovery of the twenty-first century.

"I have," he said. His tone was as firm as his decision.

Dan and Ally stopped what they were doing, intent on the conversation.

"If it is all right with you guys, I would like to choose her as my pick." There was no question who "her" was.

"Also, if you won't mind, I do not want to keep her. She belongs here, on this Island of Redemption. I would like to place her back in the chest and rebury her in the sanctuary. That place has a special significance to me." Though his voice was resolute, it held a hint of sadness.

"I am going to return and place the empty chests back into the ground. I will fill the holes and rake the sand. It will be as if we were never there. I would not want to leave the cave looking desecrated."

No one said a thing. Mark heard the waves crashing against the oceanside reef. The sound was ever present and would go on long after he was gone.

He knew what needed to be done, now and when he returned to civilization. Putting Angel away from a prying world was his gift to her. Thanks for everything she had done. No matter the archetype, for him she would always be special, his friend and teacher. Wisdom indeed.

Everything had been packed up and the boat made ready for departure the following morning. Mark went alone to the cave. It was the last day he would ever be on the island.

He took his phone, his Bible, a watertight bag, and a rake. He walked the beach alone. No dolphins, no daughter, no Carson, just him and his thoughts. Reaching the glade, he removed his shirt. Safely securing his Bible and phone into the watertight bag, he swam under the falls and emerged one last time in Captain Fick's sanctuary.

"Hello, old friend," he said to the inanimate object sitting upon the chest. "I will be leaving soon but wanted to get your photo."

He smiled, recalling the last time he tried to take her picture. But he now understood the why of her displeasure. He was sure she would not mind this photo. He opened his camera and took three photos—front, back, and a selfie.

Long ago he had followed her suggestion to read Proverbs 8—it captured her essence so well he now knew it by heart.

With the cross above his head and his back to the wall, he read the entire passage aloud.

"Does not wisdom call out? Does not understanding raise her voice . . ."

It was a lengthy stanza, but when he came to an end, he closed the book, both physically and metaphorically, and stood before the cross.

"I now understand," he said with reverence, as if talking to the Lord. "Christian faith is not about one getting a second chance. It is an entirely new birth offering a sense of peace for the living.

"Thank you, God, for giving me Wisdom. She saved me. But you know this. You always knew this."

He felt a resurgence of optimism, of hope and purpose. He placed each trunk back into the earth. He set the Goddess of Wisdom upright inside of one and placed his Bible next to her.

"Thank you, Angel."

Placing two fingers at the spot on his heart where she had laid her hand before her departure, he spoke to her. "I know you will always be right here, and I am never alone." Then with a soft chuckle, he added, "If I am still here, then He is not done with me yet."

The next few hours were a blur as he filled the holes and raked the sand, leaving it the way he had found it so long ago.

"I hope I am able to honor you with what we have found."

His words were for both Angel, his goddess of wisdom, and to Hanri Fick, the enigmatic pirate who was so far ahead of her time.

Returning to the beach, the waters were turquoise and tranquil. He stripped off all his clothes, and with only the rake and shovel, he plunged into the surf. He took the tools out as far as he could and let them sink to the bottom, symbolically cleansing him of their desecration of the sanctuary hiding behind the falls.

There were no dolphins and thus no cavalry to protect him from the sharks. But he knew he was not done yet.

God had given him a great responsibility, and Mark intended to honor all the planning that had been undertaken. He was not sure if it was the cool waters that fused him with rejuvenation or the path before him that he was now excited to undertake. But he felt primed and ready. Excitement of the prospect coursed through his veins.

It truly was time for him to leave the island.

Chapter 25

The Christakis's were now part of their conspiratorial family, a crew of equals. Maria had made a banquet to celebrate their leaving. And once again she had outdone herself. The food was heavenly, the companionship relaxed, and the anticipation of departure welcomed by all.

The following morning, sounds of parting reverberated throughout the boat. As dawn's light stained the morning, the captain was performing his final routine before weighing anchor—double-checking that the tender and raft were strapped tightly, that loose equipment had been properly stowed, and that everything was put away and the cupboards latched. They would be entering the open sea in less than an hour.

"Can I help?" Mark offered.

"Thanks, but I got it from here."

Mark interpreted this as, "It is quicker if I do it myself."

He thought of his friend Grillo, who played in a band back in Boca. At the end of the show he had asked his buddy if he could help break down the equipment, and he had been told pretty much the same thing: "It's easier and faster if I simply do it myself."

Are the guys in Preservation Road still performing together?

Live music was one of the things he looked forward to when he got back to civilization. Of course, the question of where he would live, Boca Raton or somewhere else, loomed ever larger.

"Aye, aye, Captain." Mark smiled with a salute.

The rumbling of the electric winch raising the anchor mingled with the sounds of the twin diesels. The captain expertly guided the *Serafina* into the channel and aimed for the open sea. Ally joined her father at the stern.

"Look." She pointed. Carson started barking as the pod of dolphins raced alongside the yacht.

"Goodbye, my friends," Mark called out, offering a final wave.

"Thank you for taking care of my dad," Ally shouted above the din.

Carson's barking threatened to drown out the other voices.

Dan put his arm around Ally and looked at Carson. "What she said . . ."

It was the portrait of a happy family. He considered Rachael and his other two children. He had asked the captain to let him know when the satcom was working, as he was eager to reconnect with his family.

As the island fell behind them, the kids gave Mark space to let his thoughts find closure.

"Goodbye, my Angel," he mouthed, wiping a single tear from his eye.

Being back out on the blue conjured up a slew of memories. His efforts to snag the reef, his achievement of stripping *Lil Darling* of all her valuables, and his early forays into making his place habitable. But there were few recollections of the first five years of survival. It was as if they were not worth repeating as his mind skipped forward to his first encounter with Angel.

He recalled Angel telling him that God needed that time to remove all the envious thoughts and judgments. The petty jealousies and anxieties. The lusting and resentments. The baggage that had so ingrained itself into his life that it had to be unpacked at its own pace before he could be reborn.

Eventually the island sank below the horizon. The boat plowed through the same ocean that had felt like a death trap eight years ago. He let it go. All of it. Time to turn the page to a new chapter in the book of Mark Lambert.

The trip back was expected to take ten days. The seas were calm, and the winds were gentle. The return was the antithesis of his initial voyage.

"Déjà vu all over again."

Leaning on the rail reminded him of all the times he and Davey had taken their boat from Miami to Bimini. Without exception, if one direction was calm, then the other was rough. The ocean had an uncanny knack for confounding sailors.

As typical on long voyages, everyone fell into boat rhythm. Quiet time, reflection, anticipation, introspection, meals punctuated the routines as well as each person's required time at the helm. With all five of them working as crew, it was two hours on, eight hours off.

Mark spent a fair amount of time using the shipboard computer to surf the internet. He had considered reaching out to Rachael by email but felt it would be too impersonal. How do you put everything that had happened and all that he was feeling into a mere text? He decided a phone call was the best way and managed his impatience accordingly.

He was acclimating himself to the world he had been absent from for so long. What he found was depressing—nothing had really changed. Fear-filled hate still flourished, and discord was the hallmark of most of the news sources, the world still distracted by one crisis after another.

With a world now lensed through God, will it shape what I see?

Probably, he decided.

He knew there were a multitude of things that needed unraveling, things such as what to do with the treasure. Should he trust his kids with his earth-shattering secret? Then there were the little things to resolve. When do I call my other children? Where will I live? When we land, do I get a hotel? Will it allow dogs?

He had learned in business that a shotgun approach to most things almost always ended in failure, so he focused his priorities on just one thing—the treasure.

Exploring a number of concepts, he landed on a website for the Boutique Bank of Barbados, which sparked an idea, and then a number of pieces began to fall into place.

"Bancroft Saint Elmo Gordon, that's the guy!"

With the routine established, they gathered for their evening meal. The stars above were spectacular as the nebula of the Milky Way glimmered with the glory of God.

Over the last two days they had kicked around what to do with the treasure. Ally kept dancing around the subject of him needing money, but he had been able to mostly sidestep the issue. He knew she meant well.

Dan had investigated the value of the twenty thousand doubloons they had cataloged. He used his research as a lead-in to making sure his father-in-law would never have any financial worries and would be set for life.

"Other than the ingots, the coins are all Spanish escudos minted in the early seventeen hundreds under the authority of Spain. I checked with a number of rare coin sites, and prices range from forty-five hundred to fifty-five hundred dollars each. About $100 million, give or take."

Mark let out a low whistle. "That's a lot of money."

They had discussed keeping the coins for themselves, kind of like a finders-keepers reward. He really didn't care, being more focused on guiding them into the idea that the balance of the collection should be given to the world to see, or at least put on loan.

"It is more than any of us will ever need," his son-in-law finished with a raised eyebrow.

Mark saw it for what it was, a subtle dance. Dan wanted to firm up an agreement. Do they keep all the coins, which he supposed was the end game? How do they divide them up? What are the rules of dispersal and secrecy? He could see from the expectant look in Ally's eyes that she was all in with her husband.

"I have no objection," he said with a grin. Those four words released the tension that had been building over the treasure.

Mark then threw in a curve ball. "Subject to one condition."

"One condition?" Ally asked, her brows knitting together.

"Yep," he said, the showman in him finding fertile ground. He paused to let the anticipation reach a crescendo.

"I don't want any of it. None. This was your adventure. You risked the trip, and finding me—well, that more than compensates for any help I may have offered."

"None?" Ally's words were full of disbelief, as if maybe he had forgotten that money was the substance of survival in the real world.

"Are you sure?"

"My favorite child. Trust me. You need not worry." But he could see her mind churning and a pout turn into a frown.

"Don't fret about your mother. I have no intentions of bothering her or bringing up the past. Rivers and orchards, indeed," he added with a belly laugh.

"What?"

"It's a joke," he dismissed with a grin.

Dan smiled covertly.

He had weighed whether he should share his big secret, recalling a timeless word of wisdom: *The best way to assure three people keep a secret is for two of them to be dead.*

In the end, he had asked the Christakis's if he and his family could dine in private. Tonight he would share his burden.

"Ally, Dan, I have something very serious I need to share with you. Deadly serious."

He emphasized the word *deadly* so there would be no mistaking he was not kidding. A frost dusted the discussion of doubloons.

"Both of you must swear that under no condition, and for no reason whatsoever, that you will ever tell a soul about what I am about to share with you."

"Say it." Mark emphasized, a way for them to remember their vow.

In unison they both swore to keep whatever this was a secret no matter what.

He pulled out his phone. The glass reflected the mixture of fear and curiosity on Ally's face.

"I am not kidding about this. My life will be one big, never-ending hassle if anyone ever finds out."

No one spoke. No one knew what was coming, and he could see their brains churning through worst-case scenarios. He opened his phone, brought up an image, and handed it to Dan, knowing his millionaire son-in-law would appreciate it most.

Dan stared, his eyes growing wide. His lips began to calculate, but no words came out. Mark could see him scrolling, verifying, accepting what was unacceptable, believing what was unbelievable. With shaking hands he handed the screen to Ally.

"You're not kidding . . . right?" Dan asked, letting his voice fall off. Mark watched as he mumbled over and over. He was either saying *six cents* or *sixth sense*. He had to stifle a laugh. After all, there was a kernel of truth in both.

Ally looked at the screen and then at her dad. Then back at the screen. She smiled. He knew another layer had been added to his superhero veneer.

"Okay, then," she said, trying to cover the slight quiver. "No gold for you."

Both lifted their glasses of wine. By his expression, it seemed Dan was still grappling with the information when Maria arrived and served them dinner.

As they dug into their meal, the evening breeze carried the tension away so that the stars could twinkle unfettered and without worry.

Pushing back his empty plate, Mark returned the conversation to how they should handle the balance of the island treasure, minus the coinage, of course.

"Let's recap," he began in a professorial tone. "We have discussed taking the bulk of the treasure and putting it into one or more of the great museums to make it available for all to see. The questions come down to who owns it, in what institution do we place it, and for how long?"

"I have watched you spend hours glued to the computer screen, so I assume you have an idea?" Ally had a know-it-all grin that she must have learned from her mother.

Dan nursed his drink, choosing the noble art of silence.

"As a matter of fact, I do," Mark admitted. Their relationships had fallen into a comfortable state. No parent-child awkwardness or in-law hesitations. Mark attributed it in part to their time in close quarters—and also to the adventure they had shared together. Whatever it was, he knew they would remain close no matter what the future would bring.

"I suggest we form a nonprofit and base it in Barbados. This will keep us away from the tentacles of Uncle Sam and others who will want to try to challenge the treasure's ownership."

"The nonprofit foundation will be the owners of everything, decimating claims from even the most ardent taxing authorities. And we will remain the sole trustees of the foundation. We will determine what part or parts of the assets are given on loan to what worldly institutions and under what conditions."

"When we are ready, we should approach that museum on the Upper East Side," Mark suggested.

"The Met," Ally clarified.

This roused Dan's attention. "New York's Metropolitan Museum of Art has a great Egyptian wing," he said fondly.

Having always been fascinated by the pyramids and all things Egypt, Mark liked that his son-in-law shared one of his interests. "Right, I suggest that we show them photos of . . ."

"The Golden Bible," Ally suggested, completing her father's sentence.

He was drawing them into the bigger idea. "Perfect. Once their appetite is whetted, we offer to fund a new wing dedicated exclusively to our collection *Female Pirates of the Caribbean*." He chuckled.

He knew the name played on a famous attraction, but his idea was quite different, and it was more aligned with the idea of how one person or persons can effect change if their vision is clear, and their hearts are genuine.

Hanri and Nicolette will live on as role models for a new generation.

In his vision, he saw the contrasting concepts of eighteenth-century pirates and their humane approach to fighting slavery to today's perceptions of pirates. The dichotomy of two lovers of the same sex being ardent followers of Christ would appeal to the interests of many different people on many different levels. And, of course, there was the lure of the treasure.

They had carefully cataloged each piece. Every single item had created unique quakes of exhilaration. He knew the crowds would swell for years and years to come. The exhibition would serve as an example for religious institutions the world over to reassess their Christian theology and realign it with the true teachings of Christ which was centered upon loving one another.

"I want to use the incredible wealth and beauty of the relics to attract a wide audience. And though the treasure would be the draw, the focus of the message would be on both Hanri Fick and her lover, Nicolette Rey. It should promote acceptance and reject all forms of bias and racism . . . to remind people to park their stereotypes and open their minds."

"So woke," Ally said with a starry gleam in her eyes. She seemed delighted, but he didn't really understand the context.

"Woke?"

"It's an expression of the times. It personifies a growing movement across the world. Being woke means to be aware of what's going on in your community and the world at large in relationship to racism, bias, and social injustice. I would say you already get it."

He looked at Dan as he weighed whether he should dish up the other part or let them absorb it in small bites. Mark suspected homing in on a singular religion would not fit his worldview of woke. The prudent thing to do now was to let them absorb the big idea first, then wait until they were fully committed to explain the second part of his concept. He continued unfolding his grand scheme, hoping that his salesmanship had not been dented by time.

"I envision an exhibit full of panoramas and maps, openings for the human imagination. But in the telling of her story, and the world of 1732, inevitably there will be those who will seek to retrace her adventures. And in so doing, find the Island of Redemption and turn it into an oddity to be sullied and stained. We can't allow that to happen." His voice strident, he saw they had both been startled by his loud proclamation.

"Perhaps we leave out that part?" Ally demurred.

But, of course, the Island of Redemption was the true anchor behind the grand design of the exhibit Mark envisioned. It was a perfect angle to delve into the power of prayer, hope, faith, and heaven. But he did not allude to even a hint of this . . . at least not yet. Instead, he deflected them to an alternative idea.

"As you know, after my boat electronics got fried, I was adrift for weeks. One day I saw an island way off in the distance." He smiled, knowing fate had had other plans. "Fortunately, I never came within five miles of it. But from afar, I could see it had mountains, green with vegetation. I suggest instead of dismissing such a key part of Hanri's story, we offer those adventurous types a decoy."

Fully engaged in this new aspect, Dan continued to prove his intellectual prowess by his insight. "So how far away are we?"

Mark smiled at the question. "Am I that obvious?"

Dan shrugged with a knowing grin.

"It just so happens the island is about a day's travel southwest of here."

Dan looked to Ally. "Okay."

"Great. I'll let the captain know." Mark smiled inwardly as he rose to see the captain.

Chapter 26

With morning breaking behind them, the *Serafina* cut through the mild rollers as they closed in on the island simply marked on the charts as ML900.

Captain Christakis explained it was a reference to its nautical distance from the nearest mainland, in this case the continent of South America. There were no maps of the island or the surrounding waters. As they approached, the captain slowed his vessel and set their depth alarm at fifty feet below the transom. Plenty of warning if the bottom pushed up into rapid shallows.

As they drew closer, what became clear was that the leeward side of the island had a huge, unprotected bay continuously pounded by a relentless surf. With no reefs or barriers to impede the huge rollers, they welled up into giant waves as they approached the shore. Great for surfing but not so much for anyone trying to land a small boat.

"Look," Mark exclaimed. "Whales."

When Big Daddy blew a large stream of water from his blowhole, Mark smiled. There were eleven in total. He could not tell which one was the youngest, as the calf he remembered would be at least eight years old by now.

The sighting brought back recollections of his time adrift, the whales, the highway of plankton that pointed to this island, and, of course, Old Ironsides.

Mark went into the control room and spoke to the captain. "Can we get a little closer? I want to see if we can find a place to land."

"No problem."

The *Serafina* drew close enough to see the palm trees that lined the white-sand beaches. There were no signs of habitation.

"By the look on your face, you seem to know those fellows," the captain assessed.

His demeanor was relaxed, and Mark noted that the depth gauge still showed over a hundred feet below the hull.

"Yes, sir. This big one and I had our moments. He helped still some of my loneliness when all seemed lost. You could say he was a step on the path of my redemption." His tone was one of thanks and recognition.

"Mark," the captain said on a serious note. "I did not know you before your ordeal, but the man I have witnessed could have only blossomed from a solid foundation. Both Maria and I feel blessed to call you our friend."

Mark was warmed by his comments and knew they had nothing to do with the colossal sums they had been awarded. Of course, it remained an unspoken agreement that inherent in the granting of such abundance, they were paying for discretion. But John and Maria were a class act. They would have never spoken about anything without permission. Still, secrecy was their greatest fortress. The world was full of vultures who would seize on any tear in the fabric of their accumulated wealth.

The captain slowed his vessel as the alpha male came to investigate. Mark stood by the rail and waved. Everyone on the ship, including the yapping chocolate wonder, could see the whale recognized Mark. The enormous mammal was smiling at him.

As a gesture of greeting, Big Daddy sent up a large stream of water, creating a magical rainbow to frame the moment.

Mark removed his phone and added another photo to his collection. The great blue reared up and splashed backward. Today all was right in the world.

Does God direct his creatures on what to do or where to go? Did he place this family in my path coming and going?

Again he found himself wondering about the minds of sea mammals, the will of God, fate, and destiny. Angel had explained that fate was like of puff of smoke, subject to winds of change, where destiny was more akin to the path of least resistance. Sometimes we deviated, but we intuitively gravitated back to the road hidden beneath our feet.

As they watched his old friend return to his pod, the peace they seemed to have gave him an idea. *Can you buy an island if no one lays a claim to it?*

"Let's circle the isle," the captain suggested.

The outline of Mark's plan was starting to take shape. They trolled offshore, and the waters ran deep, but the waves crashing the beach remained impenetrable. Rounding the farthest point, Mark noticed the captain had binoculars fixated on the shoreline.

"You might want to see this," he said, handing Mark the field glasses.

"There," he directed. "Where the mountain slopes into the sea."

Mark raised the glasses and saw a cut in the foothill. From this angle, the illusion of a contiguous peninsula had changed to reveal an island that had broken off from the end, leaving a narrow passage protected from the sea.

"We could land the tender there," the captain explained.

Mark sensed the old seadog had a fresh sense of adventure. And it was infectious.

"Let's do a once-around to get a lay of the topography, and if there isn't a better spot, we can return."

"Sounds good," Mark agreed, caught up in John's can-do spirit.

While circling the small island, Mark took a series of photographs to enhance the exhibit he envisioned. It did not surprise him that, like his own island, there were cliffs that were unassailable, beaches that were beautiful, and forests that looked impenetrable. In the end, they returned to the promise offered by the sliver cleaved eons ago, nature's sole access to the island.

Maria took the helm while the captain lowered the tender and tied her to the gangway. Fortune smiled with the soft swells that raised and lowered the mother ship in tandem with her daughter.

Christakis had a glint of curiosity in his eye. "Can I inquire what you are looking for?"

"I want to make sure that if there is someone else stranded that Captain John will once again be the source of divinity's will." Mark was having a bit of fun, but he quickly shifted to the outlines of his plan.

"Actually, I am hoping that if the island is uninhabited, we will substitute it. Instead of revealing where we found the actual treasure, this will become Fick's Island of Redemption."

"Be careful," the captain cautioned with a look of understanding in his eyes. He untied the line.

Dan was at the helm and pointed the craft toward the cut. Carson was on point. Mark saw that Ally had learned the art of drool avoidance as slobber whipped past her on the wind.

Approaching the pass, they saw it was narrow, the sheer walls littered with crags full of bird nests.

"Plenty of room if the currents are manageable," Dan suggested. And they were. Nature had created a tunnel outside of the ocean's force. But, of course, it was also only passable by a small boat. Larger boats would remain at the mercy of the open sea.

Aided by the inbound surf, they ran the boat up onto the soft sand. Immediately, Carson hopped out and started sniffing.

Dan stood with his hands on his hips, looking up and down the shoreline. Mark could see the "How are we going to find out if anyone lives here?" frown on his face.

"As we circled, I scanned the island. This is the only place that a boat could land. So if anyone is here, there should be evidence along this beach. Carson, go find some lizards."

It was a word she associated with sniff, smell, search. If she caught the whiff of anything, she would bark.

Walking the sand, they could see the whales out in the bay. The sound of pounding surf mingled with the chirping of birds along the forest's edge. The vibe was that there was no human habitation, but he wanted to be sure.

"Is this home, or do they migrate?" Ally asked, watching the whales at play.

Her comment triggered Mark to wonder *Am I coming or going?*

"Shall we?" he suggested, changing the subject.

Dan looked out toward the *Serafina*. She was resting easy on a generous sea. "We have about three hours of daylight left."

"Plenty of time," Mark affirmed. "If we can get to the top of that mountain, we will have a view of the entire island."

He had a déjà vu moment of Doubting Thomas fearing the island was populated by headhunters. His chuckle did not go unnoticed, but he could see that they were getting so used to his odd laughs and such that they no longer bothered to ask.

197

Chapter 27

In the end, their decoy island proved to be uninhabited. They marked the coordinates and began filling in the backstory. This would serve as the location described in Hanri Fick's diary. The story would center here.

"The place of my redemption as well as those captured by the infamous female pirates will be blurred from the tapestry we are going to weave—hopefully leaving the true Island of Redemption unmolested for decades to come."

They were all in agreement. It was a sound plan, and it was obvious this was important to him.

Now steaming ahead, they were two days east of Barbados. The dynamics of operations began to change. When they had been far out on the open ocean, the autopilot was routinely engaged, and the radar's alarm system was set at two miles. If anything came within range, a warning bell would sound, and the designated watchman would return to the bridge.

But now they had entered the shipping lanes. There were a number of freighters in the distance traveling north and traveling south, including large oil ships, small coastal freighters, luxury craft, and a host of other vessels plying the waters of the islands.

Mark was anxious and nervous. He was reentering a world that had moved on without him. Skimming news sites to get a feel of the world simply depressed him.

"Mark," the captain said, sticking his head out the sliding door. "Just wanted to let you know that I checked the satcom, and sometime over the night we were able to reestablish a link."

"Thank you," Mark replied, suddenly filled with apprehension. He was dreading the call to Rachael, but it was time.

"Ally," he said. "Shall we go call your mother?" He paused and then added, "Remember what we discussed."

"Yes, Dad. We tell no one about the treasure until we are ready."

"And . . ."

She smiled. "Of course. You need not worry. Dan and I fully appreciate the gravity of your secret."

"That's my girl."

"Good luck," offered his son-in-law.

Mark followed Ally into the radio room and closed the door. He was procrastinating. He did not really know why he was so nervous, but his stomach held bouncing butterflies, and he had to will his heart to slow down.

She dialed her mother's number. Immediately the hum of transatlantic static crackled until he heard the phone ringing. On the third ring, a female voice answered.

"Hello?" The voice was not Rachael's.

"Hey, Tori?"

"Ally! How's your honeymoon? Did you do anything exciting? Where are you? How's the yacht? Must be nice . . ."

Ally weathered the storm of uninterruptable questions, waiting for a break in the flow.

Mark noticed the smile and the bonds of sisterhood.

"Is Mom there?" she finally asked, forcing a wedge in Tori's nonstop chatter.

"Mom, Ally's on the phone . . ."

The sound of background noise gave him a pause to steel himself.

"Hello, darling," Rachael said.

The phone was on speaker, and the mere sound of her voice sent wave after wave of emotion crashing upon him. Loss, sadness, remorse, he let out a long breath, willed his heart toward normal, and cued Ally he was ready.

"How's your vacation going?" Rachael asked.

"Well, actually, better than I had hoped. I found something. Or should I say *someone*."

She looked at her dad. It was time.

"Hey, Rachael," Mark said.

There was a long pause, and static crackled, until . . .

"Mark?"

"I'll leave you be," Ally said and closed the door behind her.

Rachael's voice opened up memories of the first time they had met. How the mere sound of her could set his passions aflame. But, alas, even before he had left on this fateful trip, the ardor had long been extinguished.

"Miss me?"

She started crying, and this morphed into uncontrolled sobbing. He realized she was probably being swept up on currents of guilt and fear, worry and supposition. *What now? How does this affect my life? What about my husband, our future . . .*

"It's okay, baby. Really, I am happy for you."

Baby. It amazed him how quickly he fell into the routines they had shared. The sobbing sank to a whimper as he set out to ease her mind.

"I promise your life will not be upended. I want nothing from you, nor will I contest the divorce. The distribution of proceeds are yours forever. The only issue that might arise is the life insurance company may want their money back. But if that happens, I will cover that as well."

He had thought this out, being the minder of the pragmatic helped him keep his own emotions in check.

"Really?" she eked out. He sensed the fears abating as she accepted that the fabric of her life was not going to unravel.

"Rivers and orchards," he said lightheartedly. The comment broke the ice, and she let out soft laughter.

"That's my girl," he assured soothingly.

"You were right, of course. You were always right. I never should have doubted you."

Her words made him feel warm inside, but he knew this was not entirely correct and wanted to set the record straight.

"No, honey. There is so much about me that was not right. We both know those things. But for now, let the past stay behind us . . ."

The remainder of the call was filled with things she wanted to know and things she thought he should know. Tori talked to him almost as if he were a stranger, a distant relative she had few recollections of, not like someone who was instrumental in the life of her here and now.

He got Forest's number and asked Rachael to blaze the trail and bring him up to speed. He would call him later. The conversation ended with vague promises to visit at some unconfirmed point.

Exhausted by anxiety that had been yanking his tether in a hundred different directions, he felt emotionally drained.

"Ahh . . ." He let out a long sigh to still his mind. He closed his eyes and thought of Angel. She was the bulkhead against the coming chaos.

Near the end of the following day, the outlines of tropically colored buildings began taking shape, witnesses of entry to the next chapter of his life.

He spotted Ragged Point, the most eastern edge of the island jutting out into the ocean, and the adjacent white sands of Crane Beach. As they entered the conga line of maritime traffic, one of the things he had forgotten was congestion. Be it by boat or by car, it was a curse of man's existence.

Rounding the southwest tip of the island, he was greeted by two large cruise ships, massive containers of human cargo. From his perspective, these were new additions and no doubt both a curse and a blessing. The port was under construction when he was last here. Now it was a conveyor belt of middle America invading like locusts in four-hour stints. He had seen this scourge on other islands. It was a daily zoo.

He groaned. And they motored on . . .

Approaching the Port of Bridgetown, they saw the channel was marked by green and red signal signs. *Red right return, keep them on your starboard side.* They passed the barrier island that kept the sea at bay and motored up the channel. It was not long before they came to a berth that belonged to the *Serafina*. As dock men waved, John gave three blows of the ship's horn. It signaled he was home.

The blaring sounds and the distinctive smell of humanity continued the assault upon Mark's senses. All the while, he marveled at the colored shops that lined the quay. The mango yellows and soft sky blues, buildings topped with red terra-cotta tiles were the quintessential flavors of island life and were among the things that drew him back here year after year.

He had arranged with the Christakis's to live on board until the treasure was safely offloaded and moved to a secure location. Dan and Ally would return to New York to begin the process of bringing the right institution on board.

The following morning Mark had arranged a meeting with the president of the Boutique Bank of Barbados. A Mr. Bancroft Gordon. He hoped to engage him in multiple projects, the first being the formation of the Hanri Fick Heritage Trust, which, barring any obstacles, would be based in Barbados.

Arriving at her berth, two long piers anchored by a long promenade, the *Serafina* backed into the quay.

Tourists taking photos, seagulls squawking for scraps, and vendors hawking their wares bore witness to his arrival, but it was the deafening silence of the motors shutting down that punctuated the point. "I am back!"

A gangway was placed at the rear. All he had to do was cross a ten-foot bridge, and suddenly all his hopes and worries, anticipations and problems of his new life would begin.

Everyone was eager to step onto terra firma. It was one of those feelings you could never understand until you had spent time at sea. You risked the elements, rolled with the tide, and survived to sail another day. It was one of those exhilarating moments cherished by even the most seasoned of sailors.

He had donned his only set of fine clothes, the chinos and white shirt, but even those had a weathered look. He would need to replenish them this afternoon.

The old Trafalgar Square was just beyond the promenade. Mark could see the dolphin fountains in the center of the traffic circle and the roads lined by shops and restaurants. He also saw something else, something that caused him to do a double take.

Walking their way was a beautiful young woman whose jet-black hair shone in the sun. The way she walked and the profile she projected reminded him in so many ways of Angel, but maybe a decade older. He found himself staring as she got closer.

"Are you coming?" Ally asked, unaware that he was blocking the gangway. "Carson really needs to go," she added with a bit more urgency.

He suspected it was she, not his dog, who was more than ready. He stepped aside to let them pass. "Go ahead. I need a few minutes."

He watched Ally and Dan cross the footbridge onto the island. Though leashed, Carson led the way. As they melded into the crowd, he knew they were returning to their life. With all that had happened and all that would unfold, it was bound to be different.

Sure, they had already been well off, but now rich did not begin to describe the exponential wealth they had garnered. And all the problems that would come with it.

"Swimming pools and movie stars. Private jets and limousines. And all the things in between," he sang under his breath. The words seemed apropos, but he could not remember where he had heard them before.

His worldview had changed so much. He still saw the folly of man and the predictability of things to come, but whereas before he might have judged, now he chuckled.

His gaze remained fixed on the woman as she continued to approach. So much so, he did not hear Maria come up behind him until she shouted out something in Greek.

"Panémorfi kóri mou, πανέμορφη κόρη μου."

The woman beamed with delight, waved, and called back a similar greeting in the same language. Mark was tongue tied when she stepped onto the gangway and came aboard.

"Mark, this is my daughter, Sara. Sara, this is Mark Lambert, Ally's father."

She offered her hand, never breaking eye contact. It felt as if he was being appraised, considered, reviewed, and inspected all at the same time. Meanwhile, her quirky expression was laughing as if the world was her oyster and she had found a pearl.

"It is a pleasure to meet you, Mr. Lambert."

He found himself swooning at her demure accent. Her tone and inflections reminded him of his past island apparition. *Will I see Angel in every woman I meet?*

"Might I ask how you ended up on my parents' boat? You weren't there when they left, yet here you are."

"Sara?" He looked at the teak nameplate along the fly bridge.

She saw his gaze and replied, "Actually, my name is Seraf, which is short for Serafina. But unless you are Greek . . ." She blushed. "My friends simply call me Sara."

He could not take his eyes off her. He was not sure if it was simply her radiant beauty, her perfect face, or the long, lustrous coal-black hair firmly anchored by eyes the color of the deep-blue sea.

She appeared to be about thirty-five, but he could not be sure. She was charming, confident, and totally at ease. He found he could not restrain himself. *We only live once.*

"Perhaps you could join us for dinner this evening."

"My oh my, Mr. Lambert, you do not waste any time, do you?"

The invite was about dining on the yacht, but it had not come out that way, and he had made the offer without conferring with Maria. He had not meant it to be so presumptuous.

"I'm sorry, I was just . . ."

He tried to place her accent. The cadence was like something out of *Gone with the Wind*. Was this really her, or was she having a little fun at his expense? Beautiful women have that luxury, whereas men like himself . . . *Welcome back to the game, son. Good luck.*

He had no intention of resuming the role of a player. He just, well, he was drawn to her.

"It's been a long time. I'm sorry. I didn't mean to presume."

"No offense taken," she said in a tone that let him off the hook. With a sparkle in her eyes, she continued. "As a matter of fact, if I didn't have to work tonight, I would be enchanted to take you up on your offer. Perhaps you might consider a different night?"

"Sweetie," Maria reminded, giving her a green light. "You know you don't have to go to the bar tonight."

Mark swelled with optimism as he searched for something to say. "You work at a bar?"

"Kay's," she said, with a little less Southern belle in her reply.

"She does not work there," Maria clarified. "She owns it."

"Oh, Mother." Sara blushed, twirling her hair with a fidgety hand. "Do you know the place?" She was looking into his eyes as if he were hers for the taking.

"One of my favorite watering holes."

"My oh my."

Maria intervened. "How about dinner tomorrow night, then? We can catch up, and Mr. Lambert can entertain you with his wild tales of the South Atlantic."

Maria and her daughter had the same impish grin, and obviously much passed between them without a word ever being spoken.

"Sure. I look forward to it. I'm sorry to rush off, but I am running late. I just wanted to say hi and make sure you guys were all good."

As she turned to leave, Mark asked, "Any chance you might be going near the Boutique Bank of Barbados?"

"Sure, it's on my way. It would be my pleasure to be your chaperone." Again came that smile. Again his heart jumped like it was on a trampoline.

"I need to grab my passport. I won't be a minute."

As they walked along the crowded sidewalks, she asked a million questions. He found himself doing all the talking. Deflecting and demurring, he avoided certain topics. But he was enchanted. Seeing she bore no wedding ring, he assumed this was the second unmarried woman to enter his life in the last eight years, assuming Angel was a woman, and once again he was falling into the abyss.

"Here we are," she said, looking at her watch. "They close in an hour. I am sorry to leave you on such short notice, but I do look forward to tomorrow."

He watched as she glided away with the grace of a goddess. When she disappeared around the corner, he came out of his trance.

The building that contained the bank was old world. It was two stories tall, pink, featured cut coral lintels, and had been well maintained. He could feel the antiquity and knew from his research that centuries ago it had been a warehouse used by a British maritime company. The building had been modernized, hurricane proofed, and made secure against all comers. It epitomized the whole of this boutique institution, dependable, secure, timeless.

He entered the lobby, which felt more like a men's club than a bank. There were no tellers, but there were a number of local women who sat behind Victorian desks. Most of these were adorned with the latest computer equipment. He approached an exquisite woman of about thirty. She appeared smart and attentive, with glasses that framed an oval face and dark eyes that looked like brown pools.

"May I help you?" she asked in a singsong voice.

"Yes, ma'am. I have an appointment tomorrow with Mr. Gordon, but, if possible, I would like to open an account today and transfer in some funds."

"Please make yourself comfortable."

Though she was polite, he knew she was discreetly scrutinizing him. His clothes were threadbare, and he had a weathered, seafarer look. She clicked a few keys as she looked over her monitor.

"Mr. Lambert?" she asked. The question suggested they had a company calendar, and she had access to Mr. Gordon's appointments.

"Correct."

"I see. And you want to open an account with us?" Her demeanor thawed ever so slightly.

"Yes, ma'am."

"Do you have your passport?"

"I do."

"And you want to transfer funds into this account? Where will these be coming from?"

He hesitated. Aside from the kids, this was the first person about to get a peek at his secret.

"I understand that your bank accepts direct deposits of select crypto currencies. Is that right?"

"We do."

"Then I would like to start by transferring one hundred in Bitcoin and convert it to cash to be held in my account."

He saw her hand slip on the keyboard as she raised a knuckle to her lips to cover her surprise.

"That is approximately $6.5 million," she calculated, making a quick recovery. "May I have your passport, please?"

She entered keystrokes into the computer, and a frown spread over her face. She looked at the man across from her.

"It seems you are listed as missing."

"Dead?" he asked.

"Actually, presumed dead," she acknowledged. "It is a subtle distinction."

"Well, here I am," he said with the hint of a smile. He did not want to get into his whole life story. At least not today. He had worried that if he had been declared dead, it would open all kinds of problems. Relief swept inside. "Will that be an issue?"

"I'm not sure of your legal status, dead or alive, but your passport is current, and when I entered it into our system, there were no flags. That does not mean you won't have issues if you try and enter your country, but as far as our banking laws are concerned, you passed our requirements."

She added to her previous warning about US laws. "The minute you engage entities based in your home country, you will be brought back to the land of the living. And all that accompanies it."

She looked at him with a jaundiced eye, perhaps making sure he understood that whatever may have been lingering in the past was going to still be there.

"The zombie apocalypse." He chuckled under his breath. She pretended not to hear him.

For the next few minutes they went through the formalities of paperwork, passport, and the signing of forms and disclosures. When she was satisfied she had complied with all of the Barbados banking regulations, she inquired if he was prepared to make the transfer.

"Yes, ma'am."

"I can give you the transfer codes, and you can put them into your phone."

"I have no reception." He smiled. "Actually, I don't even have a number. May I log on to one of your computers?"

She gave him a peculiar glance. He could see she was wondering about the anomaly of a millionaire who did not have an operating cell phone. But she was now far more attentive and set him up at an empty desk next to hers. Within minutes, he was done.

"It's all here," she advised. With the sparkle in her eye, he was no longer the vagabond of her first impression.

"I know you are meeting my boss tomorrow, but is there anything else I can do for you today?"

"Actually, there is. I could use some cash, and I am also going to need a couple of credit cards. Can you handle this for me?"

"Of course, sir. We are a full-service bank. If you have an hour, I can get everything done while you are here. Do you have an address we can use to send statements?"

"Not yet. That is next on my list."

"Very good. By the way, sir. just across the way is Barbados Telecom. I am sure they can get your phone a new number. Perhaps they could even upgrade you to a newer model."

She offered a coy smile, her expression hinting at a concern she might have gone too far. To her relief, he saw it for what it was, nothing more than an informative observation, so he thanked her.

One hour later he walked out of the bank, flush with cash, credit cards, and relief that his fantasies and fortunes had not been a pipe dream. Next on his list was to see a few haberdasheries, what Americans called clothing shops.

"What do you have there?" Ally asked, eyeing the results of his shopping spree. He was loaded with bags of new clothes.

"Everything. Shoes, socks, sandals, shorts, casual wear, jeans, T-shirts, silk shirts . . . heck, I even bought a custom-fitted white linen suit," Mark said with a confidence born of wealth. He had added a white straw hat with a black band around it, sort of a cross between Ricardo Montalbán as Mr. Rourke on *Fantasy Island* and Rhett Butler in *Gone with the Wind*.

He had always wanted to try a little flair with island attire, but in the past he had always shown prudence at such an indulgence. After all, if you did not do it right, which was costly, you simply came off looking like a tacky tourist. He had done it right. Using the finest weave of silk and linen, it felt natural on him.

Now that money was of no concern, life was going to be different, to be lived. Still, he had no intention of wielding a life of self-indulgence and whimsy. There was too much to be done with the resources placed at his disposal. Angel had taught him well.

That night he and the kids dined on deck. The Christakis's had a dozen children, and most of them came by to see them. It caused Mark to wonder, *Maybe they should have invested in a television set . . .*

The captain and his wife had a home here on the island and had arranged that one of their sons, Emmanuel, stay on the ship. This was standard protocol for the *Serafina*. Someone was always on board to keep an eye on the ship, keep the curious away, and, in this case, take care of the guests still aboard. So, it came as no surprise to anyone in the marina who was familiar with their comings and goings that one of the sons was always aboard. Everyone knew them. Even the customs agents simply asked that a form be completed. They never bothered to come aboard.

It turned out Emmanuel was an excellent chef and had prepared an exceptional dinner. As they ate, the conversation flowed with a predictable rhythm and ease, but Mark was only half paying attention. His heart was tugging him toward Kay's Bar, which in his new worldview seemed another of God's little jokes.

"We have a private jet taking us back to the city tomorrow," Dan told him as he recapped their plans.

"Will you be okay?" Ally was teasing, and Mark knew why. She had already figured out he was smitten.

In the end, he donned his island flair and hailed a taxi. Ally had suggested an Uber, but the truth was, he did not know what a *Youber* was, so he stuck with old school.

"Nothing's much changed after all these years," he noted upon arrival. Kay's looked the same as the last time he was there. The wear and tear of the tropical climate was beaten back by regular maintenance and periodic paint, but that was simply a testament to its meticulous owner.

Tonight the place has quite a crowd.

He found a spot at the bar and caught the eye of a couple of younger women watching him. In the past he would have dazzled them with charm, but now . . . he scanned the tables looking for Sara.

He did not see her, but he did spot a gorgeous blonde who felt familiar. Her back was to him as she talked to one of the patrons across the way. From her demeanor she looked to work here.

Was she here last time I was here? Maybe she knows where Sara is.

He got up to approach. As the woman turned, he froze midstride. There was no mistaking those blue eyes. But her hair . . .

She saw him staring and smiled.

"Miss me already?" she asked playfully. The banter was so comfortable it was as if they had known each other for years. By the inquisitive look on his face, she must have known what he was thinking.

"It's a wig," she said, stating the obvious. "It helps keep the young bucks here on vacation from recognizing me in public and thinking suddenly they know me. Something I learned years ago."

She pursed her lips. "If they think they know you, they believe you are fair game to approach."

Her easy smile and simple banter revealed she was a master at the game and knew how to handle the tourist boys, obviously with benevolence and grace.

She acts so much like Angel . . . Did I see her the last time I was here? In the wig? Was she the model of a younger apparition? Again the same old question. Angel or imaginary friend? Seeing Sara in her wig put another weight on the right-hand side of the scale.

Stop torturing yourself. God intervened in your life, so what does it matter how he did it? For the moment, he heeded his own advice and relaxed into her company.

Chapter 28

"Mr. Lambert?" a small wiry man called up from the promenade.

He was having breakfast with his daughter and her husband on the rear deck before they left for New York. Earlier he had received an email that the package he had ordered would be hand delivered this morning.

When they were a week out, he had contacted an investigative agency to do a deep dive on the boutique bank and Mr. Gordon, to see if he or the bank was involved in money laundering or even carried a whiff of questionable dealings. This would determine his next steps.

"Mr. Johnson, I presume."

"Yes, sir. May I come aboard? I have your file."

He had already been emailed an initial report that had been more than satisfactory. But he had asked for more information on Mr. Gordon, seeking their judgment of what motivated him and his personal assets and net worth.

What he was planning would require partnering with someone whose integrity was rock solid. He believed he had found his man but wanted to be sure. The agent came up the steps and produced a bound document.

"The summary page will tell you what you want to hear. The rest is backup."

He thanked the man, who promptly departed. Opening the cover, he saw a summary that was concise and to the point. "Bancroft Saint Elmo Gordon is highly regarded in the banking world. He is financially well off, and there are no hints of illicit activity by him or his bank."

"Well?" Dan asked. They were both aware of the extent of his plans, at least those related to the treasure.

"Green light," he said, setting the file down. He raised his cup of coffee, strong and black. He looked out at the boat traffic. The marina was busy readying charters for the tourists.

Dan had set up his new phone with a VPN and an encrypted email system. They wanted absolute secrecy until they could get the treasure moved to a secure location.

"Our flight leaves in two hours," Ally reminded him. "Once we get to New York, I will call Forest and Tori. I'll organize a trip to the island in a couple of weeks."

"That's more than enough time. I'm meeting a housing agent later this afternoon. I am going to find a place here on the island. Once the treasure has been moved, I will let the Christakis's get back to their life. I understand they are going to Greece."

Mark had purchased a gray pinstripe suit but in the end decided business casual was more appropriate for the islands. No sense in projecting someone he wasn't. Although Mark weighed whether to bring his dog to his meeting with Mr. Gordon, he decided that if he was going to put his life in the man's hands, he had better know if he liked dogs or not.

With Carson in the lead and a few poop bags in his pocket, they set out across Trafalgar Square. His appointment was in a half hour.

The sidewalks were filled with morning shoppers scurrying about. Within an hour the cruise ships would begin to unload. It reminded him of the times he had returned to his childhood home of Bar Harbor.

The seaside shops will have a daily influx of eager buyers, as will the town's bars and restaurants. But the excessive crowds will become unbearable to the locals.

He had seen it all a hundred times before. Each ship would disgorge as many as three thousand people. And often there were two or three vessels in port at the same time. He knew it was the same blessing and curse the world over, especially here in the islands, where the cruise lines owned most of the local shops and stalls, limiting the actual amount of money that flowed into local hands.

With eight years of no human interaction, he had a fresh view of this onslaught. He didn't see humanity as a whole but as a collection of individuals all seeking distraction from their ultimate destination.

"Death waits for each of us and the unknown of what happens. Something most of humanity tries to keep in a fog," he reminded under his breath.

Reminiscing, he felt secure that this form of oblivion was no longer his life. Angel had told him that throughout history culture had been driven by death, but no one wanted to admit it. He now understood that how people lived their lives melded into the afterlife, and he thus planned to act accordingly.

He found a small grassy area where Carson did her business. As a conscientious pet owner, he took care of his responsibilities before making his way to the bank.

The sun was rising behind the pink building, and the sidewalk was draped in shadow. After entering through the large mahogany door, he waited in the vestibule until a woman came and unlocked the modern, brass-framed, smoked-glass interior gates.

"Mr. Lambert, welcome," she said, casting a nervous eye at the dog. He knew as a rule most islanders saw canines as part of one's security system not as companions. But he was a client, and thus she did not comment.

"She's harmless," he told her.

"I see. Please, follow me. Mr. Gordon is waiting."

Mark had the leash in one hand and the new leather valise he had purchased in the other. She led him up a wide, sweeping staircase of marble steps and mahogany wainscoting. He appreciated the old-world elegance. At the top of the stairs was a short hallway that led to a pair of ten-foot doors that were opened to reveal a grand office. And sitting behind a desk that looked like something from a forgotten age was a man who could pass for someone in his forties. Mark knew from his bio he was twenty years older.

The man stood while casting a curious eye at the dog.

"Her name is Carson," Mark said, breaking the ice as he came forward.

The banker came around the desk and bent down to let her sniff his hand. Once satisfied, he rubbed her behind the ears. Carson's wagging tail green-lighted the man, cementing Mark's decision.

"Can I get either of you something to drink?" he asked. His voice was a firm baritone, clear and naturally authoritative.

"Not right now, thank you."

"Let's sit over here by the window."

He directed them to a large couch fronted by two leather club chairs. A sturdy wood coffee table sat upon an elegant rug to complete the ensemble. The window looking out to the back of the bank had an unobstructed view of the harbor. Mark could see the boats full of tourists leaving for the day.

"Beautiful view," Mark admired. "I'm surprised it has not been developed."

"It's not a coincidence. I own the land from here to the water's edge."

Mark knew this but did not tip his hand. "Smart."

"Please take a seat. I am curious," the man said with a glint in his eye. "You have asked me to block out my entire morning, so you can imagine my inquisitiveness."

Mark smiled. He was letting the morning unfold within his mind's eye. He knew that within an hour this man's world was going to be changed forever. He opened his briefcase and extracted the file. It was all showmanship, as he already knew what it contained.

"Bancroft Saint Elmo Gordon. Harvard law, retired head counsel for one of the largest international hotel chains in the world. Star footballer for the Jamaican National Soccer Team. And now, boutique banker to a few select clients."

If the man was surprised, he did not show it. He was probably a good poker player.

"Why Saint Elmo?"

"That's not in there?" He smiled. "My grandfather was a merchant marine who died at sea. Saint Elmo is the patron saint of sailors. It was my grandmother's wish."

"I see," Mark said, sinking into his chair. "Thank you for indulging me." In a serious tone, Mark moved to the business at hand. "I am about to ask you to consider joining me on a grand adventure dealing in tens of billions of dollars. I need to be free to discuss a number of issues with you and feel assured that you will hold my activities with the strictest confidentiality."

Before Bancroft answered, he added, "There are no nefarious dealings and no laws I am looking to subvert. I thoroughly researched this aspect of you and your bank, and I was assured you are a man of the utmost integrity."

He knew from the mention of billions of dollars he had the man's undivided attention. But he could see Mark's report had him swelling with a sense of pride.

Maybe I could beat him in poker after all.

"I have a story to tell you, if you will indulge me."

For the next hour Mark told him the entire story, from his departure eight years ago to his rescue by his daughter. Leaving out any reference to Angel, he embellished every aspect of Hanri Fick's life and the treasure they had recovered. When he was finished, the man had a number of questions.

"So, this treasure. This is the billions of dollars you referenced?"

Though the man tried to hide it, Mark could see he was a little disappointed.

"One story at a time," he told him. But his tone promised there was more.

"Regarding the treasure, I would like to create an iron-clad nonprofit organization based here in Barbados. It will own the treasure. I want it bulletproof from local, national, and any international claims of ownership or taxation. Even if we need to buy governmental favor through some charitable projects, I am prepared for this." He saw Gordon raise an eyebrow.

"I am not talking about graft of any kind. That is not what I mean. Let me hold my thinking on this until we address the next item on my agenda. But money is no object as long as we are doing something that is good."

"Okay. I don't see a problem with that," the man said with a sigh of relief. "I assume you have a name for the organization and the trustees you want assigned to the ownership."

"I do. It will be my daughter, my son-in-law, and myself. The name we want to register is the Hanri Fick Heritage Trust."

"I don't see a problem. May I have a few minutes to start some preliminaries?"

He went downstairs. While he was gone, a woman came in with a tray of dark-roasted Jamaican coffee and a few biscuits, as well as a bowl of water.

"May I?" she asked.

He nodded, and she handed a biscuit to Carson, who readily accepted. Bancroft returned, and they continued their discussions.

"I have a logistics problem," Mark told him, moving to the next item on his agenda. "I have a Volkswagen-sized treasure that I need to safely store. I don't know for how long or if it will all be moved at once or in pieces."

Mark was already seeing a deviation from his original plan for the treasure, but he needed more time to explore. "I know you have a vault, but is it big enough?"

He saw the man's grin open into a wide smile.

"Finally," he said with a sense of satisfaction. It was almost a guffaw.

"Finally?"

"Yes, finally. You see, years ago, when I retrofitted this building, I had grand visions of a Fort Knox island depository based here in Barbados. So I built a massive, secure vault in the subbasement. If you build it, they will come," he said, paraphrasing a famous movie line.

"They never did. It was designed for long-term storage and is not part of our day-to-day operations. We have a separate vault and safe-deposit boxes for this. But both have state-of-the-art security. Trust me. It would be more than adequate for your needs. And it would finally give me some vindication." He said this with a hint of self-deprecation.

"Mr. Gordon." The phone's intercom carried the voice of a young woman. He went to pick up the receiver, and Mark noted the body language of satisfaction in whatever it was she was telling him. He returned the phone to its cradle.

"No surprise that the name is available. My associate has initiated the processing of your new entity. It will take about a week."

"Thank you. Now I would like to discuss something else."

"Shoot."

"As a seasoned international lawyer, I want you to look into how I go about acquiring the two islands I mentioned. I want to buy them and form independent countries, registered and recognized by the United Nations. Once done, I want to create two marine sanctuaries with the maximum radius allowed under current international laws."

"I see."

Mark could not tell if he was thinking how to do this or even if he could do this, or how it would be funded. It would require thousands of hours and dozens of lawyers from around the world costing millions of dollars at a minimum.

"This will be expensive. How do you plan to fund it?"

Mark let out a deep breath and wiped the palms of his hands on his trousers.

In for a dime, in for a dollar, he told himself. It was something his father used to say when he was fully committed.

"We will open another account, and I will seed it with an initial deposit of $100 billion."

Even the unflappable Bancroft Saint Elmo Gordon could not contain his surprise. He stroked his chin as he steadied his composure. "Initial?" he asked, making sure he understood what the man was implying. That there was more behind this amount.

"Perhaps I should explain." Mark smiled. He hoped to move the conversation quickly away from his revelation so they could get back to business.

Bancroft reached for his cup of coffee and sank deep into his chair. His face was curious, expectant, but showed a few hints of doubt.

"I have made many financial bets over the years," Mark began. "Sometimes you win, sometimes you lose. About a year before I left on that fateful trip, I had invested a quarter of a million dollars in a new currency called Bitcoin. At the time, it was trading at six cents per coin."

He could see the banker doing a rough calculation.

"Four million, one hundred, and sixty-six thousand coins . . ." Bancroft's wide-eyed awe betrayed that he was beginning to accept the man's story.

"Close. Today it is worth just under $300 billion."

The man stiffened at the thought that one of the richest men, if not the richest in the world, now sat in his office.

Mark continued with his story. "Had I been able to freely trade instead of being incommunicado for eight years, I would have sold half the coins at twelve cents. My investment strategy has always been to sell half of my stocks if they double. That way I am generally playing with house money."

"I see," Gordon replied, his attention unwavering.

"Even though this is technically not a stock, I would have stuck to my formula. Furthermore, I cannot fathom that when Bitcoin eventually hit a dollar that I would not have sold it all off. I mean, who leaves four million dollars on the table? Fortunately, God had other plans. So now we have an opportunity to do some good."

The man's demeanor returned to the prudent lawyer-banker. Mark had included him in the "*we* can do good" on purpose. And it was evident that the idea of doing God's will had struck a chord.

"I now appreciate your earlier comment about doing good works on the island. Perhaps a second foundation is in order. A place in which to operate with a semblance of anonymity so as to keep names and personalities to a minimum."

"I was thinking the same thing," Mark said, comforted that the man's thoughts hovered on the same wavelength as his own. "Would you consider your office becoming the clearing house for all of our activities? I feel confident we can come to a beneficial financial arrangement. I would not expect it to come at the expense of existing clients."

"Simply at the expense of future clients . . ." Bancroft chuckled, his understanding cementing their bond. "I am sure that will not be a problem. I assume you have given thoughts to areas in which you would like to effect change?"

"I have. I want to focus on helping Haiti. It is time we undo the harm foisted on them over the last two hundred years."

Bancroft Gordon looked at him with an unspoken query in his eye, a question on his lips held at bay. Mark suspected what he might be thinking. Many people suggested that Haiti was cursed because of a voodoo revolution that set them free back in the eighteen hundreds, a violent uprising that religious folks said was successful because of a pact they had made with the Devil - gain independence and suffer a lifelong curse. And he understood how one could assume this. After all, the Haitians shared an island with the Dominican Republic, yet that country has thrived, avoiding the quantity of hurricanes, earthquakes, and calamities that seem to plague Haiti.

Even with Mark's newly acquired lens involving angels and demons in the affairs of humanity, he knew this was only partially true. Racism was at the root of their troubles. He assumed the Black man sitting across from him knew this. He wanted him to know that he did too.

"Haiti was the first slave nation to successfully rise up against the white colonialists," he began. "They looked to the new republic of America to recognize them as a nation, but the independent nation to their north stood toe to toe with the other white nations, and eventually Haiti was forced to concede the equivalent of twenty-one billion dollars, seven times more than the United States paid France for the Louisiana Purchase, to gain recognition. They borrowed the money from a French bank and have been impoverished ever since. It is time to try to right that wrong."

"You continue to surprise me, Mr. Lambert," he said with genuine admiration. "I think I am going to enjoy working together."

"Thank you, sir. As you can imagine, this will take decades, and I won't be around forever. We will need to build a trusted team to continue our plans long after we are gone."

"Of course," he conceded as Mark continued with his thoughts.

"The people of Haiti will need to be taught skills that will allow commerce to take place with goods that can be competitively marketed on the world stage, things like hand-sewn textiles as a start."

Mark could see by the crinkled brow the banker was making mental notes as he took it all in.

"People need to have a sense of accomplishment and self-worth. We need to move them beyond feeling they are simply wards of charity. Education and training are the key. If we can get more kids into schools, that will teach them basic, industry-specific skills, and over time each new generation can learn a more complex skill set, widening the net of manufacturing possibilities and moving more money into their economy."

"I see you have given this a lot of thought," Bancroft told him.

"Yes. I have. But we must be cognizant to not look like raiders with an agenda. We must also provide a more urgent program of getting food and medical care to the people. Many are starving. To do this, we should involve some of the missionaries that already have schools and orphanages in place. We can branch out from there."

"With the resources at your disposal, I think that is a good idea. Build upon that which exists with those who have been in the trenches."

"Thank you. There is a church in Boca Raton, Florida, called Spanish River. I read an article about them doing lots of work in Haiti. They partner with a few men down there and have coordinated to build nine orphanages and schools. Apparently, they help each develop a business model so they can become self-sufficient. I suggest a conversation with a Mr. Ron Tobias might be in order. I am sure he would be a great resource to begin directing you to projects that can make a difference. We have a lot of money, but let's be prudent and maintain as low a profile as we can."

"Okay, I will get started this afternoon. Anything else?"

"No, sir. Not for now. I am likely to make a few additional deposits into my own account, as I am looking to buy a home here on the island, but they can handle that downstairs."

"You're going to live here?"

"For now," he said without further explanation. *It all depends on how the path unfolds with Sara.*

Chapter 29

Six months flew by in what felt like an instant. Mark was beyond satisfied at the progression of their plans. His choice to engage Bancroft Gordon exceeded all his expectations. The treasure was now safely crated and stored in the vault, and the retrofitting of the wing in the New York museum would be completed in a matter of weeks. Then the treasure would be moved, and he could finally let out his breath.

They had opened a small office in Haiti and were training leaders to oversee the building of schools, creating practical curricula, and they had already engaged a number of clothing manufacturers to set up shop on the island.

This, of course, required certain tax benefits from both the island government and the US. Lobbyists in both countries were achieving unexpectedly swift success. Their efforts were growing pools of hope, and Mark had no doubt divine intervention was at play. His prayers always landed in Haiti, the people, and the darkness that had a stubborn hold on the western tip of Hispaniola.

They had begun to engage the other side of the island as well. Through intermediaries, they were using common sense financial leverage to open a gap that would lead to the Dominican Republic and Haiti becoming more cooperative. And though the mountain range that separated them was a physical barrier, it was the obstacle of historical prejudice that had been rooted in place for centuries and would be the most difficult to overcome. Time, prayer, and goodwill would be required.

"One day at a time," he oft reminded himself.

Mark was learning the virtue of patience and persistence and the knowledge that God worked within His time frame, not that of humans. He would constantly remind himself of Angel's joke: "God answers all prayers; it's just that most of the time the answer is no."

Mark had bought a house high on a bluff looking out over the Atlantic Ocean. And often within his mind's eye, his view extended all the way to his island. There was a path that led down to a secluded beach where he would take Carson, and they would run, swim, and do his daily exercise. The chocolate lab had become his shadow, and most people in town came to accept her more as his companion than pet.

"Maybe my interaction with the local community is changing island perceptions. Who knows?"

He laughed as he thought of the woman at the bank who had processed his documents to open the account. She had been pretty spot-on. Though he had no skeletons haunting him from his past, when he had returned to the States to see his children and to meet Rachael's new husband, customs and immigration had been a circus. Fortunately, Bancroft had paved the way, and there were lawyers there to help him clean up the mess his disappearance had caused.

It had been awkward, and wonderful, but all a blur. He was excited his kids were on their way to see him, to meet Sara, and become part of his new life. Appreciating the blend of old and present.

He arrived at the airport a half hour before Tori and Forest were slated to arrive. He paced under the white two-story canopy. The sun was hot outside the cover. The tarmac shimmered with waves of heat rising from its surface.

The Gulfstream jet completed its taxi to the private disembarkation area, where Mark had arranged for customs and immigration to expedite the process without the need to enter the queue inside.

"Dad," Forest yelled, calling from the top of the doorway.

He rushed down the stairs, followed by his sister.

"Careful there, young buck," Mark warned. A splat on the tarmac was all he needed to have to explain to Rachael.

He had invited her and her new husband, Scott Blando, to come, but she had politely declined.

"Rachael Blando," he mused. In a way he was relieved. It gave him an unadulterated chance to reconnect with his two other children.

"Tori, my little girl," he said as she stepped from the stairway.

She had that deer-in-the-headlights stare, looking at him as if it were for the very first time, though he had spent a week with them in Boca. She hesitated, dwarfed by the million questions from her older brother.

"Dad." She sighed and started crying. "Dad."

He wrapped her in a hug and allowed her the space to let it all out.

Once the river had run its course, he ushered them to the Range Rover, and they followed the coastal route to his home on the hill.

When they arrived, Sara was there with a smile in full charm mode. He knew it was genuine. She did not have a shallow bone in her body.

He had wowed his son with tales of making a couple of mil in crypto currency, glossing over most of their questions of how he afforded his lifestyle, leaving out the billions. In part because he had no intention of holding on to this and he did not want his kids to lean into expectancy of a large inheritance.

And he laughed as he recalled Forest's comments. "Dad, Sara is smoking . . ."

He had tried to maintain a somber expression, but in the end he couldn't.

"I'm not sure that's the thing to be saying to your dear old dad, but I can't argue the point. But please don't tell your mom."

The week passed in record time. With this additional time together, they had managed to start building the bridge back to normalcy. They loved Scott, their new stepfather, but the bond of blood had been reconnected.

That had been a month ago. The treasure was still a secret known to a very select few. One of those few was Sara. Their relationship had blossomed to the point that he was wondering if she would marry him. He was in love, but was she?

"If I ask, will she say yes or run for the hills?"

His heart always beat a little faster when she was around. Like now. She was on her way over, and they were going to swim at his beach today.

He had been toying with the idea of another project and had invited her to discuss it, something similar but separate from the Fick exhibit. She was a good businesswoman who could see things he often did not. He had grown to value her practical counsel.

"Knock, knock." Sara walked in and was met by a hundred pounds of chocolate attached to a wagging tail. As usual, Carson had one of her stuffed toys in her mouth, in this case a manatee.

"What a pretty girl you are," Sara cooed as she stroked the happy dog. Mark was out by the pool, and her entrance nearly knocked him off his lounge chair.

"Is this to your liking, Mr. Lambert?"

The only thing sexier than her voice was the white high-cut bikini she had on. He noted it was strikingly similar to the one Angel had worn when she no longer paraded around clothing-optional. This triggered a mental reel of the progression of apparel Angel had worn as their relationship achieved new levels. Quickly it spun from her unabashed nakedness through the bikini, then the one-piece, to the sundress, and ended with the elegance of the final outfit she had worn the day he was rescued.

"Neiman's?" he asked, recalling their banter that day at the lake.

"Why, Mr. Lambert, how could you possibly know that? I ordered it online to surprise you, and it just arrived this morning."

He saw the small pout she now sported, as if she had been cheated out of dazzling him. She stood with her hands on her hips as the sun shone upon her bronze body. The look in her eyes grew mischievous and the smile on her lips impish. Taking back complete control.

Eventually they made their way down to the beach, had a swim, and then lay on the blanket he had retrieved from the cabinet installed at the base of the path.

"I understand your parents are returning from Greece next week. How are they doing?"

"Mom's having a ball," she said, shaking water from her hair. The lustrous, coal-colored locks shimmered in the island sun.

He was enchanted.

219

"She's seen practically every relative we have throughout every one of the islands. Dad, on the other hand, is eager to get back to his mistress and away from the clan."

"Hmm." Mark laughed. He knew she was referring to the *Serafina*. "It's actually something I want to talk to you about. I need to go back to the island and am hoping that your mom and dad would be open to another charter."

He paused, the blood rushing behind his ears sounding like a freight train. He felt clammy, and his stomach fluttered with nervousness. "I would love for you to come with me."

She did not say a thing as she toyed with her hair. The impish grin that always hooked him crooked up one side of her mouth.

"May I ask why?"

"Why? Because I enjoy being with you."

She laughed at him. "No. I mean, why do you need to go back to the island?"

"Oh." She had a way of making him feel like a little boy.

"There are actually two things. We are making progress in determining how to acquire ownership of the island. The quickest path would be if we could successfully deem it as a sovereign nation. And to do that, I need to go and lay claim. To plant my flag."

"You have a flag?" She giggled with surprise.

"No. Not literally. I need to affix a notification in a prominent place dated with the years I spent living there, and then we lay a claim of ownership."

"We're gonna need a flag," she said with excitement. "Of course I'll come, you big goof. Did you really have any doubt?"

She pushed him to the sand, and it would be a while before she let him come up for air. Eventually, he was able to free himself.

"I need to keep a safe distance from you so I can finish my thoughts," he said as he caught his breath.

She wasn't listening. She stood and went into the ocean.

"Come on in," she pleaded, but he ignored her.

When she returned, he handed her a towel. "Now, may I get to that other thing?"

Even though they had been together for over six months, he still could not take his eyes off her. His memories of Angel were being juxtaposed against Sara, and soon he could not distinguish one from the other. He knew Sara had some inexplicable likeness to her.

"God sure does have an interesting sense of humor." He laughed under his breath.

She gave him a curious look. "Does he now?" She grinned, unaware of what he was really thinking.

"I left one piece of the treasure behind," he explained. "It was the one piece I chose as my own. I want to go and retrieve her. As a matter of fact, I want her to be the anchor of a different exhibit."

"Her?" she said with mock scorn. "I'm supposed to share you with another woman?"

Even in fun it made him feel good.

"You know, you are more than any man could hope to handle. I am just happy to have an excuse to be around you."

She leaned over and gave him a gentle kiss and whispered softly in his ear, "I will go anywhere you go."

Chapter 30

Weeks later they were dropping anchor in the bay when Carson started barking. As the dog ran wildly back and forth, her tail became a danger to anything in its way.

He had expected a strong reaction, a little remorse and nostalgia at returning to the island. But he was in love now, and that more than anything else ruled the currents of his passion. His focus, instead, was sharing what he could and letting the rest lie undisturbed.

"Look," Mark said, giving Sara a little turn.

"Dolphins!" Her face lit with joy. "I love them."

"Not just any dolphins," her father said, joining them at the stern. "Mark's dolphins."

Seeing the frantic nature of Carson, he added, "I better get those stairs down before that dog of yours jumps overboard."

Mark heard John chuckling as he walked away. "That dog still thinks she's a puppy."

Carson knew he was talking about her, which only encouraged more yapping, more pacing, and more chaos. No sooner had the winch stopped whining than Carson flew down the stairs and, with a giant leap, was in the water.

"What in the world?" Sara gasped with alarm.

"Watch." Mark knew what was going to happen.

Flipper got under Carson, who let her legs hug the side of the mammal, and they took off. The other dolphins rallied around with jumps and backflips, splashes, and cacking. All the while, Sara was speechless, perhaps for the first time since he had known her.

"Best friends," he explained. This went on for some time. Meanwhile, John had been going about prepping for shore. He lowered the Zodiac and brought it to the bottom of the stairs.

"Grab your suit," Mark told her. While she went below, he placed a shovel and empty bin in the bottom of the inflatable, as well as two engraved plaques and a container of bonding agent.

As they approached the shore, the dolphins delivered Carson as close as they could. She slid off Flipper and rode the small waves onto the sand.

"I want to see everything," Sara told him. She had brought a flag they had designed as well as a pole they could plant it with.

"Let's take care of business first, then we can do the Mark Lambert Castaway Tour."

He pulled the raft up onto higher ground.

"It's been less than a year, but nothing seems to have changed," he told her.

He noted that the birds still flitted in and out of the forest. The insects still buzzed in the grassy glade, and the large boulder at the edge of the grass where he had slept his first night was still firmly ensconced in place, as he suspected it would still be hundreds of years from now.

"There." He pointed, directing her to the large rock. "That is where we will bond our plaque."

They took one of the brass notifications and fastened it prominently to the stone. It listed his name, the dates he had lived on the island, and a few other salient points, including contact info.

Engraved on the plaque was a flag. It had a cross in the upper left quadrant and the silhouette of an angel below.

"Can I?" Sara asked. She unfurled the flag, which was stark white with red ornamentation and had been made of materials designed to outlast the elements. "In the name of the Father, Son, and Holy Ghost, by this flag we stake our claim."

Mark had come to learn the entire Christakis family were devout Christians and that her dad had once been a deacon at the Greek Orthodox Church. That was before retiring as a successful doctor and following his dream of becoming a licensed captain.

John and Maria where on the *Serafina* filming the event, technically as archival proof to be submitted to authorities, but they were privy to his secret plans and so had an ulterior motive.

Sara jammed the post into the ground. It had been designed with two-foot pegs in the middle. Mark climbed aboard and stomped down until the pole was three feet into the island.

"Shall we?"

Carson led the way as if she were simply returning home. They came out of the forest, and Sara saw the lake for the first time.

"It's paradise." There was a trace of awe in her voice. She had heard all his stories, but now she was able to frame the picture. "But lonely," she imagined aloud.

Mark chose to stay silent. He was not sure if he would ever reveal the truth.

Maybe someday.

They swam and made their way into the cave. He saw she was struck by its simple elegance. The translucent water of the falls shimmered its gossamer tranquility.

"I'm gonna be a while," he told her with shovel in hand. "Perhaps you want to explore a little and keep Carson company."

At first she would have none of it. But as the monotony of dig, dump, dig, dump grew tedious, she had a change of heart.

"I'll let you know once I recover the Goddess Wisdom, and together we can push all the dirt back into place."

Time moved slowly, but eventually he was shoulder-deep in the freshly dug hole, where he opened the chest and recovered his goddess. At first he had been excited, anticipating being able to contrast the similarities the figurine had with his memories of Angel and the woman who now owned his heart. Instead, he found disappointment.

Is my mind playing tricks on me?

He recalled the first time the statuette had been revealed and the vertigo that was set off by her striking appearance. He had been sure Angel had been reincarnated from an inanimate object.

But now, he found himself laughing. Looking at the cross etched into the wall, it all made sense to him.

That day at the bar when the mature woman was leading him back to her place, he had seen a vision of beauty floating across the floor, moving from one customer to another. The smoldering depth of her blue eyes had caught his attention and burned deep into his memory. She had been the catalyst that freed him from the fog of lust and had given him the stamina to withdraw from the older woman's hold on him.

This statue looked nothing like Angel or Sara. He began to realize he had conjured her up from the brief view of Sara when she was in her blonde wig. But he also knew, as always, God had his plans. And none of this was accidental.

"Thank you," he said aloud, unaware that Sara had surfaced behind him.

"Thank who?"

She spied the platinum statuette and with gentle fingers traced the contours of the elegant carvings. It was a thing of beauty and was in all likelihood priceless.

"So, this is your goddess."

Mark, whose emotions ran unchecked, did not answer. Instead, he busied himself putting the place back together. She joined in.

"Let's place the other plaque here in the metal chest."

They had discussed that if their claims of ownership were ever challenged or their fixed plaque somehow disappeared, they needed to have a backup in place.

They worked together like a well-oiled machine. As Sara finished brushing the sand back to its natural state, she stopped. He saw that something shiny had caught her attention.

"Look." She smiled, holding up a gold ring.

"I'll be?" His expression was all surprise. "See if it fits."

As she worked it on to her finger, Mark got down on one knee.

"Ms. Serafina Christakis, would you honor me by being my wife and my partner? By fulfilling my life as the better half?"

"Mr. Lambert, you are a most peculiar man. Cagey, but peculiar."

Time stopped. His breathing stopped. Even his heart paused. She had not said no. But she had not said yes either. The universe held its breath.

Please, God, Mark repeated a thousand times in his mind. *Please!*

"Yes. Today, tomorrow, and forever, I say yes."

She wrapped her arms around him, and though the pause in the universe had resumed, time was at this moment meaningless.

That evening they dined with his future in-laws. And that night Sara asked if they could sleep together in his bed on shore.

"Now that you are making an honest woman out of me . . ."

He was reliving every erotic fantasy that had played out when he was alone on the island. And he had had quite the imagination. He was in love, and he knew she was too. He realized that by mortal standards, God had gone through great lengths to bring this relationship to fruition. Mark inherently knew that in God's lexicon, one plus one was far greater than two. It was apropos that the nonprofit trust they had formed to do good works had been named the Ingodwe Trust.

It was meant to cause people to think. Once they got it, they would never forget. He recalled seeing the arrow pointing to the right in the word FedEx. It was hidden in plain view between the *E* and the *X*. Once you saw it, you always saw it. Their campaign had been "Moving Business Forward." He wanted something just as clever to state their mission.

It was God that was the root of this trust, and he wanted it to be emphasized in everything they did, for those who got it to always remember, "In God We Trust."

"Before we leave, there is something I need to do." He told her this with an air of adventure, having asked John to make the tender available so they could go to the back side of the island.

As part of the castaway tour, he would show Sara his lost vessel, then round the point to the beach in which Ally, Dan, and Carson had first landed. He had never made it out to that old house on the peninsula, and curiosity was calling.

It surprised him that events had kept him away from exploring. But at this point in his life, he knew there was a reason for everything. It would be something they could discover together.

"There she is, my old friend." He pointed, looking over the side at the watery grave. The ocean was so clear, it looked as if you could reach down and touch her. He knew from experience, though, it was at least ten feet to her rail.

"This is where I managed to hook the reef. *Lil Darling* was hard upon the coral for five years, something that I had latched onto as a link to my past. When the hurricane hit, she slid out of my life. It was years until I had the courage to reenter the ocean, and I found her sheltered here, resting in a watery cocoon."

Though he had earlier told her about how he had maneuvered onto the reef and the loneliness that followed her demise, this was a key moment in the tour of his life of solitude.

226

He revved the engines, and they passed the jutting promontory that distinguished the south end of the island. Sara was sitting in the rear with Carson at her side. With her wild mane whipping in the breeze, he saw that she might need a few lessons from Ally about slobber avoidance.

"Gross!" he heard over the wind. He laughed, but quietly. No need to suffer the wrath of a woman's scorn.

The waves were rollers that smiled with gentleness, and they made quick time to the white sands of the little cove.

"Over there," he shouted, his gaze sweeping the beach toward the tiny house built on the farthest end of the point. He did not risk the unknown of a submerged coral head or hidden rocks and thus landed at the same place where Dan had originally come ashore.

They were in no hurry. Sara was enjoying every moment together on this magical island. And he could see she had no idea of the fountain of thoughts that flowed through him.

Each step he took reminded him how special this island was. The old house on the point had always been there, reminding him that God had been in his life long before he had been with God.

His time here had stripped away the things that prevented him from being a better man. God knew he needed to change, because the woman who was to be his wife would not have accepted anything less. *Is this the road called destiny? Where there are no coincidences?*

As she chased the dog through the surf, his heart beat a little faster, and his grin grew a little wider. *I am blessed.*

Catching up, they left the beach and starting climbing on the rocks demarking the point.

"Careful," he warned, taking her hand, lifting her onto an aged path. It was worn by the wind and rain and felt as if it had not been trod upon for centuries.

Carson spotted lizards and now seemed consumed with a fantasy that she was some sort of great and feared huntress.

"Stalking fear in the heart of Lizardlandia." He chuckled. As far as he knew, she had never caught one, but hey . . .

Standing outside the hovel, it appeared to be made of ribs from the ruins of a ship sunk long ago.

"This place looks old," Sara said, running her fingers over the ancient wood.

"Perhaps a schooner was wrecked and some of it washed ashore."

"Come on, let's go inside." She grabbed his hand, and his curiosity way ahead of her.

The rough-hewn building stood alone. It was the only evidence of human intrusion, a faint whisper that someone had been here long ago, maybe hundreds of years or more. It was hard to tell. The wood had been petrified to the texture of stone. The floor was coated in soil, and the inside of it was so dark, everything was draped in shadows.

Mark removed a board, letting sunlight stream through dust motes disturbed by their presence.

"Mark. Look at this."

Propped in the corner was a large piece of wood. Her attention was drawn by a message that had been diligently carved into the plank.

"It's in English." She then read aloud:

"In the year of the Lord 1799, our ship floundered off this point. High seas dashed us upon hidden shoals until we broke apart and perished. I, Xander Stewart, am the only survivor. Our holds full of gold and silver now rest upon the floor of Davy Jones's locker."

"I must confess something that may cause you to question my sanity, for surely I have done the same on many occasions. This island has transformed me. Whether by imagination or divine intervention, I am blessed that an angel with long locks of fiery red hair and emerald eyes like a jaguar has kept me company and guided me until my recovery."

"Her wisdom was more precious than any gold or silver could ever be. So for the finder of this message, I leave the treasure for you, as I shall store mine up in heaven. May God be with you . . ."

Behind the plank sat the deteriorated remains of a Bible. Like himself, Stewart had left behind a guide for the next soul brought by God to this island. Mark stood transfixed, the tapestry of his time here broadening on so many levels.

He felt Sara watching him.

"She kept you company as well, didn't she?" Her tone was gentle. There was no judgment or question of sanity.

Has my expression said more than I intended?

"Yes." The single word transferred mounds of information that needed to be shared if they were to have an honest life together.

"And this is why the statue is so important?"

"Perhaps."

He thought of the man's description of his Angel. Xander was Scottish, and the reference to a fiery, red-haired goddess would have been in keeping with that man's own fond memories. Maybe she is real. Perhaps she is all things to all men. Or maybe she is imaginary, an apparition God designed for each of our unique attentions. *I doubt I will ever know for sure.*

"She saved me," he admitted. "If not for her, I do not know who I might have become."

"God saved you," Sara reminded him. "For me."

She took his hand in hers, and they stood quietly as the sea rolled past the point and the wind tipped the treetops. Two people, lost in time, their love a bond that crossed everything.

"He mentions a lost treasure. Do we care?"

"How much wealth can a man accumulate until he becomes corrupt?" he asked, quoting a passage in the Bible. "'It is easier for a camel to pass through the eye of a needle than it is for a rich man to enter heaven . . . I have more treasure than a man deserves."

He caressed her face and kissed her. With a heart brimming with thanks, he knew he had found peace, a peace that one can only experience when you are right with God.

What is it Angel had told him? Following Christ is not a form of hell insurance, but a life with one's mind at ease, a heart full of hope and the sting of death accepted as the inevitable journey home. They returned to the ship and departed the following morning.

Chapter 31

The wedding was meant to be a small affair, which by Greek standards included a dozen siblings and their families, extended families, aunts, uncles, cousins, and neighbors of cousins.

On his side were just his three children, Dan, and his friend Davey and his wife. He made it a point to be especially indulgent with Leslie, David's wife. He regretted that years ago he had unleashed his anger at her, actually referring to her as a bitch when he was stewing in his wallow at Kay's. She never knew, but he made it up to her anyway.

All told, a mere three hundred people, give or take those who came uninvited, attended.

Bancroft was to be his best man. As the number of self-invited dignitaries, local constabulary and politicians continued to pile up, the venue was moved to one of the grand hotels. The foundation had generously paid lavish amounts to keep all their guests wined, dined, and happy. After all, he was ecstatic, so why shouldn't they be as well? All of it was blanketed under the guise of a gala for the Ingodwe Trust.

Mark's instincts remained keen in wanting to stay off the radar screen. He did not need to be known as anything more than a moderately successful businessman who had managed to cobble together a few million bucks and retired to the islands, no big deal in the global scheme of things. Nothing to see here, folks! And of no concern to the alphabets, a term he used to describe most government agencies.

Bancroft's job had been a little more difficult. No bank, let alone a small one in the islands, could disguise $100 billion. But he was smart, and the work they did in Barbados and the surrounding islands, as well as their success in Haiti, soon blunted perceptions of ill-gotten gains.

Banky, the name that only close friends were allowed to use, had devised a reemergence strategy for Mark. He leaked his story of the surviving castaway to a few local papers in the States. Next he took copies of his death certificate and divorce settlement and filed eight years of individual tax returns.

Mark accepted from his friend the copy of the death certificate, a memento to his time gone. It had triggered all those conversations he had had with Angel. The river of societal consciousness flowed quietly.

"I, too, will die," he said to no one. It was not a worry or a fear in disguise but a recognition of inevitability. A beacon to remind him that one day, he will truly be home. And that here and now was temporary. A place to fulfill the will of God by casting unconditional love for his wife, his family, friends and for the world at large. "Do good," he reminded himself.

Once Banky's plan was completed, Mark's passport was renewed, and though he would need to file taxes on moneys he deposited into this own bank account, he was now able to sink back into obscurity. All this was done so that the love of his life would never be dragged into some unknown future problem because of him.

". . . and do you, Mark Lambert, take Serafina Christakis to be your lawfully wedded wife?"

There were hundreds of family members who had every eye on him. He knew they were there for her.

For him, those words sealed another blessing from God. "I do," he said, never breaking eye contact with his soul mate.

"You may kiss the bride."

The gathering watched as Mark and Sara celebrated their union with a kiss.

"Ladies and gentlemen, may I be the first to introduce Mr. and Mrs. Mark and Sara Lambert." And so another page turned in the book of Mark Lambert.

The honeymoon would start in New York City. *Female Pirates of the Caribbean* was to open next week. Already there was a buzz around the exhibit as photos were strategically meted out to the press.

Months ago, after their return from the island with his goddess safely secured, he had discussed with Dan and Ally a desire to create a second display focused on the presence of angels among men and centered on the Goddess of Wisdom. It would have more religiosity than he knew Dan would be comfortable with. He also knew expanding into the battle between good and evil and the hierarchy of God's emissaries engaged in the war for souls would distract from the message personified by the life of Hanri Fick and Nicolette Rey.

Both kids gave him their full support, and together he and Sara created their masterpiece, melding into like minds.

Bancroft made numerous trip to New York to negotiate the details with the museum, and it was agreed that this would open six months after the primary exhibit and with less fanfare. Or so he thought.

"My, what a turnout," Sara said with mild bemusement. It was the opening gala for the *Female Pirates of the Caribbean* exhibit. Stepping onto the red carpet, she dazzled in a silver off-the-shoulder Oscar de la

Renta gown. The wattage of her smile overwhelmed the flashing cameras, and nary a man could take his eyes off this vision of loveliness.

"Who is she?" echoed whispers from the paparazzi.

He, on the other hand, blended with less sensation in his uniform of black tux and tails.

As they ascended the stairs, questions of who they were mounted, but in keeping with their desire for anonymity, they had arranged early on for all-access credentials, the type held by fewer than a dozen individuals. Transcending VIP, these were "whatever they want, whenever they want it" credentials.

"After you, my lady," he said. The Fifty-Fourth Street entrance led into the Heyman Lobby, a grand entrance of tall ceilings and marble floors. From deep within the building, sounds of gaiety reverberated off the stone walls. The further one descended into the bowels of the gathering, the louder the murmurs of merriment grew.

Mark and Sara were instrumental in the design of the Fick exhibit, suggesting changes here and there, giving final recommendations and approval to the accompanying light show and soundtrack. It was Ally's wish Sara place her imprint along with their own.

Anchored by the craftsmanship of a distant age and thrilling the guests with the knowledge that this was purported to be the richest collection to have ever been gathered under one roof, it was the powerful message of love that was driving the euphoria of the crowd. Something that a reporter would later summarize in an article penned for *The New York Times*.

"Come, let's see how they are progressing with *Angels Amongst Men*." Arm in arm, Mark led his wife down the empty corridor.

In a wing far from this one, they were met by a pair of security guards who immediately recognized them and ordered the gate lifted and the lights to be turned on.

"Hello, George," Sara said to the main guard. He was in charge of keeping this private until they were ready for its opening months in the future.

"Ma'am." He smiled, his demeanor conveying a genuine respect for both of them.

Beyond was a large room spaciously divided by a long, lit hallway. At the far end, Mark saw *The Goddess Wisdom* perched on an ethereally lit throne. Above were synchronized lights of stars twinkling in a moving cosmos as reenactment of the big bang unfolded upon the ceiling.

This was their collective endeavor. For him, it fulfilled a much different interest than the Fick exhibit. He knew that too much at once would diminish both, and he looked forward to the fall, a mere six months away, when they would return to show this exhibit to the world.

He stood transfixed, studying the movement of the constellations. But something did not feel right. Then, in an epiphany, he recognized that the stars above, though accurate in their portrayal, did not convey a sense of the galactic year, of the rotation of the twelve constellations of the zodiac that formed the ages of humanity.

"You know, darling, I think we can improve on this," he suggested of the rotating stars above. "I think we need to emulate the movement of the constellations so that the public understands the great wheel of time, the twenty-six-thousand-year precession of the equinoxes. I think it will help remind us all how small our time on Earth is, and hopefully inspire some to use it wisely."

It was all part of the angelic worldview he hoped to share with the public, maybe even capturing a few souls along the way.

Behind her, carved into a midnight-black alabaster wall, were the commanding words that shimmered with quicksilver. To many, knowledge being personified as a woman would seem arcane. But the mesmerizing glint and shine of the phrases drew most people to absorb them in their entirety.

Does not wisdom call out? Does not understanding raise her voice . . . ? At the highest point along the way, where the paths meet, she takes her stand; beside the gate leading into the city, at the entrance, she cries aloud: To you, O people, I call out; I raise my voice to all mankind.

You who are simple, gain prudence; you who are foolish, set your hearts on it. Listen, for I have trustworthy things to say; I open my lips to speak what is right. My mouth speaks what is true, for my lips detest wickedness.

All the words of my mouth are just; none of them is crooked or perverse. To the discerning all of them are right; they are upright to those who have found knowledge. Choose my instruction instead of silver, knowledge rather than gold, for wisdom is more precious than rubies, and nothing you desire can compare with her.

I, wisdom, dwell together with prudence; I possess knowledge and discretion. To fear the Lord is to hate evil; I hate pride and arrogance, evil behavior, and perverse speech. Counsel and sound judgment are mine; I have insight, I have power. By me kings reign and rulers issue decrees that are just; by me princes govern, and nobles—all who rule on the earth.

I love those who love me, and those who seek me find me. With me are riches and honor, enduring wealth, and prosperity. My fruit is better than fine gold; what I yield surpasses choice silver. I walk in the way of righteousness, along the paths of justice, bestowing a rich inheritance on those who love me and making their treasuries full.

The Lord brought me forth as the first of his works, before his deeds of old; I was formed long ages ago, at the very beginning, when the world came to be. When there were no watery depths, I was given birth, when there were no springs overflowing with water; before the mountains were settled in place, before the hills, I was given birth, before he made the world or its fields or any of the dust of the earth.

I was there when he set the heavens in place, when he marked out the horizon on the face of the deep, when he established the clouds above and fixed securely the fountains of the deep, when he gave the sea its boundary so the waters would not overstep his command, and when he marked out the foundations of the earth. Then I was constantly at his side. I was filled with delight day after day, rejoicing always in his presence, I rejoicing in his whole world and delighting in mankind.

Now then, my children, listen to me; blessed are those who keep my ways. Listen to my instruction and be wise; do not disregard it. Blessed are those who listen to me, watching daily at my doors, waiting at my doorway. For those who find me find life and receive favor from the Lord. But those who fail to find me harm themselves; all who hate me love death.

As Mark read them aloud, the phrases flowed like an incantation that delivered them to another time, and another world. And in truth, it was. For beyond this wall resided seventy-two statues of the most famous of God's emissaries, with seventy-two different adventures taken from their exploits through time.

"From the Book of Enoch and the plea of the watchers . . ."

"Who fell from grace by the flood of Noah," she said, as one on their mission.

"To the Book of Daniel where Gabriel was held up by the Dark Prince of Persia until Michael's arrival to free him from his confrontations. This allowing him to go and answer Daniel's prayers."

He admired the broad canvas they were painting. "All these stories will likely be unknown by the audience."

"Until they come here," she said with appreciation. "Then they will be thrilled, enthralled, and walk away a bit more educated about the invisible war."

"And hopefully see some of the true cause and effect that shapes the world they live in."

"Yes, indeed." She smiled, taking his arm in hers.

The overall exhibit chronicled the fallen angels who commingled with the daughters of men and the abomination of giants called Nephilim that were born to roam the earth. Those whose souls were destined to the dimension of demons after their physical bodies perished in the great flood.

Walking with an eye to improving what they had already created, they examined each story, the anterior displays, and augmentations. The lighting, soundtrack, nothing was being left to chance or someone else's interpretation. This was their vision. Actually, to be truthful—it was mostly his.

"You have quite the imagination, Mr. Lambert."

She always addressed him by his last name when he was in trouble or, conversely, when being complimented. And with her fiery temperament, sometimes he wasn't sure which was which. He decided a little background would cover a multitude of questions.

"When I purged *Lil Darling* of everything of value, there were two books I took, the Bible and a novel by Chris Reynolds called *Lost Secret of the Ancient Ones*."

"I must have read both a hundred times. Everything I learned about angels, the cosmic war, the watchers who fell from God's grace, was either from the Bible or woven into the story of a heroine who was destined to save humankind from Satan's imminent clutches. I love that book."

"There are no coincidences," she said, strolling with him arm in arm.

"Amen, love. Amen."

Satisfied, but still looking to improve upon it, Mark made numerous notes to enhance the developing exhibition. Once finished, the guards were instructed to drop the security screen with no public entry for months to come.

"Hello, my favorite child," Mark said as he approached his daughter. They had joined the gala and all of the commotion that came with it. Ally looked too sophisticated to be his little girl. He was proud of her, though a little melancholy at all the years he had missed. She was his first, and if one had to be truthful, she was his favorite. He had proof—she was still listed in his phone that way. Every time she would call, it would light up with "My favorite child."

"Hey, Dan," Sara said with an extended hand. He kissed it with a genteel savoir faire. "Great party."

A waiter appeared, and they were all handed a fluted glass of champagne.

Mark made a toast. "To love, tolerance, humility, and family. May we be instruments in the glory of God."

It was Dan who surprised him.

"Amen."

The following morning, they lay in bed at their sumptuous suite at The Mark, which Sara had chosen because of its name and standard of luxury. While his new bride poured coffee from the room service tray, Mark opened a digital copy of that day's *The New York Times* and located the review of the exhibition's debut.

The Island of Redemption
By Gregory Hazel

As a journalist, I view religion as a catalyst that influences history. I do not know if there is a god, and I certainly do not ascribe to having a relationship with any unproven benevolent being. But as an educated citizen who has more than a rudimentary knowledge of the three great religions that dominate the Western worldview, this display has done more to give me introspection and a leaning than any other event I have ever covered.

Let's start by stating the obvious. The reliquaries displayed in the *Female Pirates of the Caribbean* exhibition are among the greatest treasures ever found throughout all of history. The inexplicable beauty among the bevy of these priceless relics can only be experienced by seeing them. Each magical. Each radiant. Each the envy of Midas himself. It is hard to conceive that these creations could have been fabricated by the hands of mere mortals.

The Golden Bible deserves to be seated beside Ireland's *Book of Kells* as one of the greatest literary creations ever made. As visiting Mecca is for Muslims, seeing the *Female Pirates of the Caribbean* is something one must experience at least once in one's lifetime. It will change you—and I suspect, like myself, you will be better for it.

But it is not the sum of the treasure that moved me, but instead it is the story of Nicolette Rey and Hanri Fick and the Island of Redemption that sinks into your soul and surrounds your psyche with an offering of peace and hope. It is the story of two lovers, both women, who defied the dictates of their time, their religion, and the tide of history itself.

Among the major religions then as now, many have been usurped by institutions called churches or synagogues or mosques. Rules have changed to reflect the times, and interpretations have been engineered often for political power or to gain control. But in this case, the lives of Hanri Fick and her lover, Nicolette Rey, personified the teaching of the gentile Messiah called Christ, transcending religion while still showing the grace and glory of God.

Christ said above all things love thy neighbor. He did not place one sin above another in a hierarchy of rights and wrongs. And his offer of salvation was, and is, open to all.

For like each of us, these two unique women were human, bearers of sin and slaves to their appetites. Hanri loved Nicolette, and her passions were inflamed with sin when Nicolette was unjustly killed. But even then, she gave Nicolette's killers a final opportunity for absolution.

When slavery was practiced the world over, these two did not get 'woke.' They bore the mantle of accountability. Called pirates, a disparagement placed on them by others, they took action to free as many human souls as chance allowed. And when they interdicted the slave traders, they did not send them to the gallows or a watery end; instead, they showed compassion and placed them upon their Island of Redemption, where they were given time as well as motivation to reflect on their lives. Then they were returned to the world, perhaps becoming one more light in the darkness.

Captain Fick had lost her true treasure when Nicolette died an unnecessary death. The riches on display were never hers, and she saw them as nothing more than blood money. Her riches, she expressed, were being stored up in heaven.

I must wonder about the depths of their Christian idealism. Can we learn something from them? I find this exhibition may be the catalyst for my own redemption. Perhaps here, in New York City, now rests an Island of Redemption. It has given me pause to reconsider my life, a Rubicon that each of us must cross at some point.

"Did you know you move your lips when you read?" Sara said sarcastically.

"Well . . . did you know that you snore when you drink?" His reply was a good-natured ribbing.

"I do not snore," she said with faux indignation. "I purr."

He handed her the electronic pad.

"So how did we do? Does the media hate us?"

"You tell me."

The man's insight was more than he could have hoped for. He wondered if their next display would get as warm a welcome. *Whatever . . .*

"What shall be shall be," Mark said in acceptance that some things are out of your control.

As his children had, she had grown accustomed to him thinking out loud. When she was finished with the article, she pulled him close, and they ducked under the covers and returned to the throes of passion. Eventually he made ready for his appointment. Stepping from the luxurious shower that may have lasted a bit longer than necessary, they confirmed their afternoon as Mark finished dressing.

"Let me help you with that," Sara offered, tying his tie. "You look very handsome, Mr. Lambert."

"Well, I hope to impress. After all, it's a big day."

With his untold legion of lawyers, Bancroft had brought the formation of a new island nation to the steps of the United Nations. There were no competing claims, and the charitable work of the Ingodwe Trust had not gone unnoticed.

"What are your plans today?" he asked as he prepared to leave.

"Shopping." She grinned. "You know what they say, when in Rome . . ."

He laughed. In this instance, he was glad he had to be somewhere else. They agreed to meet for drinks at Baltazar's at five o'clock and let the night unfold from there.

Chapter 32

Sara had done a fair amount of damage to the retailers of New York City. He knew because the driver had texted him a smiley emoji amid an image of a dozen shopping bags.

She arrived at the bar, and he ordered a bottle of Chassagne-Montrachet. He poured a glass for her as he nursed a Fresca. She produced a package from her bag.

"What have you got there?" he asked, eyeing the bundle she laid on the table.

"A gift."

"For me?" His love for her flowed from his smile. He removed the wrapping. It was a book.

Ghost Gold by Chris Reynolds.

"It's the sequel to *Lost Secret*," she said, quite smitten with her choice. "I figured if the first book of the Manna Chronicles could lead you to create a world-worthy exhibition of angels among men, then what would the next in the series spark you to do?"

He laughed. The cover was dominated by a stained-glass window above an altar upon which rested a blue glass chalice.

"I look forward to indulging in the continued adventures of Maya Harrington," he said with a smile. He reminisced how, like himself, the heroine of *Lost Secret* had a unique destiny painted by God long before time began. He felt a strange kinship with the author.

"Thank you, my love. You never know where inspiration will come from," he said with the lovelight shining in his eyes. "I, too, have a gift." He could see her face light up with delight.

"Oh, please do tell, kind sir."

He simply could not get enough of her playful ways, the teasing voice, and the flair in which she lived life. He had never felt this alive.

"We have nothing but time. And money that exceeds anything we could ever come close to spending, so I would like to take you anywhere in the world you want to go. And we can stay for as long as you like."

"Anywhere?" she asked, her mouth crooked with mischief.

She was privy to his billionaire secret, but it had neither surprised her nor impressed her. And for this, he loved her even more.

"Anywhere," he confirmed.

He saw the arch of her brow he had come to learn meant she was giving it some serious thought. Another tell. But it was her answer above all answers that caught him by surprise.

"I want to go home. I miss our dog."

"Anything for you, my lady, I love you even more today than yesterday, but I will leave some room for tomorrow."

Chapter 33

The following morning, while flying back home, he received a text from Bancroft.

'Congratulations, Mr. President. The nation of Angelica has been accepted as a sovereign country recognized by the United Nations. Furthermore, they have approved a National Heritage Marine Sanctuary that by international law extends outward for twelve miles.

'Because the lands are owned by Mark and Sara Lambert under a land trust based in Barbados, you are now its official governing body and free to form whatever type of government you deem appropriate.'

Mark sat and let the news marinate. The road from his past to this day had been long and punctuated by events set out by the hand of God.

"Congratulations, my darling. I know this brings you great satisfaction. Perhaps . . ." She paused, putting a finger to her lips. She turned to look into his brown eyes.

"Maybe one day you will tell me about her?" It was not an ask or a need, simply a comment if he ever wanted to share . . .

He considered this. The transfer of title, the ownership of a nation, and the name they chose together, Angelica . . . "There is nothing I will keep from you," he said to his betrothed. "Ever."

He began his tale on the day of the hurricane. He did not stop until the day he was rescued. He knew that telling her was a way of resolving what still felt unresolved. Though Sara was everything to him now, he still felt the loss as Angel drifted in and out of his memory, each time further away.

But he was ready for the next chapter in the adventures of Mark Lambert—a duet 'til death do us part.

"You know," she said, her expression bearing gratitude that he had finally unloaded his burden and the impish grin displaying a bit of the mischief he loved so much. "International law defines that the treasure off the shore of Angelica is rightfully the property of the nation upon whose territory it rests. Perhaps another adventure?"

With a lascivious smile he concurred, but not necessarily the adventure she was contemplating. "Do you know what the 'mile high club' is?"

He loved her, and she loved him back. When the flame of passion was spent and the onslaught of slumber came unbidden, the drone of the engines created a hypnotic hum, and he held her as she drifted off to her dreams.

While holding her close, his mind wandered. *She seems to know my thoughts, just as Angel did.* He accepted without question that God had unfolded everything that brought them together, and he was forever grateful. This was the peace he knew came from being right with your Creator.

But the practical side of him needed to find closure, to once and for all decide if Angel was real or just a long-running hallucination. He had never landed on a definitive answer. Until he did, it was a Gordian knot that would always seek untying.

He opened his phone to the photos. Scrolling back from last night's exhibit, he continued to finger swipe as he went back in time. The night before, his kids visiting, he and Sara revisiting the island.

Continuing, he scrolled back to shots of his decoy island. Big Daddy gave way to his personal photos of the island taken before he had been rescued. The dolphins, Carson on the beach, Ally and Dan at the falls, the treasure . . .

Eventually, he came to the first picture he had taken since he got the phone to charge. He recalled the day perfectly. It had been raining for a week. Everything was wet.

Angel was swimming, and I took photos of her in the lake, he thought, reliving the moment. She was angry with me, so I deleted them.

He gently stroked the hair of his bride sleeping beside him and smiled as he sank deeper into the recollection. He recalled Angel asking for the camera followed by his panic, him pleading. Her surprising him as she quelled his fear.

"You are quite the stud muffin, Mr. Lambert. Don't think I haven't noticed."

Then she made him pose for a photo by the falls. Staring at that photo, the strangeness of her admission once again flooded him with a satisfied feeling. His eyes remained glued to the image as he wandered through memories of that special time in the redemption of Mark Lambert.

He considered the whisper in his ear, the very last thing she ever imparted to him.

Jesus promised to get you safely to the other side, but He never assured the waters will be calm.

"No doubt," he said, appreciative of her accumulated wisdom.

Sara opened her eyes. "No doubt what?"

She saw him eyeing the screen, seeing him standing by the falls.

"My sexy husband," she cooed. "Can you send a copy to my phone?"

~ Finale ~

An Author's Epilogue

Many times people tell me, "I think my life would make a great story." And no doubt, some probably would.

Since I believe we are all part of God's tapestry, it is fair to say there are no ordinary lives. Some may seem more interesting than others, but this is because of who we are, where we have been placed in the scheme of God's plan, and the zest for adventure that was breathed into our spirit.

The realist in me knows that most personal stories are of interest to only a few good friends and one's family. To chronicle them is most often simply a vanity project, another way of extending mortality beyond the final curtain.

So, instead, I created Mark Lambert, the protagonist of my vanity project disguised as a novel. Most of the stories of his life are based on real events. The whale bump and the surrounding pod. The decades' old floating glass buoy. The plankton highways and the Bimini lobster march. These are all real experiences. I plead mea culpa on the illegal lobster harvest in Biscayne National Park.

The navy father, the deceased mother, Annapolis, Carson, Ally, and Forest . . . all true, but no Tori. Sorry, two was what God gave us. And of course, Sara, my wife of a different name, whom I have loved for more than thirty-five years.

I grew up assuming I was a Christian, not saved, but more as a descriptive element. I believed in God, but then again, so does the Devil. I moved to Pacific Palisades in the late nineties, and when a neighbor passed, we went to her church to pay our respects. Located in the cafeteria of Malibu Elementary School, the setting stretched my idea of a house of worship.

The congregation of Malibu Vineyard was very intimate, numbering less than a hundred people, but it was full of well-known actors and actresses. I did not expect these people to be the religious types.

"I can do this," I remember telling my wife after chatting it up with Brooke Burns, an actress from *Baywatch*, and a woman who shares the looks, beauty, and kindness of Angel.

I, of course, was referring to joining that church, probably for all the wrong reasons. My wife showed great wisdom in her simple reply. "I'm sure you can."

I now know, when God wants to get your attention, he provides the path best suited.

Months later, we were driving home from church when I was overcome with a wave of emotions so strong it caused me to pull off the road. With tears streaming down my face, both my children and wife grew concerned.

"I did not commit suicide," came the clear voice of my mother. She was speaking to me of things that only I could hear. "I would never leave you like that. I was sad, your father was always at sea, and I often took pills to sleep. These were accumulative in my day and, well . . . God knew it was time to bring me home. Know that I watch over you and pray for you and your family every day."

This is the day I became indwelled with the Holy Spirit. Trust me, I never ever thought I would be that guy. As I look back at my reckless behavior and understand how my choices led me to where I am today, I can see God was always there, protecting me from myself and nudging me in the right direction.

Mine has not been an ordinary life. And I suspect neither has yours.